Praise for *A Sinister Love*
(also by Spencer Hixon)

"...laugh out loud funny; whimsically adorable; I read this in one sitting... "

—*Betwixt the Pages*

"*A Sinister Love* masterfully blends the supernatural with the profoundly human, crafting a narrative that is both entertaining and emotionally resonant... challenges the traditional boundaries of genre fiction... a worthy addition to any reader's collection."

—*Literary Titan*

"A very entertaining read, with a healthy dose of fresh, unique world-building that takes on so many supernatural tropes and characters of Sinisters, Dexters, and mortals in-between."

—*JD Donnelly, Goodreads.com*

"I want to download Surli as my phone companion! The storyline keeps you reading and it's easy imagining yourself in the scenes. Looking forward to more from this author."

—*MydNyte, Amazon.com*

"I was most impressed by Hixon's knowledge of Scripture (both canonical and apocryphal), demonology, and angelology, and by the creative liberties he took with the lore... Hixon is also has a gift for description; whether describing a bookstore or a machine of demonic design or a portion of heaven, he does so in a way that helps the reader to really *see*."

—*Jennifer Fulton, Goodreads.com*

"This book is about mental illness, at its heart. It's about grief and depression and anxiety and fitting in...and not fitting in... I found this book decidedly just plain fun... I would definitely recommend it to [paranormal romance] fans... the romance is solid and the obstacles are both internal and external. Scribble is an interesting heroine and her viewpoint is the right choice for the book. I'd definitely read the sequels."

—*JenniferRP / Views of Other Planes*

Fate & Fortune

SPENCER HIXON

Fate & Fortune © 2025 Spencer Hixon

www.spencerhixon.com

ISBN: 978-1-959544-21-0

Fate & Fortune is a publication of

FÆROS PUBLISHING
Austin, TX

This edition distributed through KDP.

Cover art by Graziel Joanna Tallongon

Interior art by Graziel Joanna Tallongon and David Hixon

FÆROS PUBLISHING is an imprint of Wootton Major Publishing, LLC

www.woottonmajorpublishing.com

Trigger Warning:

*This book includes depictions
of abuse, rape, and PTSD.*

To mom, my real-life superhero.

Chapter 1

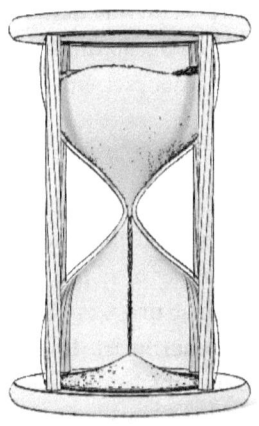

Getting Tied Down

They say that your life flashes before your eyes right before you die, but I can tell you from experience, that isn't true. The only thing that flashed before my eyes was a falling key reflecting the headlights of the five-ton pick-up truck that shot down the blind alley towards me like a bullet down the barrel of a gun.

The high-pitched squeal of metal scraping along brick wall sent a cold shock through my body—a constant reminder of just how close that death machine of steel and rubber drew. I couldn't even feel the pounding of my heart as the thunderous growl of the diesel engine rattled my bones. Whether by chance or destiny, I somehow managed to catch the key in mid-fall and shove it into the rusty lock of the door before me.

I tried turning it, but the old knob merely slipped beneath my sweaty palms.

"Shit! Shit! Shit!" The mantra did not help but I continued chanting it anyway. Given the thick coating of rust, that door probably hadn't been opened in my lifetime, which, by the way, would be ending in the time it took for that affront to nature on wheels to cover the short distance between us. I gripped with all my might and turned the knob.

Never once did my life flash before my eyes, but even if it had, it was a life that my death would prevent from ever happening. You'll understand what I mean soon.

They also say that dead men tell no tales, yet here we are. Yeah, I die in this book, spoiler alert. But it would be a very short book indeed if the main character gets killed on page one. Talk about jumping the shark. In order to really appreciate why I'm bothering to write this all down (not to mention *how*), we have to start at a Northern Virginia bar in the late '00s, two years from now.

Don't worry. We'll get back to that pick-up.

*   *   *

"It's not like you to drink anything harder than cough syrup, Alex. You're not trying to get drunk on me, are you?" the bartender asked as she put the bottle of Korbel California Brandy on the bar near the shot she'd just poured me. She wore a black tank top with an image of a Gray Raven—that was the name of the place—tastefully positioned over her heart. It did an excellent job showing off her heavily inked arms. She'd had the septum piercing for only a year but it fit her so well that it felt like she'd been born with it. Her dark-brown, gamine hair (something a toddler with hedge trimmers might have cut) completed that "tough girl" look she pulled off, and pulled off *well*.

"I'm fine, Naomi," I said. "Besides, it's supposed to be a celebration! Hunter should be here soon."

"Here? Isn't he supposed to be, I dunno, getting ready for the wedding or something? It's in a few hours."

"Apparently he didn't have a bachelor party and wants to 'enjoy his final moments.'"

Someone called for her, but she put a finger up in his direction without turning away from me. "He's not planning on having his party here, is he?"

"He said something about a bar crawl with all the groomsmen."

Naomi shook her head with a smirk. "Maybe I should be more worried about *him* getting drunk before the wedding. As the official ambassador for women everywhere, I'm ordering you to make sure he stays sober, got it? And that goes double for you. I think Amanda would be more upset if *you* show up drunk to her wedding."

"I'll do my best," I said.

"Swear. We don't want a repeat of a certain Homecoming party, do we, Mr. Pineapple P—"

"—I swear! I swear!" I put up my right hand up and crossed my heart with my left.

"Good." When the same customer became belligerent and tried to get her attention again, Naomi put her hand out in his direction once more, but this time lifted a *different* finger. "I'm talking to my *brother!*" she shouted in his direction. It may not have technically been true, but "foster-siblings" was close

2

enough for us. "If either of you does turn up drunk, trust me, I'll hear about it."

The moment she turned away to serve the guy on the other end of the bar, I downed the shot in a single, burning gulp, quick as a rumor, and poured myself a new one before she could turn back. Already, I could feel my ears heat up.

She looked over her shoulder and eyed me and the drink with suspicion. "And don't be late. The church is on the other side of town."

I waited until she finished pouring a beer and turned to hand it to her customer before I hurriedly drank the second shot. Or tried to. Once it hit my throat, I ended up in a coughing fit and put the shot glass back on the bar top.

I'd only poured half a shot more before I noticed her watching me. Putting the bottle back down, I feigned innocence with an over-the-top smile. Naomi narrowed her gaze as she approached. "How many have you had? One or two?"

"Oh, is that one new? The lizard?" I asked and pointed to her upper arm tattoo of a tastefully nude woman wrapped in serpent's coils.

"What? Yes, it's new, and it's not a lizard. That's Eurydice and the snake, you dolt, and—*give me that bottle, Alex!*" We both grabbed for it, but she proved the faster and snatched away the distilled nepenthe with a "Ha! How could you not know about Eurydice? I thought *you* were the one who graduated college." After putting the bottle away, she held her hand out to me. "Keys."

"What?"

"I know you, Alex. Two is your limit. There's no way I'm going to let my little brother—who can't hold his liquor—get behind the wheel and kill somebody. Keys. *Now.*"

I pouted at her like a kid, but soon wilted under her gaze and handed them over. "Fine."

She frowned at me and pocketed my keys before returning to her bartending duties. "You *just* swore you wouldn't get drunk, Alex."

"But I'm not drunk!"

"And it better stay that way. I mean, a *bar crawl*? What the Hell is Hunter thinking?" After finishing with another order, she walked back over to me. "I'll drive your car over to the church when I get off and you can drive me home."

"I drove you here," I said with a smirk.

She ignored me. "Does your plus one have a car? You should give her a call."

"Uh, I don't have a plus one," I confessed. "Besides, my apartment lost power last night, so my phone's dead."

"Wait. You don't have a plus one?" She planted herself on the bar in front of me with a soul-burrowing stare. "You seriously couldn't think of anyone, not *one* person who would want to go to an all-expenses-paid wedding funded by the *Pace* family? We're talking open bar, chocolate fountains, expensive wine, *filet mignon.* No one?" When she pointed at herself, I felt more than a little guilty.

"I'm sorry, Naomi. I should have asked you. I've had a lot on my mind."

She scoffed. "I may look like a gruff bitch on the outside, but inside beats the heart of a delicate *woman!*" she said with as much drama as she could muster. She even had the back of her hand against her forehead.

"Maybe I can sneak you in," I suggested.

"Nah, don't worry about it. I'm just joshing ya." The playful smirk was proof that she hadn't been serious... at least not *too* serious. "It'd be weird. Though I am surprised you never go on any dates. You're cute. Enough." She winked and returned to her work.

I examined my half-empty shot glass absent-mindedly. "I just haven't found anyone yet."

"HA! Don't give me that. You aren't even looking. If you need help, I can hook you up with someone. It's about time you got over Amanda."

With how suddenly I felt the blood leave my face, I was sure I looked like one of the undead. "Wh-What are you talking about? We're just friends."

"Dude, I've known you, what, fifteen years? I can read you like a comic book. I've known all about your crush since—" She'd been cleaning a shaker as she talked, but when she looked at me, she stopped. "Oh. It's not just a crush is it? You're really in *love* with her, aren't you? Welp, sucks to be you, then." Ah, sisterly love. So caring. Of course, I'd never told anyone what I really felt about Amanda; I hadn't even admitted it to myself, not until Naomi spelled it out like that. "Is that why you're pregaming so hard before Hunter gets here?"

"It's not like that!"

She grinned from ear to ear. "The more you protest, the more I'm gonna ship the two of you together in my head," she teased. "I remember catching you two asleep against each other when you were *supposed* to be studying for Professor Sapper's chemistry class. Didn't you fail that one?" My awkward expression was answer enough. That devilish smirk of hers would have been insufferable if she hadn't been so damn accurate. "You know, you two were always cute together. If she looked at *me* the way she looks at *you*, I'd have dragged her to my bed—"

"*Naomi!*" I kept my voice low, even though I didn't recognize anyone else at the bar. "She doesn't think of me like that. Would *you* want to go out with me?" She wrinkled up her nose in obvious distaste. "See? Amanda and I, we're not just friends, we're *best* friends, and I'd never do anything to compromise that. I'm here to support her on her big day and... I just thought a little liquid courage might... help."

"What do *you* need liquid courage for, Al? I'm the one getting hitched to the ball and chain." Hunter appeared at my side without warning. I panicked internally, wondering just how much he'd heard. But he didn't show any sign that he'd heard something incriminating. He wore his tux, though the bowtie lay

4

limp over his shoulders. It looked like it was tailored just for him by some big name no one's ever heard of. Despite being hours away from his wedding, he still had his blonde hair in an unkempt cut only the rich could afford. And, as always, there was that debonaire smile people loved; only, it seemed a little off to me that day.

"It's not for me," I quickly lied and then pointed at him. "It's for the condemned." I got a wry smile in return.

"Don't *I* get a say in my last meal?" Hunter patted my back and took the seat next to me before addressing my surrogate sister. "Naomi, how have you been? How's business?" He grabbed a handful of bar nuts and started popping them into his mouth one by one.

His charisma, which seemed to charm nearly everyone, usually didn't work on her. They rarely got along. But this time she smiled all the same. "It's going pretty good."

"Hey, I'm really sorry that you didn't get an invite," he said. "No hard feelings? Amanda wanted to keep it to family and close friends only. You know how she can get."

"It's fine, Hunter. I'm a big girl. I'll get over it."

"How she can get?" I asked. "What do you mean?" Before Hunter could answer, though, someone sat down on his other side. It was TJ, his best man. The two had been friends since before they were even born. I say that because their families had been friends for generations. It was no surprise they dressed the same, did their hair in the same style, and even sounded similar. If someone put on a Hunter look-alike contest, TJ would have won.

As the two of them chatted for a bit, Naomi leaned in closer and said, "I'll leave you guys to your 'male bonding'." She made air-quotes with her fingers— an impressive feat while she held someone's drink without spilling it. "Let me know when you're ready to order something. Some *food.*"

As she went to the kitchen to grab someone's lunch, an imposing but stout figure took the seat on my other side. Diego resembled a Belgian Draught Horse; same physical prowess, and he wasn't much smarter than one either (his words, not mine). There wasn't a tuxedo on Earth that could have fit his build without taking *some* punishment. But of all the groomsmen, Diego was my favorite and the only one I was friends with myself. He gave me a small smile, but beyond a "Hey," it felt like he avoided looking at me.

Next to him sat a tall, gaunt man in his twenties with lank, black hair and pale skin. Between that and his bulging eyes, he always looked like he was standing at the edge of the grave. I swear, in that tux, he looked just like an old-time undertaker. We called him by his last name, "Glass", but I never knew his first name. In fact, the only thing about him that I was sure of was that he scared the shit out of me. Unlike Diego, he had no problem staring.

Thankfully, Diego distracted me from that stare by pointing at the half-full glass that sat on the bar in front of me and asking, "You gonna finish that?" I shook my head and leaned back so he could take it. Before he had a chance, however, Hunter snatched the golden libation and downed it.

"Ugh. Should've known it'd taste like shit." When he saw us looking at him, he added, "What? I'm just joking with you guys! Condemned, remember?" he said, pointing to himself. The way he grinned made me think he was trying to keep some sort of secret, but not a fun kind.

"Why wouldn't Amanda invite Naomi? She's practically family." I hadn't meant to say it as loudly as I did.

Hunter leaned in and spoke conspiratorially. "She told me she didn't like trans people." Then he went right back to his conversation with TJ like he hadn't just said something atrocious.

The statement was so absurd, I sat in shock for a full minute. "Jason is trans," I eventually said, and then repeated it louder so he would hear it over TJ. "Her brother is trans." How could he not have known that?

Their conversation ended abruptly. "Hey, talk to her! She's the one who said it, not me. I'm not like that."

"Are you the one who's been spreading that rumor about me?" Naomi asked, coming out of the kitchen holding a plate of food. She went straight to us instead of to whatever hungry customer was waiting for his burger. "I'm not trans." For the first time, he didn't have an immediate response. He'd just started sputtering words when Naomi cut him off. "You should go, before I call the manager."

It was a standoff Hunter would lose. "Come on, guys. Let's get out of here. We've got other places to be, anyway." All four of them got up and shambled to the door. "You coming, Al?" It was then that I realized that they were my best chance of getting to the wedding in time, bar crawl or not. But the last thing I wanted to do was insult Naomi by going with someone who'd said such terrible things. I looked at her for approval and she gently nodded before pointing to her eyes and then to me.

"Y-yeah. I'm coming." I gave Naomi a look of both apology and thanks before springing to my feet to follow them outside.

*　　　*　　　*

I soon found myself sitting in the back of Hunter's pick-up truck. It had an extended cabin so it could seat five and still had that fresh-from-the-factory smell. I hear it comes in cans, now. But it was spotless inside and might as well have been new, despite being several years old.

My body was squeezed between Diego and Glass. With Hunter in the driver's seat and TJ next to him, we headed off in relative silence. Ten minutes later, I realized we were heading out of town and that forboding sense that something was off came over me again, far stronger.

"So, uh, where's the next bar?" I asked.

"It's a bit of a drive," Hunter replied.

Several more minutes passed and we turned onto a pothole disguised as a road snaking through a forest. The thick canopy made it look like dusk.

"How'd you get your parents on board?" TJ asked out of nowhere, almost like it was scripted. He sounded nervous. "Didn't your dad hate her? I mean, it's not like she's in the same tax bracket."

"Took a while," Hunter replied. "He can be a real prick, I'll give you that. But we came to an agreement."

"Yeah?"

Hunter looked at me in the rearview mirror for a moment before answering. "You were there last night, TJ. He makes me a board member so long as my charity-case-of-a-wife gives us some good publicity. Plus there's the prenup."

Pin pricks covered my body as ice crystals formed in my blood. I glanced between the two men on either side of me but didn't dare bring any attention to myself. There had to be a way out.

"How did you get a girl like her anyway, man?" Diego asked stiffly.

"Patience. You've gotta start out sweet, then make her doubt herself. Soon she'll be second guessing everyone else. Once she believes you're the only one she can trust, she'll let you do anything."

"Anything?" Diego asked. "Like, chores and shit?" Blessed idiot.

Hunter snickered and looked at me again. He sounded *different*. "Let's just say that I'm the reason she's not wearing white today, despite her protests."

"Why's that?" Diego asked, which was followed by a smack on the back of his head by Glass.

They outnumbered me, and something told me that speaking up at that moment was a Bad idea. Capital B. No bar awaited me at the end of this ride. Wherever we were headed, I knew I didn't want to be there. I would have felt sick, or enraged, or devastated, but Hunter kicked my nerves into high gear by turning sharply onto an even bumpier dirt road. Fear, however, was not my strongest emotion. No, I felt useless, used. If this was what Hunter was really like, then how did we miss it for so long? What hadn't I seen?

"Do you think she knows about you and Diana?" Glass' voice was scratchy and his breath stank like dead fish.

Hunter scoffed. "Are you kidding? She's not that smart. Hell, I fucked Diana last night and she didn't catch on. I've been banging Sam for years without her noticing."

"Sam, the Maid of Honor?" TJ asked.

"Oh yeah. And they weren't the only ones. It gives me such a *rush* to fuck someone right under Amanda's nose. If we hurry, I might have time to do Diana again before the wedding starts."

The car abruptly stopped. There were trees, rocks, and sky. In short, we were nowhere.

After getting a nod from Hunter, Diego got out. I tried to slip behind him, hoping to make a run for freedom, but Hunter blocked the way with that dangerous smile on his lips. Glass pulled my arms behind me with surprising strength. "You know, Al, I tried to get her to hate you for years," Hunter said softly. "She cut nearly every other friend off after I got in her head. But Amanda never changed her opinion of you. You're the only thing keeping me from having complete control." The cabin rocked some while Diego rummaged around the bed of the truck. Glass pushed me down face-first on the leather seats.

"I even tried giving you hints to not show up and yet you still did. I mean, I never expected *you* to show up for a bar crawl. Hmm. She'll probably miss you for a while, but I'll make sure she gets over it."

"Won't they be looking for him?" Glass asked.

"Pshh! This guy? The guy who ran away from a dozen homes and went globetrotting on a whim? I'll just say he—"

The conversation stopped when Diego returned with some rope, which he promptly tied around my wrists. Struggling did nothing, but I gave it my all. I called Diego's name but Glass quickly shoved a cloth in my mouth. The sticky *RIP* of tape caused me to stiffen. Thankfully, it only went over my mouth. At the same time, Diego tied my legs together. I looked at him in betrayal and he glanced away, over to Hunter. After getting another nod, he carried me out of the vehicle over his shoulder and sat me down with my back against a boulder. I figured it was better to comply than to fight someone who could effortlessly turn me into a Jackson Pollock. Deftly, Glass ensured I was one wallet lighter.

"Can't have you causing a scene at the wedding, you understand," Hunter said loudly. I got the impression that was meant for Diego more than for me. Then he squatted in front of me and spoke more softly. "Now you just sit here and think about how much fun I'm going to have with your crush tonight." He knew. *Of course* he knew. "Maybe I'll get her to moan loud enough you'll be able to hear it all the way out here. Goodbye, Al."

He, Diego, and TJ all headed for the truck. Once their backs were turned, Glass grabbed my hair and knocked the back of my head against the boulder. Stars burst into view and obscured everything else for a while.

"Isn't it a bit much for a prank?" Diego asked. "You didn't *really* cheat on Amanda, right?"

"Of course not, Diego. It's all just part of the hazing! After this, Al will be like our brother, you'll see."

"But will he be okay?"

"He'll be fine. I'll send someone to get him after the wedding is over."

Then they drove off, but Hunter's parting wheeze of a laugh lingered in my mind. "Hehhehheh!" I had a feeling no one would be coming.

* * *

Okay, I know what you're thinking. It's the old "best friend is marrying a jerk and the hero has to stop the wedding" trope. It's been *done!* It's *hackneyed!* And you'd be right. But this isn't some Hallmark movie with a bit more violence and cursing. Hell, I don't even think I'm the real hero of this story, not after the shit I did. No, this story gets a whole lot stranger before the day's end.

Chapter 2

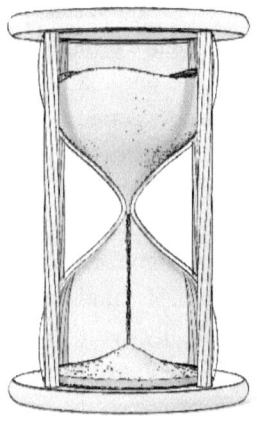

Contract Tracing

You might think that having your mouth taped shut is just to keep you quiet, but you'd be wrong. Do it right, like Glass did, and breathing becomes the real issue. It's the cloth that's the secret. Getting a lungful of air becomes a challenge when panic has your nose running like a faucet. And when you're struggling to breathe, you aren't thinking about how to escape. Thankfully, I'd taken Captivity Survival Training due to my job and knew how to keep myself calm.

Once the dust from the truck had settled, I focused on releasing my hands. Slipping them out of the rope was surprisingly easy. When Diego had tied me up, I tensed every muscle in my body as hard as I could to make myself bigger. After relaxing, it only took a few tugs to get out of the now-loose rope. From there, removing the tape was a snap—just don't do it too quickly if you value having lips. The rope around my legs practically fell off.

Getting out of there, however, was not so easy. It wasn't like I was lost. Okay, technically, I *was* lost, but all I had to do was follow the roads back to civilization. Simple. With Amanda's wellbeing in my mind, I took off at a run.

Jog. It was a jog, okay? Look, I'm not *that* out-of-shape, but I'm not exactly in-shape either. Coach James would be *so proud* of my fifteen-minute mile. The next mile took even longer. I'm pretty certain the squirrels overhead were laughing at me. By the time I'd made it to the end of the dirt road, my head hurt,

I had a charley horse, and I had to double over on my knees to catch my breath. So much for my Olympic debut.

Most of the rest of the way, I could only walk. And think. Surely he had some contingency plan in place in case I escaped. Recalling the conversation they had in the truck, it didn't take long to figure it out. Gaslighting. Play it off like some boys-will-be-boys joke; after all, no one really got hurt. Make me look like an idiot who can't tell the difference between unlawful restraint and harmless fun. It'd be my word versus his, a formerly homeless man versus an up-and-coming young business mogul. If I took this to the press, it would be social suicide. And at that moment, I did not have the will for such a fight.

The new road before me ended. Somehow, while occupied with my thoughts, I'd made a wrong turn. After that, it must have taken two hours of jogging, walking, and wheezing before I finally made it back to civilization. But with no money or phone, I had no ride. The church was on the far side of town; there was no way I'd make it there before everything was over. My apartment, though, only took another hour or so to reach on foot. As I plodded through the lobby of my building some time later and slumped into a chair in the corner, every muscle hurt and an elephant had begun to dance a jig on my skull. The ticking of the lobby's clock set the elephant's tempo.

"Oh, Mr. Petersen!" The security guard, Manny. He had just arrived at his station in the lobby. "When did you get here?"

"What time is it?"

"4:15," he said without having to check.

"That's when I got here. Ugh. Damn it. Do you have a phone I could borrow?" Although Manny let me use the lobby's phone, I quickly realized that I only had Amanda's number memorized, and there was no way she had it on her at that moment. I tried to leave a message, but her mailbox was full—undoubtedly from well-wishers congratulating her. Any time now, Amanda would say, "I do," to that snake and I was helpless to warn her. How could I have failed my best friend so badly? I hung up and pressed my hand against the wall to keep myself steady.

"No luck?" Manny asked. I shook my head. "You look terrible, Mr. Petersen. Are you okay? Do you need some help?"

"No, Manny. I'm not okay, and I don't need help." Thank God for elevators. Not having to navigate the stairs made the pain of the elevator's obnoxious *ding!* worth it. I rummaged around in my pockets as the elevator took me to the top floor, then remembered that I didn't have my keys. Or my wallet. The lift opened onto a nondescript hall that might have been found in any middling hotel. You'd never guess the door at the end led to the penthouse stairs. Thankfully, we had security pads next to our doors. I tried punching in my code while squinting because of the headache. It took a few tries to remember it correctly since my

12

key fob usually took care of it.

As far as penthouses went, it was definitely on the lower end of the scale. It wasn't much bigger than most apartments, but at least it had a decent view and the amenities were nice. Not that I used them much. Since my job required plenty of traveling, I was gone about half of the time. No one greeted me as I ascended the steps to my apartment, not even a pet. I'd been planning on getting a cat, but I travelled too much. The first thing I did was drink enough water to bathe in. Then I tried to assess the situation, but my headache made thinking a chore. So, I took some pain-killers, even though they probably wouldn't start working for another hour. A sizeable and sensitive bump on the back of my head revealed itself when I lay down on the couch. I thought about calling for a ride, calling someone else at the church, even calling the cops (though they usually just made things worse in my experience), but my phone's battery was so far gone it refused to even turn on until it had some time to charge. If I somehow *did* get a ride at that very moment, chances were damn good that Amanda and Hunter would have left the reception for their honeymoon by the time I arrived. The best plan was to wait for the phone to charge enough that I could call someone who would hand me over to Amanda. When I checked my phone's battery a few minutes later, however, I discovered that I didn't live as alone as I thought—*something* had chewed up the charger's wire, rendering it useless. *fml*. I was down to my final option: tell her everything when she returned from her honeymoon. In two weeks. But just thinking about her being married to Hunter...

Naomi was right. It was time I got over Amanda.

The reprieve of sleep would have been nice, but the headache and heartache wouldn't be letting that happen anytime soon. I gave up trying when a church bell outside struck six. Instead, I oozed off the couch and sat down at the computer. My headache was a bit better, at least good enough that I didn't have to squint at the light. I opened my browser. Social media. I wasn't interested in the posts and pictures—I just wanted the instant messaging.

Naomi, you still at the bar?

Yup. 'sup buttercup?

I left my credit card there.
Can you bring it by later?

Sure thing, I'll c u 2nite
How'd it go?

Dunno. I never made it.
I'll explain later.

Oh shit! U ok? Not drunk, r u?

I'm not drunk. I'll be fine.
Since you have my card, go ahead

13

and charge me for
a round on the house.

Awesome. Thanks, bro!
I'll come by after work.

I leaned back in my seat and heaved a heavy sigh while unconsciously pulling a watch from my pocket. I thanked God that it hadn't been taken. The thing came straight out of the 90s—a children's wristwatch with a dinosaur motif. The band had lime green, bright yellow, hot pink, and electric blue dinosaurs all over, interspersed with random shapes and lines, but the colors had faded with age. On the face, a Brachiosaurus serenely picked leaves from the top of a tree. A digital display hovered next to the prehistoric giant's head, but it didn't show any numbers—the thing hadn't worked in years. Instead of looking at it, I ran it between my fingers like a fidget toy. It always calmed me and brought me comfort. "Guess I should get dinner," I said and slipped the watch back into my pocket, but before I had gathered enough mental momentum to actually get up, I heard a chime from my computer, so I checked it.

What're u gonna do now?

I dunno. TV until I pass out?

I mean, u staying in town?
Can't imagine u would wanna
hang out here. I hate 2 c u go
but I wouldn't blame u 4 moving

Never thought of that.
Not a bad idea.
It's not like I wouldn't visit, right?

Y not go back 2 Scranton?
Isn't that where u went
when u ran away?

I traveled all over the place.

Well, u *were* gone a few years.
Anyplace stand out?

I hadn't thought about that time of my life since before I started college. It hadn't been a bad time or anything. In fact, the experience could not be equaled, and as a fifteen-year old who'd only known DC streets and foster homes, it was the perfect mix of freedom and security, novelty and routine. But nowhere ever really felt like my home. Exotic locales, fly-over states, busy cities, they all failed to become the place I belonged. I returned here for that very reason. Still, she had a point. I didn't particularly want to stay around where I might run into Hunter or Amanda. This might no longer be home, either.

I closed my laptop and headed to my bedroom, to my closet. Somewhere in that apartment I had pictures stored away, pictures I likely put someplace "smart." Usually, I can never remember where my smart someplaces are, but this time I got lucky. I clicked my tongue against the back of my teeth as I took a mental inventory of everything in my closet. Under some hanging shirts I found a rubber-top storage bin about three or four feet long and covered in dust. "Aha!" I couldn't lift it, so I just dragged it along the carpet out to my room and sat down on the floor next to it. The lid popped off with a little effort and the scent of memories and aging paper escaped and infiltrated my mind.

Memorabilia and books sat neatly inside. As I looked through them trying to find pictures or a reminder of a place I'd forgotten—a potential fresh start—I uttered things like, "Good Lord, I remember them," and, "Damn, I was young!" and, "God, that's embarrassing," and, "Where was that?" I pulled out a yearbook and thumbed through it out of nostalgia. A pattern emerged. In every picture of me, I could find Amanda, and vice versa. She almost always had a sketch pad. I almost always had a pencil behind my ear.

Why is it that when you start looking through old things, you inevitably get distracted? I had finished torturing myself with feelings that didn't know when to die and slammed the book down. A moment later, I found what I had been looking for: a prehistoric, hard square of plastic—a Zip disk. Of course, my computer didn't have any way to *read* a Zip disk. "There's gotta be my old Zip drive around here somewhere..." I muttered while putting everything back into the bin. The yearbooks wouldn't fit. Things had shifted. I reached inside to find the culprit and pulled out a little wooden box, one I didn't recognize.

"What's this?" The box stood four inches long and two inches high, a bit larger than a bar of soap, and had a small lock on it. I didn't have the key. Even though I took everything out of the bin again, I still found no key. Time to think outside of the box, pun intended. I kept all my unused wires, electronics, and random bits in another bin, and, after raiding it, I had procured both my Zip drive and a jeweler's kit. You'd be surprised how useful those little screwdrivers can be.

An hour, one adapter, and a driver download later, I sat in front of my computer watching a slideshow, alternating my attention between the pictures as they flashed by, and the box I held a tiny screwdriver up to. Who needs a key when you can just take the hinges off? It took a while, but the little screws eventually gave up the ghost, at least on one hinge. I worked on the second, but started noticing another pattern, this time from the slideshow. I wore a charm on a necklace in quite a few of them. Why didn't I remember owning the thing?

When I got the box open, that very charm tumbled out into my hand: an hourglass with real glass and sand in it, about an inch tall. The glass bulbs were supported by a small frame made of silver. The charm felt and looked delicate.

My memory again stirred. I had blocked out that day, the day I ran away for good, but it hadn't been erased. Bits of it came to the forefront of my mind. I'd hidden on—no, *under* a bridge. I was fifteen.

Two well-dressed women had approached me from out of nowhere, identifying themselves as Lady Luck and Dame Destiny. I'd been too young and too naïve to avoid them, keep moving without talking to them. Later, I thought I must have dreamed the strange encounter.

I'd long given up on the slideshow at this point, instead concentrating on the hourglass, turning it over again and again. The memory may have been slow to piece together, but eventually it all returned to me. Eight years had passed since those two approached me with those snake-oil smiles. They had a contract. I'd signed it. Preying on my vulnerability, they offered me irresistible candy: to change my fate and reverse my fortune.

I know it sounds crazy. Even *I* thought my mind had gone over the edge. But I could remember *so much*, even the voice of the pale woman who called herself Destiny. *"Now, if you ever want to cancel this contract and undo it all, just come and tell us. This amulet will bring you to our home. Simply break it. But be careful with it. You only get one, and it will not be replaced."*

The hourglass felt heavier in my palm as I recalled such weighty words from so many years ago. But it took me less than a heartbeat to make up my mind. Delusion or not, I had no attachment to the hourglass any longer, I was clearly unhappy with how things were turning out, and breaking a piece of glass sounded rather therapeutic. If canceling the "contract" would ease some of the heartache, it was worth whatever riches I might lose. So I threw the hourglass as hard as I could against the floor.

The glass in the pendant shattered into a thousand tiny shards and the sand inside exploded from it. It released more sand than I thought the thing could hold. A *lot* more. Sand covered the floor, the walls, the furniture. In a state of panic, I tried to get to my vacuum cleaner but couldn't trudge through it all—I didn't think anything would actually *happen!* The room groaned under the stress of such weight. "My insurance won't cover this!" But the sand didn't care; it kept coming. It buried the bed, blocked the window, and covered the walls. As more and more of my body disappeared beneath it, I finally realized what peril I was in, but it was too late. A sudden wind turned the domestic desert into a vortex of chaos with me at the center. Sand filled my eyes, my ears, and my lungs.

*　　　*　　　*

Just as quickly as it arrived, the vortex left, blowing everything away. The first thing I noticed was that I was standing on stone tiles, not the carpet of my apartment. Then I looked up. Shelves, each supporting two long rows of hourglasses, surrounded me. Every timepiece stood around five or six feet tall, with silvery metal frames much like the pendant had had. The shelves had been separated into aisles and the aisles into sections, almost like barrios with wide thoroughfares between the different blocks. Overhead, signs with labels like "Reish and Sigma" hung from a ceiling so high, I could barely make out any details. "There are more things in Heaven and Earth, Horatio," I muttered to myself while looking around in awe.

A sound caught my attention. People were working some ways down the nearest aisle, so I decided to talk to them. As I headed their way, I realized that no two hourglasses I passed were exactly alike. Their shapes, frames, and even the color of the sand in their upper bulbs differentiated one from another. A few did not have any remaining sand to fall. The one thing that they did all have in common, though, was that once the sand passed through the middle to the bottom, it turned black. I wanted to spend more time admiring the sand timers but someone behind me said, "'Scuse me!" in a child-like voice. I muttered an apology and stepped aside, only to find that it was, in fact, a child, probably ten years old or so. He wore a hospital gown that had been tied so as to prevent anyone seeing his backside. In his hand, he held a black bag half his size, sporting a silver hourglass icon. Once at the timepiece I'd been admiring, he climbed some steps against its side, opened a hatch in the top of the glass, and began pouring black sand from the bag into it. When the dark grains were in the upper bulb, they turned the same brilliant blue as the rest of the sand inside.

The strange work he diligently performed was not the most striking thing about him. Neither was the manner in which he moved and held himself, which would fit an adult far better than a child of ten. The most striking thing was that he was utterly devoid of any color, body and clothing. At first I thought he'd been covered in dust, but when I looked at the other workers nearby, all of them lacked any hue whatsoever. A great deal of them were children, though none of them acted like it. Several wore hospital gowns, but I also saw one in pajamas, another in a swimsuit, and yet another wearing their Sunday Best. A young woman in a sari helped an elderly man wearing a yukata to pour sand into an hourglass. It was as if they'd been plucked out of the world at random times.

"Oh! We have a guest!" I looked around to see a slightly overweight man dressed in a Victorian-era shirt and vest with a silver-gray pocket watch chain across his belly. Great care must have gone into make his English-style mustache as immaculate as possible. His sleeves had been rolled up to the elbows and kept in place with black ribbons. Nothing in my experience had ever looked—nor sounded—so *British*. Like the others, he was only a collection of grays. The ladder he stood on was a rolling library ladder attached to a rail that spanned the entire long aisle. He held a slender scoop made of glass inside one of the hourglasses and carefully removed a bit of the golden sand before pouring it into a black bag held up by a young girl.

"Let me finish and I'll be right there. Don't go anywhere!" he said. As soon as he emptied the scoop, he shut and latched the little hatch, hung the scoop on his belt, then pulled out a fabric measuring tape and pressed it up against the glass to determine the sand's height. Then he pulled an antique pocket watch out from his vest pocket. What I thought was a chain turned out to be some sort of thin braided cord that connected the watch to the vest. When he pushed a button on the side and then lowered his gaze to the level of the sand, I realized it was a stopwatch. He pushed the button again with an exaggerated movement and checked the time. "Excellent." After pocketing the watch, he stepped down the ladder, and stood before me.

"Welcome to the Halls of Time. You look a bit lost. Where are you trying to go, sir?"

Any words I tried to make got stuck in my throat. When the shock of what had happened began to wear off, I could finally begin understanding his question. "I... I'm looking for... Lady Luck and Dame Destiny. I think. What is this place? Who are you all? What are all these hourglasses for?"

A hint of disappointment flashed briefly across his face. "The Sisters? Ah. I know where to find them, but it is too far to walk. If you'll follow me." We then proceeded to walk anyway, passing aisle after aisle of hourglasses. "This can all be a bit overwhelming to newcomers. We are souls either lost or indebted to Chronos, the Lord of Time. I'm responsible for ensuring that each sandglass has the proper amount of sand and drains at the proper rate." My other question remained unanswered.

I didn't see how we could possibly escape the limitless chamber, but in minutes we were standing in a warehouse looking at a small fleet of the strangest vehicles I've ever seen. Each looked like one massive wheel nearly ten feet tall with a wide tire. The long bench seat was on the *inside* of the wheel, with a joystick and lever in the center. In front of the joystick sat the engine, enclosed in metal that had a steampunk look (except for the pull cord). Small mirrors helped the driver see directly in front of the wheel. Circling the rim at regular intervals were twelve bronze numbers, making it look almost like a giant clock. A sign hanging overhead labeled them as "Chronowheels." I recognized them as monowheels. It didn't look particularly practical.

As I sat beside him on the nearest Chronowheel, the Englishman put on a set of aviator goggles that had been looped around the joystick and said, "We have an hour's journey ahead of us. Do try not to fall out—I'd like to get back to my work quickly." Apparently, seatbelts were an invention that had yet to make it to the Halls of Time. When we started off, the seat rocked back and forth slightly, but soon it stabilized and the hourglasses passed by in a blur. It had its own lane in the hallways between the barrios, and a good thing, too. That thing was crazy fast, almost like it was warping space-time around it, so the lane kept the workers safe and focused on their tasks. You had to be eagle-eyed to read the overhead signs before they passed by. When it turned, the wheel leaned but the seat stayed upright, stabilized like a gyroscope.

The Halls of Time didn't exactly have an entrance—it just seemed to fade from stone floors and vaulted ceiling to black sand and gray sky. The sky did not have a sun or clouds, just endless, drab gray. Like London. Perhaps that's why it was around room temperature there. The view before me was straight out of a sci-fi movie, one of the stranger ones. The ground was nothing but jet black sand that rose to distant mountains, only they weren't actually distant, nor were they mountains. Since the sand absorbed almost all light that touched it, I had a hard time discerning sand dunes from each other or telling how far one was. More than once my eyes crossed on their own. After a few minutes, they adjusted and I could make out the narrow path before us that wound between midnight hills. Here and there I spotted workers, measuring out sand on silver scales or pouring it into black bags. The Englishman and I passed the time in relative silence; he focused on driving, while I tried to process everything around me.

An hour must have passed before we banked sharply and headed towards a gate, where the sand ended. Beyond it, I saw two very different worlds separated by a road. On one side it looked like Vegas, complete with gaudy casinos and flashing lights, and on the other, boring courthouses and libraries. On one side, ostentatious outfits and colorful water displays, on the other, tall Doric columns and leonine statues. Although people went about their business on their respective sides, no one took any notice of us.

The Englishman parked us right between a library and an outlandish casino shaped like a massive six-sided die, then turned the engine off. "This is your stop. Good luck," he said and gave me an impatient-but-polite smile. I took the hint. He wasted no time leaving once I'd disembarked.

"Alright, then. I'm just going to meet the immortal personifications of abstract human concepts. Nothing to be afraid of." Despite the little pep talk, I remained where I stood, like a nervous shrub.

Out of the library strode a stern, well-kept woman. I recognized her as Destiny, though I hadn't remembered her height: a good head taller than me. Her skin—pale as the pages of a book—had no flaws or blemishes. She even had her somehow-whiter hair tied into a tight bun, not a strand out of place, and held it all together with a pencil. If I hadn't recognized her, I'd have said she was in her twenties. A pair of simple glasses framed her curious, dark eyes. Like I remembered, a well-fitting pencil-skirt and matching suit jacket clung to her slender frame.

"I thought I felt a mortal enter The Between," she said. "What brings you here? It's Alexander, correct?" A smug grin made an appearance on her lips for about a second.

"Alexander Petersen-with-an-s-e-n." I replied by rote. Enough people misspelled my last name that my preemptive correction had become part of it. "I've come to..." My wavering voice squeaked. I coughed.

"Yes?"

I took a deep breath and closed my eyes. It didn't really help. "I've come to... c-cancel my contract."

"Is that so?" Her grin returned. "Then we are going to need to summon my Sister." I don't know what I expected, a spell or some sort of teleportation. I certainly didn't expect a smartphone. She pulled it out of who-knows-where and began typing away on the screen with her thumbs. "Come inside, Alexander Petersen-with-an-s-e-n. *She* will join us shortly." That smug grin had thankfully turned into a playful smile.

The size of the library she led me to boggled my mind. I stood on the steps just trying to take in its enormity. I wouldn't have been surprised to discover it held every book ever written, and a few that hadn't been. Yet, like a massive T.A.R.D.I.S., the vast athenaeum inside was even larger. I had to pop outside for a moment just to be certain. Along the walls stood endless rows of bookshelves that stretched out of sight above us, far higher than the roof should have allowed. More literary Towers of Babel filled the distance, but between us and them lay a maze of shorter shelves that moved around, creating pathways and cul-de-sacs as they went. Not only were other people working throughout the place, but a flock of ravens had decided that it was a good place to roost and would pay their rent by assisting the librarians. Destiny beckoned me down the steps of the entrance and straight to a room along the wall with a door labeled FATUM. More bookshelves covered the room's perimeter and left not a single inch bare. She stood behind a large, wooden desk that had nothing on it save for an open laptop and a Newton's Cradle that clacked away and probably had been clacking away since time immemorial. My nerves wouldn't let me sit, so I remained standing behind one of the chairs off to the side, like I could hide there.

"It's been eight years, two months, and three days, is that accurate?" As she talked, she opened one of the drawers of her desk and looked through it.

"I suppose so."

"Tell me, what makes you want to cancel our contract after all this time?"

Before I could answer, the office door opened and a woman walked in hurriedly. Lady Luck, like her Sister, was taller than I remembered, but, unlike Destiny, she had bronze skin that contrasted beautifully with her freely flowing blonde hair. Gold rings and necklaces adorned her, just shy of too much. The casual sundress she wore showed off plenty of flesh while dark sunglasses hid her eyes. She sported a small beauty mark on the left side of her chin.

"Where is he?!" the woman demanded and planted her hands on the desk.

Destiny pointed at me and Lady Luck spun around. "Alex! How good it is to see you again, child! My, how you've *grown*." She lowered her shades and let her gaze travel the length of my body. I shuddered, both from some primal excitement and the unsettling sensation of being ogled like a prized bull.

"My Lady, I'm here to cancel my contract." For some reason, I found it easier to talk with her, but her eyes still made me feel like prey, or a prize.

Destiny pulled out a legal document from a drawer and spread it out on the desk. She cleared her throat. "'I, the undersigned, do hereby and hereon accept a full and complete reversal of my fate and fortune so long as it does not upset the Divine Plan, to be carried out by Dame Destiny and Lady Luck, until the sands of my life cease their flow. Signed, Alexander David Petersen.'"

Luck anxiously chewed on her lower lip. I never thought someone like *her* could have frazzled nerves. "My dear boy, let's not be hasty. Consider everything that's happened," she said and walked behind me with her hand on my shoulder. "You were on the street, an orphan, a runaway." She put her sunglasses on my face and scenes from my life immediately filled my head. "It hadn't even been an hour before you found that nice watch that you pawned for a couple hundred dollars. Anything you needed just seemed to fall into your lap. And on your eighteenth birthday, you won the lottery. Remember? Your foster father was arrested. You traveled. You were accepted into college. You have friends that love you. Even though you put all that money aside, your coffers still somehow remained full. How can you give all that up?"

"But," the Dame spoke up, "if you don't ask to cancel the contract, you and Amanda will not end up together. She will marry Hunter, who will most likely continue to cheat on her. And, you will never marry."

"Never?" I asked, pulling up a little on the sunglasses.

"Oh, please... There are plenty of other girls out there. How do you know there isn't a better one just waiting for you to find her? You are merely twenty-three!" Luck took her glasses and leaned back against the desk.

Destiny, however, had the answer ready to go. She held a simple, white, hardcover book, a book that looked nearly identical to all the others in this room, a book with *my* name on it, and flipped through its pages. "I'm afraid there is not, Sister. Amanda Shields is, in fact, his soulmate."

"*Soulmate?*" Luck repeated. The shock in her voice was reflected in her face.

"Yes. Before he signed our contract, they were destined to fall in love, marry, and be together until their final day."

I took a step back and grabbed at my chest. As I recalled the times she comforted me or had my back, the times I made her smile or laugh when nothing else could, it felt like pieces of a puzzle were slowly falling into place. When we were apart, she was always on my mind. After trying to get over her for years, all I'd really done was bury how I truly felt about her. For ages I wanted to confess, but she was my best friend—if she didn't feel that way about me, confessing could destroy our friendship. Had there been signs I was blind to? Might she actually develop feelings for me? And now, because of a stupid decision I made as a teenager, she was marrying a monster.

Lady Luck spun and slammed her hands down on the desk. "You neglected to share *that* little tidbit, *Sister*."

"You did not ask."

Luck glared at Destiny before drooping her head in resignation and sighing. "Fine. This is your decision, Alex." She straightened and faced me. "Will you choose your fate," she said, holding a hand out, palm up, "or your fortune?" She put her other palm up. "Do you want to go back to being penniless, friendless, and hungry, but married to your girl?" Amanda's face appeared over her right hand. "Or would you rather keep your penthouse and your riches and your friends but give her up?" An image of a pile of gold appeared over her left. "I mean, you could have any girl you want!"

"What about Amanda?"

The images vanished as she dropped her hands. "Any *other* girl you want! What kind of life could you have given her—"

"No, I mean, will my decision change her fate as well? Cause I'll go back to being penniless if it means that Amanda won't end up with that jerk. In a heartbeat."

"I cannot guarantee anything, Alexander," Destiny said. "But that is the most likely outcome. Your fates are bound together."

"Then do it. I want you to cancel the deal."

All at once, Lady Luck's coy smile and Destiny's more serious expression traded places. "Well then, that is that," Destiny said, turning to Luck. "You lost the bet, Sister of mine."

"Bet? What bet?" I asked. For the third time that day, I got the feeling that something was terribly off.

"I believe you owe me one soul." Destiny's delight was nearly palpable as she watched Luck bend over the desk and start writing something out on a slip of paper she'd removed from the same drawer. The pale woman kept her eyes glued on the promissory note as she spoke to me. "We had a bet. Luck believed that you would wish to keep your riches at the loss of your future mate. I believed otherwise." The moment Luck finished, Destiny snatched the paper away with a satisfied grin.

"I don't care about some bet you two made! You said you would cancel the contract when I asked, and here I am asking." My attention didn't stray from the document that remained intact on the desk with my shaky signature still on it.

"We most certainly did not," Luck said without looking at me.

"My contracts are binding, Alexander," Destiny said. "We cannot simply 'cancel' one. Now if you wish to enter into *another* contract with me—"

"What!? No, I don't want another contract with you! I demand you cancel this one like you said you would!"

When Lady Luck turned to face me, she had a cutting scowl. "Lies are a *human* shortcoming. My Sister and I have never lied to a mortal in our entire existence, and we are not about to start for a kid like you. When King Gustavus Adolphus and I made a deal that he would not die while riding in battle, I honored it. I made sure he fell from his horse first! When Julius Caesar asked that no *one* would betray him, I honored it. There were over sixty conspirators!"

How many times, I wondered, had the Sisters followed the letter of their law to trick mortals? To play with them? "You used me..." I said as I sat in a chair with my face in my hands. Knowing that I was just a toy for the universe to kick around made me feel truly insignificant.

Destiny came up beside me and put her hand on my back, but her touch did not soothe. "I am sorry to have made you feel this way, Alexander. It was not my intention. I like you. You're the first human I've dealt with who shared his fortune with others. Is there something I can do for you, some water or something to eat?"

"What I want is justice. A trial." They looked at me in confusion. "I want someone impartial to hear my case. Is there anyone like that?"

"We cannot bring this matter to a human court," Destiny replied.

"How about a non-human one? Surely, you two aren't the only ones with power here."

Luck folded her arms and looked to the side. "There's our Kin, Chronos."

"Take me to him."

Chapter 3

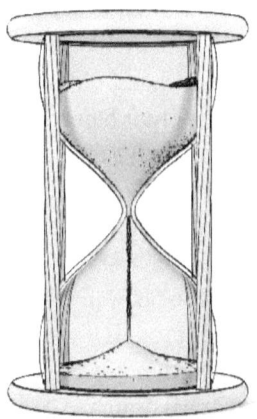

The Timelord

Chronos didn't act anything like the Sisters. At least they *pretended* to be human. The aged body he wore was the most human thing about him. He sported an ancient Roman-style toga, but went barefoot. Age had turned what hair that remained on his head white, yet he had a youthful face. His dark skin made his long beard stand out particularly well. Although his eyes lacked any pupil or iris, I knew he was looking at me. In his hand he held a massive scythe. He didn't have a well-defined outline, but rather it looked blurred, like a thousand different versions of him tried to occupy the same place and posture. He stood in the Halls of Time in front of the largest hourglass anyone had ever seen, so massive that its top reached the ceiling a thousand feet up, or more. Luck and Destiny waited at my sides as he looked at me with a dead expression.

"I told you not to leave the manor," he said slowly. "No, you haven't been there, yet. You will want me to act as judge. Why are you here? You lost your case."

I hadn't even said anything yet. "I don't know what you mean. I've never met you before." Only my growing anger kept me from being too cowed to talk.

His eyes fluttered for a moment. "Apologies. Alternate timelines can be hard to differentiate from each other." When his white eyes stared into mine again, I felt my skin crawl. With how expressionless his face remained, I got the impression that he had no emotions. His outline sharpened. "You have a case to present?"

Luck nudged me. "Yes," I said. "I believe Luck and Destiny lied and misled me. I—"

"Come."

"Follow him," Destiny insisted when I did not immediately obey.

I'd never felt a truly irresistible order before. It was disconcerting. I followed where he led, but not because my body acted on its own or anything. Instead, my mind had been made up for me. To say that I didn't have a choice in the matter would be inaccurate. Like a gift, the decision was mine, even though it was given to me.

Chronos led us to a door on the far wall of the Halls of Time. I didn't even know it had a wall. As we walked through it, we were treated to a very different scene. A garden surrounded a rather serene but palatial manor, the sort I expected to see in a British historical drama. All the plants in the garden looked, well, fake, but they had clearly been watered and the stench told me they'd just been given a fresh bed of mulch. I wondered what an immortal being like him wanted a fake garden for. Beyond the manor I could only see a dark gray, no horizon, like he'd made this patch of reality for himself but never bothered to finish it.

"Time and space always have been, are, and will always be under my complete control here. This is my Domain, my Realm. The Between is a neutral place my Kin and I reside in. But even here, there are rules I must follow. I cannot lie to a mortal. I can neither take nor save a mortal's life for personal reasons. I cannot interfere with the work of my Kin, nor they with mine. I also cannot directly interfere with mortal matters. Although I can weigh the evidence, if I deem that the Sisters are guilty, there is only so much I can do." He spoke without inflection, further solidifying my theory that emotions were foreign to him.

He led us into his manor, which looked more like a museum than a home. Artifacts from across time filled every corner and shelf. I recognized many of them. A spartan shield marked as *Leonidas I* hung next to a Japanese sword labeled *Honjō Masamune.* On one shelf sat a crown labeled *Llywelyn* next to what I believe were the stolen Crown Jewels of Ireland, though they were only labeled as *Vicars.* I half expected to run into the Ark. But some things I didn't recognize at all: a massive bell, a varied collection of crosses, a pile of ancient scrolls. I figured that some of those I couldn't recognize had to have come from the distant past. Or perhaps the distant future.

I tore myself away from the historical artifacts and caught up with Chronos. "I understand. But if you hear my case..."

"I will do better. I will see it." He led us all to a small room rather like an elevator without buttons. "Row Reish, Section Sigma," he said. I certainly didn't feel any movement, but with a cheerful, "ding!" the doors opened a moment later onto a large, semi-circular room with dozens of mirrors. They were evenly spaced along the curved wall, each separated from the others by little walls on either side just long enough to obscure them from each other. In the middle of the room, a symbol was painted on the floor, rather like a cross with a semi-circle on one end. He led me to a mirror with a bronze frame and a plaque with my name on it attached to the bottom. "Alexander David Petersen's contract with Lady Luck and Dame Destiny," he said and tapped it with his scythe. The reflection it had been showing vanished.

A scrawny teenager somewhere around fifteen sat under an overpass. He wrapped his arms around his bent legs and rocked back and forth, sobbing. Out of nowhere, Destiny and Luck walked up to the boy and started asking him about his misery, but he only responded by shaking his head.

Chronos waved his scythe and the encounter which lasted minutes unfolded in seconds, but slowed down near the end.

They brokered a deal. Destiny bent over while Luck held a contract against her back and offered the boy a pen.
"Just sign here and everything will be different, you'll see."
"What is this about sand?" he asked.
"It basically means until you die," Destiny explained. "I have to write it that way. It's like a legal thing."
After a brief hesitation, the youth said, "Fuck it, what've I got to lose, right?" He signed the document with a trembling hand.
As soon as he did, Lady Luck snatched the pen from his fingers. "Now, if you ever want to cancel this contract and undo it all, just come to us and tell us."
Destiny carefully folded the contract and put it into a briefcase she had open on the ground. When she rose to her feet once more, she held out an hourglass amulet. "This amulet will bring you to our realm. Simply break it. I only have one, so you should only do so if you want to cancel the contract."

We continued watching until the Sisters left the scene. Chronos tapped his scythe on the ground. "I'm afraid they were quite clear," he said. "They asked you to tell them if you wanted to cancel the contract. They never claimed that they would do so." I felt a sense of despair take hold of me, but only for a moment. "However, I do not believe this is the whole story. What was your state of mind? What brought you to this point?" He waved his scythe and the scene rewound quickly, and kept rewinding beyond the bridge. It displayed younger me lost in the streets, then running in tears, then the home of the family fostering me at the time.

"No, no, that's far enough! Don't go back any further!" I pleaded, turning away, but Chronos just ignored me. He made it start to run forward again. I shut my eyes tight. But that didn't stop me from hearing what was going on.

"Mr. Lancie... I mean 'Dad.' Why aren't you at work?" The young man's voice held a tinge of fear.

"I heard you had a half day and didn't tell us, so I decided to come home early. What? Don't you want to give your dad a hug? Come here. I told you to come the fuck over here you little bastard."

"Please stop," I begged Chronos. I walked behind a neighboring partition, trying to get away from it, but still I could hear the struggling, the metal clink of the man's belt as it hit the floor, the screams of pain and terror. Even with my hands covering my ears, I could still hear it all. It played in my head as well as in the mirror. "I said STOP!!" I didn't know if I directed that to Chronos or the memory of the man who assaulted me.

"Very well," Chronos said. The mirror went silent.

Destiny came to me and put her hand on my shoulder. Despite her paper complexion, she somehow looked pale. "I... I didn't realize. It's... different to see it than it is to write it in my books. I'm sorry," she said with perhaps the first display of genuine empathy I'd seen from any of them. When I looked over at her I felt anger, but I just cried into her shoulder.

"I do not find fault in the Sisters' language, nor in the language of the contract. However, you two did not fully explain the consequences of signing the contract. It is also apparent from what we've just witnessed that he was in an extremely delicate state, which you failed to take into account. Given these circumstances, as well as his youth, I believe that the validity of the contract is questionable at best."

I pulled away from Destiny and tried to dry my cheeks. Eight years on and it still made me a shaking mess. "What does that mean?" I asked, coming back around the corner.

"It means that though I cannot change what has been done, I believe you should be given the chance to change things yourself."

"How am I supposed to do that?"

"There is only one way," he and Destiny said together, nodding at the mirror.

Chronos cleared his throat as he briefly glanced at Destiny. "The looking glass will show you any point in your past. Step into it and you will enter into your past self. You will be permitted to relive and rewrite any point of your life as often as you like, but only as far back as the signing of the contract, until you decide to remain in a new timeline or return to your original. If you accept this offer, the pages of your Book of Fate from this point forward will be erased. Is that agreeable, Destiny?" She nodded.

I couldn't believe his words. Then again, I was talking to literal *Time* itself, cried on the shoulder of Destiny, and had just watched the past like it was a home movie; *anything* was possible. "What if I change things too much?" I asked. "I mean, if I fix the past, then I'll never have come here to fix the past in the first place."

"There is no paradox here, Alexander Petersen. The Between is outside the space-time you are familiar with. You will simply be stepping out of your own timeline and into a brand new one."

"What about the old one? I don't want Amanda to—"

"It will remain in stasis until this matter has been settled. If you choose to stay in an alternate timeline, it will replace the old one."

"I'll do it!" I said it so quickly that I practically cut him off.

Chronos lifted his hand. "As always, there are rules. Rule 1: you will not be permitted to grossly alter the course of history or otherwise try to capitalize on your knowledge of future events except where it pertains to your contract."

"No cheating on exams, no 'sure bets', no sports almanacs, that sort of thing," Luck explained.

"Rule 2: *your* time will not stop advancing."

This had me concerned. "What do you mean?"

Just a tip: if the fabric of reality is ever folded over you, I recommend you sit down first. I stood in that room of mirrors in one moment, in the next, hourglasses surrounded me and I felt sick and dizzy. Lady Luck helped me sit on the floor so I could put my head between my legs. "Warn a guy!" I protested.

When I felt well enough to stand, Chronos walked over to one of the hourglasses, the one with bright orange sand. Beneath it, a plaque displayed my name and birthdate.

"This is the time allotted to you, Alexander Petersen. Once the sand in the top is gone, you will pass on to the Afterlife. When you move through the past, every hourglass will adjust to the new time except for yours. I will not add sand to yours as long as our agreement lasts. This is how much time you have left and no more. Relive one day and you will die one day sooner. Go back a year, and you will lose a year at the end. Once you go back, you can either live through the remainder of your life from that point or return here. But do not think yourself invincible. The actions of mortals keep us busy, adding or *removing* sand, and believe me when I say you are still quite mortal. Death does not always care if there is sand remaining."

Over my head, a sign marked the location. "Row Reish, Section Sigma." I looked down to the hourglass next to mine. Its design seemed nearly identical, but it had teal sand, not orange. Amanda's name and birthdate—the same as mine—were printed beneath it. "Oh, it's Amanda's! What are the odds?" I said.

"Pretty good," Destiny replied. "I *said* you were soulmates, didn't I?"

"Hey. Why does mine have so little sand? She's got like ten times as much. Most of these have a lot more sand than mine does."

"Everyone gets what they are given. You have approximately one-and-a-half decades remaining," Chronos replied, like he'd just told me to expect rain tomorrow or something.

"What?! You mean I won't even live to see 40? But I exercise! ...I've been meaning to anyway. I eat well—well enough at least! What the hell is going to happen to me? You've got to be joking!"

"I cannot *joke*. At present, you pass on to the Afterlife somewhere between ten and twenty years from now. So, you will have to decide. If you go into the past, you will die at a younger age than if you remain in the present."

"Rule 3: when you return..."

Letting my mind wander while Chronos explained the rules might not have been the smartest idea. I couldn't help but reflect on what I had done with my time and what I had planned on doing but never got around to. I suppose knowing how much time I had left actually made me lucky, but I didn't feel lucky. I expected to be scared, horrified, or disheartened, but when the initial shock of it wore off, determination won out more than anything else. "Fifteen years..."

"Pardon?" Chronos stood stone still but I knew he was not pleased at my interruption.

"If all I've got are fifteen years, then I want to use them to help my soulmate. I'll do it. Besides, I'm only going to have to go back a day or so to stop the wedding."

"Very well." With a movement of Chronos' scythe, the hourglasses melted away and we were in the Mirror Gallery once again. I leaned against the wall and felt nauseated. None of this was doing my headache any favors. When I had recovered, Chronos held out a small piece of metal for me to take. It looked rather like a key, but its shaft was smooth and round with a single hourglass-shaped prong. The same symbol on the ground made up the hole in the key's head, which had my name printed on one side and the location of my hourglass printed on the other.

"This key will fit into any lock. But whatever door you unlock with this key will lead you back here to your mirror. Keep it on you at all times."

I gripped it firmly. "Thank you. Oh, and one more thing. How do I know your Kin aren't going to interfere?" I asked, receiving a scoff from Luck and a sad sigh from Destiny.

"They are bound to the agreement. Before you begin, be aware that there may be repercussions and complications which arise unexpectedly. You will need to handle them as they come." Chronos stroked his beard in thought. "But not alone. You will be given a handler. I believe you've met." As if summoned, the door opened and the Englishman approached with a bow. "You may call him 'Arbiter.' If you have concerns, take them to him, and remain here at my manor. I must go handle a matter that is beyond your ken. Do not expect to see me."

"Good luck, handsome," Lady Luck told me with a wink, not actually upset at my query.

"Do be careful," Dame Destiny said.

* * *

The three of them left. Suddenly, I realized that I didn't know what to do next. "I should've listened..." I muttered, then saw Arbiter staring me down with a stern expression, waiting for me to do something. I now had to entrust myself into the hands of a man I knew next to nothing about. He didn't seemed too happy about it, either.

"Ahem. It doesn't work if you don't set a destination, Master Petersen," he explained after what felt like minutes of awkward silence.

"Ah. Right. How did he do it?"

If there's a British way of rolling your eyes, Arbiter had mastered it. "Simply tell it what time you want to return to."

I faced the mirror, key in hand, and walked up to it. When I saw my reflection, I had to pause. Running my hand over my goatee, I turned my head this way and that. The short, black mop of hair on my head had dirt in it. More of it caked my face. To be honest, it almost looked like I had a tan—something my pale skin had never accomplished before. The dark rings around my eyes reminded me that I'd spent most of that day trudging along the side of the road trying to hitch a ride or being escorted through a desert. No wonder Arbiter looked at me funny.

"If you prefer, I can show you to your quarters instead," he said.

"My quarters?"

"Yes, sir. Your lodging. Your room." He had the voice of one explaining the definition to a child.

"I know what 'quarters' means. I didn't expect to have a place to sleep is all.

Does Chronos get a lot of visitors?"

"You are the only guest at the moment," he said. "His manor houses many of those who work for him, though."

"Well, sleep sounds tempting, but let me figure out how this thing works, first. Um... Mirror? Show me back to the day before Amanda's wedding. Let's say... noon."

Our reflection shimmered and was soon replaced by a different image.

A pre-teen Alex crouched before a chalk line on the ground, his body tight and ready for action. Next to him crouched a girl of about the same age, with wavy, dark-brown hair and wearing a tank-top. Other pre-teens surrounded them.

"I'm gonna beat you this time, Naomi!" Alex said, glancing over at her.

"Heh, fat chance," she replied, her eyes glued to the chalk line on the other end of the school parking lot.

"GO!" someone shouted, and the two took off like springs that had just been released.

"What's this? This wasn't yesterday. Is it broken?" I asked.

Arbiter either hummed or sighed; I wasn't sure which. "The mirror is connected to you. Until you learn to control it, you will need to *concentrate* on the time you want as well."

"Why is it showing me this time? I wasn't thinking about it."

He shrugged. "Something in your 'subconscious' I suppose, if you believe in that rot."

The scene mesmerized me, so despite it being the wrong one, I continued to watch.

Alex and Naomi ran at full speed, but Naomi was clearly getting ahead. When Alex looked over at her, he slowed down without warning and changed direction. Though the other kids protested, he ignored them and sat down on the steps of the school next to an auburn-haired girl who was crying into her knees.

"Amanda? What's wrong?" He panted and put his hand on her back.

"I'm a terr-err-errible per-person!" she sobbed without looking at him, but eventually leaned against his side. When Naomi noticed, she shooed the other kids away.

"Only if you keep telling lies like that one. What did you do?"

Her response was muffled, so she repeated it loudly. "I stole something, alright?! My parents are going to kill me." But after a few moments of silence, with young Alex rubbing her back, she lowered her knees, revealing her freckled face and button nose. She kept her gaze on her lap. "Mrs. Vista's fossil. I took it from her classroom and accidentally dropped it. I just wanted to borrow it for a little." Sitting in her lap were two pieces of rock which, when put together correctly, formed a curved claw. When she saw them, she began to cry again.

Alex picked a piece up and turned it over a few times, inspecting it. "Yup, that's a fossil, alright. I'm sorry, Amanda, but the law is very clear on this." She looked up at him confused. He handed the piece back to her, but then took her hand in his and used the other to chop at her wrist. "Oh yes. Thieves get their hands cut off. I suppose this is a first offense, so maybe just one *hand will do. This* is *a first offense, right?"*

Amanda looked at him in horror, then a laugh burst through her tears. She rubbed at her eyes. "How dare you make me laugh..." she said, but smiled at him. Her demeanor completely changed in a matter of seconds. "What if it's not my first?"

Alex straightened and pointed his finger to the sky. "Then it's off with your head!" he announced in his best impression of the Queen of England, which sounded nothing like her. They both giggled for a while.

"I have to tell her," Amanda said after the giggle-fit ended. "I'm going to turn myself in."

"But you can't do that!"

"Why not?"

"Because I'm turning myself in first!" Alex quickly grabbed the fragments and jumped to his feet, running into the school.

It took a moment for Amanda to realize what just happened, then she followed him. "You can't do that! I'm the thief!"

"You took the blame for her?" Arbiter asked. A bit of softness had crept into his voice.

"Yeah. I had detention anyway," I replied.

Arbiter cleared his throat of any empathy. "Perhaps that is why you saw this scene. You were willing to make a sacrifice for her then as well as now."

"Perhaps. I guess I should try again. Mirror—"

"You needn't address it."

"—show me the day before the wedding at noon." I crossed my fingers as the scene changed.

A pre-teen Alex sat beneath a blanket in an abandoned metal shed that stood in the middle of the woods. He held a backpack to his chest as he munched on a power bar. On the floor, a book lay open, but he wasn't reading it. The only light came in through glassless windows that looked like they hadn't been in the shed's original blueprints, but were crudely added later. Without warning, the door opened to the trees beyond. Alex gave a start, but when Amanda walked in, he blushed and looked away from her.

"Alex! You're here! Thank goodness! I've been looking everywhere for you."

"I'm running away and you can't stop me," he said curtly.

Amanda walked inside and sat down next to him. She had been carrying a backpack overflowing with cereal boxes and bags of chips. A few spilled out. She looked at him with worry. "Why?"

"Nobody cares about me." Alex pulled the blanket around his shoulders more. Amanda just worked her way under the blanket with him. He didn't resist.

"I do. Plus, if you leave, who will Praeli raid the goblin castle with?"

"I'm sure you can find someone else to play with," Alex said, but looked regretful the moment he did.

"I don't want someone else to play with. I want you! Just, next time, let's remember to actually equip our characters." Her grin proved impossible to frown at as it broke through Alex's attempt at scowling. "Happy Birthday, by the way." She slipped a handmade bookmark into his hands. It had a drawing of a creature with the head and torso of a dappled horse and wings, legs, and tail of an eagle, all filled in with colorful marker. Beneath, it said, "Page the Griffohip".

Alex looked down at the bookmark and let out a stuttering laugh. "I didn't get you anything."

"You could... not run away?" Her wide smile brought a little grin to his lips.

"But—"

"Or else I'm coming with you. You know you can't stop me."

"But—"

"I've got a map of Canada with me, if that helps."

I sighed. "We called that our 'Sanctuary.' She was the only one who remembered my birthday that year."

"I take it you did not run away," Arbiter said.

"Not that time."

"It seems *she* saved *you*."

"Yeah, she did that a lot." I looked away from the mirror and cleared my throat. "This thing isn't working."

"It... is possible your memories are jumbled up somehow," Arbiter said.

I thought back on the day I signed the contract and how thoroughly I had blocked it from my mind. "I, uh... might have some repressed memories from my childhood."

"Try again, but this time visualize what you remember."

"Alright." I took a deep breath and stared long and hard at the mirror. "You are going to show me yesterday. At noon. On my couch. Nothing else, got it?"

The image changed. It worked. There yesterday-me was in the mirror, sitting in front of the TV. "Are my arms really that scrawny?" I reached a hand out, and the moment I touched the mirror's surface, I found myself sitting in my living room with the TV on. I was in the exact same position as I had been in in the mirror, only that key was still in my hand.

It took a moment to realize what had happened. When it sank in, elation ran through me and I giggled like a kid. My headache was gone, too. All at once, I jumped to my feet and *whooped!* It felt like I'd been given a super power.

Suddenly, Queen's *You're My Best Friend* started playing from the cellphone on the end table next to me. That euphoric feeling vanished. I remembered this. Although that was Amanda's ringtone, it wasn't Amanda on the other end. It was Hunter, inviting me for drinks with the groomsmen.

"Hello?" Honestly, I have no idea why I answered it. Morbid curiosity, perhaps.

"Hey, Al. It's Hunter. Listen, me and some—"

"No, I won't join you! And I'm telling Amanda all about your affairs." I growled.

There was silence on the other end. Apparently, he didn't like being talked back to. "Heh, I wouldn't let my guard down tonight, if I were you. Do you honestly think Manny isn't already in my pocket?"

The security guard. He'd always acted like such a professional, but when I thought about the reach the Pace family had, I knew I had to take that threat seriously. The calm manner in which he said it was a lot more frightening than if he'd gotten angry. I ended the call and tossed the phone on the couch. That's when I realized I'd been holding the key so tightly it left a mark in my palm. "Let's see how this thing works..."

Chapter 4

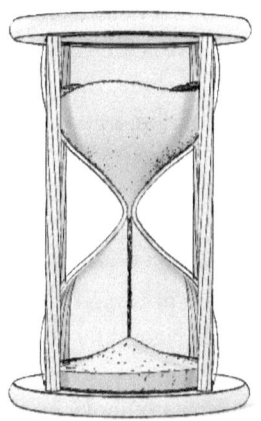

Hunting Hunter

"Amanda?" I asked into my phone with just a hint of desperation.

"Alex?! Hey! It's been so long! How are you? Are you coming? *Please* tell me you're coming." That joyful, playful timbre her voice had always sent my pulse into overdrive. She might not have been good at singing, but by God did I always love to hear her try.

"Hell yes, I'm coming! Lord, I've missed the sound of your voice." My kitchen-pacing stopped when I realized that had slipped out. For weeks, we'd been seeing less and less of each other. I'd told myself that it was because of her wedding planning, but deep down I knew that wasn't the real reason, nor were Hunter's attempts to keep us apart—I was subconsciously trying to save myself the heartache of seeing the love of my life married to another.

"...I've... missed you, too," she said softly. "A lot. A month is too long. I'm really glad you called." Only once before had I heard such a soft, intimate tone from her—we were both half asleep then—but it wasn't half as powerful as this.

"Why is that?" My voice cracked a little as I asked.

"Alex... I... owe you a dig, don't I?" That intimate quality disappeared. "We should schedule it!"

I knew there was something else on her mind, not that it would have taken a genius to figure that out. But I also knew Amanda better than anyone else, and she needed me to keep asking. I leaned my back against my fridge. "What if that's the wedding gift *I* got *you*?" I joked. "But that's not what's really on your mind, is it? I'm here if you want to talk about it."

I held my breath as I waited for her delayed response. When she did respond, her voice had softened again. "You're right. It's just that... I've been feeling really down. I keep regretting things I've done, things I haven't done. I feel trapped. I'm worried that we're growing apart and I don't want that."

"You two are growing apart?"

After a brief pause, she said, "No, us. You and me. You're still my best friend... right?"

"Always," I said. "No matter what." It was only after I spoke these words that my brain actually caught up. I'd kept myself booked for a month so I wouldn't have to see them together. I'd told Naomi I would skip town. Some best friend I was turning out to be. "Amanda, I—"

Before I could continue, she quickly spoke up, perkier than a moment ago. It was her defense for when she didn't want to hear something. "So what did you call for? Or did you just miss me that much?"

I took a deep breath and released it. "Funny that you mention regrets. The reason I called is about Hunter."

"It's Hunter."

"Yeah. I heard him talking—"

"No, I mean it's Hunter, here. He's back early from the wedding planner. Ugh! I've got to go."

"Amanda! Wait!"

But it was too late. "I'll see you at the wedding," she said and then hung up.

It was hard feeling completely defeated, at least at first. I'd talked with Amanda, after all! Not only did I get to hear her voice again, but she gave me such hope, and she still had that sprightly spirit. After going weeks without any contact, it was painfully obvious now that I was still head-over-heals in love with her, or at least with my memory of her. But I was no closer to warning her about him than when I started.

I put my phone away with a heavy sigh and took out the key Chronos had given me. Since hanging around wouldn't achieve anything, I left my apartment and started looking for a door. Not just any door would do. Sure, technically any door *would* do, but how boring! I clicked my tongue against my teeth until the perfect portal caught my eye. "Aha! That one looks entertaining." The chosen candidate: an overhead door. So far I'd tried the key on my bathroom door, a rotating door, my car, three random apartments, and a locking cabinet I had to crawl through. They all worked. I squatted to fit the key into the padlock—would that even count?—then lifted the door above my head and took the key out.

Everything looked like a normal storeroom until I stepped through. As I crossed the threshold, I appeared back in the little alcove of my mirror and chuckled. You've gotta take whatever amusement you can find in a situation like this.

"Hm. Another failure? And what did you learn *this* time, sir?" Arbiter asked once I arrived back in the Mirror Gallery. He kept his nose buried in *The Old Man and the Sea*. At his feet sat a stack of books I'd seen him reading since I started this whole affair. The titles *Faust, The Sun Also Rises, Futility*, and *Rabbit, Run* stood out to me. Subtle. He looked up briefly with the same forced-polite smile as usual, then returned to his book.

Despite how infuriating his passive-aggressiveness was, I kept myself calm with a deep breath before answering. "Not great. I'm pretty sure Hunter's been keeping her phone. I mean, I must have called nearly a hundred times at different points over the last two weeks and this was the first time we spoke for more than two sentences! Texts don't get through. Hunter must have threatened me a dozen times by now. She's disappeared online. She's never at her apartment. And when I ask her parents, her mom gets on my case—I didn't realize how scary that woman can be. Mrs. Shields practically accused me of being a drug-dealing pimp! Where did she even get something like that? This should have been solved by now, but no matter what I do, everything turns out the same! Somehow I've created my own personal *Groundhog Day*."

"That's nice, sir. Have you tried phoning her *again*?" Arbiter licked his thumb and turned the page. "You could make it an even hundred."

Another deep breath. "I suppose I could just blurt it out. I'm sure that'll go over well. 'Hey Amanda, it's Alex. I think Hunter's cheating on you. By-eee!' She'd probably just think I'm jealous."

"Aren't you, sir?"

I folded my arms over my chest. "No! ...Maybe. But that's not why I'm doing this."

"Hmm. Perhaps the young lady simply does not wish to speak to you," Arbiter said, eyes still on the book.

I sighed and leaned against the partition between my mirror and the next. "Yeah, I've wondered that myself. I don't know how this whole 'soulmate' thing works, but if she really doesn't want to see me, maybe... Could Destiny have been wrong about us?" My headache from the day I arrived began to return, making it hard to think. "Ugh. I don't know *what* to do."

"Does this mean you're *finally* ready to quit?"

For some reason, that riled me up. I slowly lifted the book out of his hands and stared at the Englishman. "You could at least *try* sounding less hopeful about it. Look, I'm a stubborn man with limited time on the clock, so you might as well stop entertaining the notion of me *ever* giving up. I don't know what I did to get this attitude from you, but we're going to be stuck together until I see this thing through. We can either keep up like this and make each other miserable or we can try to get along."

Arbiter looked flustered as our eyes met. "I have been perfectly congenial! I... I am not a nanny. I simply wish to get back to my work. You're not the only person who has an agreement with Chronos, you know."

This intrigued me. "You? How long have you been working on yours?" I ventured.

He began silently counting out on his fingers. "By my time, it's been nearly fifty-seven years. By yours... Well, I started in the year eighteen hundred and eighty-seven. And you are from the twenty-first century, am I correct?"

"That's correct. But how can that be? There's a big time gap there."

"Sir, you are standing in the home of Chronos, the Lord of Time."

I nodded and rolled my eyes in a "I suppose that's a good point" manner. "I guess I must seem a bit strange to you."

"Indeed. But I have seen many things stranger than you in the past fifty-seven years." His body relaxed a little and he sighed like he wanted to get this over with. "But I suppose we have a few similarities. I, too, had to meet with my lover clandestinely."

I'd never really gotten much out of him before, so I couldn't let this opportunity go by. "Really? What did you have to do?"

"I remember tossing pebbles against the pane of his window in the middle of the night. Once I had to use a disguise to spirit him away for holiday." Arbiter had stopped looking at me. I'm not even certain whom he was talking to.

"That must have been difficult." His defenses seemed to have slipped some. Yet, if I wanted him as my ally, I knew I had to proceed with caution. "Is he why you're here?"

"Yes," he answered after a pregnant pause. For the first time, I got a genuine expression out of Arbiter—at least a genuine one besides mild annoyance. It was a bittersweet look, the kind only complicated memories can draw out. "I'm paying the debt of our borrowed years."

"Were they worth the price?" I asked.

He scoffed at me indignantly. "Of course they were."

"Then will you help me have my time with Amanda?"

Arbiter looked down at the key in my hand for a while before letting out a long breath. "All right, sir. I will try. To begin with, you should put that key on a chain to wear close to your heart. I can't help you very well if you are stuck there. Here." He pulled out his stopwatch from inside his vest and removed it from the long, silver cord that kept it secure. Then he slipped the cord through his vest button hole and disconnected the fabric measuring tape case from the other end.

40

After putting the watch and tape back in his pocket, I handed him the key and he attached it to the cord. To finish, he brought the cord into a loop using the clasp.

When I examined the thin plait, I realized, "It's hair?" The intricate weave was bound on either end by metal cuffs, one with a clasp, the other with a short metal chain, which was where the key had been strung.

Arbiter nodded. "A mourning chain. I will try to find a more suitable replacement. Whatever you use must come from Earth or it will not return there, but you have to bring it with you from here, or else it will stay on Earth, so options are limited."

I put the key on and hid it under my shirt. "That's very nice of you."

"*Promise* me you will not lose it," he said with a firm tone. "It is personal."

"I promise."

He nodded in approval of my vow. "Now, if you want my advice, you have been pursuing the wrong person. Wouldn't it be more efficacious to track your rival?"

A light switched on in my head. "You mean, make Hunt*er* into the hunt*ed*?" I said with a shit-eating grin.

Arbiter closed his eyes and rubbed his temple. "...Yes. You had mentioned meeting him at a public house once. Can you think of any other time you know Hunter was not with her? Perhaps you will be able to see Amanda while he is with his mistress."

"I think he said he was with Diana the night before the wedding. If I can just figure out where they were, I can get proof."

Arbiter rocked back on his heels. "You are American. Do you still have a tradition of a dinner before the wedding day, sir?"

I swear I could hear angels singing the moment that first ray of actual hope shone down on me since this whole ordeal started. "Yes! The rehearsal dinner! Thank you, Arbiter. Oh, and you can call me Alex."

"Thank you, sir, but no." Well, at least I had made progress.

"Mirror, show me to the afternoon before the day of Amanda's wedding to Hunter."

*　　　*　　　*

I had no problem finding the rehearsal. I went to the church and waited all afternoon and into the evening. The wedding party arrived, and an hour later they filed into cars. I followed them to a restaurant in D.C. renowned for serving expensive Italian food, mostly to rich customers who could afford to take two hours for a meal. There weren't a lot of places that still required a coat and tie. I didn't dare show my face in there with Hunter around, but I hoped I'd be able to follow him and Diana to wherever their illicit affair would play out. I waited in the parking garage for them to return. It was my first stakeout.

Around the first hour, I began questioning when I had last slept. It was strange going back and forth between worlds—I had to keep two sleep schedules.

"Sir? There's no overnight parking here."

I jerked awake to find a teenage rent-a-cop at my window. I couldn't see any other cars in the garage.

"Sorry. I didn't realize how tired I was," I said and started up the car. As soon as I could no longer see him, I pulled out that wonderful key that could make everything better. "Huh, silver hair," I said as I inspected the cord. I then got out of the car, and used the key on the car door. Within a minute, I was crawling into my own bed the evening before. I had to make sure my phone was fully charged, after all.

Despite being overly tired, I could barely sleep that night. Whether due to stress, fear, or anticipation, my brain just refused to shut down. When I finally did fall asleep, the sun was already up. I didn't get out of bed until after noon. "Ugh. Okay, self. Since I know they'll be in the restaurant, perhaps it's best to keep tabs on them from inside. At least I know what time they'll leave the church. But, first things first," I said to no one in particular. "I need a disguise." Yes, I've always talked to myself; it helped hold back the loneliness a bit. I went to the bathroom and ran a hand over the goatee I'd had since high school. After shaving both it and my head, I bought a pair of fake glasses to complete the disguise. I was sure I'd done a damn good job of making myself look a lot less like myself. Hopefully.

I arrived at the restaurant early and got a table just outside of the private room that had been reserved. When the wedding party started filtering in, I held a menu up to my face, just in case. Amanda followed behind Hunter. I couldn't help myself and watched her walk in. She had reddish-brown hair the color of dark redwood that fell to her back with bangs covering most of her forehead. Her cute, button nose and cheeks were sprinkled with freckles. They helped emphasize her youthful vitality. The gray v-neck shirt she wore displayed just a hint of her modest bust while also showcasing how toned her arms were. No one else in the room could compare. But those green eyes, which had always been full of joy and mischief, held a sadness that betrayed the light smile on her lips. Believe me when I tell you it was hard to not jump up and hug her right there.

Before long, everyone from the wedding party had sat down to eat: Glass, Diego, TJ, and Hunter on one half of the long table, Amanda, Sam, Diana, and Tilly on the other. Amanda's 17-year-old brother, Jason, sat with her parents and grandparents on the bride's side of the room, while the other side looked like a "Who's Who" of Fortune 500 companies. So much for the "close friends and family only" policy Hunter had told Naomi.

"Mr. and Mrs. Shields, I can't tell you how good it is to see you both here tonight." Hunter gave his speech after the main course. As he spoke, he poured white wine into a glass. "When you welcomed me into your home, you treated me as if I were one of your own. Before I knew it, you were like family to me. When I learned about the cancer, I was only too happy to open my heart—and my wallet—to you." That got a few giggles from some, though I didn't understand why. I knew Mr. Shields had been in and out of the hospital for several years because of cancer, but he looked pretty good that night. "You've treated me like your son ever since." I managed to change positions so I could see him with the side of my eye. And damn it, they were eating out of his hand, metaphorically speaking. "A toast! To health and to family!" The party cheered and raised their glasses.

It hurt to watch someone who'd tied me up and cheated on Amanda earn her family's undeserved adulation. I lost count of the number of toasts they gave throughout the night, though that might have been because I didn't really want to hear so many speeches on the many virtues of Hunter Pace. In fact, most of the toasts focused on Hunter, as if most of the guests had come to support the Pace family.

A man with more than a few streaks of wisdom in his hair rose and lifted a glass. "Mr. Pace, you have done exemplary volunteer work at the Phoenix Women's Shelter. Your family's donations have kept us running for decades. So, I'd like to offer a toast to you and your family for your charity work. To your charity!"

Good Lord, did they have to treat him like a saint? Oh, did I mention that Hunter's family had money? Lots of money. *Oodles* of it. The Pace fortune was *old* money that made my fortune look like a child's allowance. Their company made parts for satellites, many of them in national defense. "Keeping America On Pace" was their slogan. The crowd on the Pace's side dressed in expensive, tailor-made clothing, likely imported from some European country, while the few on the Shields' side had probably never even been to a tailor. And judging from the way his clan paid so little attention to hers, it was clear to me that not everyone really cared for this wedding. Hunter's dad, who looked like he was still forty, hadn't participated or shown any interest in the evening, beyond eating that is. This was, from what I understood, par for the course in his family. So, when he rose and demanded everyone's attention, I was surprised.

"Son, you've been moving up the echelons of Pace Enterprises at a prodigious *pace,*" he said, earning a chuckle from the party. I could see who came up with their slogan. "It was always my intention for your sister, Tilly, to take over for me someday. But now I believe you two deserve an equal shot. That's why I am putting you both on the Board of Directors at Pace Enterprises. I am also prepared to bankroll your own company as subsidiary to Pace, making the integrated circuits we use in our products. Tilly, you will head a company that manufactures our motherboards. Whoever has the more profitable business when I pass on will be given my shares of Pace Enterprises."

Though that got mixed applause, I was mortified. Did families always set each other up for conflict, backstabbing, and failure? Surely they just broke several laws, right? And no mention of Amanda or the wedding? Hunter thanked him, but shot a glance to the young blonde woman who sat catty-corner to him, Tilly.

When Amanda got up to talk with her seventeen-year-old brother, Jason, Hunter didn't waste any time before redirecting his affection—he and Diana smiled at each other once her back was turned, like they delighted in some mutual secret. Hell, he even *winked* at the bridesmaid. I got out my phone, but didn't get the chance to record the flirty glance before Amanda sat back down next to him. Someone started clinking a glass. Another joined in. Soon, the whole room demanded that the happy couple kiss.

It wasn't just a peck. Hunter had practically pulled her into his lap and she put her hands on his chest. Watching it made my guts twist in a knot. The kiss ended, everyone went back to their conversations, but Hunter kept pulling her closer for another kiss, and Amanda was pushing herself away. I felt a fire and ire I'd never felt before try to take over my thoughts as I watched her struggle.

When she finally got away, Hunter hit his fist on the table. Enough voices died down that I could hear him over the remaining conversations. His glass fell over and water spilled on his best man, TJ. "Look what you did! You bumped my arm," Hunter growled. Amanda recoiled. My mental image that they were a happy couple began falling apart. Hunter was usually so good at being friendly; an outburst like that was out of character. After a moment, he regained his composure. "If you'll excuse me, I need to get some air." I'd never seen that expression of apprehension on Amanda's face before.

I lowered my head as he walked past my table. The volume of the conversation returned to its previous level. When I glanced back in at the party, I couldn't find Amanda at first. Then I saw her, her gaze fixed on me. Had she recognized me? Her deep-green eyes lingered for several moments before she turned away. My imagination went to the worst place first: she didn't want me there. My logical brain protested, told me that she just kept her eyes on Hunter as he walked away. Or maybe she thought I looked familiar. That didn't change the sense of shame and dread I felt. Mark private eye off my list of dream jobs.

*   *   *

The evening went on, and the lasagna I'd forgotten I'd ordered arrived. I had to at least make a show of eating it, but it didn't hurt that I was starving. It was difficult keeping track of both Hunter and Diana while eating the most delicious lasagna on the planet (I've checked). At some point, Hunter returned and the party turned to chatting and milling about. It was that time of a party where it began slowly shedding the less-essential members. I was *forced* to order tiramisu to keep up the ruse. As I dug into the dessert, I overheard Hunter speaking softly to Diana as they stood just outside the party room, two booths down from mine. They weren't speaking softly enough.

"She said that?" Diana whispered.

"Oh yeah," he replied. "I mean, treatment is *expensive*. So, I can see where she's coming from. Still..."

"But to wish your own dad was *dead* so he wouldn't be a burden to the family? That's awful!" I quickly found her dad on the far end of the room talking with Jason. He looked healthy as far as I could tell, and the two of them were smiling. Maybe Hunter was talking about someone else?

"I completely agree. I told her I'd pay for it, but she doesn't want to be a burden on *me*. You know how Amanda gets." Well, there went *that* theory.

I scanned the room to see where Amanda was, but it was her mom that caught my eye. Though she stood at a wet bar on the inside of the room refilling her water from a silver decanter, she had to have been close enough to hear them, especially if I could, and Hunter had to have known it as well. She looked pale and disturbed. When she walked back to her husband, I could have sworn I saw Hunter smirk.

Maybe five minutes later, Hunter quietly slipped away from the party room and headed towards the bathrooms. But when Diana did the same thing a couple of minutes later, I decided to turn my phone's video recorder on and follow her. This could be it, the evidence I needed! Although I stayed back a respectable distance, it didn't really matter. As soon as she got to one of the single-person bathrooms, she knocked once, then moved to the next one and knocked again before letting herself in. When I moved in closer, I noticed that there was no light shining beneath the door of the first bathroom. Just outside the second bathroom door, I heard voices. Though muffled, I could make out enough to tell they came from two people; a man and a woman. It sounded like Hunter.

I had a hard time making out any specific words. But moans eventually replaced the mumble of conversation, along with other amorous activity. *Vigorous* amorous activity. A spank and subsequent gasp of pleasure from Diana were crystal clear. After a few more slaps, her sounds became less like pleasure and more like begging.

I had heard more than enough. When I got to my car, I checked the video. I finally had the proof: Diana entering the bathroom, then audible voices. "It's all here. Now what?" I couldn't take it back with me to Chronos' domain. I was going to have to get it to Amanda on the first try or relive the entire day yet again.

*   *   *

The church opened early that day so it could be decorated. Finding the room reserved for the bride to prepare in took no time at all. It was the only classroom decorated with white streamers on the door. I quickly scrawled a coded message on the dry erase board inside and left it in plain view.

ROY G BIV, Praeli
-Tamlarian

Sure, the colors of the rainbow are not hard to figure out, but to anyone other than Amanda, it would just seem an odd note left over from some church event. We'd never told anyone about the characters in our favorite online game where we used to chat, flirt, and dream together. I stopped seeing her as just a friend in those chats in between raids. That's where I fell in love with her.

Next, I had to hide and I already knew the spot. I'd seen that the classroom across the hall had a door featuring Noah's Ark beneath a rainbow, hence the note. It was unlocked. Inside, two circular tables with munchkin-sized chairs took up most of the room. It smelled like crayons. Clearly, they weren't expecting to use this room. I knew Mrs. Shields would never allow Hunter to see her daughter before the wedding, so all I had to do was wait.

And wait.

Three hours really isn't that long in the grand scheme of things. But I worried that I'd get caught, plus the prospect of actually seeing Amanda again made my heart race. So much waiting with so much fear and hope exhausted me, and since I didn't get much sleep again, I didn't know if I could stay awake for three hours.

"Alex?" She slipped into the room and shut the door behind her. Hearing her voice alone made my heart leap for joy. Who needs coffee?

"Amanda, I'm here!" I'd taken up post in a spot hidden from the door's small window. Although she kept the lights off, I could see her clearly from the light in the hall. She wore a gray t-shirt and sweatpants. The red hairband I'd given her years ago kept her hair back. Her makeup sadly obscured her freckles, but that goofy grin of hers more than made up for it in cuteness.

"Alex! It *is* you!" She nearly knocked me over when she hugged me, then squeezed tightly. There's nothing quite like a powerful hug. I swayed back and forth with her, one leg to the other, as we laughed. When she released me, she

46

leaned back and rubbed her hand against my bald head. "What happened to you? Get in a fight with a sheep shearer? I'm sorry to tell you this, bud, but you lost," she mused. "I *thought* that was you last night. What is this, a disguise?"

Some of her makeup had rubbed off onto my shirt, but I didn't care. "Don't you like it?"

"I think I prefer the hair and goatee. You should've consulted your best friend, first! We... *are* still best friends, right?" It was the second time she'd asked me this, though in different timelines. It felt good knowing she was just as worried about drifting apart as I was.

"Of course we are!" I said without hesitation.

"Then why did you tell me you weren't coming? I was so worried I'd done something or said something to hurt you..." She was the one who looked hurt.

"When did I say that?"

"In that letter," she said, blinking with confusion. "Didn't you send it? You said you were leaving the country for good."

"Are you kidding? I wouldn't miss this for a pack of pachycephalosauruses! Besides, I haven't written a *letter* since the 20th century!"

The worry just melted away from her face. "Then you must *really* want to see me." I was sorely tempted to tell her I did, but from what I could tell, Amanda still thought of me as a friend.

"Hunter told me *you* didn't want me there," I said.

She punched my shoulder lightly. "That's absurd. Of *course* I want you at the most important event of my life! You know, if you wanted to come to the rehearsal dinner, you could've just asked. You didn't need to go all Billy Zane on me and sneak around."

"Actually, there's another reason for that," I said. "I know it sounds ridiculous, but I found out that Hunter has been planning to tie me up and leave me in the woods if I tried to come. I just had to see you before the wedding, and that was the only solution I could come up with! I can't even *begin* to tell you what I had to go through just so I could see you today. Seriously, I wouldn't even know where to start."

She gasped. "Hunter wanted to do what!? He couldn't... ...would never..." I could *see* her going through her own thoughts and memories looking for something. "If you're lying... No, I trust you, Alex." Amanda's eyes widened. "Oh my God, he *has* been lying to me! Has he this whole time?! Do you think *he* wrote the letter? What else has he lied about? Was Naomi ever selling drugs? He even had pictures. I... I don't know what to believe..." The fact that she still trusted me gave me hope. We'd promised not to lie to each other when we were kids, and we had done our best to keep that promise ever since, though at times that meant some awkward silences.

"It's bad, but there's a silver lining," I said. She still stared off into space, distraught and muttering, so I foolishly tilted her chin towards me. "There's still time. You can..." The instant our gazes met, she calmed down. If the eyes are the windows of the soul, then what if you look into your soulmate's? There was a spark in my mind; I felt a connection with her. Everything else faded away, including the rest of that sentence.

Her eyes grew wet. "Alex, there's something..." Fear was in her eyes, even as she looked into mine with wonder. Both her body and voice were tremulous. "Alex~ I..." I wasn't surprised when a tear broke free and blazed a trail down her face. But when she cupped my cheek in her hand and kissed me, I was taken completely off guard. Believe it or not, no one had ever kissed me before, and if I didn't fix things, no one ever would again. It started awkwardly: neither of us moved our lips, I held my breath, and our noses got in the way. Regardless, I felt my confidence rise and pressed against her lips more firmly. She parted hers. I did the same. A deep kiss followed immediately after with more passion than before. Her fingers curled against my chest and gripped my shirt. The moment I ran mine through her hair, she let out a soft moan. When our lips eventually separated, she bit mine with a gentle tug, then pressed her face against my chest.

"I'm sorry," she said, at least that's what it sounded like muffled against my shirt.

"H-how long have you been wanting to do that?" I whispered between heavy breaths. My pulse refused to calm down. Every nerve in my entire body tingled. The kiss may as well have been a marathon.

She leaned back and lifted her eyes to mine. "A while," she whispered. I wiped the tears from her cheeks. Her makeup was a lost cause by that point. "Please don't leave, don't hate me. I was too scared to tell you."

"Tell me what?" I whispered back. Neither of us could speak any louder.

"How I feel about you."

I eagerly kissed her. She gasped and went rigid. After a few seconds, her body relaxed, she tilted her head, and her arms slid around my neck. Just as the kiss ended, I began playing with her hair. "God, I wish we'd done this sooner," I said.

"Me too. I wanted to every time we leaned against each other, hugged each other, smiled... Actually, Alex, I keep dreaming that it was *you* waiting for me at the altar." She laid her head on my shoulder.

I couldn't believe what I'd just heard. "It's not too late," I said. "You're not married, yet. And you're not the only one who's dreamed that..."

Pain showed in her eyes as she sharply pulled back from my shoulder like she'd seen a snake. "You don't really want me. I'm... I'm damaged goods. I'm not worth it..." I didn't know where this came from, but it burst out of her in sobs.

"You're not damaged goods, not to me. I don't care about that. It doesn't change how *I* feel about you."

She pressed her cheek to my chest and the sobs slowly subsided. We must have spent ten minutes like that without a word between us. Words were unwelcome.

Speaking of unwelcome, we eventually heard her mother in the hall. "Amanda? *Amanda!* Has anyone seen my daughter?" She sounded pissed.

Amanda whimpered. "She's been furious at me since last night but she won't say why."

"I bet it's because last night she overheard Hunter say you wished your dad was dead."

"What?!" She bit her lip and leaned in closer to whisper. "What? I never! I may have said that I didn't want him to be in pain, but that's totally different!"

"So he's still sick?"

She nodded and pressed her face against my neck. "Remember that rare cancer he got?"

"I thought he was in remission."

"It keeps coming back," she said. "I hate seeing dad so weak. We can't afford the treatment, so Hunter's paying for it." I felt a twinge of guilt. I had no idea of their plight.

"I'm so sorry." We held each other tighter as her mom's calls faded down the hall.

"Can't we just stay here, like this?" she cooed softly. "We can build our first house together using Legos."

I chuckled. "With all the Play-Doh, making babies will be a snap!" She laughed lightly and leaned back so we could see each other better. Once more, she had a smile. That's when I remembered the whole reason I wanted to meet her like this in the first place. That smile would not last long.

I cleared my throat. "Listen, Amanda, there's something important I have to tell you. It's about Hunter," I said and pulled out my phone. "He's been cheating on you. A lot. He's just using you. He and Diana—"

"Again?" she whispered. I expected shock, or tears. Not this. All that work for nothing.

"You knew?"

She nodded. "I wasn't sure, but I thought I heard them together once. He doesn't know I did. I've suspected about him and Sam for a while, too."

My brain blue-screened. After a quick reboot, I said the first thing that came to mind. "Then leave him. I love you, Amanda! We—we can go down to the courthouse right now and get married, just the two of us."

Her voice quaked and she turned her face so I couldn't see it. I didn't need to. I could hear the sorrow. "No... we can't."

"What do you mean?"

She let go of me and sank to the floor. I joined her. "I *have* to marry him. I don't have a choice. He says I'm the only person keeping him from hurting himself. He has my family worshiping the ground he walks on. We're indebted to him. He's been telling awful things about you—I knew they had to be lies. If I even *think* about leaving, he says he'll spread rumors about me, too. And, and..." She started crying again and leaned back against the wall. "He's *threatened* me. He's threatened my *brother*. Once, he saw that I'd called you. Jason didn't come home from school the next day. It was only that night when we found out Hunter had picked him up and took him to some arcade. Mom thought Hunter was being a good boyfriend; they kept saying I was reading too much into it. But he told me to stop calling you after that, Alex. He screens my calls. He destroyed my art because he says I should be dependent on him. He hardly lets me out of his sight. I'm scared. I'm so scared of what he'll do if I don't marry him."

"What about if you *do*?" Before that moment, I had just thought of Hunter as an aggressively possessive philanderer. But the more she spoke, the worse my image of him became. I never dreamed he was such a psychopath. "Do you think he'll stop or change?"

"I—I don't know."

"What if we call the cops?" But as soon as I asked that, I knew the answer. Unless there was evidence of abuse, they couldn't do a thing. And that's assuming the Pace family *doesn't* have a cop or two on payroll. "Or maybe the press? No... We can... There must be *something* we can do!"

"Amanda, where *are* you?" her mom called from just outside the room.

She shook her head and wiped her cheeks. "I tried everything. I put off the wedding for so long, as long as I could... There *is* one thing you can do."

"Anything."

"Forget about me, Alex."

"I can't..." I whispered.

She pushed away from me. "Go! Find happiness for the two of us. Stay away from me. I don't want the man I love to get killed!" A confession of love, in any other situation, would have made me the happiest man alive. As it was, I felt like I just died inside. She got up and walked over to the door, then looked back to me with a sad smile. "It should have been you. I wish I'd kissed *you* that day." And she was gone.

Chapter 5

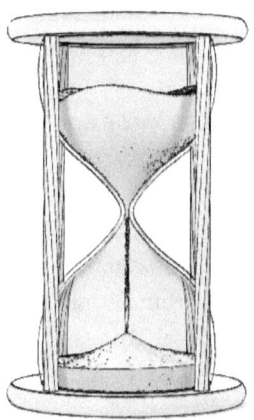

Taxi Troubles

"Master Petersen? Are you all right?" Arbiter's normally soft voice almost sounded worried. "I saw what happened, sir. You have my deepest sympathy." I heard him sit next to my supine body. His hand touched my shoulder. "Do you... wish for a refreshment?"

I took my arm away from my face. "She loves me." It had taken a while to sink in.

"I'm sorry, I didn't catch that."

"She loves me. Amanda loves me! And she kissed me, Arby! She practically told me she wanted to marry me!" I sat up and ran my hand over my face. "All this time she's felt the same way I have."

"*Arby?* Ah, um, congratulations, sir, but, you *did* hear the rest of that conversation, correct?"

"Yes. She's trapped. I had no idea Hunter was *that* bad."

"He sounds like a bedlamite, a reprobate, a—"

"A real monster."

Arbiter smirked. "Come now, I think something a bit harsher will fit him better. Arsehole?" he said as he helped me up.

"Narcissist. But that's the problem. I don't know how to deal with someone like that. I hate confrontation. I used to just run away."

"And now you can't because someone you love depends on you," he said.

"And who loves me! I still can't believe it. She actually loves me! I've got to help her! I'm the whole reason she's *in* this situation."

"Do you have an inkling of how to do that?"

"No. Yes! ...no." I winced and knocked my knuckles against my skull like it would rattle loose some amazing plan.

After a moment, the Englishman spoke up. "She mentioned something about a kiss."

"Yeah. Pretty sure she meant the day she started going out with him. I had a chance to kiss her but I... chickened out. That night, at a party, he, uh, didn't. But that was, what, four years ago? Damn, she really did stall that wedding." I'd begun talking to myself, though Arbiter could hear me. "If I go back that far, I might not even make it to thirty-five! My destination needs to be more recent."

"Sir, perhaps if you get some sleep it will help. I have prepared your room in the manor." I reluctantly agreed.

*   *   *

It felt like I slept for days. Accurately determining the passage of time in that place, Between-time as it were, just couldn't be done. I knew I must have spent a good week reliving the past, but how much of my remaining time did I use planning my next moves while in Chronos' manor?

"Good morning, sir. There is breakfast ready for you downstairs." Arbiter flung open the thick curtains that blocked out the constant light. My room, which he always prepared for me, looked the way I would expect a 19th century Victorian gentleman would prepare a room. It had large windows that overlooked the faux gardens, a four-poster bed, two ornately decorated, plush chairs that likely had never and would never see use, several pieces of furniture containing unknown items, and a small table that held an electric lamp (which was the most modern item there).

"Ugh. Morning? What time is it?"

"Funny. Time to get up, sir. Feel better?"

With a wry smile, he went around the room tidying things up, even though they certainly looked tidy to me. But it was more than simple tidying; he measured distances with his tape measure to ensure everything was *precisely* where it belonged. If the furniture had shared the same grayscale Arbiter had, I'd have thought I'd walked into an old black and white murder mystery.

"Any thoughts pertaining to your next move?" he asked.

"Too soon to tell. I need coffee."

He chuckled. "That is another proclivity we share."

"Say, were you a butler before?" I got out of bed and touched the bump on the back of my head. I knew some amount of time must have passed in that strange world between worlds because it didn't hurt any longer. My clothes, too, always returned to the ones I had on when I first came there. Thankfully, he did my laundry every other night. Instinctively, my hand went to my pocket and I smiled when I felt the old dinosaur watch.

"Head footman. I was second in command of the household. Why do you ask?"

"Just trying to learn more about you."

"What about yourself?" he asked.

"Me? I'm a travel writer. I go all over the world and blog about it—that is, I write articles about my experiences and put them up where the whole world can read them. I tried novels but I didn't have the patience."

Arbiter turned to leave. "I know what a blog is, sir. And I think you will find that patience is a virtue of age."

"Then I'll be lucky to get any." As he closed the door, I got in one final question. "Arbiter, how much time have I spent so far?"

"It's been nearly a month by your clock." He almost sounded apologetic. "It is very easy to lose your sense of time here."

*   *   *

"Mirror. Show me. When Hunter. Proposed. To Amanda... Please." So far, the mirror had shown me breaking my arm in the 6th grade (it doesn't matter how much they dare you, don't do jumping jacks on a sheet of ice), sharing my food with a kid during my first night on the street, and sitting in detention as Amanda made googly eyes at Brian Reynolds in 10th grade. I didn't know what I expected this time, but it certainly wouldn't have been an image of me dressed up as Gomez Addams standing in line to get my badge at a major gaming convention.

"What is that?" Arbiter asked.

"That's GameDay Con," I said. "I remember this now. Me and my friends flew a thousand miles to be there and Amanda never showed up to the airport. The only good thing was that Hunter had already paid for everything."

"No, I mean, what is that?" He pointed to a tall lump of hair.

"Oh, that's Jack. He's dressed as Cousin It. Diego was Lurch. I went as Gomez. There were seven of us. We were all dressed as members of the Addams Family, and Amanda was supposed to go as Morticia."

Just the look on Arbiter's face told me how strange he found us all. "And Hunter wasn't going to be there? I wonder why not."

I chuckled, but kept my eyes on the mirror the entire time we talked. "Oh, he used to come with us. A few times. We were all friends. Then he just... stopped."

"Is that so? Not a very constant friend."

"Now I remember what a shitty trip this one was. Since she wasn't there, I ended up sitting out in the hall most of the time." When I got a quizzical expression from Arbiter, I added, "Oh, I don't do well with crowds. Amanda had a way of keeping me calm. I could usually handle them if she was with me. Even so, I never went into the exhibition rooms. But this isn't the right scene. Is my mirror defective, or is it just me?"

"It looks like you are the right age, and she is not present. Is this what you were doing when Hunter was proposing?"

"What do you—Oh! Yeah, that's right. He apparently showed up at Amanda's house talking about some big surprise and convinced her to stay behind. I never found out where it all happened. We never really talked about it. She just sent me a text later saying she was engaged. You see, Amanda and I... we had our first fight a few days before."

"Soulmates can *have* fights?"

"We sure can. It was so stupid, too. It started with who was older. But since I don't know what time I was born and we share the same birthday, we decided to just say I was born at noon. Well, it turns out she was born at 10 a.m. on the dot... in Mountain Time. She said she's still older, even though that's noon Eastern Time. It became this whole thing. But when I said she was lucky her parents were still alive to tell her when she was born, she ran off crying. Oh. Oh no." A sudden realization made me freeze for a moment. "...That was because her dad was sick, wasn't it?"

Arbiter nodded. "That would be a safe assessment."

"Oh God, I can't believe I said that to her. I figured I was the reason she didn't go to the convention with us. We were stuck there all weekend, so I had plenty of time to feel guilty." I paced the floor in a circle, focusing on the pattern of the stonework underfoot while my mind excavated ancient memories. "Even if I left from the convention right away, I wouldn't get back until that night... That's far too late to do anything. Mirror, show me that morning, eight a.m."

As the image of an airport terminal appeared, Arbiter leaned in close. "And what is your plan here? To interrupt the proposal? I do not think that is going to do very much good."

"I remember Amanda telling me that she wanted to break up with him but didn't know how. A week later they were engaged. I need to know what happened." With that, I walked into the image without waiting for Arbiter's reply.

It's strange stepping into your past. The emotions of my past self took over, fresh and strong. At that time, I mostly worried about the fact that Amanda hadn't shown up. We sat in an airport terminal, all checking our phones. The flight had started boarding and she still hadn't replied to any of my texts. When I called her parents, I just got a busy signal.

"Hey, forget her. She's not coming, Alex, and we're going to miss our flight," my friend Xiao told me, but I just ignored them. Instead, I shirked the security warnings and left all my luggage behind as I took off. I could just make out Jack's voice protesting in the distance, but they would have to go to the convention two men down.

I'd nearly made it to the airport parking lot when I remembered that I hadn't parked there. I hadn't parked at all. I had long forgotten that fact, but now it appeared fresh in my mind after stepping into the past.

"Aw shit, that's right. It's in the shop." For once, it hadn't been my fault, either. My car had been parked in a parallel parking spot. When I got back to it after running my errands, I found an anvil sitting in the middle of a crater that had once been my car's roof. A literal anvil. Like in the cartoons. I had to admit, it actually impressed me.

By the time I got to the pick-up zone, I was out of breath from all the running. Thankfully, I discovered a taxi right there, waiting for someone like me to show up. I jumped in and tossed all the cash I had onto the front seat. "I'm in a hurry." The driver gave a nod and wink and started off before I'd even given an address.

When we got to her apartment, it dawned on me that she hadn't moved into it yet. She still lived at home and wouldn't move in for another month. Thankfully, her parents lived nearby.

To my driver's credit, we got to their house in record time. We probably broke a few laws along the way, most of them laws of physics. As soon as the taxi stopped, I jumped out and ran up to the house. Mrs. Shields greeted me at the door. She was a petite woman with boundless amounts of energy and a wicked protective streak. When she was on the rampage, the military moved the DEFCON down a number. But the curious smile she gave me let me know I would be safe from her wrath. For now.

"Alex! What are you doing here? Are you looking for Amanda?" I nodded. "I'm sorry, dear. She left with Hunter. He said he had some surprise for her."

"Did he say where they were headed?"

"Sorry, no. But he said they would be back late tonight."

"Damn!" I patted my pockets, but no phone. "Seriously? I just had it!" I looked back at the taxi, but it had already left. "Um, can I use your phone?"

She hesitated and became a little stiff. It was enough to make me wonder if I actually *did* risk incurring her wrath for something I'd forgotten about. "I can call her if you like. Is something wrong? I thought you'd be at the airport by now." She went to the wall-mounted phone in a nearby hallway. Mr. and Mrs. Shields always updated their technology... eventually. They just didn't trust things like cellphones and computers. When she picked up the phone's receiver, even *I* could hear the dial-up modem screaming through the line. How were there people in the world who still used dial-up? She quickly hung the receiver back in its mount.

"Hon, are you on the internet?" she called.

"I'm trying to find out what channel the game is on!" her dad replied from somewhere inside.

"Well, we need to use the phone!"

Thirty awkward seconds passed before he called, "Try it now!"

Mrs. Shields picked up the receiver again and dialed. A moment later, we heard the muffled theme to Jurassic Park playing nearby. She peered around the corner into the living room.

"Oh no! She's forgotten her phone!" she cried. "It must be between the couch cushions."

Of course. I sighed and thanked her. I would have to try again—and now that song would be stuck in my head for hours. "May I use your bathroom?" She slowly nodded. I removed the key from around my neck, somehow fit it into the round keyhole in the bathroom door, and stepped into The Between.

*   *   *

"Back so soon?" Arbiter asked as I stepped onto the stone floor of the Mirror Gallery. He'd pulled up a Victorian-style chair, had a new book open (*The Odyssey*), and was sipping on tea.

"Yeah, yeah. Don't worry, I got this." Before I continued, though, I glanced back over my shoulder at his monochrome self. "Is that... Earl *Grey*?"

"It is my own blend of Assam and Darjeeling." He turned a page.

Comedy is hard.

I took the mirror back to a couple of hours earlier. When I came out the other side, I sat in Jack's van as some of my friends were getting out of it in the airport parking lot. They let me ride with them since my car was out of commission.

"I'm sorry guys, I just remembered that I left my wallet at home. Go on without me! I'll get a later flight!"

"What are you talking about?" Naomi asked. Her Wednesday Addams costume fit her tone perfectly. Granted, that was just how she dressed and talked at that phase in her life. Come to think of it, I'm not entirely sure that was a costume.

I didn't give her any answer. I just ran straight to the taxis. It must've been a slow travel day, because I saw the same driver sitting there, waiting. Again, we reached Amanda's home with such speed that a Ph.D. dissertation could be written about it. And again, I missed her by *that* much.

"That was quick," Arbiter said. The book was still open in his lap, but he was looking down at his stopwatch.

"I'm close! Mrs. Shields said I missed them by fifteen minutes."

I went back to the same moment. Jack, Naomi, Diana, and Xiao had just taken the luggage out of the van. This time I waited. When Jack tried to use the key fob to lock the van, I grabbed it from him. "I'll buy you a new one!" I shouted and climbed in. Obscenities, and a few rude gestures, flew at me when I drove off, but without having to run to the arrival gates I had to be saving at *least* fifteen minutes.

My hats off to that taxi driver. If I ever see him again, I'll be sure to give him a massive tip. Somehow, he had been able to make it to Amanda's house and break the land speed record at the same time without being seen by any cops. Me? Not so much. I made it just in time to see Amanda going out to Hunter's truck, but I had collected an unhappy officer on my tail. When he was finished with me, Hunter and Amanda had left and I owed the county enough to buy another plane ticket.

*　　*　　*

"Don't. Say. A thing." I barely even gave Arbiter a passing glance before I turned back to the mirror. "Take me to... four o'clock that morning." The scene changed to my room, with me fast asleep in bed. "Here goes nothing," I said.

"Um, sir, that's not going to work."

I didn't give him a chance to explain before I stepped through.

And woke up to my alarm clock. I grabbed it and could just make out "6 a.m." when I squinted at it. "What the hell? Ugh. Of course, I was asleep." I grunted my usual morning grunt while I got out of bed and went for my phone. Perhaps I still had enough time.

Half an hour later, a taxi (not the same one) arrived just as Jack rolled up to the idling zone in front of my apartment building. "Uh, my car is ready and I'm going to pick it up. Meet you there," I called to Jack as I climbed into the taxi cab. We pulled up to see Amanda getting in Hunter's truck as he went around to the driver's side, but when he saw me get out of the taxi, he approached me, instead.

"What are you doing here, Al? Shouldn't you be on a plane?" He put his hand on my chest. It seemed innocent enough a gesture, but when I tried to push past him, he easily checked me. "Don't ruin this for me," he said under his breath. Everyone loved Hunter's smile, but at that moment his smile was a warning.

"Let me go," I sternly commanded. "I know what you're up to, I know what you've been doing. And who you've been doing it with." That got his attention. I thought I wanted his attention. I didn't.

"Oh yeah? And *who* would that be?" he asked with sudden malice. As he spoke, he removed his hand from my chest and jabbed me quickly in the solar plexus, just beneath my sternum. It didn't take much to knock the wind out of my lungs. "Now get back in your ride and leave."

I couldn't breathe for several seconds, but with empty lungs and a body that refused to cooperate, it felt more like several minutes. Hunter took a step back and opened the taxi's door for me. Once I was able to gasp for breath, I felt rage growing in my head, blurring my vision a little. Without warning, I slugged him across the jaw. "That's for tying me up!"

The movies don't really convey just how painful it can be to punch someone. Not only did my fist strike his mandible, but his mandible also struck my fist, right between the knuckles. When Hunter hit the ground, I held my hand between my legs in pain. The bit of blood on it felt like mine more than his. Hunter glared and kicked me in the shins, then scrambled to his feet and swung a punch at me. I managed to block it with my face.

The world reeled. I pushed away from the taxi and threw myself at Hunter, knocking him back to the ground. He could fight a lot better than I could, but I had a lot more to fight for. The two of us rolled around on the ground in a struggle to gain the better position. I rained punches down on him with all my strength once I'd pinned him to the ground, but he put his arms up and defended himself. With a shot to my chin, he got on top and put his hands around my neck. My instant reflex, to grab at his fingers, just made him squeeze harder. It only stopped when we heard the screams.

"Hunter! Alex? Stop it! What happened?" Amanda rushed to her soon-to-be fiancé and pulled him off of me. He looked a bit roughed up, but generally okay. Better than I felt. The taxi driver helped me to my feet.

I coughed and tried to say something, but Amanda's mother came running out of the house, shouting. "Amanda! I saw it all! Hunter was opening the door for him and out of nowhere Alex just hit him!"

Hunter smirked at me briefly before holding his jaw with a pained expression and a groan. He hammed it up real good, like a true soccer star.

I tried to use reason. "Mrs. Shields, I didn't—"

"Hunter had just been telling us how jealous and dangerous you were. I didn't believe him, but it's true! Go away, Alex! You're no longer welcome here!" Mrs. Shields stood between me and Hunter. The look Amanda gave me—incredulous, hurt, angry—was worse than any broken fist or busted nose.

The lesson today, kids, is that violence is rarely the answer.

They took him into the house, leaving me on the front yard as the taxi driver looked for his first aid kit. I waited for them to come back out, tried to get in a word of apology, but in the end Amanda and Hunter got in the truck and drove off. I had messed up. Again. And to top it all off, I got to see Hunter pull Amanda into a kiss just before they left. Once they disappeared from my sight, I headed for their house. I could see my reflection in the glass storm door. A train might as well have hit me. I sighed and took the key from around my neck to put it into the lock.

*   *   *

The good thing about returning to Chronos' manor was that the pain in my nose and hand immediately disappeared. Emotional pain? It liked to stick around.

"That didn't go according to plan, I take it," Arbiter said with a hint of schadenfreude. He closed his book and set it on a little side table next to his tea.

"I'm not in the mood." I had to think. Thus far, *all* my plans had failed. Doubt about this entire affair crept into my thoughts. Had I made a huge mistake? I clicked my tongue on the back of my teeth.

"That was a dangerous stunt. I nearly called on Chronos when you assaulted him."

I scowled. "He's the one who threw the first punch."

"...And you shouldn't be using the key in front of others. Don't you recall Rule number 3?"

I knew letting my mind wander back then was going to bite me in the ass someday. I smiled innocently. "Refresh my memory?"

Arbiter gave a defeated sigh. "*Americans.* Rule number 3: Do not let anyone follow you through the door. There is a brief window of time before the way closes."

I thought back on all the times I'd used the key. "I don't *think* anyone has. But won't they just show up right here? Surely Chronos can put them back."

He got to his feet. "No, sir. The key opens the way, but everyone comes through their own looking glass. Did you not wonder what all the others were for? You must be careful that no one sees you."

"Well, I guess it's better to learn about it now than to have it happen."

"Yes. At the present moment, I think you should get some rest. You have been at it a full day." Only after he mentioned it did I realize how damn tired I was.

"I will, but not yet. I've got an idea. And I'm not going to fail this time."

Chapter 6

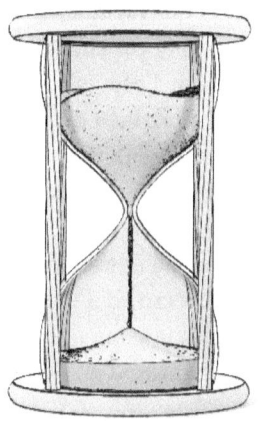

Strike Out

I sat in a used Toyota idling on the side of the freeway with my eye on the dashboard clock and my fingers drumming on the steering wheel. The car cost me a pretty penny, not to mention I had to go back a full day in order to get it in time, plus the day spent learning I was too young to rent one. On the other hand, that did let me set my alarm for whenever I wanted and give my friends ample warning that I wouldn't be making it. Only God knows how many times I bought that car.

A few times I'd tried to warn Amanda about Hunter before he arrived to pick her up. Tossing pebbles at her window backfired when the neighbor's dog woke up the entire block with its barking. The moment I heard police sirens, I got out of there. Even if I got to talk to her without his interference, she didn't know what to believe or what to do. Whatever changed the tide in her heart must have happened later that day, a day that I hoped I wouldn't need to relive yet again. So, I decided that the best course of action would be to simply shadow them. At least if I got caught, Hunter couldn't pummel me.

Shadowing them, though, proved to be more challenging than comics make it seem. Eventually, I'd stopped counting the attempts. I had no trouble following them all the way to the interstate, but that's where I either lost them in the traffic or Hunter saw me. I did manage to get a little further each time, though. Believe me, nothing pisses you off quite as much as having to redo an entire day just because you got cut off on the freeway by a truck. This time I'd thought ahead and parked near the last place I'd seen them. Sure enough, his massive pick-up shot by me and I quickly followed.

The traffic was insane, especially for that time of day. After nearly losing them again, we ended up at a Major League Baseball stadium—Camden Yards. The Orioles played there, but to be honest I didn't know much more than that. I only knew about the Orioles because of all the banners they had on display. Ever since that skinned knee I got in 5th grade from trying to slide into first base, sports and I had not been on talking terms.

Parking took ages. Finally, I stood at the entrance and watched Hunter and Amanda disappear into a sprawling crowd. I'd never seen so many people in one place before, all standing close and moving towards the massive gates. Without warning, I was transplanted from the real world into an old memory.

Adults twice my height surrounded me in an impenetrable wall. None of them noticed me. Nor did I recognize anyone. No matter how many times I called for them, my foster parents never came to my rescue. All the sounds of the carnival drowned out my voice. Panic set in and I started running. Soon, I no longer recognized the rides and shops nearby. Even when I collapsed in tears, I got no sympathy from the strangers around me. Someone tried to grab me, but I bit him and ran. Even though it got dark, the bright lights and loud crowd kept me awake. The feeling of dread gave way to need, the need to eat, the need to sleep. But the only food I could get my hands on came from the fly-and-bee-infested trash.

"Oh fuck no." Even being this far away from the throng made me feel sick. I'd have sooner walked through the gates of Hell than through the gates to the baseball stadium before me. Running the dinosaur watch through my fingers brought me some calm. I swatted away the unearthed childhood memories and stepped back. When the throng thinned, I figured, things would be easier.

I found a man a little bit away from the crowd going through his tickets, counting. "Hey, any left for sale?" I asked as I jogged up to him.

He looked at me like I'd slapped his mother. "I'm not a scalper. These are for my family," he said and turned his back to me.

"Oh, no, not yours! I mean, are there still tickets available to the game? Do you know?"

He looked over his shoulder and chuckled. "You kidding me? This game sold out within minutes. Good luck getting in."

"Sold out?" I looked around and realized what all the signs and flags advertised—the American League Division Series. "Aw crap." Sports might be somewhat foreign to me, but at least I knew that the Division Series was a big deal. Finding a scalper would be more than a little hard considering the recent crackdown they'd been under.

The prospect of having to go back weeks or months just for a 5 minute window to buy the tickets made my guts start to wrench, especially considering that I may have to do it dozens of times. Buying a ticket was a nonstarter. I could have tried to catch Hunter and Amanda on the way out, but I had a feeling his proposal would happen during the game itself. I wandered the cold October sidewalks beyond the old warehouse that lined one end of the stadium, deep in thought. At some point, I passed a bar with a TV showing the game. Although I didn't care much for baseball, I had nothing better to do while I waited. My mind wandered. I didn't even have a plan for when, or if, I did catch her in time. I'd been so obsessed over finding this moment, I'd almost forgotten the real reason I was doing it. I had to convince her of the truth, not confess to her. Laying my own feelings aside, I resolved myself to make this about helping her leave Hunter. The Seventh Inning Stretch had just started when I saw a live feed aimed on Hunter and Amanda with a heart framing the screen. Hunter knelt on one knee and held up a ring in front of tens of thousands of people. Millions, if you counted the people watching from home. After all, they didn't bring all those cameras for nothing. Amanda's face turned so red I thought she would faint, but I knew her well enough to recognize the trepidation and worry she tried to mask. I stood and watched helplessly while Hunter's devious plan unfolded. If he asked her in a place like this, surrounded by judgmental, expecting eyes, she would definitely say "yes." Amanda would never embarrass someone like that, and she never went back on her word.

Sure enough, a gentle nod had the crowd bursting into cheers.

I turned away; I was done torturing myself. So, I promptly pulled the key off my neck and found a door marked "Employees Only." A plan of my own began to form.

*　　　*　　　*

I didn't need to go back months, or even to the day before. Now that I knew about Hunter's secret destination, I could just take the train and head straight there after breakfast. Early that morning would suffice. This time, I went prepared. I replayed the day a few times just to scout things out. That's when I got a break and met Samson. This was such a stroke of luck that I briefly wondered if Lady Luck herself was interfering, but as long as she was on my side, I didn't care. Samson worked one of the many vendors at Oriole Park. Unlike his namesake, this Samson could not tear down a corrugated cardboard box, let alone a temple. The scrawny teenager with twigs for arms had spent the morning getting high with his friends before he remembered that he had to work. When I promised him I would cover his shift, the kid practically threw his uniform at me. No one questioned the food vendors. His boss didn't even notice, either. And best of all? They had access long before the crowds showed up. Samson undoubtedly lost his job later that day.

During my break, I went to work locating them. The man at the gate hadn't been lying about the game being sold out, and just looking down at the backs of over 45,000 heads started to trigger anxiety. But it didn't take long to find where Hunter and Amanda were seated: the top row. I don't know if Hunter preferred seats so far back or if this was all the stadium had left, but I was happy to see them there and not buried in the crowd. The entire time, Hunter was watching the game while Amanda had her eyes on her lap. Then, in the sixth inning, he left her there with a wad of cash in his hand and headed towards Eutaw Street, near the private offices. My guess? He either left to ensure the Jumbotron focused on them or was hoping to buy some large nachos—maybe both. Who knows how far a bribe that size might go? But with him leaving Amanda alone, I saw my chance and took it swiftly, despite how close the crowd was.

My nerves got the better of me the instant I sat down next to her, but at least being with her made the crowd more bearable. She was hunched over a small sketch pad in her lap, drawing a picture of Gomez and Morticia. A well-used tin pencil box with a Triceratops on the cover sat on top of the backpack at her feet. Even though she was only using pencils as a medium, she still created something dynamic, with shading and depth and emotion. I hadn't seen her work in so long I'd forgotten the extent of her skill. When she lost her focus and saw me, though, her face lit up and she put the pencil box and pad into her backpack.

"Alex!" The greeting reminded me of how we used to be, but a distance quickly sprang up between us and she looked down at her lap. She hadn't forgotten about the first fight we'd ever had, and feelings were still sore. "What are you doing here? I thought you'd be at the con by now."

"I thought I would be, too." I closed my eyes and thought back on that kiss she gave me in the Sunday School room. But that wouldn't be for another two years in this timeline, if it happened at all. "After you ran off the other day, I felt terrible. I couldn't let it go like that, so I want to apologize. It was insensitive."

A shy smile briefly snuck its way onto her cheeks. "You don't have anything to apologize for," she said, but then narrowed her eyes. "Wait, how did you know I was here? Was it Jason?" I wasn't sure how to answer her, so she filled the silence herself. "Alex, did you follow us here?"

"I... yeah, kinda. I tried everything I could think of to get in touch with you."

She frowned at me. "That's not okay, Alex. You don't just follow a girl like that so you can talk to her."

"But this is important," I protested.

"It's stalking. Did you skip the convention for this? Am I just a prize you're trying to win so *you* can get in my pants?"

"It's not like that. This isn't about me!"

She raised her voice in anger. "Don't be a creep, Alex!" A moment later, she winced at her own words.

It hurt to hear that. I realized it was true, but it still hurt. "I'm just trying to warn you about Hunter. And if you never want to see me again after I've said my peace, then so be it!" Something I said gave her pause and she calmed down a little.

"What *about* Hunter?"

I took a moment to collect my thoughts before answering. "He's sleeping with Sam. I overheard him talking about it. And I don't think she's the only one."

Any anger in Amanda's eyes turned to pain and shock. "Alex... are you sure?" I nodded. "I... I knew I wasn't crazy," she said to herself. "The way they look at each other when they don't think I can see them... When she said she was on a date and I couldn't get ahold of him for hours..."

Being the harbinger of bad news is not fun, but at least she still trusted me to tell her the truth. "He's manipulative. I know he's trying to make you think he's the only one you can trust, but you can't buy into it." As she hung her head, I remembered my promise to be her friend and only her friend. If we were ever to become something more, it would be her decision when. "Please stand up to him, Amanda. Don't let him control you. I mean, come on—we both know you hate baseball." I rose to my feet, but as I turned to leave, she took my hand and tugged.

"Don't... Don't leave, Alex. Please."

I sat back down next to her. "I'm sorry to—"

"I'm scared," she said just loud enough for me to hear.

The shock of it paused time. "Of what?" I asked eventually. The following silence between us was not exactly awkward, but it *was* intense. "It's okay. You don't have to tell me." Perhaps my presence was all she needed at that moment.

But she leaned forward and whispered, "Him. He threatened me today. In the parking lot. It scared me. We were in his truck. He... put his hand on my thigh and moved it... up. When I told him I didn't want him to touch me like that, he threatened me."

The news sent waves of heat and cold throughout my body. Her comment about being damaged goods sprang to mind. I held her hand in both of mine. "He tried to assault you?"

"It wasn't like *that*..."

"Are you okay?" I whispered.

She nodded at first, then shook her head. Tears fell onto our hands. "No. He's the only guy who wants to be with me and he scares me. I think he's going to propose but—"

"He's not the only guy who wants to be with you," I informed her.

"Yes, he is," she said, shaking her head. "Guys don't want a weird, geeky tomboy like me. I've been rejected *so* many times by—"

"*Cariad.*" It was an endearment our two online characters adopted for each other long ago. "I promise you he's not." Even though I had decided I would only be her friend that day, the pet name slipped out before I could stop it.

"What did you call me?" she asked and turned her teary, emerald eyes to mine. I repeated myself and brought a hand up to brush the tears from her cheek. "~Alex..." Her voice wavered as she spoke, but not from sorrow any longer.

I don't know how long we were like that, but when I felt the urge to kiss her, alarms went off in my head. *Friends! Just friends!* I cleared my throat and lowered my hand. "Amanda, you need to stop worrying about if anyone wants to be with you. What is it *you* want?" I asked. It was definitely a case of, "Do as I say, not as I do." Any remaining anger or sadness disappeared from her face as surprise at the random question took over instead. "What goals do *you* have in life?"

"Me? No one's asked me that in years." She closed her eyes and took a moment to think. "I want... kids."

"And? I know that's not all."

The corner of her lips turned upward for a moment. "I want to draw. I want to make art that inspires and entertains and educates. I want to help my family. Hmmm... I want to travel. Oh, and I want cats. Three of them. And one dog." She opened her eyes and looked into mine with awe. "And I want—"

"What is it you *need*?" I interrupted, concerned about what she might say while looking at me like that. "To make those goals happen, what can't you do without?"

Amanda lowered her gaze to our hands. "I need materials. I need money. I need time. But... more than that, I need... someone who dreams with me, who encourages, inspires, and pushes me."

"Does Hunter fit that description?" She slowly shook her head. "So, why can't *you* be that person yourself?"

"What are *your* goals?" she asked me suddenly, instead of answering the question.

I grinned at her. "Well, right now it's to save you from a lot of pain in the future."

66

She smirked. "You can't predict the future, Alex. Plus, you're dodging the question."

"Am not!"

"Are too!"

"Am not!"

"Respect your elder!" We both giggled. I'm sure the people sitting next to us thought we were crazy. I, on the other hand, knew we were.

The fact that Hunter could return any moment spurred me on. "Amanda, I'm sorry for stalking you. And I'm not trying to win you over. We're best friends, no matter what. Right?"

The crowd began to cheer at an exciting play, so we leaned in closer to each other to be heard.

"But what if—" The rest of her words were drowned out.

"What?"

She tried talking again, then shook her head and pulled her sketchpad back out, along with a pencil from her case. As she flipped through the pages of her sketchpad, I noticed a recurring theme: me. She had sketches of me sitting in class, laughing with friends, smiling, studying. Another thing I noticed was that Hunter was conspicuously absent from its pages. She found a blank sheet and started writing, then handed me the pencil as she showed me.

What if I don't want to be friends anymore?

I looked shocked and started to write, *Did I hurt you that much?*, but halfway through the word "hurt" she snatched the pencil away.

By adding one word and a caret, she turned her question into, *What if I don't want to be just friends anymore?*

This wasn't turning out the way I expected it to. My resolve began to dissolve. *What about Hunter?* I wrote.

She bit her lip before replying. *You showed me that something else scares me more. I hope you can forgive me for being such a coward.* Her lettering, usually neat and loopy, looked rushed, like she wanted to say things faster.

I took the pencil. *I'll forgive anything if you forgive me for being a creepy idiot. What are you afraid of?*

This time, she leaned over the pad so far as she scribbled that I couldn't see what she was writing. When I moved closer to get a look, she suddenly lifted her face to mine and kissed me fully on the lips. She even brought a hand up to my cheek to keep me from escaping it, not that she needed to. After the initial shock, I slid my palm over the side of her neck and kissed her back. There aren't a lot of couples that can claim they've had more than one first kiss. I cannot recommend them enough and think every couple should have as many first kisses as they can get their hands on. However, unlike our "first" first kiss, we kept ourselves to just one. When it ended, I could see fear in her eyes as she uncovered what she'd written.

I'm so afraid of losing you if I tell you how in love with you I——

After the crowd settled down, I realized that I hadn't felt my usual fear for a while. I began to get an idea of what soulmates were all about. But despite being able to hear each other, I still wrote out my reply; it was easier than speaking the words out loud.

Ditto. I've been scared shitless about confessing.

Amanda bit her lip as her eyes dropped to the sketchpad, then a bright smile formed and she looked up into my eyes.

"I love you. Jinx!" We both spoke in unison and laughed. Amanda planted another surprise kiss on me, even better and more passionate than the first. Both her hands held my head like she hungered for more. When our lips parted, she kept close and said, "I've been hiding it for years." But she quickly leaned back, looking worried.

"What's wrong?"

"It's Hunter. He's jealous of you," she said. "I don't want him to hurt you."

"Why would he be jealous of me?"

"I think he knows you're more important to me than just being my best friend. You—you should leave before he sees you."

I felt a sinking feeling in my heart. After the confession and kiss, this was... anticlimactic. "You're... staying? With him?"

She held her arms across her belly and looked away. "We can love each other at a distance. Alex, I... I shouldn't have kissed you. I'm not going to cheat on him. We've been together for two years. I owe it to him to—"

"You don't owe anything to anyone!" I said loudly, then softened my tone when I saw that I was moments away from making a scene. "Amanda, this is your choice. I've told you about what he's doing. If you decide you are okay with it... I'll still be your best friend. But nothing more."

I stood up without another word and left her there, my mind reeling. Had Hunter already gotten his hooks in so deep that she couldn't get away... or did she still love him? As I contemplated whether or not to stay in this timeline or just return to my original, I didn't notice someone step right in front of me and stop. I nearly ran into Amanda, but she put her hand to my chest and pushed me back.

"What's wrong?"

Although it'll probably get me in trouble for saying this, the angry glare she aimed at me was *incredibly* cute. "Alexander Petersen! How *dare* you walk out of our conversation just so you can get in the last word! You always do that!"

I stepped back, but she matched my speed until my back was against a pillar.

"I-I-I don't always, do I?"

"You do. You think you can just kiss me out of nowhere and then run off?"

"But you ki—"

She gripped the front of my vendor shirt and twisted it into her fist. "That I would *cheat* on someone? It *infuriates* me that you think I would do that!" Enter, a scene.

"Where is this coming from?" I asked, at a total loss.

She growled (cutely) and jerked me so I hit the pillar again. "*You're* the one who told me to stand up for myself. Well, this is me standing up for myself! You think I can just throw away two whole years of a relationship with someone simply because we *like* each other?" Another thump against the pillar. She was stronger than she looked. "Or that it'd be *okay* telling me my boyfriend is actively cheating on me with my high school friend and then just leaving?" *Thump!* "Or that I would let my *best friend* give me the *best kiss* I've ever had *in my life* without facing any consequences?" This time, instead of thumping me against the wall, she pulled me forward into a third, somewhat violent kiss which involved her entire body pushing against mine. I'd never been so turned on before.

"Fffffffuck it," she groaned as our lips parted. "Take me to the convention Alex, right now. Before I come to my senses."

Amanda didn't need to ask twice. I swept her up off her feet and we both laughed loudly as I carried her out of the stadium. For the first time, I felt like life made sense, that it was *good*. I was already formulating a plan to keep her family out of his reach when I came to Eutaw Street, the same place Hunter had been headed. I put Amanda down and we quickly walked hand-in-hand to the northernmost gate, Gate H. It was on the opposite end of the street from the offices, but we moved fast. Once we made it past the gate, we were home free!

Almost.

"Where are you lovebirds off to?" I recognized that scratchy voice.

"Glass!"

He appeared from out of nowhere and forced us both behind a large concrete column, away from prying eyes and cameras.

"How do you know who I am?" he asked as he pushed my shoulder against the column. I heard the distinct *click* of a switchblade flicking open. I went still.

"Leave him alone, Glass!" Amanda cried. She tried grabbing the blade, but he slashed it towards her and she jumped back in the nick of time.

"Hunter said he couldn't trust you. He said I could do whatever I want to the piece of shit you're spreading your legs for."

I decided I did not like Glass very much.

"Just let us go. Take my wallet, there's cash. I can get you more—"

He scowled. "I don't care about money. I want revenge." It was hard to tell how much of his threat was real and how much was bluster. He surely wouldn't try to murder someone with a knife just outside the gate of Camden Yards. But at the same time, I couldn't guess what he wanted revenge at *me* for.

"Don't hurt him! I'll do anything! Anything Hunter wants!" Amanda cried.

I'd like to say that no one witnessed all of this, but plenty of people walking to and from their cars just looked away and walked a little bit faster. Living on the streets as long as I did, I wasn't surprised. No one wanted to put themselves in harm's way for a perfect stranger. I felt the blade on my belly.

"I'll be sure to tell him that," Glass said. "He'll be very pleased with you tonight. But before I let you go, I have a message for you from Hunter." He was looking at me when he said this. His breath still smelled like fish. The knife moved away from my belly. "Don't show your fucking face around Amanda again." His hand covered my mouth as the knife sank into my thigh, every horrible inch of it. It was the first time I'd ever been stabbed. I truly can't describe the feeling. The pain made me light-headed and nauseated. 0 out of 5 stars: would not recommend.

* * *

It may not have seemed like it, but that gave me the advantage. The next day, that is the next time I lived through the same day, I did everything identically, more or less, but with one difference. I knew Hunter had gone to Eutaw Street, and Glass was just outside Gate H, so I took Amanda in a different direction, to Gate D on the exact opposite side of the stadium. It might take a few tries, but he couldn't have had all the exits covered. Once we got home, we could be together, she could even get a restraining order on him to keep her family safe.

"So, it's really true. You *have* been cheating on me." Hunter stood watch at Gate D, barring our exodus yet again. Glass and TJ were next to him.

"Wh-what are you doing here?" The blood drained out of my face.

"I could ask you the same thing." I didn't know if this new, almost submissive attitude was more or less disturbing than the times he was being malevolent. When he looked at Amanda, I could've sworn there were actual tears in his eyes. "Here I've gone out of my way to have a special time with you and *this* is how you repay me?"

"No, Hunter, it's not like that." She squeezed my hand a bit tighter but I could feel her trembling. "You scare me, sometimes."

"Is it because of when I touched you? Come on, babe. You know you liked it. Remember when we talked about this? About our fantasies? You said you liked showing off in public. Role playing. That's all it was."

I can only imagine the level of embarrassment Amanda was going through at that moment. Her face turned crimson and she looked away from me, but her hand stayed in mine. "I didn't... That's not what I meant."

He gasped. "Did you think I was going to—? Mandabear! Is that really what you think of me? It was just a little fun! A game! I'm sorry that you took my intentions the wrong way. Please, let me make it up to you. Let me prove myself to you. I promise I'll do whatever it takes."

"I don't..." she uttered. Her grip faltered.

With her eyes cast to the side, I doubt she saw the quick flash of a smile on his lips. I tried to interject, but he interrupted with, "Don't our two years together mean anything? I love you, Amanda. Just give me one more chance. I *need* you."

"Well, *she* doesn't need you!" I declared.

Hunter just ignored me. "I thought you were better than this. I thought I could *trust* you, that you were the kind of girl who would *never* cheat on someone."

How did he know to throw her own words back at her? She lowered her gaze to my feet and muttered, "I'm sorry." As she let go and walked over to him, I wasn't sure if she was apologizing to me, to Hunter, or to herself.

"Come on, let's get out of here," he said as he put an arm around her. They all walked past me, Glass and TJ in front, Amanda with her eyes shut, and Hunter directing a sinister grin at me. It made no sense. How had I lost? In stunned silence, I watched them go back to their seats and felt my heart being trampled with each step. Honestly, I preferred getting stabbed in the leg.

*   *   *

"What the Hell happened, Arby?" I asked with my head against the wall. "It's not possible. He had to have been in two places at once! They both would have!"

"Was he able to monitor your movements? It is my understanding that such facilities are well-surveilled." He was seated again, this time with several short piles of books beside the chair. *Catcher in the Rye* lay in his lap.

"I don't think so. Maybe? Ugh, yeah, I suppose that's a possibility. But they were waiting for us! And they couldn't have known we'd leave from that gate."

Arbiter actually sounded like he cared. "It *is* very concerning, sir. Are you sure you did everything *precisely* as before? Even a little deviation could have a monstrous effect."

"No," I said, trying to convince myself. "This is no butterfly effect." I replayed everything in my head, but refused to believe that something as silly as knocking someone's drink off the counter could make any real difference in so short a time. "I mean, either I'm going crazy or... shit! What if he followed me here once? He could've been listening in on our plans!"

"*Your* plans, sir," Arbiter corrected. "I did warn you about Rule 3."

"What do we do? Can we check around here and see? Where's his looking glass?"

Arbiter got a bit flustered when I said this and stood. "I'm sorry, no, I cannot allow that! It would be far too dangerous and Chronos would never reveal the location of his looking glass."

"Dangerous? How?"

He hesitated. "I am quite certain that if it breaks, it will be exceedingly bad. It's never happened *before*, but there's always a first time, and I don't want to be the man in charge when it happens. Plus, the knowledge gained from looking into it would most certainly be a violation of Rule 1!"

"But what about him? He could be making major changes to the timeline! Chronos said that was not allowed, either."

"For you. If he is in The Between, it is very unlikely that he will manage to return to Earth. Any damage he does here, Chronos will be able to repair, eventually. Anything that happens here is a consequence of your agreement."

"But he could be dangerous!"

Arbiter's gentle demeanor did wonders to soothe my nerves. "Master Petersen, the chances that he is here are slim, and if he *is* here we will catch him. If you want my opinion, it was likely a breach. I hear they happen all the time."

"Breach?"

"Yes, sir. A timeline breach. Rule 4. Too many visits to the past, particularly to a single point in time, can cause different timelines to interfere with each other. They manifest in many ways. Usually it's a sense that something has happened before. I believe the term nowadays is '*déjà vu*.' That could explain why they were at the second gate. But sometimes, going back too frequently to the same time can cause objects and events from other realities to spill through. These we refer to as 'rifts'. They can be as large as an earthquake or meteor, or as benign as a missing sock."

"...or an anvil on the roof of your car?" I asked and started to wonder if I had caused, or would cause, my own car to be destroyed.

"Precisely. More often than not, people call them 'Acts of God.'"

"I'm not sure God has anything to do with Hunter. Chronos doesn't have a bet on me, too, does he?" It started to feel that any deal with these beings could only have a bad outcome. "No, I suppose he's not the betting type. I just need more time." Great choice of words.

"Speaking of time, sir, you're about a year down now. You could simply continue from this point and fight for her. Or, even just be present for her. It took great patience and persistence before my beloved realized I was even interested in him."

"I get the impression that's not going to work. You heard him; he's got his claws in Amanda pretty deep and he knows it. Now... Now I might have made things worse! What if he gets impatient and pushes her boundaries harder? Hurts her?" I slid to the ground and held my head in my hands. "Whether it was a breach or he was just watching me on the security cameras, going back to that day isn't going to change anything. He'll always win."

It must have been awkward for the Englishman, but he slowly sat down on the ground next to me and stiffly patted my back. "She is a special girl indeed to deserve such dedication." I appreciated that he was trying. "How did you two meet? Perhaps it will help to reminisce about the good times."

"Let me think. I was being passed from home to home. I was maybe...eight? She was always just there, a constant friend. Pretty much my *only* constant." I looked up at the mirror and got to my feet. "Show me third grade, when I first met Amanda. Will it show me that far back?"

And there I was, a third-grader heading to a seat in the art room at the end of the school day. "Oh, I remember Mrs. Paladino," I told Arbiter. "We had made clay sculptures and they were sent to the kiln the day before."

Students sat at tables, listening for their names so they could collect their creations from the twenty-something teacher in the front of the room.

"The classroom's a lot smaller than I remember," I said as I examined the memory. "And I could have sworn Mrs. Paladino was in her forties!"

Arbiter chuckled. "It is not unexpected for a child to see a different reality than we do."

When I looked over at him, he wasn't watching the mirror, but looking at me with a hint of pride, or perhaps amusement. "I suppose I'm still a child in your eyes," I said.

"Indeed, you are, sir. But it can be refreshing to see things from a child's perspective."

"Jonathan. Michael. Zoe. Amanda." Out of nowhere came an adorable, befreckled girl to the teacher's desk. The unicorn the teacher handed her looked like it had perpetually skipped leg day and become overweight, but none of the other sculptures in the room could compare to it.

More names were called until every student had their sculpture, every student but one. The bell rang, marking the end of school. As most of the kids got up and packed their backpacks, Mrs. Paladino softly said, "Alexander," and beckoned him with a finger. A scrawny kid missing several of his front teeth bounded to the front, but his smile didn't last long. "I'm so sorry about your cow, Alex. It broke in the kiln." Instead of a clay sculpture, Mrs. Paladino handed him a paper bag.

Back at his desk, he carefully took out the contents—several pieces of pottery covered in cracks. Young Alex began to cry, then rushed to a corner of the art room behind some easels and squatted down with his arms around his knees. Most of the kids ignored him. Mrs. Paladino got up from her desk, but stopped when Amanda headed behind the easels herself. The girl came up behind Alex and put her hand on his back. The effect was nearly immediate; he calmed down and rubbed at his cheeks.

"I saw you making your bull," she said. "I really liked it. With the flames, it reminded me of the Red Bull from The Last Unicorn—"

"—The Last Unicorn," he said at the same time she did. He sniffed.

"It's my favorite movie!" she exclaimed. "I didn't know what to make until I saw you working on your bull."

His eyes crossed just a little. "It's a movie? I thought it was just a book."

Young Amanda gasped. "It's got a book too?! Ooh! Can we read it together? You can bring it over to my place! And then I can bring the movie to yours!" Amanda's eyes shone like starlight. The enthusiasm pouring from her made Alex crack a smile, but that smile faded when he noticed some of the other kids looking at them.

"B-but you're a girl..."

She swiftly punched him in the arm, but not hard. "And you're a boy! And I'll punch anyone who says we can't be friends!" she announced.

Though Alex rubbed his arm, that smile returned. "Friends?"

"Where's your Red Bull? I wanna see it," she said, looking around.

"There." He pointed to the broken pieces on the desk.

"Oh no! It broke? Now who will go after my unicorn?" She pointed to her desk where the unicorn stood, albeit only three of its legs reached the desk at any given time. The boy's smile once again faded, like it was an engine Amanda kept trying to start. Then he buried his face in his knees again.

"What's wrong? I'll help you glue it together," Amanda said.

"It's not just that. You can't come over. I'm going to a—a new family again," he blubbered.

Instead of asking any questions, she silently hugged him until he calmed down. The young pair stayed put, even when they were the only ones besides the teacher left in the room.

"That sounds awful... But maybe they'll be a better family," she said softly.

He shook his head. "I doubt it."

"Don't give up. I'll still be here for you. Maybe I can help."

"How?"

74

"...Do you like dinosaurs?" she asked out of the blue. When he nodded, she took a dinosaur watch off of her wrist and gave it to him. "Brachiosaurs are my favorite. Keep it. When you're sad, look at it and you'll think of dinosaurs instead. That makes me happy!"

I took the dinosaur watch out of my pocket and ran my thumb over it. "I still have it. It's comforting to know it's there, like a link to my past, you know?"

Arbiter stepped up next to me with a knowing smile. "I do. Although, were I a betting man, I would bet you no longer think merely of dinosaurs when you look at it."

Young Alex blinked his tears away as he accepted the watch. "Thank you," he said with reverential awe. "Um, wait here." He got up and ran to his desk, grabbed his backpack, and pulled out a metal pencil case. It had a grazing Triceratops on the lid. Then he hurried back to her, holding it out. "Here."

The freckle-faced girl took the proffered case and held it like a holy relic. "Wow. Hey! This makes us dinosaur buddies!"

He examined the watch now on his wrist. A small smile formed. "Paleo-pals," he countered.

"Ooh, I like that!" She put her hand out to shake. "I'm Amanda."

"Alex," he said and took her hand with a sniff and a grin.

For just a moment, it seemed that young Amanda's eyes looked at me through the mirror. *"Don't worry,"* she said. *"You've got me, now!"* I stepped back and the memory faded. My heart was beating a mile a minute.

"We were pretty much inseparable after that," I said. "No one had ever shown that they cared about me before."

"Hrm. I do believe I'm beginning to see how you two are soulmates," Arbiter said. "That was *cloyingly* cute. Come on, then. Let's get you prepared for tomorrow." I shot him an odd look. "You have a 'paleo-pal' to rescue.'" He gave the friendliest grin I'd ever seen from him.

Chapter 7

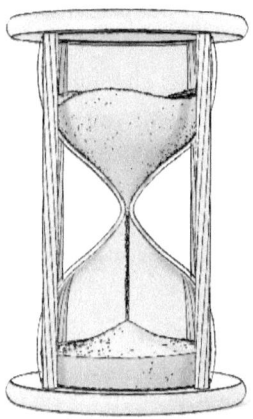

Lucky Breach

I had to move forward. If Hunter really had followed me to the Halls of Time, I'd figure it out soon enough. Arbiter reminded me that it didn't mean that he would win; it just meant I'd have a fight on my hands. If Hunter hadn't followed me to the Halls of Time… then something bigger was happening.

I decided on a different tactic: get in good graces with her family. If I could get them on my side, their support would be invaluable. I had to make them see what Amanda saw, to show them that I was still the same as when they cared for me that one Christmas. And I knew just how to do it.

"Take me to when Hunter said he would pay for Mr. Shields' medicine."

Alex sat at a desk in a bare study room, typing away on a laptop. Mozart's Salzburg Symphony No. 1 played over its speakers. The setting sun cast a warm glow over the scene.

"How do I know this really is the right time?" I asked. "What if the mirror is acting up again? I mean, I wasn't there when Hunter paid for the medicine."

"We won't know for certain unless you check," Arbiter replied, "but the mirror has not been acting up as of late. Your looking glass is connected to both you and the appropriate timeline, so it should be fairly good at narrowing down when an event occurred. If it was only tied to your memories we would see things from your point of view. Plus, well, memories are usually rather faulty."

"Do you think... it could show me my dad?" I had no memories of the man, and only a few of my mom, so the prospect of seeing him for the first time was exciting.

Arbiter frowned. "I'm afraid not. I already attempted it while you were asleep in the hopes of surprising you. It seems you and your father have never met."

"I sort of suspected that would be the case."

"Sir, may I suggest we return to the task at hand? If Hunter is offering to pay for the medicine at this moment in time, stepping into it will not do you much good, sir," Arbiter warned. "Perhaps you should consider going an hour or two further back?"

"I just wanted to get an idea of when it happened, but I don't intend on going back only an hour. Mirror, take me to one week earlier," I said.

Xiao, Jack, Michael, and Alex sat around a table in the back of a game store. The room had a dozen tables, most of them empty. Groups of college kids gathered to play a collectible card game on some of the others.

"...I float six white mana and four red mana," one particularly excited college kid said. "Now I cast 'Shatterstorm', and because of my lattice turning everything into an artifact, every permanent is destroyed." Groans of despair erupted from a card game table. "Now I cast 'The Cheese Stands Alone' with my remaining mana and I win!"

"Not again, Gerald!"

Alex smirked as he heard the chorus of complaints behind him but turned his focus to the board game in front of him. A game board made up of cardboard tiles designed to look like rooms lay spread out on the table with several figurines on top.

"Alright Xiao, now draw an 'Omen' card," Michael said. "You have to roll the dice next and compare the result to the number of omen cards we've already drawn. But since this is the first one drawn, there's a pretty good chance you're safe. All you've gotta do is roll at least a one."

I turned to Arbiter. "Wish me luck."

"If you think She will help you, I wish you all the Luck in the world."

This time I jumped into the mirror and "landed" sitting at the table with my friends. The game had just started. I cleared my throat. "Sorry guys, I gotta use the bathroom. I'll be real quick."

"We'll wait for you on your turn then," Michael said.

I apologized again and rushed off towards the bathrooms, but they were occupied. So, instead I pulled out my phone and stepped out of the back of the store. Some conversations shouldn't happen via text. No, this again called for direct voice-to-voice chat with Amanda. I dialed and held my breath as I listened to the electronic ringing, then, "Hello!"

I practically did a little dance of joy when I got through. Okay, I really *did* do a little dance of joy, but if you embarrass yourself in an empty lot, did it actually happen?

"Amanda! It's Alex!"

She giggled on the other end. "I know it's you, ya goof. You're in my phone. So what's up?"

I felt my heart race, my stomach do somersaults, and my nerves get jumpy. You know, all the typical "head-over-heals" in love stuff. *Deep breath.* "I heard that your dad's sick again."

Amanda's tone quickly changed to something more serious. "Yeah. We just found out a week ago. It's... cancer. It felt like he was sick with something for a while. Now we know what. I was going to tell you myself, but I've been so busy with commissions and classes and work..."

"It's okay, I know you're busy. How *is* work, by the way?"

"Awful. I hate working retail. Maybe you can come by the store? It really sucks that we don't have any classes together this semester."

"Tell me about it," I said. "I've come by a few times but you're never there when I am."

"I can text you my schedule!"

"Um, listen, Amanda, I know medical bills can be tough. How are you guys hanging in there?"

"Actually, since Hunter offered to pay for the treatments this morning, I think we'll be okay. I'm so lucky to have him."

"I... Wait. *This* morning?" I sighed as I figured the mirror was playing tricks with me again. Since I was planning on returning to The Between, there was no harm in trying to warn her now. "Amanda, listen. Hunter's not a good guy. He's got girls on the side."

"What? You're just mistaken. He would *never* cheat on me. I know we haven't seen much of each other recently—"

In the background I could hear Hunter's voice. "Mandabear, come on or we're gonna be late!"

"I've gotta go, Alex. We'll talk soon." And she hung up.

With Amanda still enamored over Hunter in this timeline, I did not want to wait here until things turned sour. So I put the key in the back door of the game store and walked through.

Don't give up. Amanda's words still resonated with me.

"This *is* most unusual," Arbiter said as he ran a cloth over my looking glass.

"You don't say." I knelt on the ground, my pants in my hands as I wrung soapy water out of them. Next to me sat the now nearly-empty culprit: a bucket and mop. I could still smell the unique blend of Windex and furniture polish that greeted me via cloth-to-the-face the moment I had stepped into the Mirror Gallery. I was sure he'd done it all on purpose.

"It is unlike any breach I've seen," he said in all seriousness, like he hadn't just witnessed me blindly flailing around the place with a bucket on my foot.

I grunted and strained as I twisted the cloth over the bucket, getting out the last few drips I'd be able to manage. Then I whipped the pants out and inspected them. "What if I wasn't specific enough with the mirror? Did it make a mistake again?" I said.

Arbiter used a second cloth to dry the surface. "The mirror is, in your lingo, 'user-friendly'. Well, yours not so much. There *is* the distinct possibility that it was misbehaving." Then he stepped back from the glass, inspecting his handiwork.

"Well, I know there's one way to make certain, if I can only figure out how to explain myself to her." Sitting, I put both legs into the pants at the same time— no one-leg-at-a-time here!—and got to my feet to finish fastening them. Though the pant legs were a bit cold, I'd be able to manage.

"What do you have in mind?" He brought my sneakers over so I could slip them on, even though one of them was sopping wet. I *hate* wet shoes.

"If I go back to whennn-Nng!! Nope." It was too much for me. I proceeded to shed both shoes and socks, opting for the barefoot approach. When Arbiter noticed the footprints I left behind, he stiffened slightly. I'm pretty sure I saw his mustache twitch.

"If I go back to *when* he was diagnosed, I'll definitely get to talk to her before Hunter does, plus I'll know if the mirror is glitching."

"That sounds logical," he said and slowly reached for the mop. "Do you wish to finish drying first, sir?"

"I'll air dry. Mirror, take me to the moment Amanda learned that her father had cancer." I didn't even look at the scene but kept my eyes on Arbiter, grinning slyly. With my fingers spread, I pressed my full, wet palm against the mirror's surface right where he'd cleaned. Whether my touch ever made it dirty or not, I'll never know for sure, but I like to imagine it did.

I found myself sitting alone in a study room going over Spanish vocab. Although no one else was around, I decided to wait a few minutes before calling.

If that was indeed the moment she learned of the diagnosis, I didn't want to interrupt. She would need some time to process. Eventually, I dialed. It rang several times.

"Hello? Oh, Alex." There was definitely a somberness to her tone.

"Amanda? Hey... Are you okay?"

"I don't know. I'm glad you called. I could really use someone to talk to."

I felt a pang in my heart when I realized she hadn't called me right away when this happened the first time. But I knew we could make up for it now. "Then talk to me."

"I'm so sorry I didn't call you right away," she said. "I think I was too scared." The statement struck me as an odd one. Wasn't *this* "right away" now? If anything, it felt like she had answered my *thoughts*. Perhaps this was another aspect of having a soulmate, but she shouldn't be answering questions about a different timeline.

"Dad has cancer. I'm in the waiting room right now," she said.

"Oh no... I really can't imagine what you're going through. Do they know how bad it is yet?"

I heard her sniff. "No, not yet. We... They're coming out." Several tense minutes passed as I tried listening in, but everything was too muffled or distant to make out any voices. Then, "Alex? Are you still there?"

"I'm here. What's up?" I asked with bated breath. I knew the answer, but that didn't change any of the emotions.

"Some good news. They might have caught it in time. And Hunter's here. He said he'll pay for all the treatment."

I wish I could say I was shocked, but half of me expected this. The implications, though, terrified me. My mind raced through all the explanations, and I always came up with one conclusion: Hunter had a key of his own. And that meant he might have made a contract with someone, too.

"Alex?"

"Sorry. I'm here. I'm glad your family won't be footing the bill." There really wasn't any practical reason to stay in that timeline, yet I couldn't bring myself to leave her in distress like that. Doomed timeline or not, it was still Amanda. "Tell me again about the time he accidentally put on your mom's lipstick?"

We talked for hours.

*   *   *

Lady Luck didn't exactly have an "office." The casino she called home had no resemblance to the dusty office where Destiny worked. The general aesthetic reflected the building itself: dice. There were light fixtures shaped like dice, dice patterns in the carpet, dice-shaped glassware, and even a giant die slowly rotating as it hung from the ceiling like a disco ball, sans the disco. On the main floor sat row after row of slot machines with their flashy displays, blackjack tables, craps tables, poker tables, roulette wheels, Big Six wheels, and every other game of chance devised by man. It even had a fully-stocked bar, a buffet, a small stage in the corner, and an actual champagne fountain. Everything I expected to see in a casino was there. Everything but people.

"Lady?" I called out. No response. "Lady Luck? Fortune?" I went to a blackjack table and idly dealt out cards. Sure, it's a simple game, but you have a better chance of winning a game of blackjack than any other game in the casino, if you know what you're doing. "I'm playing a game without you!" I called. For the house, I placed a card face down and a Queen of Hearts face up. I then dealt cards for myself. Ace. Two. Jack. Seven. All Clubs. "Guess I'll stay."

"Push." Lady Luck turned the dealer's face-down card over, revealing a second Queen of Hearts. It was like she'd always been there. However, instead of the loose sundress and hat I'd seen her in previously, she wore a dealer's uniform consisting of a white shirt buttoned up all the way, a gold bowtie with a pattern of green four-leaf clovers, a visor made of clear, green plastic, a black vest that emphasized her bust, and a green and gold sleeve garter on her right arm. She kept the visor low so I could only see her eyes by looking through it. "Care to try your luck again?"

I wanted to be angry with her, but her playful smile and flirty gaze made staying angry rather difficult. Finding out I could entice her to show herself by offering a game did not hurt, either. "I already told you I wasn't interested in another deal."

"No deal, Alex. Just a friendly game. I'll wager a kiss," she said and winked.

"I'm not here to play games."

"Is that so? Don't make me double down." I just gave her a serious look. "Such a wet blanket. You may be the first person in history to refuse a Good Luck Kiss from Fortune herself. Tell you what, if you win, I'll give you a kiss. And if you lose, all I ask is that you return for another game later." She coyly bit on the tip of her finger in an altogether alluring display.

I rapped my knuckles on the table with a smirk. She girlishly squealed with delight as she began dealing again. "Everything is a game, Alex. The question is, what game are you playing?'"

"A game where I get answers."

She dealt me a three, face-up.

"Ah. An interrogation, then? Want to tie me to a chair? I'll warn you, no one has ever been able to tie *me* down. But there's always a first time," she teased.

Dealer face-up, four.

"I was hoping for more of a conversation than an interrogation."

Face-down, ace. It had been ages since I played blackjack with a facedown card; perhaps Luck was old-fashioned.

She gave me a little pout. "And I'm just supposed to give you the answers with nothing in return? How is that fair? Or fun? What if I want something only you can give me? Surely Lady Luck can get lucky sometimes," she purred.

Face-down, dealer.

The way she licked her lips and lifted her visor slightly so she could look me over had every muscle in my body going tense. She giggled. "Oh, you are a fun one to tease. No wonder that girl likes you. For the record, I do, too, Alex." She scrunched up her lips and moved them from side to side as she appeared to be judging me. "All right, I suppose I should give you a chance for what we've put you through."

From thin air, she produced a golden coin and turned it for me to inspect. The obverse had a horseshoe, and on the reverse, a sundered horseshoe. "One coin flip. Whichever side is up when the coin comes to rest determines the outcome. Heads, you can ask me *whatever* you like. Tails, you enter a new contract with me."

Though I did not like the prospect of another contract, I nodded and she flipped the coin high into the air. As it spun, I thought of how no contract with her would be a good idea, how she'd likely obey the letter of the contract to twist things in her favor. If she could do it... why couldn't I?

With a sudden burst of speed, I snatched the coin out of the air. She stared at me, dumbfounded, as I pressed the coin against the table, horseshoe side up, and withdrew my hand.

"You *dare*... That's ch— ...It's against..." she stammered.

"It *is* at rest now," I said and grinned widely.

Arms akimbo, she glared at me, but it turned to a slow smile. "Turnabout is fair play. But don't think you'll be able to get the better of me so easily next time. Ask away."

A sense of relief hit. My gamble had worked. I tapped the table in front of me to resume our game. "Hit. First, I need to know, do you have some sort of deal or agreement with Hunter Pace?"

With a single, well-manicured finger, she slid a card over to me. An eight.

"No. I have no deal or agreement with Hunter Pace."

"How about a bet with him?" I asked.

She arched an elegant eyebrow as if impressed. "No bet, either," she replied.

"Then you aren't helping him? Do you know who is?"

Luck's hair flowed in gorgeous waves as she shook her head. "You know none of my Kin can directly interfere. And we cannot lie to a mortal, either. You aren't accusing me of being *naughty*, are you?"

Tap. "Hit. Can you blame me? You lost a bet with Destiny over me. Everything I try is a failure, and now Hunter is showing up where he shouldn't be. *When* he shouldn't be. And you seem to be rather skilled at... creative rules-lawyering."

She carefully placed a card in front of me and let it go with an audible flick. A five. "Stay," I said with a wave.

"You flatter me! Destiny and I have many bets, and one soul is a relatively small wager. There are so many realities, Alex. I get to try every option, every angle. So while it is possible that Hunter is getting in your way somehow, I can guarantee you that in none of the infinite universes out there am I assisting him."

With a coquettish smile, she glanced at her face-down card and drew another card face-up, an ace. "Stay."

I revealed my cards. "Seventeen. But it makes no sense. He'd have to be in two places at once. He's always a step ahead. It feels like I'm being cheated."

Lady Luck "tsked" and waved a finger at me. "I may be many things, Alex, but I am not a cheater. Like I said, 'everything is a game.' But games don't always have a clear winner or loser."

She used her ace to flip over the other face-down card, but quickly placed the ace on top of it, covering its value. "And sometimes the game isn't what you think it is."

She picked the two cards up and turned them over. The card on top didn't belong in a deck of playing cards at all, but rather in *Uno*: "reverse."

"I suggest you take a moment and get a better look at the cards on the table."

As she stepped back, the casino suddenly filled with people playing at every table and machine. It was loud, glaring, and overwhelming. Lady Luck disappeared into the chaos. It felt like the walls were closing in around me. I had to get out of there. If this was her way of kicking me out, it worked. But before I left, I picked up the cards she left on the table. Instead of an ace, the card simply said, "Don't give up" in thick red lipstick. And I couldn't find a four, only a Queen in its place; instead of a standard suit, it had an icon of a paintbrush. The queen herself held a sketchpad and had Amanda's face.

Chapter 8

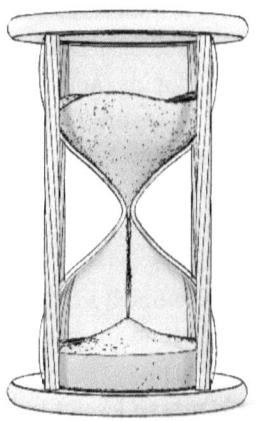

Amanda Hug and Kiss

"I am no expert, sir, but perhaps instead of speaking ill of Hunter, you can try to impress the girl yourself," Arbiter said. I appreciated that he had begun trying to help on his own.

"I know, Arb, but... how?"

Arbiter laughed. "I'm afraid I have never understood *women*, sir. But as the Bard of Avon once penned, 'to thine own self be true.'"

Those words got me thinking. "I haven't felt like *my own self* very much since I got here," I said as I scanned through the timeline of my life in the mirror. "I hate all this spying and just... *reacting* to whatever Hunter does. It was really nice just talking with Amanda on the phone."

"Is there a time when you were comfortable together? When I first met Charles, he intimidated me and I was nervous and reticent. You have to remember, sir, that in my day, a love like mine was forbidden. Outlawed. It was dangerous. I could not know if it was even safe to let *Charles* know how I felt, just as he might have deemed the risk too great to let *me* know of his affections. Every time I saw him, I was filled with shame and grew flustered.

"One night, word was sent that his sister had passed. She had been convalescing for many years, so news of her unexpected death was particularly difficult to bear. They had always had a tight bond. When he traveled to her home in Newcastle, I decided to take the risk and joined him as he mourned. It was the first time I had ever seen him so *vulnerable*. Witnessing this Adonis among men on his knees, weeping, helped me to see him as one of us *lowly mortals*. I had put him on a pedestal hopelessly out of my reach instead of seeing him as my fellow man with needs and desires and shortcomings. As a matter of fact, these flaws, apprehensions, doubts, and eccentricities only deepened my affections for Charles. Yet, I gave up on the idea of wooing him. He did not need a lover; he needed a partner. Once I shed him of his godhood, my genuine self emerged. And that was when he began to notice me. Years later, he told me that I had always been that 'perfectly precocious and pretentious youth' in his eyes until that journey north."

Arbiter had never opened up so much to me before. When I looked back at him, he was drying his cheeks with an intricately designed silk handkerchief. "What happened?" I asked.

He turned his back towards me, so I went to him and put my hand on his shoulder. Even though we'd been working together for months, I knew precious little about him—not even his real name. I wasn't about to give up this chance to learn about his past.

"His sister was not the only one who had been ill. Death took him from me a few short years later. I was approached by Destiny. She told me there had been a mistake, that we were meant to have more time together, so she brought me to Chronos. I begged him to bring Charles back to me, but he refused. When Destiny told him that the death was untimely, however, Chronos offered me an opportunity. I could stay and live out the rest of his days with him here, but when he passed on, I would need to remain and pay for it with time and a half.

"I spent nearly forty more blissful years with him while managing Master Chronos' estate. Charles had always been fond of the green world, so I thought a garden would be nice, but plants do not grow here. The artificial garden was meant to bring some of that green world to The Between. Now it serves a dual purpose: as a memento to our love and as a *memento mori*." He let out a heavy breath. "I am fifty-seven of my years into payment. Soon, my clock will wind down. I will get to pass on as well and... hopefully see Charles again."

There are times when words just get in the way. I rubbed his shoulder and got a smile, a genuine smile. Minutes passed in silent reflection. He broke the silence with a sniff. "I am sorry for rambling, sir. I did not mean to 'get emotional' with you."

"It's okay. Trust me, I understand how the past can bring out unexpected feelings. But being sad can be a good thing. Fifty-seven years... So that makes you a hundred years old?"

He used the handkerchief to wipe his nose and put it back in his pocket. "I've been here nearly a hundred; I'm about one hundred and thirty-eight, though I don't really feel older than one hundred and twenty, sir," he said. I was sure that was a joke, but he was very good at playing the straight man. So to speak.

"You don't really look older than a hundred and twenty, either. And you know you can call me Alex."

The wrinkled nose was all I needed to see to know what he thought of that. "I think I will hold fast to my druthers. Though I doubt my story helps your predicament in any way."

"I don't know. It might have. I think the last time I saw her really act like herself was at the end of sophomore year." The cogs started turning. I looked around the otherwise-empty Mirror Gallery and lowered my voice to a whisper, just in case. "It was about five or six months after she started going out with Hunter. There was an artist field trip program we were preparing for when he called. I remember that it was the first time since she'd started dating him that she looked sad and hurt. Mirror, take me to the day Amanda and I were planning our trip." I turned to Arbiter and said, "Here goes nothing," before blindly touching the mirror's surface.

A giddy feeling filled every piece of my soul, so powerful that I broke out in laughter. When I got ahold of myself, I discovered that I was in my old dorm. The immediate memories of that time flooded in. This wasn't the day we had planned our trip; this was the day Amanda started going out with Hunter.

I would have gone pale if I could have, but the dread of knowing I had somehow come to the *last* point in time I wanted to visit simply could not compete with the pure joy I felt that night four years in my past. After all, I had nearly kissed the girl of my dreams a couple of hours before and had no idea what would be happening later that night. The only reason I wasn't still with her was because she had gone to a party and I hadn't.

"Fucking mirror," I muttered to myself. As I reached for my key, a thought stayed my hand. "Wait. I know it's a ways back, but what if I actually go to that party?"

*   *   *

As soon as I stood in front of the frat house for Sigma Pi Iota, I remembered the reason I hadn't gone to that party. It hadn't even been a month since that very fraternity had expelled me from their ranks. Flashes of a Homecoming party gone horribly wrong haunted me. The karaoke. The streaking. The punch bowl. *Especially the punch bowl!* And all in front of the chapter president. That was the first—and the last—time I'd ever gotten drunk. Thanks to rumors, I became a campus legend the rest of the semester, just not the good kind. As far as any party on campus went, I was *persona non grata*.

"Aw shit." Before I even had a chance to devise a way inside, Jaxson, the "bouncer", saw me. He was not as large as Diego, but he knew how to fight. Plus, we had a history. He gave me a warning glare and shook his head. I pointed at myself questioningly, and he nodded, then shook his head again.

I wandered off aimlessly, or at least that's what I wanted Jaxson to think. Once I was out of sight, I ran through the adjoining snow-covered grass lot and went to the back of the frat house. The oppressively loud bass pouring out of every crack in the walls was more than enough to obscure any sounds I made as I snuck up to the deck. The deck itself was a story up, with a single flight of stairs on the other side as me. And sitting on the top of the stairs was Jaxson. Or his doppelgänger.

Trust me when I say that I tried everything to get into that place: distractions, disguises, windows... Rain gutters, by the way, weren't designed to hold up a human. Fort Knox would have been easier to break into. It was not a raucous soirée that would have made infiltration much easier. I even sent Amanda a text, but she never responded. An hour later, I leaned my back against the wall beneath the deck. I was about to give up when I heard the sliding glass door to the deck above open and Hunter's voice getting louder.

"...No, thanks. I'm allergic to peanuts. Ladies first... You look so down, Amanda. At a *party*. Is something wrong? Do you want to talk about it?"

"Oh, it's nothing important," Amanda replied in her "it's definitely important" tone. I both wanted to hear their conversation and wanted to be miles away from their conversation. But if I stayed, it would be spying again, so I began sneaking away across the side yard.

"It's Alex." With my name on Amanda's lips, I froze in the shadow of a tree. Had I been caught? "Yet *another* in a long line of rejections." I turned around and saw them. They were leaning on the railing at the side of the deck, looking out in my direction, but they did not see me in the dark. I dared not move.

Hunter was as handsome as always, but instead of that suave smile he usually had, he was gazing at Amanda with a genuine—or perhaps well-practiced—look of concern. Amanda wore a silver dress that fit her perfectly, with just the right balance between modest and sexy. A few flakes of snow fell from the trees nearby. Overhead, the clouds parted, revealing a crescent moon and a sky full of stars. It quickly became one of those romantic moments that come out of nowhere to ambush you.

"Really? I'm surprised. He seemed like he was into you," Hunter replied.

"We're just friends." I could hear how hurt she was, even though she was trying to hide it.

In retrospect, I should have let them see me and left, but the emotions running through my heart just then—anxiousness, apprehension, and a cold dread—kept me paralyzed. Also, I think we've established how much I torture myself. Even though I knew what was coming, I could still feel my spirit slowly fracturing.

"Just friends? It sure doesn't sound like you were 'just friends.'"

She sighed. "I guess... I don't know. Sometimes I feel like half of me is missing. I thought maybe..."

"Maybe he was your other half?"

Amanda shrugged. "We've been friends since the third grade. I guess if something was going to happen, it would have by now."

"Didn't he go missing for years? If I was your other half, I certainly wouldn't have left you behind like that."

"You?"

I shifted my weight to make an escape, but a branch cracked beneath my foot and I went still. Hunter looked out into the dark, right in my direction. "Well, yeah. I'm not blind, like all those idiots who couldn't see what was right in front of them. Their loss."

Amanda looked over to him with a raised eyebrow. "What do you mean?"

"A beautiful girl like you with such amazing skills? I mean, your art is astounding, you know just about everything, and I've never seen anyone say the alphabet backwards so fast! Imagine how many D.U.I.s you could get out of," he teased.

His joke was rewarded with a laugh and one of her patented goofy grins. "Oh? And what about you? You're handsome. You volunteer at the shelter. And you were pretty good in there singing, 'Sweet Home Alabama'! Surely you have a waiting list of girls wanting to date you."

"Only if they're approved by my dad first. Besides, I'm not out here with any of them." His voice lowered a little. "Next time, join me at the mic. I bet we'd make a pretty good couple."

I shouldn't be here. I should go back to the manor.

Amanda may have been too far for me to see her blush, but I knew that look she gave him. "You think so?" His hand moved to hers. Her fingers spread to make room for his.

I need to leave now. I don't want to see this.

Some generic, soft romance started playing from inside. "May I have this dance?" Hunter asked and soon the two of them were in a light embrace, swaying, gazing into each other's eyes.

Now's my chance. I don't want to be here for this. MOVE!! No matter how much my mind protested, my body refused to obey. Like I said, self-torture.

As they drew closer together, it felt like a claw squeezing my heart. Her hand went to his cheek. Their lips met.

Now, I've seen them kiss before, but not as often as you'd expect—I think Amanda avoided kissing him around me. But this felt different. It was the moment I lost my chance to Hunter. I'd never experienced *real* heartache in that timeline, but this moment dwarfed all the heartache I'd felt in any other timeline as well. *Watching* my soulmate share her first kiss with Hunter, as opposed to having her tell me they were dating, was a whole new level of pain. It manifested as ice needles flowing in my blood, starting from my left hand and spreading up and into my chest with each heartbeat.

Having a soulmate was turning out to be more of a curse than a blessing.

The pain did break me from my mental paralysis, however, and I finally turned and ran. Behind me, I heard Amanda exclaim, "A-Alex!?" but I didn't stop until I was in the Mirror Gallery. The anguish did not go away. Arbiter knelt beside me as I collapsed into his chair, my face in my hands.

*   *   *

"Sir, you are certain you are feeling up to it?" Arbiter asked as we stepped into the Mirror Gallery. "It has only been a day."

"Yes. I have to do this," I answered. "*You're* the one who has been stressing out. The only way I can get over this feeling is to keep moving forward."

"You *are* allowed to mourn, Master Petersen. A broken heart should not be ignored." At some point, he had upgraded from books to an eReader, which he had tucked under his arm as he carried a tray ladened with supplies for, in his words, "a spot of tea": a kettle, teapot with cozy, two cups, teaspoons, napkins, sugar cubes with tongs, cream, a candle warmer, several scones, a platter of small sandwiches, macarons, some shortbread, jam, lemon curd, honey, a roll of digestives, and, of course, a selection of teas. Some folks stress-eat, some stress-bake. Arbiter stress-*Britished*.

"It's nothing new. In case you haven't noticed, I've been doing nothing *but* getting broken-hearted since this began," I said. "I learned a *long* time ago that going forward is the best remedy. By the way, where do you get the ingredients for all that food? Do you guys even need to eat?"

He placed the tray on a side table next to his armchair and retrieved the eReader from under his arm. "Strictly speaking, no. We are still mortal, but these are not our normal bodies. They do not require food or sleep. However, many of us eat and sleep anyway for a variety of personal reasons. Mother Gaia brings whatever we need."

I stood in front of the mirror and stared it down. "Mother Gaia, huh? Who's that?"

"She is one of the Kin. Her realm is Earth."

"You mean there are more?"

He stepped up beside me and put a hand on my shoulder. "There are, but now is not the time for a lesson on the inner workings of The Between! If I'm not mistaken, you were attempting to find some sort of... planning meeting?"

"Yes... but how do I know if I can trust this damn thing? I am *certainly* not jumping in again without looking first."

"I do not believe it was *entirely* a malfunction. Part of you must have felt you *needed* to go to that time for some reason. Or perhaps that was the last time you truly felt like your own self. We will simply need to be more cautious in the future."

"'In the past,' you mean," I joked.

"Hmm. Perhaps a fortnight in repose is needed after all..." He delivered the line with perfect seriousness, but under his mustache was a grin.

"Alright, then. I can do this. Mirror, show me when Amanda and I were planning our D.C. trip."

The mirror showed a slightly younger Amanda and Alex sitting in my old dorm, figuring out what they were going to do and see in Washington D.C. that summer. Arbiter chuckled when he saw the decal on the back of my old laptop—a depiction of Magritte's *Son of Man* where the apple had been replaced with the glowing icon of my iMac.

"Do you want to go see the Washington Monument?" my past-self asked while scanning through a travel website. He sat in the middle of a couch with his laptop open on the coffee table before him.

"Meh, not really. Too touristy!" Amanda didn't even look up from her sketchpad as she answered. She sat on the couch corner, dinosaur pencil case next to her, all curled up, and wearing a red hair band and matching, oversized t-shirt she'd once "borrowed" from me. With how she sat, the shirt almost completely obscured her black gym shorts.

"Yeah, that's the point. We are *tourists! Come over here. We can work on the comic after."*

"Is something wrong, sir?" Arbiter asked in concern. "You look feverish."

I paused the scene. "What? No... I'm fine. I just forgot how cute she was that day." I took a few deep breaths to calm down. "I don't get it. How did I go so quickly from feeling sad to..."

"Infatuated, sir?"

I nodded. "It's like I'm on some sort of emotional rollercoaster."

Arbiter cracked a sly smile and leaned in closer. "You are in love. And I do believe you find her more than merely 'cute'. Sir."

If there was a time I was most attracted to her, it was that day. She looked so warm and soft, her legs were almost entirely on display, and I could tell she didn't have a bra on. "Yes, you're right. I very much wanted to be with her."

"Biblically?"

I'm sure this whole conversation had me blushing. "Biblically. But that's not helping me at the moment, is it?"

Arbiter walked over to his seat and put his hand on the back rest. "You mentioned a comic. You were working together?" he asked. The change of topic was a much-needed distraction.

"Yeah. It was silly. We dreamed of making a webcomic and earning just enough money to get by. Nothing came of it, though."

"I thought you were wealthy," Arbiter said.

"Yes... and no. I never told her how much I had and never flaunted it. I was planning to give most of it away, anyway. Not that it's worked in the past."

"I thought you told me you lived in a luxury flat. Did she never visit?"

I winced as he called out my hypocrisy. "Maybe I flaunted it a little. I never should have bought that penthouse. No, she never saw it."

I resumed the scene.

"Well there's always the Smithsonian museums," past-Alex told her.

"Meh." Amanda tilted her hand side to side before erupting in giggles. "Of course, silly! I know you want to see the dinosaurs. Almost as much as I do," she said in sing-song. Even though she didn't look up from her pad, past-Alex clearly had her attention. "I'm still gonna take you on a dig someday."

"Sure you are. What about the National Gallery?" he asked as he continued searching the site, idly clicking his tongue on the back of his teeth.

"Any good exhibits?"

After some searching, he shook his head. "Not while we're there. Oh! But the Hirshhorn has an exhibit on Yoshitaka Amano that week!"

"Shut-up-and-take-my-money! Really? Quick, get tickets!" Amanda said, slowly looking up from her pad. She soon tossed it to the coffee table and scooted next to him, clutching a couch pillow to her chest.

"Aaaaand done! Let's see... Oh, there's the Spy Museum. I've heard it's fun."

"Yeah, but that one costs money," she replied.

"I can pay for it. I mean, experiencing DC is part of the reason we're going." When he looked over at her and saw the expression she was giving him, he nodded. "Or this isn't just about the money, is it? Amanda, I know you want to be able to pay your way, but we might not get another chance like this."

"We don't live that far away from it." Her voice sounded like she was distracted. "You know I don't want you spending money on me."

Past-Alex sighed. "But I want to."

"Pause! Pause!"

"Sir?" I'd all but forgotten that Arbiter was there.

"It's... it's nothing. Oh God, Arb. I remember it so clearly. She was *insanely* sexy, she smelled so damn *good*... and she was dating Hunter. Ugh! I wanted to make a move, I *should* have made a move!"

"Unless I'm mistaken, you still can, sir." He gestured towards the mirror in an "after you" pose.

I stared at the scene intently. One of the funny things about the mirror was that the events didn't occur from my point of view, so I got to see myself in the third person as it were, the way someone else would. Thanks to the new vantage point I could see something this time that I hadn't noticed before: Amanda's eyes fixed on my neck with such *desire*. Her hair spilled out around the hairband and fell over her shoulders, one of which was completely exposed by the shirt, showing off more freckles and toned muscles. She looked rather coy as she bit her bottom lip.

"Yeah," I said absently. "I can." But I didn't move. Believe me, I tried. My feet remained fixed to the spot.

Arbiter looked at me expectantly. "Well?"

"If I go back now, that's over three years I have to relive. Three years of classes and cancer and dealing with Hunter... not to mention Professor Sapper."

"Ah. And here I thought you would do *anything* for her. Maybe you are a little nervous with the way she is looking at you." I didn't have to take my eyes from the mirror to know he was smirking—I could *hear* it.

"I'm not nervous!"

"It's nothing to be ashamed of. Every schoolboy gets nervous around women. Even those like me."

That was all the motivation I needed. With a deep breath, I steadied myself and entered the mirror.

Chapter 9

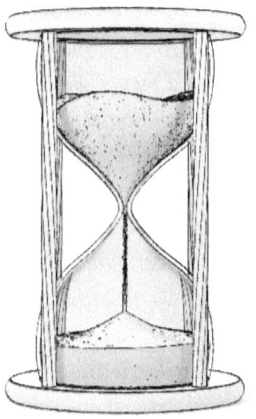

Good Call

I had tried to prepare myself for the onslaught of emotions and memories from that time, but what I wasn't prepared for was a couch pillow to the face. It was accompanied by the magical lilt of Amanda's giggles. I did not remember this happening before, but I wasn't about to start questioning things at that moment.

"No spending money on me. That's for my boyfriend to do," she teased.

I quickly reached to the other side of the couch and grabbed the remaining pillow. I bopped her in the face with it and grinned. "...and best friend," I countered.

Amanda gasped at me. "Curse your sudden but inevitable betrayal!" Soon we were trading cushioned blows. The computer took a hit and slid across the coffee table, then teetered on the opposite edge. Amanda rose to her knees on the couch for a height advantage, so I changed tactics and surrendered my weapon. Instead, I went straight for her sides with bare hands. The next few seconds were a jumble of laughing, tickling, and teasing, until she pushed against me hard and rolled us both off the couch and onto the floor with her landing on top.

As she gazed down at me, I could see whole galaxies in her eyes. Our bodies pressed together in dangerously pleasant ways that made shifting around an exercise in resisting temptation. The scent of apple and cinnamon that clung to her would be forever associated with this moment. My hand had been trapped between us, and moving it free caused it to brush over one of the peaks that pressed hard against her shirt. We both trembled at the sensation. She grabbed hold of my hand, but didn't let it go.

I honestly don't know how long we lay there, each holding the other captive, sharing our breath. One minute? Thirty? This was an experience I somehow missed out on the first time. It wasn't something even best friends did. I felt the same spark as I had on the morning of her wedding. We'd crossed the line into something different and I didn't know if we could—or wanted to—go back. There was no more fooling myself into believing that I was doing this as just her friend.

A cellphone alarm broke us free and we both gasped like we'd been holding our breaths the entire time. Amanda leaned up, one hand on my chest, and grabbed her phone on the table.

"Oh, I promised Sam and Diana we'd go out for lunch," she said and moved to get off of me, but neither of us let go of the other's hand. She looked down at me and bit her lip hard.

"Amanda... stay. Stay with me," I softly asked.

She gripped my hand tighter. "I... I want to. But we... we can't do this..." she whispered.

"Why not? We love each other," I stated, and from the way her face nearly glowed with embarrassment, I knew it was true. "I've been in love with you since we were kids. You were the only one who stood up for me, who pushed me to do better, who stayed around. You've been so supportive of your brother. I can't think of anyone else I would've confessed to breaking the teacher's fossil for. You've been an incredible role-model. You're funny, inspiring, creative, smart, kind... I judge my days on whether or not I get to see you. Remember when we used to leave random notes of encouragement for each other? Finding one always made me smile. After Brian Reynolds stood you up for someone else, you still wanted him to be happy. And I'm pretty sure you kept Praeli at the same level as Tamlarian so we would always be able to play together. Amanda, you amaze me."

Amanda didn't respond. I finally released her hand and caressed her cheek. "You're more than just my best friend, Amanda. When you started going out with Hunter, it killed me inside. It made me realize just how much you mean to me. I never had the guts to say it out loud before."

Instead of a look of affection, she appeared conflicted. "Alex... Why?" she whispered. "Why couldn't this have happened sooner?" A tear fell partway down her cheek.

"Hunter's going to call soon and tell you not to go to D.C. He's going to say something about a yacht. Please, don't let him talk you out of this trip."

"Alex, you know I'm loyal to—" Hunter's timing was impeccable. We both sprang to life when her phone began to play, "Every Breath you Take". "It's Hunter..." We picked ourselves off the floor, sat down on the couch, adjusted our clothing. I rescued the still-teetering computer while she answered. "Hello?"

Her expression changed from surprise to bewilderment. I put my hand up behind my ear to indicate I wanted to hear. She hesitated, but eventually nodded and placed the phone on the table, turning on the speakerphone.

"...-on't think it's a good idea. It's not safe there. D.C. has a high crime rate."

I woke my computer up and opened a notepad, but couldn't think of what to type to her.

"It'll be fine, Hunter. It's not like we're going to be wandering the streets or anything," she said.

"Of course babe, but you know me. I worry about you. Isn't that my job?"

"Yeah, but nothing's going to happen! There's going to be a whole bunch of us! And it's only for two weeks." She squeezed my hand briefly, reassuring me.

It took Hunter some time before he responded. "Hey, remember how I told you that my father didn't approve of us dating? It's more than just that. He was already pissed at me for going to a different college than the one *he* picked out. Last week, he went ballistic when I told him we were still together."

"Again?"

"Mm-hmm. He wants to control my whole life. He said I had to break up with you or he's cutting me out of the will and Tilly will get everything. What an asshole. I told him I didn't care about the will, that I would rather be with you, and now he's blaming *you* for destroying the family. When I stood up for you, he said that for all he knows, you're just in it for the money."

Amanda sighed. "He hates me that much?"

"It's not that. He just doesn't know you. He hasn't approved of you. Remember, everything I do has to be *his* idea. Nothing *I* ever come up with is good enough for him."

The conversation took a turn I hadn't expected. Even *I* almost felt sorry for the guy. For the first time, I was glad I didn't have any parents imposing their will on me. I stayed quiet, so quiet that I really did hold my breath. Amanda looked at me with a mixture of sympathy and guilt. "I'm sorry, Hunter. It's terrible that you have to put up with him. He really does have the whole family under his heel."

"Tell me about it. I'm lucky I've got you to keep me sane. I told him that he'd change his mind if he got to know you and convinced him to go with us for a week out on the family yacht on Lake Erie. Ever been out on a yacht? No, I suppose not. Well, it's our six-month anniversary coming up, so that gives us the perfect excuse."

The moment he offered the yacht, Amanda's eyes widened and she looked at me questioningly. "I don't know. Trapped on a boat with your parents for a week? That doesn't sound very relaxing. Isn't there another way?" When she put it that way, I could see how hard the decision to go would have been, how much influence he already had on her.

Hunter laughed, but it wasn't the usual wheeze I'd heard from him. "Trust me, I don't want to be stuck there with that jerk either, but I don't see any other way. You have no idea how hard it was to get him to agree to this. I'm already giving up *half* my inheritance just for this chance."

My fingers hovered over the computer's keyboard, but I still couldn't think of anything to say, at least not anything helpful. Despite my confession, I had no idea what Amanda was going to do. It didn't feel right demanding anything from her. I leaned back and felt for the key through my shirt, but once I had a grip of it, doubt crept into my thoughts. All this time, I'd been trying to control her choice. *Her* choice. Hunter had manipulated her on the previous trips to the past—or rather, to the future, relative to this moment—but now, today, his claws weren't quite in her yet. This time, it was a more even playing field. She knew how I felt. She knew how Hunter felt. As he continued talking, I made up my mind that if she chose him, I would stay and be there for her, help her however I could. I let go of the key.

"But this is so sudden, and I've been looking forward to this trip all semester," she replied. Then she leaned over to the computer and typed out one letter at a time: *how did u know?*

"This might be our only shot. He's planning on pulling a few strings and having me removed from school and transferred to Dartmouth. We'll never see each other again! But if I can show him the real you, I'm sure he'll change his mind. Our relationship depends on this!"

Whether or not his words were true, I could see the effect they had on Amanda. She looked away from me, shrank into herself, and hung her head. No, I was not going to win her heart that day. *Whatever your decision, I'll support it. I'm here for you,* I wrote. As I typed the words, it eased some of the guilt that had been building in my mind, but feeling less guilty didn't really make this any easier to swallow.

Amanda took a deep breath and reached for my hand. She was trembling and her voice wavered. "Maybe it's better if we take a break."

The meaning of what she'd just said took a while to sink in. I looked at her in disbelief, unsure that what I'd heard was real. She kept her eyes on the computer screen.

Hunter's response, though, was immediate. "A break? After all I've sacrificed for you, for *us*?" His voice had lost that piteous quality that made it easy to empathize with him. "I've put so much of myself into this relationship, can't you do the same? I might not even *be* here by the time you get back from D.C.—is going on this trip really worth more than our love?"

Amanda's posture changed, and her mood with it. She was emerging from the submissive, unsure girl Hunter made her feel like and gradually returning to herself. "I don't like that you're using our relationship as leverage. You think I haven't sacrificed for us? That I haven't been invested in us?" she asked.

Hunter never lost his stride, but there was a desperation in his voice he tried to hide. And desperate people make mistakes. "The way you go on about 'Alex', sometimes I wonder." He mocked her with my name. "You swore he's nothing more than a friend to you, but he's always been a wedge between us. Are you sure he's not trying to steal you from me? You should be more careful around him. I once caught him spreading rumors about us, but when I talked to him about it, he just blew me off."

"You said the same thing about Xiao. I even had a fight with them about it!"

"Where do you think Xiao got the rumors from? I once overheard Al say he was going to make you another notch on his bedpost. You can't trust him."

My mouth hung open at such wild accusations. *I've never done or said anything like that!* I wrote. But Amanda didn't see it; instead she rose to her feet and began pacing.

"Well, I do! He's my *best friend*. We've been through a lot together and I know him better than he knows himself! He'd *never* behave like that. He and I, we're a package deal. And if you don't believe me when I say nothing's happened between us, then maybe you don't know me as well as you think you do."

I hadn't seen her defend me like that since the tenth grade. I was in utter awe of her and her fiery spirit. She plopped herself back down next to me with an exasperated sigh. A moment later, though, she pulled my laptop into her lap and started typing furiously.

Hunter went from desperate to injured. "See? He's *already* between us. You know I love you, Amanda! I can't live without you. Don't let him get in your head."

"It's not about him. I—"

"Why are you being such a narcissist? Please, think of me for once. If you leave, I'd have nothing left. You're the only person I've ever loved, the only one who's ever loved me! Dad hates me, he doesn't let mom ever speak to me, Tilly only cares about herself. Please, Amanda. You're the only good thing in my life."

Talk about textbook manipulation. Amanda turned the screen so I could see what she'd written: *I'm sorry. He's never spoken to me like this before. I know you haven't done the things he said. Btw your mouth is hanging open.* I'd been slack-jawed the whole time. Had she even seen my expression, or did she really just know me *that* well?

"You're scaring me, Hunter," she said sternly. "I won't be held responsible for *your* happiness. I have enough trouble finding my own. Besides, you've known about this trip for months. You said you supported it. It's not fair to—"

"Of course I do, babe! You know that!" His words sounded like an accusation. The way Hunter changed emotions so quickly was nearly as impressive as Amanda's newfound strength. Needless to say, this was *not* how the scene played out the first time. The only real change I'd made was letting Amanda know how I felt about her. Then, all I could do was watch helplessly on as a butterfly created a hurricane before my eyes.

Amanda the hurricane was getting angry. "Stop interru—!"

"You can go next year. I promise!" he interrupted. "I'll even go with you! But I may never get a chance with my dad like this again. Once he gets to know you, everything will be perfect, you'll see!"

"I don't want—!!"

"Without you... I'm nothing. Life wouldn't be worth living. I might even—"

Amanda gasped. "*Hunter!* I—I'm sorry. I don't think I can be with someone who says things like that so easily. We're... We're *through*, Hunter!"

I couldn't believe it. Amanda just stood up for *herself*. Pride filled my heart, at least until she pressed her warm body against mine. That left me with a very different, but equally as powerful feeling. She closed my still-agape maw and turned my head towards the screen.

I've wanted us to be more than friends since we were 12. I thought **you** *didn't want to be. Can you forgive me for not telling you?* she wrote.

I nodded, a goofy grin on my face, probably as goofy as the one on hers. But Hunter's tirade continued. "Mandabear! You don't mean that! Don't you care if I die?"

She sat straight up and pulled at her hair. "Ugh! Hunter, I'm fed up with all your guilt-tripping! Well, you know what? Fine. I admit it. I *am* in love with Alex! I have been since before you and I even met. But we've never done anything! I've been loyal to *you!* Maybe it's time I found out if he loves me, too."

"I knew it," Hunter said in a rather menacing voice. "I *knew* you were cheating on me with that limp-dicked simp."

There must have been a blush on my face because after hearing her confess, I felt my entire head heat up. But a thought came to me, a gamble. If he'd been with her future bridesmaids, how far back had that gone?

Ask him about Sam, I typed. Amanda looked devastated. Sam had been her friend since high school, and became her closest friend after I ran away. Amanda had depended on her to be her confidant, which made Sam's betrayal so much worse.

"What about Samantha?" The line went silent. "I know she had a crush on you once. Have you... have you been seeing her?"

The depths of anger and hatred in that man's voice gave me chills and made Amanda blanch. "Who the *fuck* have you been talking to? It's Al, isn't it? Didn't I tell you he's been spreading *lies* about me? You know he and Naomi—"

"Leave him out of this; he's never been my boyfriend! Is it true, Hunter? What will Samantha say if I call her?" she asked.

He didn't miss a beat. "Oh come on, Samantha's not even my type! You know she likes to make shit up for the attention. Remember—"

"*Hunter Pace!* You've really been cheating on me!?"

"It's not like that, babe. I was drunk and she came onto me! It was a one-time thing! Nothing would have happened if you'd just put out."

Amanda yelled, "*I can't believe I trusted you!*"

"...Are you on speaker phone?" he asked after a moment of silence. "You're with Al right now, aren't you? I can't *believe* this shit!" Loud knocks and bangs came over the line. Something glass shattered in the distance, followed by repeated cracking thuds, like wood hitting wood. He screamed as the thuds continued, sometimes joined by more shattering glass. "I'm gonna *kill* the motherfucker!" he yelled, the words starting loud, interrupted in the middle by a *SMACK!* and *crack*, and ending far off. "God damn little shit screwing my girl! Ruining everything!" More words, mostly cursing, faded away and ceased with the **SLAM** of a door.

I reached for the phone and hung up. After a few seconds of stunned silence, Amanda moved her arms around me and pressed her face against my neck, weeping. The laptop slipped to the floor. We held each other until she calmed down. "I'm so sorry," I said. My voice cracked.

She shook her head against me. "No. Thank you. Thank you." She kept repeating it softly. When I asked her what for, she looked up at me and rubbed her cheek dry. "For finally telling me. For helping me stand up to him. For showing me what he's really like. I suspected he liked Sam, but he kept making me doubt what I'd seen or accusing me of not trusting him." With a slow exhale, she sat up and held onto my hands with a death grip. "I should have listened to what my head was telling me, not my heart."

"The heart is fickle," I said as I squeezed back. "And the head can overthink."

She sniffed and gave me a soft smile. "At least they agree right now." This felt new, like starting a new chapter in a book. Everything was going to work out.

"Are you okay?"

"Yes. I'm all right. But we can't stay here," Amanda said. "I'm sure he tracked my phone."

"You don't think he'd *really* try to kill me, do you?"

She bit her lip. "I've seen him get violent before. He might try something. They go hunting, so he's got access to all kinds of guns."

"That's all I need to hear." In seconds we were up and I dragged out my suitcase from the bedroom closet. "Guess he's living up to his namesake," I jested. I needed something to break the tension.

"Ha. Ha." Once I had the suitcase open on the bed, we started throwing whatever essentials and clothing we could think of into it.

"Why did you start going out with him anyway?" I asked. That kiss they'd shared on the deck left a lot of questions unanswered for me.

She sighed but kept packing. "Do you remember the day Hunter and I started dating? There was that party?"

"Yeah." How could I forget it?

"I asked you to go with me, but you said you couldn't. I kept trying to flirt with you all day but you never flirted back. And then we were standing out there in the snow and holding hands and I thought you were going to kiss me. I was *so sure*, and the moment was perfect. But... you didn't. You just gave me a little hug and left. I thought you were rejecting me, that you wanted to stay friends."

I shook my head. "I was scared. When I was being passed around from home to home, you were my only real friend, my anchor. I didn't have any good role models for relationships so I was sure I'd mess things up. And what then? What would have happened to our friendship if I broke your heart? Could we go back to just friends? I wanted to be more, but being friends was safer. It was stable."

"What changed your mind?"

"I realized that I was already in love with you. There *was* no going back."

She gave me such a sweet smile. "I guess we were both scared. I kept talking myself out of telling you how I felt. Every date I'd ever been on ended in disaster, and if I hurt you... I was worried you would run away again. I'd lose you a second time, and I didn't know if I could handle that.

"At the party that night, Hunter was funny and charming and sweet and kind. I went out to the deck to get some air and he joined me. We talked about all those first dates turned disasters, about how lonely we both felt. When you—when I *thought* you had rejected me too, I felt so vulnerable and alone. He made me feel wanted and safe. And then we danced... and we kissed. I didn't think anyone else could love me. He was good for me, I thought. I remember how terrified I felt when I saw you running away."

We both stopped packing for a moment and looked at each other in confusion.

"I said I couldn't make it, remember?" I said.

"Yeah, that's right. That must have happened in a nightmare. Why *couldn't* you make it, anyway?" We returned to packing.

Her explanation made sense, so I did my best to ignore the worry growing in the back of my mind. "Do you remember the Pineapple Pecker?"

"You mean the guy running around campus with pineapple rings on his—!" She put her hand over her mouth. "That wasn't *you*, was it?"

I know I should have felt ashamed, but her grin made me feel proud instead. "Yup. First time I got drunk. Got banned from every party on campus, *especially* Sigma Pi Iota."

She giggled as I zipped up the suitcase, but when I headed to the door, she caught my arm.

"What is it?" I asked.

"Run away with me, Alex. Right now."

"Wh-where should we go?"

She picked up her phone and went to the window. The blue rectangle of plastic and glass spun majestically on its maiden voyage, flying over the heads of students below, and finally landing in a bush unceremoniously. I gasped—I knew how hard she'd worked to afford that thing. "Anywhere. Away from here." The moment she got close enough, Amanda pulled me from the door and rose onto the balls of her feet. We shared our first kiss.

Again.

And let me tell ya, third time really is the charm. This one was no slow build-up, but a supernova—all the passion of the others crammed into a matter of seconds. I never knew a kiss really *could* steal your breath away. But the threat of being hunted down, shot, stuffed, and mounted on Hunter's wall kept it short. Without another word, we left our old lives behind and embarked on a new one.

Chapter 10

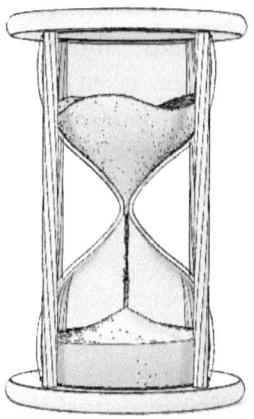

Isla Del Encanto

One of the advantages to having money is that running away, unlike the last time I did it, is a very easy thing to do. But when you're running away from someone who also has money, your options aren't limitless. Shelters were an absolute no-go; the Pace family owned most of the ones in the area, anyway. Motels were not particularly pleasant—or safe—places to spend a night on the lam. Any expensive hotel in the city could easily have someone willing to report our whereabouts back to the prestigious Pace family if they asked. Instead, we went to a two-star local chain called *Lodge-N-Comfort*.

We walked hand-in-hand into the pleasantly decorated, chic lobby. At the front desk stood a plump man in suit and tie. He spoke with a thick South African accent.

"Welcome. Do you have reservations?" He began typing on the computer.

"I'm sorry, no. We'll take whatever room is available." I pulled out my wallet.

Amanda put her hand on my arm. "I'll pay for it," she said.

"It's not a problem."

"It actually is a problem, sir. I'm afraid we're full up for the night. There's a conference in town. I could put you on the waiting list in case we have a last-minute cancellation."

"Oh, for crying out loud," I grumbled, determined to give Amanda a soft bed that night. "I am NOT letting a setback like this get in the way, not after making it this far." The manager didn't get a chance to protest. I was on my phone immediately. "Sufiya, please? Alexander Petersen-with-an-s-e-n."

"Who are you calling?" Amanda asked.

"My travel agent." But when I heard the confusion in Sufiya's voice on the other end, I remembered that I hadn't taken her on as a travel agent yet. Well, I decided to fix that. "Sufiya, my name is Alexander Petersen. With an s-e-n, yes. I got your name from a business associate of mine and was told you're the best travel agent around. I'd like to use your services. Yes, I'll hold."

"Alex! Travel agent? That sounds expensive." Amanda pulled me away from the front desk as she spoke.

"Remember when I told you I won the lottery?" She nodded. I gave her a guilty smile. "It was $7 million."

*   *   *

Getting to a safe hotel with vacant rooms may have taken a lot longer than I expected, but once Sufiya was on the case, it became a breeze. In fact, it was such a breeze that everything else that day, including the city we arrived in that night, had become a blur. All I knew for sure was that the city had about 200% humidity, the hotel was near the ocean, and my knowledge of Spanish was proving to be invaluable.

"Yeah, I know it's late," Amanda said with my phone up to her ear. "I hope I didn't wake you. No, Mom. I'm fine... It's about Hunter. I broke up with him this morning." She paced around the suite trying to dry her hair and talk on my phone at the same time. She wore a rainbow-splashed shirt from the airport, which proudly declared, "Puerto Rico: Isla del Encanto" printed above and below an image of the island. It went down to her mid-thigh. I, on the other hand, lounged in a white robe embossed with the hotel's logo, aimlessly flipping through TV channels looking for nothing in particular. After a brief pause, Amanda's cheeks glowed red and her gaze turned towards me. "It's because... I'm in love with Alex. Yes, Petersen! Do you know of any *other* Alex? ...From church? But, she's a girl... *Mom!*"

"Hello, Mrs. Shields!" I said loudly.

"Yes, Mom, that was him. No, we aren't doing anything like that! *Oh my God, Mom...*" She covered her face, but that didn't hide her blush from me. I had stopped looking at the tv and just gazed at her. Perhaps it's a soulmate thing, but no ever got *close* to turning me on the way Amanda did. Everything from the way she moved to her nubile figure barely obscured beneath her shirt to the way she looked at me between her fingers with that coquettish smirk excited me. But when her cheeks lit up again and she turned her back to me, I discovered that my robe wasn't doing the greatest job of obscuring *me*. My face heated up as I quickly fixed it.

A knock at the door put me on high alert. I got up to peer through the peephole. "Ah. Room service." I opened it and a porter wheeled in a cart that carried several packages. As Amanda talked with her mother, I tipped him, then went through the packages once he left. When we had opened our suitcase after getting to the room, we'd found that, in our rush to pack, we had forgotten most of our toiletries, I had neglected to pack pants, and Amanda lacked nearly *any* of her clothing, particularly underwear. The packages had most of the items we needed. Like a model in a fashion show, I held up random articles of clothing to my chest to show them off. I even strutted a little.

Amanda still had her back turned and didn't notice. "Don't worry about that, we've got it covered. ...We're in Puerto Rico... It's ok! We're fine, we made it! ...No, mom. It's part of the United States. The water is-snnk!!" When she turned around and noticed the black chemise I held against my chest, she put her hand over her mouth to stop from laughing, but that little snicker still escaped. "Behave," she mouthed at me and threw her towel at my face. "It's nothing, Mom. So, about Hunter. I think he's dangerous. I'm concerned that he's going to try something. His family own guns, so—."

"A gun!?" Mrs. Shield's response was so loud, even I could hear it, and Amanda had to pull away from the phone for a second.

"Uh-huh. He sounded *very* upset. It's probably not safe there tonight. ...Yes, we're serious. We think you should get somewhere safe. We'll pay for it. Uh-huh. Alright. Love you, too! If you need me, call Alex's phone. I'll talk to you tomorrow!" Before I had a chance to walk back to the cart, a heavy, Amanda-shaped weight wrapped around my back. "This is serious!" she said as her arms and legs squeezed me from behind.

I stumbled and fell back on the bed. If I hadn't known better, I'd have thought she took a few wrestling lessons with how well she had my arms pinned, but eventually she let go and we lay side by side. "I know it's serious. I really do. But right now, I think we could both use a little levity and a bit of stress-relief. We've done what we can. Hunter can't get us, and your family has been warned. They'll get somewhere safe, I'm sure. Everything else is out of our hands."

"I don't know how you can act so cavalier about it," she said and punched me in the arm. "I'm scared shitless."

I rubbed where she'd punched. "Me too, and I lived on the street more than once as a kid. I've seen some shit. When I was scared, there were two things I turned to, and humor was one of them."

"What's the other?"

"Thinking of my soulmate."

She lay her head on my shoulder and pressed her palm against my chest. I never knew how much I had craved her touch until then. "Soulmate, huh? Well, *soulmate,* there's a time and a place for making each other laugh."

"How did you cope, then?" I asked.

"When you were gone?" She buried her face against me for a moment, muffling her response. "I didn't." She never spoke much about what she did the years I was away, and from the shame in her voice I wasn't surprised.

"And when I wasn't?" I asked and started running my fingers through her still-damp hair.

"Well, just being with you is a big help. Mmmm... that helps, too." Her fingers traced over the key I still wore. "What's this?"

I'd gotten away with calling her my soulmate, but as her delicate fingers outlined the key on my chest, I became very aware of how dangerous this might be. "That? ...A wise old friend gave it to me when I was far from home. He said I should wear it at all times and it'll help me overcome the sins of the past."

"Ooh, cryptic much? Your friend sounds a bit out there."

"Oh, he is."

She lay her hand over the key and snuggled into me more. "I didn't know you believed in good luck charms and all that. Is it helping?"

"Mmmmm... Actually, it is." We lay there for a while before a question that had been rattling around in my mind spilled out. "If you knew I only had a few years left to live, would you still want to be with me?"

Her body tensed slightly. "Why? You aren't sick or anything, are you?"

"I don't think so."

I felt a soft kiss on my shoulder. "Good. And yes, of course, I would. But you better not die on me anytime soon, or I'll march straight into Hell and drag you back myself!"

"Hell?"

"You heard me!" She leaned over me with a smug grin. "That's where people who don't tell their best friend about having $7 million end up. I thought it was a few thousand!"

"Well, *after* taxes and fees, I'm only getting a little over $100k a year for the next thirty years, and most of that is going into—ow! Don't pinch!"

"Then don't play the victim, here! That's still a lot of money!" She settled against me again and silence fell over us for a time, enough that I thought she had fallen asleep when I heard her voice again. "So why didn't you?"

"Tell you?"

"Mm-hmm." She slid her leg over me and shifted until she was laying on top of me, folded forearms on my chest supporting her chin. My hands slid along her back. I was keenly aware of how she was straddling me, and there was a good chance she could tell.

Her body rose as I took a deep breath. "Because it's not mine." When she gave me an inquisitive look, I explained. "It was amazing to have at first, but... how could I keep all that money—money I didn't deserve—when I knew so many good kids who didn't even know when they would get to eat again? So, I decided I wanted to use it to start a foster home for kids. Teens, mostly."

She leaned up some to look at me. "That sounds perfect for you. You wouldn't happen to need a cute assistant, would you?"

"Sure, do you know of one?" My tease earned me another light punch to the arm. "What about you? Any secrets from when we were apart?"

With a huff, she said, "No. When you disappeared I was worried sick. I checked our sanctuary every day to see if you were there. I grew depressed and always felt alone. I... had a lot of first dates with guys. Dozens. Never had a second." I could see in her eyes that there was more to be said, but I did not want to press her. "Art and your travel blog kept me sane."

"You read it? I should have gotten in touch with you before I left."

Amanda lay her head against me again and let me play with her dark-red hair. "So how'd you get by all those years?"

"I found this funny-looking pocket watch just laying on the ground with no one around, so I pawned it. That kept me going for a while. Every now and then I'd get an unexpected windfall like that. Then someone I met said he had an extra plane ticket to L.A. and offered it to me."

"Just like that? And you didn't even know him? Sounds to me like he was being a Good Samaritan. Either that or a predator."

"Yeah, I was curious about it, too. But I had nothing to lose. We talked a lot on the flight over. He said it was meant for his son who died. Unfortunately, once we landed, he just disappeared."

She put her lips out in a pout. "That's so sad."

I sighed. "It was. He asked me to hold onto his laptop bag and then never came back. I must've waited 12 hours. I couldn't get any information on him. The only thing in the bag other than laptop stuff was a post-it note that said, 'it's yours.' Even the laptop only had an operating system, like it was new. I wish I could remember his name." The more I talked about it, the more I wondered if Luck or Destiny was involved somehow.

"Definitely a Samaritan. Or a ghost. Ooh, could he have been *your* dad?" she teased.

"Yeah, right. I think he was too old to be my dad. Not that I've ever met him."

"So is the laptop how you started your travel blog?"

I nodded with a grin. "Yup! I turned it in, but he never claimed it, so I got to keep it. I wrote a... pretty scathing review of a hotel that went viral, and then I kept getting hits. People liked no-budget travel. The ads kept me afloat, so I kept traveling and writing. You know, I tried to email you a bunch of times, but they kept getting returned with an error."

Amanda sat up, still straddling me. She had her hands on my chest, and the way that shirt hung loose on her threatened to reveal more of her than I'd ever seen before. I was both intensely aroused and nervous as Hell. "The school changed their whole email system after you left. *You* should have put your email on your *blog* somewhere!" she started tickling my ribs with a playful grin.

"Ack! I did! At the bottom!"

"Well *I* never *saw* it!" She giggled as she kept up her assault. After years of practice, she knew *exactly* where I was most ticklish. I squirmed wildly beneath her and grabbed her wrists. The tickling stopped but we kept grinning madly at each other. Slowly I moved her arms over my head and she lowered into a long and long-overdue kiss.

Certain things a man should keep to himself, particularly when it comes to sharing a hotel room with the girl of his dreams. Unfortunately for me, none of those things happened that night. The woman who had been trying to keep herself pure did a marvelous job of testing her own boundaries before we both fell asleep from exhaustion.

The song *You're My Best Friend* woke us an hour later. It was the ringtone I'd set for Amanda and her parents. It went to voicemail, but when the phone rang again a moment later, she sat up at the edge of the bed, threw her shirt on, and answered it. The conversation was mostly one-sided, with Amanda only getting in a few soft words now and then.

"That was dad," she said once the call ended. "It's Hunter. His friend TJ broke into the house before they had a chance to get out. Dad says he had a gun. But everyone's safe. Apparently he wasn't expecting them to be awake and ran. The neighbors called the cops on him. They're looking for him now."

Neither of us could sleep, or even relax, after that. We kept the phone close by and held each other for comfort—levity was not an option this time. As the sunrise painted the sky and ocean in brilliant pigments, we got a call that TJ had been caught and arrested. Around noon, we learned that he'd squealed pretty easily and thrown Hunter under the bus. Hunter had indeed given the order.

Amanda and I spent the rest of the week together on the island, getting updates from her family often. We did manage to enjoy ourselves despite it all, but this was one trip I did *not* blog about. When we heard news that the judge in the case had a chip on his shoulder and wanted to make an example of them, that he'd denied them bail and wanted a swift trial, we finally felt safe enough to return home. Meanwhile, Amanda and I were together in paradise, we were in love, and everything was how it should have been.

Yeah, this sure sounds like a happy ending, and I wish I could say that we lived happily ever after, but that would make me a liar. If you're not sure why, go reread the first page.

Chapter 11

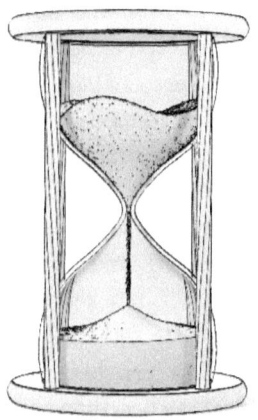

It All Comes Crashing Down

One Year Later:

The words "Sips & Blips" lit up on the storefront ahead as we approached. Amanda practically vibrated with excitement and anticipation as she held onto my arm with one hand and clutched a wrapped present in the other.

"You look like you're about to explode," I said with a smile. I was only doing a marginally better job of hiding my anticipation myself.

"I can't help it!" she exclaimed. "I just really want you to see the mural I painted!" She wore a burgundy off-the-shoulder dress that made her green eyes even more striking as she beamed at me. Her usual bangs and ponytail had been traded out for freely flowing locks that fell just to her shoulders, parted in the middle. Ever since we started going out, she began wearing flirtier clothes that showed off more skin than she used to. She claimed it was because she "felt more comfortable" in her body. I didn't quite know what that meant. It was one of many topics I looked forward to talking more about, someday soon.

"I will! It's not going anywhere," I said. I had opted for a deep-blue, button-up shirt and nice slacks, though she insisted I keep the top two buttons open. "I'm happy Diego's folks let us come before the grand opening. Something tells me this place will be crawling with people afterward." Of course, I happened to *know* it would be, which was why I'd never been inside it before, in *any* timeline.

Naomi and Xiao emerged from the closed double doors and held them open for us. They wore matching shirts and vests; not Naomi's usual, but still fit her personality perfectly. Xiao was non-binary, and ever since the two of them became a couple, they had both started experimenting with different styles for both genders. But I knew the real reason Xiao was there. Because Xiao's parents had come from China, their strict, academically focused upbringing had resulted in the best computer programmer I knew. As Amanda hugged Naomi and I hugged Xiao, I quickly whispered into their ear, "Is it ready? Did you test it?"

"Oh yeah. It's better than you expected. You'll love it."

Sips & Blips was a combination bar and retro-arcade. The walls were a dark gray, but a temporary wall on wheels blocked Amanda's mural from view. The place had once been a service garage and still kept the open concept plan, but instead of cars and tools, it had flashing lights and a long bar along the back wall. Customers could order a drink at the bar, then carry a little flag on a suction cup with them as they went from one classic arcade machine to another. Servers hunted down the flags to deliver their drinks. At least, they would in a few weeks when it properly opened. Today, in place of servers and customers, though, were a bunch of our friends, more than I was expecting but not enough to be anxiety-inducing. Most of them were playing old arcade games.

"How many people did you invite to this?" I asked her as we stepped inside. "I thought it was just going to be a few."

Amanda's grin turned a bit sly, like she knew something I didn't. "Well, we have a lot to celebrate."

As if on cue, Diego approached us with a drink in each hand. "Congrats on the webcomic," he said as he handed us the drinks.

"Thank you. What's this?" I asked and looked down at the old-fashioned glass filled with liquid sunset. I hadn't planned this part.

"Your favorite. Tequila Sunrise," he said as he pointed to Amanda's drink, then pointed at mine. "*Virgin* Tequila Sunrise." I scoffed at him, then saw Naomi over his shoulder with a huge, shit-eating grin on her face. She raised a glass.

Amanda laughed until the scowl on my face cracked into a laugh of my own. "She knows you too well."

As we walked, I strategically and nonchalantly aimed her towards the row of games facing the bar itself. "I can't believe the webcomic is actually getting hits," I said, trying to make conversation to hide how nervous I was.

"Do you think we should unveil it now?" she asked with a bounce.

"Your family isn't here yet. I think we should wait for them."

"Oh, but I want you to *seeeee* it!" She leaned against me and looked at me with a puppy-dog gaze. "Please?" She managed to be both cute and sexy at the same time.

My will would not last long under such an assault. It wasn't the end of the world to show her my surprise later, but I wanted to do it *before* her family got there. "Tell you what. How about you play a game first, and then we'll do the unveiling." She pushed her lip out in a pout, but I still had an ace up my sleeve. "Oh, is that Galaga?"

Amanda had a complicated relationship with the 1981 space shooter game. In it, waves of alien ships flew around the screen into specific formations and tried to shoot the player's space ship at the bottom. She had studied the game and knew the best strategies, like letting a ship get captured so you can rescue it later. Unfortunately, she was also terrible at it. Instead of letting that dissuade her, however, she never turned down an opportunity to try again.

"What? Where?" I pointed it out to her and she chewed on her knuckle as she had an inner debate. "...I suppose just one game. But then we're unveiling the mural!" She practically ran to it.

I thought I was being smooth and had everything under control, but as Amanda put her things down on the table next to the machine and stepped up to it, my stomach did nervous flips. "Let's do 2-player," I suggested. With that button press, she unknowingly triggered my devious plan. I put my drink down and started fishing around in my pockets. When I didn't immediately feel the small jewelry box I panicked. I had been *sure*—

It wasn't in the box! I pulled the empty container out of my pocket and plunged my hand in deeper, muttering a soft prayer. The ruby-set ring I'd picked up earlier that day was nestled in the folds of my wallet. I swallowed hard as I removed it and held it out in front of me.

"What's going on? This thing is busted!" Amanda complained. "Look! The aliens aren't dying if I hit them! This isn't..." She put both her hands against her mouth with a gasp. Over her shoulder, I could see that my plan had come to fruition; the alien ships did not go to their normal formations, but rather formed the letters, "MRY ME?" The ships in each letter spun in unison, one letter at a time. The screen went blank and a prompt appeared showing two options, ">YES" and ">ALSO YES."

My voice cracked as I uttered the words, "Amanda Heather Shields, will you marry me?"

She turned, hands still covering her face, but didn't answer. In the back of my mind, I wondered if I had asked too soon, but my fears were soon dismissed as she pointed behind me to the mural over the bar.

Naomi and Diana took the hint and pushed the mobile wall away, its wheels squeaking as it went. When I turned, instead of the expected scene of 8-bit space ships in virtual battle in front of me, she'd painted the words, "Alexander

Petersen, will you marry me?"

When I turned back around, she was smiling, crying, and nodding as she held out a simple golden band. Sure, it's not traditional for guys to wear engagement bands, but our relationship was proving to be anything *but* traditional.

*   *   *

We didn't play a single game that night, but spent the whole time talking, getting congratulated by friends, and flirting with each other. By the time we left the building around midnight, Amanda had already planned half the wedding and was working on the honeymoon.

"We could go back to Puerto Rico again, but we've already been there!" she said and slipped her hand into mine. "Of course, we don't have to actually *go* anywhere to have a pretty amazing honeymoon..."

When she mentioned Puerto Rico, I realized that the engagement had distracted us from the second most important reason we'd gone on this date. We were a few blocks from the barcade, walking through the abandoned downtown streets back to campus, so at least this time we wouldn't have an audience.

"Oh, um... Happy Anniversary, by the way," I said and stopped walking. "I wanted you to have this..." I pulled the key out from under my shirt and removed it and the cord from around my neck. Then I took her hand and placed the key into her palm.

"Your charm?"

I nodded. "I'm... not going to need it anymore." Though she couldn't have understood the full gravity of the gesture, that I was choosing to stay in this timeline with her, she acted like she did.

"Alex... This is very important, isn't it?" But instead of taking it, she turned my hand around and returned it to me. "It was entrusted to you."

I smiled and put it back in her hand. "And I trust you, so I will entrust it *to* you."

She inspected it with admiration. A look flashed across her face, like she remembered something. Then she once more took my hand and pressed it to my palm. "Then, I am entrusting it to *you*, at least until the wedding."

She closed my fingers around it, then her eyes widened. "Oh crap! *Your* gift! I left it back there!" Walking backwards, she stepped away from me with hands in front of her. "Do not move a *single* inch. I will be right back!" Then she ran the way we had come, calling over her shoulder, "NOT AN INCH!"

I smiled as I watched her turn the corner. "Another big reveal?" I asked the empty street, half expecting her to return with something huge. Or perhaps some*one*. If she'd found my dad...

"Hello, Alexander."

A figure stepped out from a nearby alley and started walking towards me. I couldn't quite make out his face, but I knew that scratchy voice quite well. It was *not* my dad.

"Glass?! What do you want?" I stepped back as I heard the *click* of a butterfly knife being opened.

"You know my name? Then maybe you already know why I'm here." I matched his pace to keep him out of arm's length.

"N-no, not really!"

"Hm. You ruined my family. Does 'The Glass Hotel' ring any bells?"

Normally, I'd need to go to my blog to recall a hotel or restaurant that I'd been to, but not this time. My post on The Glass Hotel was the whole reason my blog became popular in the first place.

"I see that it does," he said.

"I-It was just one bad review! There were rats! The whole place smelled!"

"It was your article that triggered the investigation that got our hotel shut down. And my parents arrested."

Something clicked into place. That smell. The smell of decay. I only had about a quarter of a second to contemplate the implications before Glass lunged at me with the knife.

I jumped back. The thought of Amanda returning while this madman came at me kept me focused. I had to lure him away, to keep him from seeing her, too. I'd rather he killed me if it kept Amanda safe.

When I turned to run, he followed. Every alley I passed was blocked by *some*thing: piles of trash, misplaced dumpsters, closed fences. It wasn't any better on the other side of the street. Up ahead, construction blocked the road. I didn't have time to climb over the barriers, not when I could hear Glass' breath a few feet behind me. Thankfully, I saw an alley just before all the construction that looked clear.

As I ran down it, I realized two things: Glass had stopped following me and it was a blind alley that ended in a twenty-foot brick wall. Lights flooded the area as a diesel engine roared into life behind me.

I hadn't been leading Glass away—he'd been corralling me into an ambush!

"Hehhehheh... go get the tarp, Glass."

I spun and saw Hunter leaning out of the cabin of his pick-up. A construction barrier was crushed beneath it as it blocked the only way in or out of the alley. He sat back down in the driver's seat and revved the engine, making the entire vehicle shake with bloodlust.

I looked at the brick wall, desperate for any escape. On one of the side buildings, wooden steps led up to an ancient, metal door. Was he really going to crash that truck to get me? I looked back at him. "You're crazy! You're fuckin' crazy!" I didn't waste any more time and started running for the only egress.

The truck's tires spun, creating a noxious cloud around it. I leapt up the half-rotted stairs and reached for the door knob. It was locked. Hunter careened down the narrow alley. Sparks flew from it as the side mirrors scraped the brick walls.

"Shit." The key. It was still in my hand. I tried to jam the thing into the lock, but it slipped between my fingers. "Shit! Shit shit shit shit *shit!*" The sound of my impending death drowned out my own voice. I desperately grabbed at the falling key. Time slowed down. The blinding headlights reflected off of it as it tumbled toward the ground. I put everything I had into grabbing it. My finger caught on the cord and sent the key into an upward arc. The way I caught it and shoved it completely into the keyhole with one fluid motion was straight out of a movie. I tried to turn the knob with a sweaty hand, but rust held it fast.

Just then a burst of adrenaline kicked in. I gripped the handle so hard it hurt. With more strength than I thought I had, I turned it. The door swung inward.

I saw a flash of black feathers.

Then I felt the deadly impact.

Chapter 12

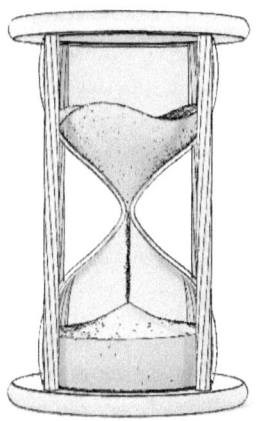

Dead Man's Party

I was dead.

At least I thought I was.

When I opened my eyes, a figure stood over me, light streaming from their every pore. But as they moved closer, I realized that the light, which gave them a holy aura, was actually coming from behind the figure. As my eyes adjusted, a mustache faded into view. Arbiter looked down at me from in front of my mirror. The light had come from Hunter's headlights shining through the mirror itself.

"That, sir, was an *extremely* close call."

"Arbiter?" He helped me to sit up, but every attempt to get me to my feet failed. I was in shock, *real* shock.

A good ten minutes passed before I managed to piece myself back together. When I did, I realized Arbiter was sitting beside me.

"Holy shit. Arb. I *died*. He killed me! He actually killed me! What did I do wrong? I thought he was in jail!"

Arbiter nodded stiffly. "He *was*, sir," he said. "But he served his sentence."

"What?" My mind still needed time to recover, so it took me longer than it normally would have to figure out what had really happened. "Shit, that's right. They never found the weapon he gave RJ."

"Correct. Additionally, he may have received time off for good behavior or been granted parole. I don't doubt but some well-placed donations to the right officer, judge, or politician aided him also."

I finally got to my feet and went straight to the mirror. "Damn it! Well I'm going to make sure he gets what's coming to him. Mirror, take me back to the day before," I demanded. Nothing happened. My own reflection stared back at me. "Hey, what gives? Mirror, show me the day Hunter was released from jail."

"That is not a request it can grant you. You should know that." Chronos' voice rang in the little alcove. He'd been so still that I hadn't noticed him. In all this time, I'd only dealt with Arbiter. Chronos hadn't made an appearance in the year and a half since I started.

I turned to look at him directly. "What do you mean? Why not?"

"The looking glass can only bring you back to the time of your most recent exit or to a point along your original timeline. You cannot use it to—"

"Then take me back to the alley!" I shouted to Chronos.

"Sir, I advise—" Arbiter began, but a thump of Chronos' massive scythe against the ground silenced him. The scene in the mirror showed me at the moment of impact. Turning the scythe this way and that, Chronos navigated the scene in the mirror. Blood spray thankfully obscured some of the carnage, but not enough of it. From what I could see, several of my internal organs were attempting to become external ones. And the way my back was bent against the vehicle's bumper couldn't have been healthy.

"I am here," Chronos said, "because you left your world at the very moment of your death, Alexander. Even *I* was unsure if you would enter my domain or if my Kin, Azrael, had taken you to his. I came to see for myself."

"Azrael?"

"The Angel of Death."

Very few people get to witness themselves getting killed and live to tell about it. If every out-of-body experience is like this one, my recommendation is to avoid them at all costs. I couldn't tear my eyes away from the horror show. "You mean, if I return, I'll die? But... it's been a year. We just got engaged! Amanda's going to expect me to be there when she returns! What if they see her?!"

Arbiter put his hand on my back. "I know that no amount of condolences can ease the pain you must be feeling. If it means—"

I grabbed Arbiter by the vest and pressed my face against his shoulder. Don't let anyone make you think that grieving isn't something men do. Arbiter went rigid for a moment, then patted and rubbed my back.

"*No!* We were so happy. I was so close..." A big part of me just wanted to crawl into a bed and stay there for the rest of my life. However, the longer I thought about it, the more determined I became. I knew in my bones that I could get it right this next time. She'd chosen *me*, after all. "Fuck. I've still got, what, thirteen or so years left, right? Now I know what to do. I'll make sure TJ doesn't ditch that gun. I'll keep tabs on Hunter the entire time. I'll find Glass before he can find me. I'm not going to give up!"

I'm not sure when Chronos left, but by the time I'd psyched myself up enough to relive the day Amanda and I ran away, I couldn't find him anywhere. "Good luck, sir," Arbiter said before I stepped through.

*   *   *

This time around, I did things right. I managed to show Amanda what Hunter was really like, but instead of flying off to some tropical paradise, we went to her parents' house. I called the cops early so that when they showed up, they caught TJ trying to smash his way through a window. He had no chance to ditch the gun this time. And he still squealed.

Even so, it had been a harrowing night for all of us and no one slept. The following night, Amanda didn't want me to be alone, so I slept at her parents' house on the fold-out couch in the basement. I was grateful that Amanda snuck down there when everyone else had gone to sleep. I'd been antsy, either because I worried about her safety or because it was the first night in months that I *hadn't* slept with Amanda at my side. With her there, sleep came quickly.

I dreamed that night. I was trying to reach a door that kept getting further and further away while a giant truck ran me down. I somehow made it through the door, but on the other side, Hunter and Glass were waiting for me. They tied me up and pushed me down a slide that turned to sand. I fell through an abyss. Amanda was falling next to me. The ground rose up. I reached for her.

"Amanda!" I jerked awake, trembling. The pillow was damp with sweat.

"Alex?" Apparently I had woken Amanda as well. "*Cariad*, it's okay. It was just a nightmare. You're safe. I won't let anything happen to you." She stroked my hair and cheek while lying against my side.

"Hunter was after me, and then you were there and... I'm sorry if I woke you," I told her.

She smiled and kissed my shoulder. "I don't mind." She settled back down, using my shoulder as a pillow and rubbing my bare chest. "Go back to sleep, love." We were both halfway there when she muttered something.

"Where's your charm? I gave it to you to keep safe..."

I probably would have been more aware of the fact that Amanda had just clearly remembered something from another timeline if the message itself hadn't been so alarming. I looked down at my chest but her hand was the only thing on it. Had I dropped it, or put it on the side table? I scanned my memories in a desperate attempt to recall where I'd put the key.

When I remembered the last place I'd seen it, my blood ran cold.

I had unlocked the door in the accursed alley with it... but was "killed" before I got the chance to take it back out of the lock. The key was lost to an alternate reality that Chronos had sealed away, and now I was trapped in this one.

Way to go, dipshit.

I didn't get any more sleep that night.

*   *   *

For about a week, everything little thing made me jump. Amanda, bless her, was so patient with me. The worry that Hunter or Glass would appear out of nowhere and come after me consumed my thoughts. Without the key, I had no way to get back or restart if things turned sour. There were no 1-ups, no save points. I was like everyone else. This was my last chance.

Naomi invited me over one night for a "get together". I hadn't accepted her invite any time before, but since Amanda was going to be there, I decided to do it this time. Naomi hadn't yet begun bartending, so she needed guinea pigs to try out her attempts at making mixed drinks. No, I wasn't planning on getting drunk—I was there to be emotional support. I thought the party was supposed to be a small affair, just a few friends over for some cocktails, but I could hear the commotion from down the street. The open door to her apartment was blocked by a mob of people outside it with more spilling into the parking lot. None of them looked familiar.

I stopped in front of her place, staring at the crowd. Panic filled the pit of my stomach. I tightly gripped the watch in my pocket. "Hey, Alex! Come on in! I've got a Rusty Nail with your name on it! I promise it'll only be one!" Naomi shouted from the somewhere in the throng.

"Ah. A rusty nail. Sounds... painful. Just one?" There'd been no chance to slip away unnoticed. She materialized out of nowhere and took my arm, dragging me into her apartment.

"Just close your eyes, you'll be fine once we get inside!" she said. Even though I did so, my ears rang with the noise and my skin churned from all the bodies that kept jostling against me. But once I was inside, it really was far less crowded than I thought and I opened my eyes again. She led me to an island of calm where she'd set up a table in front of the passthrough between the family room and kitchen. Naomi herself slipped into the gap that separated them. Both the table and the ledge behind her displayed every kind of liquor known to man, and then a few more. As a makeshift bar, it was quite impressive and must've been rather costly. This was dedication. She'd even put out a dish of bar nuts.

"Who are all these people?" I asked. Although I stood a few feet from her, I still had to shout to be heard.

122

"Friends, neighbors, coworkers. Here, tell me what you think!" She put an old-fashioned glass, half-full of some golden liquid over ice, into my hand. I took a sip and was surprised how sweet it tasted. Heather, honey, and a hint of spices balanced out the peaty scotch. I had to admit, Naomi knew what I liked. I nodded in approval. "You've been so stressed lately, bro. Tonight is all about letting that weight go. Here, I'll introduce you to some new friends. Just *no streaking!*" She could be very insistent.

"What?" That corner was peaceful, so long as I didn't think about having to go back through that mob outside to leave. However, she took my hand and started leading me to a group in her apartment. There were still quite a few people we had to work through.

It had been a long time since she saw my enochlophobia—fear of crowds—in action. Over time I'd gotten better at managing or avoiding it, and Amanda was a huge help. But I'd already felt a growing sense of panic just from getting inside, and the people in her apartment had my fear right on the edge of getting out of hand. Then, a glimmer of hope.

"Special delivery!" Naomi said as she pulled me to the group of people in conversation, right into Amanda.

"Hon, you made it!" Amanda's voice calmed me considerably. Her hand sliding around my back made the sense of panic evaporate. Without her, a panic attack could last for hours. But with her as my rock at my side, I felt calm in a matter of seconds. "These people work at a local press. Let me introduce you."

I usually had no trouble remembering people's names, but that night, the litany of monikers and appellations bounced out of my brain instantly. Without warning the world shifted. I stumbled, dizzy and light-headed. The whole room continually drifted to the left, like I stood on a listing boat no one else was on. Someone took the glass from my hand.

"Looks like he's had too much to drink," one voice said, but Naomi reassured them that I hadn't had more than a sip.

"Oh no! Alex, is it a panic attack?" Amanda asked. I nodded. "It's ok. I've got ya. Breathe. Let's get somewhere quieter."

Every step felt like an ordeal as Naomi and Amanda guided me out of the party and into a bedroom. I sat down on the bed and put my head between my knees while Naomi opened the windows to let in fresh air. Amanda sat beside me, rubbing my back.

"I don't get it," Naomi said. "Being with Amanda always stops your PTSD."

"I haven't seen an attack like this since we were kids," Amanda replied.

Naomi sat beside me. "Shit! I'm sorry, Alex. I shouldn't have dragged you inside. I thought you'd be fine once I got you two together. How can I help?"

"It's okay. Give me a few minutes and I'll be alright. I'm already feeling better," I told her. A powerful sense of weakness hit. Something about it all was wrong: the attack was getting stronger, even though I'd escaped the crowd; being with Amanda always made it better; and physical weakness—that had never happened before. With each wave, my vision warped worse and worse. Immediately my mind went to Hunter. Was he trying to poison me somehow? But I quickly dismissed it as paranoia.

"You look terrible," Amanda said. "Naomi, help me get him to the bathroom." Even through the attacks, I could hear the tremor of poorly masked fear in her voice. I appreciated that she didn't want to scare me, but I knew it had to be bad for Amanda to try hiding it from me. Thankfully, I only had a few feet to make it to the bathroom. Once there, I leaned over the sink and hung my head. Another wave of weakness passed through me. When I looked into the mirror, I fully expected to see pale lips and sunken eyes. But instead, I saw a gray, well-dressed Englishman looking back at me from the Mirror Gallery. Concern creased the wrinkles of Arbiter's brow.

"Arb?" I asked in a hoarse whisper. Whether he could hear me or not, I certainly couldn't hear him. He placed a piece of paper against his side of the mirror. He had *perfect* handwriting, even backwards. Of course he did.

Hunter is in The Between. Come quick.

Chapter 13

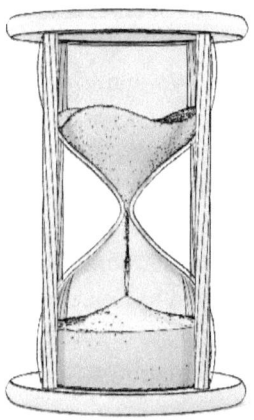

Final Arbitration

If I hadn't been pale before, I certainly was now. My hand clutched at my chest, but that didn't make the key magically appear or anything. While Hunter did who-knows-what in The Between, I couldn't do a damn thing about it. This couldn't have been a coincidence.

Arbiter's image faded and transitioned into my reflected expression of shock. My lips were the same pallid shade as my piqued flesh. I looked like a paper cut away from being a corpse. The girls helped me leave the party, with Naomi making way before us. The other guests must have thought I'd seen a ghost—or would soon be one myself. They weren't far off on either account.

Amanda helped me back to my dorm room. She kept me upright through each strength-sapping surge. We didn't say anything the entire time. My mind kept itself busy trying to figure out if I had any options to get to Arbiter, any options at all.

When we got to my dorm building, I started to realize that whatever was happening, this may well be it for me. Hunter had already killed me once.

"Are you sure you're going to be ok? Should I call an ambulance?" Amanda asked as we stood outside my door.

"Maybe that's a good idea. Will you stay with me? I don't want to be alone." I didn't have to check to see if my roommate was there; he'd never moved in.

A few minutes later, we sat on my couch as she talked to the 911 dispatcher on the phone. She held my hand tightly and put the phone down. "An ambulance is on the way. Is it getting any better?"

"Some. The waves aren't so frequent. At least it's not getting worse right now."

"Your color is coming back..." We shared a moment of silence before, "Alex, can I ask you something? Remember back in high school? 10th grade? When you just disappeared? I thought we'd never see each other again. What happened?"

Another wave hit me before I could answer. Each left me feeling more and more drained, but the weakness did not last long. When I recovered, though, I didn't know how much to tell her. All those rules Chronos gave me, yet I never swallowed my pride and asked him to repeat them. I could not recall one that explicitly *forbade* me from speaking of the other world, but I decided not to risk it. "I don't think you met my foster family at the time."

"The Lancie family?"

I nodded. "You remembered that? Mr. Lancie... abused me, so I ran away."

She gasped. "No!"

"His wife must have known about him. She went out of her way to keep him from being alone with me. That day was a half-day at school. I didn't tell them, but he must've figured it out. He was there when I arrived."

Amanda leaned against me. "That sick bastard! He always gave me the creeps. I wish I could go back and stop it."

I smirked at the irony. "I'm sure you would if you got the chance. I'm just happy to be with you now."

She snuggled against me. "What made you decide to go to college?" she asked.

"Oh, you know me. When I was told the only place for foster kids was prison, I had to prove them wrong. Plus, when I saw you at orientation, I just *had* to go," I said, only half-teasing. "Amanda, do you remember back when we met?"

"Of course I do! You made the bull but it broke in the kiln. And then we became paleo-pals!"

I laughed lightly. "You remember that, too? You know, I still keep the watch on me." An epiphany struck and I sat up with renewed vigor. "I kept it on me..."

I rushed to my bedroom as fast as my tired body could go, which involved running into some walls. Amanda trailed behind me to help.

"What is it?"

"Help me get this storage bin out!" Together, we pulled an old bin out of my closet and emptied its contents onto the floor. "It should still be here in *this* timeline..." I didn't care if anything broke, in fact I wanted it to break. "Look for a little wooden box!" As we roughly searched the pile, the box tumbled free. "Ah!

There you are, you little bastard," I said gleefully. I picked it up and ran to the bathroom. Then, with all the strength I could gather, I threw it on the tile. The box itself remained unharmed, but I did hear the distinct sound of shattering glass coming from within it.

Nothing happened.

"What're you doing?" Amanda asked as she walked in behind me.

I sighed and picked the box up. A little trickle of sand fell from the gap between the body of the box and its lid, then stopped. "Being an idiot, apparently."

Suddenly the lid's lock snapped open. Sand gushed out from inside, coming so fast that I dropped it. In seconds, the sand covered the floor.

"What the hell is going on, Alex?" Amanda cried. She held onto the door frame as more sand pushed us away from each other. It whipped into the air like a dust devil and forced me back. "Alex!" she called. We reached out for each other, fingers outstretched, but before we touched, a blizzard of sand covered everything and then blew away. I once again stood among the endless shelves of hourglasses.

*   *   *

I wasn't alone, but Amanda was not with me. Halfway down a nearby aisle, I saw Arbiter... and Hunter. They were talking. Hunter's back was turned to me, so I moved as quickly and, more importantly, as *quietly* as I could. How he had survived in The Between for so long I never found out, but he looked dirty and unkempt and had grown facial hair. He made a sudden jerk and I realized he was holding something—no, some*one*. He pressed the edge of a switchblade up again the neck of one of Chronos' gray workers, a girl in a private school uniform. She looked scared.

"I told you to fucking empty it! I'd do it myself if I could touch the fucking thing! Stop stalling! Killing that bastard is the only way I can get home!" On top of an hourglass—*my* hourglass—knelt a boy in a monochrome hospital gown. Both the boy and the girl were young, maybe six or eight. The boy glanced over to Arbiter as if unsure, then slowly lowered his arm into the access hatch in the lid of my hourglass. He pressed his face against the lid and strained to reach what little sand remained in the top bulb. The hatch was not big enough for him to reach any deeper. His glass scoop sang out a brief, crystalline note as it lightly grazed the top of the sand. He pulled his arm out and tossed the thimbleful of sand in an arc onto the floor. The very instant it left the hourglass, the orange sand turned black and I felt a little more of my time slip away from me.

Arbiter stood in front of Amanda's hourglass a few feet away from them, his arms raised in a placating gesture. "Let them go, Hunter," he said. "They have nothing to do with this. I'm the one working with Alexander, not them. If you let them go, you can take me as hostage, instead."

Hunter looked him up and down. "Your arm is long enough. I propose a different deal. *You're* gonna get up there and take over. You, kid," he said to the boy. "Give him that." The boy looked at the scoop, nodded, and obediently climbed off the hourglass.

No one noticed me, as far as I could tell, but I didn't know how much closer I could get without being seen. A good fifty feet lay between us. There was no cover; hourglasses filled every possible spot on the low shelves. *Why isn't Chronos stopping this?* I thought as I crept along with my fingers crossed.

With Hunter's attention on the boy, the knife had drifted away from the girl's neck. All at once, she grabbed Hunter's knife arm and bit him. Hunter cried out, but the girl managed to twist herself out of his grasp and make a run for it.

"You little shit!" He tried to grab the girl, but missed, so he quickly lunged for the boy instead to pull him off the side of the hourglass. The moment Hunter's hand touched the hourglass, though, he pulled it away quickly with a cry of pain, like he'd been shocked by it. The boy took his chance and jumped to the ground to scamper away.

He didn't get far before Hunter grabbed him by the hair and pulled him back. As the kid started crying, Hunter pointed the knife to Arbiter. "Get over there! Fuck that thing stings!"

In all the commotion, I'd come within ten feet of them. Arbiter noticed me over Hunter's shoulder and nodded before slowly moving towards the hourglass, towards Hunter.

"Only the hourglass' owner and the nigh-dead can touch them," he said as a means of diversion. He kept talking as I tiptoed closer. But I hadn't been paying attention and my arm brushed up against the hourglass next to me. I felt searing pain, like intense heat and extreme cold at the same time. Though I pulled my arm away as fast as I could, I still hissed. Hunter turned towards me.

The Englishman displayed a burst of speed that middle-aged body of his had no right to possess. He lunged at Hunter with a piercing yell and grabbed his hands. The boy fell and ran as the two men struggled for control over the knife.

"I will *not* let you hurt Master Alex -*unggg!*" That was not the sort of grunt you'd make from exertion. I booked it towards them. Arbiter stepped out of the way. How I wanted to coldcock Hunter, but I had yet to win a fight with him, and that was when I hadn't been drained. So instead, I charged. My shoulder dug into his side and my momentum carried the two of us right up against the metal frame of Amanda's nearby hourglass, scooting it up against the one behind it. He screamed in agony as I pinned him to it, but soon rolled away and fell to the ground.

Her hourglass teetered, threatening to fall, and I reached for it out of instinct. It wasn't until I had it stable on the shelf that I realized I wasn't feeling any pain from touching it. But I did not have time to ponder this, or even to savor my victory. I heard a yell, then metal hitting the stone floor behind me. I turned to find Arbiter slumped against my hourglass, bleeding gray blood all over the lower chamber. One hand grasped his gut. The bloody knife lay on the ground in front of him.

"Arbiter! Don't pull it out!" I cried, even though it was too late. I fell to his side but was at an utter loss. This was far beyond any first aid I'd ever learned.

He held his hand over the wound tightly. "Master Alexander. You found your way back."

"We've got to get you to a medic or something! Do you have doctors around here?" I asked. "Where the fuck is Chronos?"

The Englishman shook his head. "This... is a mortal affair... He will not intercede... or save a life. I have bandages and alcohol back... at the manor. Help me there. A Chronowheel is not far."

I had to admire the man's strength. He tried to walk, but I quickly went to his side to support him. As he guided me towards the Chronowheel, I glanced over my shoulder to where Hunter had fallen. He was down on hands and knees, crawling away. Behind him, a glint of metal on the floor caught my eye: a key on a silver cord of braided hair. It must have fallen out of his pocket in the struggle.

No, I didn't even think about going back for it. I looked forward, instead, to the Chronowheel.

When we got back to the manor, Arbiter looked pale. Well, paler. It's hard to tell how pale someone is when they are in gray-tone—especially when they're British. But it didn't look good. In the small, elevator-like room, he strained to speak. "Row Aleph, Section Ming." When the doors opened a moment later, we stepped into a room of mirrors identical to the one with my mirror in it, only all but one of these mirrors looked ancient and cracked. Their surfaces were severely desilvered, like dark clouds obscuring any reflection.

"What are we doing here, Arb?" I asked, afraid I already knew the answer.

His breathing had become labored and he panted between sentences. "My *real* name is James Covings. Help me to my looking glass. I want to see Charles one last time."

A chill ran down my spine. "Hey, now. None of that talk. You're going to be fine. Heck, I don't even think you *can* die working for Chronos."

"I am still mortal. My hourglass is nearly spent. We all have to pay the Ferryman. Not even Chronos can stop it. Hurry."

I did as he asked. Once at his mirror, the unbroken one, he asked to sit in front of it, but did not have the strength to remain upright for long. I sat behind him, one arm around his chest to support him. I had never noticed the scent of bay rum on him before.

"Show me... Charles." The mirror image faded and I got to see Arbiter—James—in color for the first time.

James lay in bed with a jaundiced appearance. Sitting next to him and holding his hand was a man with dark hair and intense, tear-filled eyes.

"James, the priest is here," he struggled to say. A man of the cloth stood behind him.

"Will you stay, Charles?" James asked before coughing, getting a nod in response.

"Priest?" Something wasn't adding up.

"No, not this one," he said. Before I had a chance to question him further, the scene changed and I found myself engaged in it.

"Five minutes, thirty-seven seconds," Charles said. He looked every bit the proper butler, with impeccable dress, stern expression, and dark, well-kept facial hair that ran from ear to ear but left his chin bare, instead passing over his upper lip. He held a silver stopwatch in his white-gloved hand. "That is thirty-seven seconds too slow, Mr. Covings."

A younger James, dressed to the nines, stood nervously at attention. His slicked down hair was dirty blond and shone with hair oil, though his mustache had quite a bit of red in it. They were in a well-appointed Victorian dining room at a table meticulously set for a proper English breakfast. "I'm sorry, sir."

Charles pocketed the watch and walked around the table slowly, inspecting each place setting with a measuring stick. "Do you know why I ask for such punctuality, Mr. Covings? It is because little delays throughout the day add up. At the end, it comes out of our leisure time, and I would prefer we spend it... at leisure." He looked up at his subordinate with a subtle interest.

James' face flushed. "'We,' sir?"

Charles walked up to him, standing closer than polite society would expect, which only made James blush harder and stand more rigidly. "I am pleased that you are paying more attention to the matters of toilet, James, but I find Macassar oil to be unsightly and ruins the upholstery. I prefer hair to be in its natural state."

James met his eyes for a moment before the second footman arrived. Charles cleared his throat and stepped back. "You did well. Now, set it up again and we'll see if we can't speed things up a bit."

"I was... so enamored of him. That was the moment I first wondered if my feelings might be... reciprocated." James coughed and winced. I helped put more pressure on the wound.

"Let me get some help," I said, but he shook his head.

"No, Alexander. It is my time." He nodded to the mirror, which began showing a new scene from his life. We watched Charles take him to see his sister Eliza as she lay in bed, suffering from consumption (which I later discovered is tuberculosis). She gave her brother the same mourning cord the key was on, made from her own long, silver hair. It was there, with his sister, that Charles first confessed he was in love with James and wanted the two most important people in his life to meet while there was still time. That night, James confessed while on the train home. But then came a memory that I had not expected.

James had been feeling weak and went to see a doctor. Though they could not show each other affection in public, Charles was nevertheless at his side when the doctor told him he, too, had consumption.

"James, Charles wasn't the one who died, was he?"

"No. I am sorry I was not forthcoming, Master Petersen. Alex." His voice was weak and he took heavy breaths between words, but he still spoke eloquently. "It took years for me to succumb to the disease. But I could not simply leave Charles alone like that. My desire was so strong, Dame Destiny noticed it and asked Chronos to let me work for him instead of passing on to Limbo. Chronos could not prevent my death, but I had plenty of time remaining, so he offered to let me watch over Charles, protect him like his guardian angel for the rest of his days. In exchange, I had to work for him for time and a half. I will be reunited with him soon; my payment is nearly complete."

I am not ashamed to say that I cried with him that day. We watched even more scenes from his life, as well as many scenes from Charles' life as James watched over him. I knew his deal with Chronos differed from mine when I watched James walk alongside his lover in a ghostly form. Dark spots began marring the edges of the mirror's surface.

In time, he put his hand over mine and placed his stopwatch in it. "I'm proud to call you my friend, Alex," he said softly. "Don't weep for me." As the scene in the mirror faded into our reflection, the tension in his body relaxed, his breathing grew shallow.

He inhaled deeply, though I could hear gurgling when he did. Then Arbiter's—no, *James'* body went stiff in an instant. It was an unnatural stiffness, like he was frozen in time.

I heard Chronos' voice behind me. "He will be going to his mate in the Afterlife soon, Alexander Petersen. Why do you mortals mourn this?"

I looked back at him. "Because I'm going to miss my friend." I couldn't say anything more without choking up.

The funeral, if you could call it that, took place right there at his mirror. Luck and Destiny arrived after a few minutes. They claimed they wanted to check in on me, but I had a suspicion that they had another reason for being there. Destiny, at least, looked surprised at what had happened—not, perhaps, at his death, but the manner of it.

Quite a few of Chronos' workers joined as well, to pay their respects, including the children he'd rescued from Hunter. Word spread quickly, it seemed. Chronos sliced the air with his scythe and the image in the mirror changed.

James moved slowly down a Victorian hallway, holding on to whatever furniture was nearby. He wore his full uniform sans jacket, though it must have taken quite an effort for him to put it on. In the bright, crisp morning sunlight, James' skin and eyes were yellow and several veins could be seen through his flesh. He coughed from time to time, but stopped in front of a large, curtained window and held a handkerchief up to his mouth. A fierce coughing fit hit him. When he pulled the cloth away, it was stained with blood.

Charles had been speaking with a priest at the end of the hallway, but when they heard his coughing, they both rushed towards him. Charles cried out, "James! What are you doing out of bed?"

A raised hand stopped the butler in his tracks. "I do not want to pass on while lying down. Let me work beside you once more." Another coughing fit came, leaving him gasping for air. This time, it did not pass quickly. James reached out towards Charles, but his strength gave out and he fell, grasping onto the curtain. Charles and the priest ran to him, managing to catch him as his hands lost their grip.

"James!" There was fear in Charles' voice as he fell against the wall and slipped down to the ground with James in his arms. In the chaotic movement, James' hand had become tangled in Charles' stopwatch cord and it tore free.

"I'm sorry, Charles. I don't want to leave you on your own," James wheezed and put his empty hand on his lover's cheek. "I'll be waiting for you." His fingers slowly slipped down and off of Charles' chin.

With a tap of his scythe on the ground, Chronos halted the scene. "This is the moment I removed him from the world. Now, the last grain of sand falls and he must return. Azrael will only allow me to delay for so long." He then waved me towards the mirror.

I couldn't do anything more. First I kissed James on the forehead, then I carried his time-frozen body to the looking glass. The instant his hand touched it, he vanished in a flash of light. Another thump of Chronos' scythe and the scene before us played on. James spasmed, then went limp in Charles' arms. But I could see an ethereal hand move over his eyes for just a moment and a black feather fell on his breast. I shivered.

"Was that—?"

Chronos nodded. "Our Kin, Azrael. It is rare to see him."

The scene went dull and the mirror grew dark with rot and cracked. The workers all left. I hardly noticed. Instead, I thought of that hand, that ghostly, decaying hand. The vision had been brief, but it was not something easily forgotten. What flesh remained on it was mottled and pale, but most of it was discolored muscle and bone. That was the hand that would soon pass over my eyes and take me. I could *feel* each passing second like a grain of my life falling to its final resting place and adding its weight to my already burdened shoulders. Despite having just lost my friend, I was suddenly very worried about myself.

"How much time do *I* have left?"

"Approximately 1 year," Chronos immediately replied. "And I will not restore the sands that have been spilt. That *is* what you were going to ask next, Alexander Petersen."

"W-what!? Why not? It isn't supposed to be this way! Hunter—"

"There is no way for you to know what was *supposed* to happen, Alex," Destiny said. "That is my purview."

"And *how* it happens is mine," Luck added.

"We three are all in agreement," Chronos said. "Our arrangement had risks. This is one of them."

I scowled. "If you know what and how everything is supposed to happen, why did you even have a bet on me?! Why did you ruin my life for nothing? Was it for some sick entertainment? Some twisted game?"

"Sometimes things aren't clear, even to us," the Lady said. "Games can have many players, and the game pieces aren't usually privy to their player's designs."

I turned my back on them and crossed my arms over my chest like a child having a tantrum. I mean, I couldn't do anything to them, after all. They could just use me like a toy, a plaything. But I still wanted answers.

"But that *wasn't* the question I was going to ask," I said, turning to Chronos. "I wanted to know how you could let Arby—how you could let James die! You're the master of time!"

The three shared a meaningful glance as Chronos leaned his weight against the scythe he carried. "We are forbidden from taking or saving a life that is not in our line of duty. Death is not under my control, and I am not permitted to interfere with one of my Kins' work. As far as this matter goes, my role is to keep the timelines and make certain everyone receives their *allotted* time before passing to the Afterlife, but I care not about the trivialities of where that time is spent or what someone does with it. Azrael receives Divine Orders, guides souls to the Veil surrounding the Afterlife, and repairs the Veil once a soul has passed through. If he takes someone before their time has ended, they either work here in The Between or he brings them to his realm of Limbo and they become, in human terms, 'ghosts.'"

Destiny added, "I read the Divine Plan and write what happens in everyone's story, past, present, and future. When something unexpected happens, I make adjustments to keep to the Plan as closely as possible."

Then Luck said, "And I determine *how* that all happens, especially the unexpected parts. That's why Destiny and I work so closely together. There's also Gaia, Fear, Dream, and the Muse, but I doubt you'll ever meet them."

"I'm confused," I said. "I don't understand. It sounds like you are all at odds. How can that be when you say you can't interfere with each other?"

Destiny cleared her throat. "We often are at odds. And we often work in tandem. When one of us makes a final decision in their domain, we all respect it. And, humans have free will, which lets them interfere with all of us. We try to keep things in balance. Suffice it to say that we each play our role, and James' role has ended."

"Yes, yes," Luck said. "We seem callous and uncaring and cruel and confusing. You humans seem that way to us. The only one of our Kin you might get any *real* sympathy from is my Sister."

"I see..." I couldn't think of what to say—my brain went back to my impending death. "So, I really only have one year left?"

I thought I had come to terms with my approaching demise, but with so little time left, all the sorrow, regret, anger, hatred, guilt, and fear that I'd been keeping deep inside all fought to get to the surface. Some people say that so much overwhelming emotion can numb you. I wasn't numb—God, I wish I had been. I fell to the ground, hung my head, and held my hands against the top of my skull. And I stayed that way, ignoring everything around me. Despair had won out.

*   *   *

At some point I fell asleep. When I finally came to, I realized that everyone had left except for Destiny. She sat next to me on the ground, lost in thought.

I looked at her with what I hoped was the sourest expression I'd ever given anyone. "Why are you still here?"

She hadn't been looking in my direction and jerked when I spoke. "Alex. I'm sorry. And I feel guilty. Those aren't normal emotions for me."

"I didn't think any of you had any *real* emotions," I said and rubbed my cheeks with the base of my palms.

"We do. We can feel joy, pain, sorrow. We can even fall in love. Guilt, however, is pretty unusual. I did not realize how... hurtful my words and actions would be."

I stretched my aching body. Remind me not to fall asleep on cold stone tile again. "You said that before."

"Yes. I justified my actions by telling myself I only did what was necessary, but now I think my actions were wrong. I want to make amends, but even I cannot unwrite what has passed. I can start by saying I'm sorry for what I did to you. And since I can't lie, you know it's true." The last bit she said in a more light-hearted, joking manner. She seemed to be a lot more human than before.

Hearing that from her doused most of my anger. "You mean you're not infallible? I thought you wrote everyone's future."

"I do, but sometimes a strong-willed human like yourself messes things up and I need to do a lot of rewriting. I try to guide the story a certain way, but none of us truly knows what is going to happen, not even Chronos. Just don't let him know that. Oh, I have something for you." She placed a key with a silver cord in my hand, my key. "I found it near your hourglass."

I sat there, staring at the key, turning it over to inspect it from a new angle. "So Hunter really did use my key to get here."

"Most likely. The Hunter of that timeline shouldn't even be here, but since he likely used your key, he's bound to your reality while here. Right now," she said with a sigh, "your story's ending is unknown. And it may be against my interests, but I can offer help."

Her words soothed me, somehow. It's nice to think of your life as a story someone else is so engrossed in that they just want to sit down with you at your lowest point and comfort you. I huffed and smiled from the corner of my mouth. "If I didn't know better, I'd say you liked me."

Destiny's pale cheeks shaded like yellowed, aging paper. "Don't flatter yourself, Alexander. My heart lies with another. And we both know who holds yours."

I nodded as I put the key on over my head. "Can I return to her?"

"You mean where you left off? I'm afraid not. You broke the pendant in front of her, which Chronos would *not* be happy about. And you might soon agree that returning to that time is not such a good idea."

"What do you mean?" I asked.

"I mean you need to take a moment and think things through." She stood up and straightened her skirt. I realized for some reason that she didn't tower over me any longer—perhaps she never had. Had she changed, or just my perception of her? In fact, I could easily mistake her for a normal human. Even her skin had a hint of color now whereas it didn't before. After typing something into her smartphone, Destiny looked at me with a smile. "You will still need someone to guide you and I've got the perfect person in mind. You know, there's a reason Luck and I approached you that day under the bridge, Alexander. It was part of a deal."

"*Another* deal? With who?" I got to my feet slowly, but I felt like all my strength and will had been sapped, and not from the missing sand.

"With me." The voice, which came from the door behind me, belonged to a woman. She walked over to Destiny and stood by her side. Like the other humans in this place, she had no color, only grays. She looked like she was in her thirties, with dark, wavy hair that fell past her shoulders. Strangely, she wore a generic superhero costume, complete with cape. Despite the unusual outfit, something about her voice, her face, and even her scent felt familiar.

"Alexander, let me reintroduce you to Carey, your mother."

Chapter 14

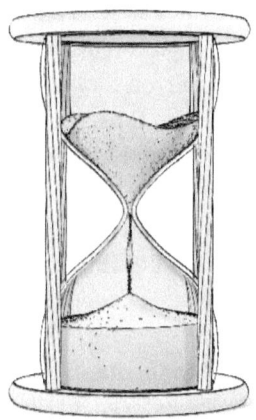

Mother Deadest

I stood there with my mouth hanging open like a trout about to get hooked. I had not seen her since I was just a toddler, yet somehow I knew her. "Mom?"

She called my name and a flurry of emotions suddenly welled up inside of me. If someone really wanted to understand how the moment felt, the awkwardness, the joy, the sorrow, they would have to live through it for themselves. As I stated earlier, certain moments a man keeps to himself.

Part of me just wanted to stay there forever with my Mom's arms around me, making up for all that lost time. I felt like that toddler again. Somehow, memories from my life I'd long forgotten returned to me.

"How is this possible?" I asked softly.

"When Luck and I placed a bet on you, your mother's soul was the wager," Destiny said. "It was never very clear which of the two of us your mother was indebted to in the first place."

"May we show him?" my mother asked.

Destiny nodded and led us back to the elevator-like room. In seconds, we stood in front of my mirror. James' chair sat there, a silent monument to his vigil over me. The pile of books still sat there too, with the eReader on top. As we passed by it, I became morbidly curious about what he'd been reading last, so I picked it up.

When I went to the title page, Destiny yanked it out of my hand, but not before I saw *my name* on the cover. "H-hey, is that—?"

She put it on the chair and pushed me forward with a hand on my back. "Didn't anyone tell you not to tempt Fate?" she said with a sly smile.

"If this place is outside time," I ventured, "then does that mean—"

We all stopped in front of my mirror, looking at our own reflections. "I don't know, Alexander. I haven't written on those pages yet," Destiny explained. "But my library holds many, *many* things, not just Books of Fate. That book might be from another Alexander Petersen, or may not even be from your reality. And unlike my Kin, I am bound to *actual* reality. Best not to think about it too much." She put her hand out, then touched her fingertips to the silvery surface before us. Our reflected images shivered and changed.

The moon's pale veil of clouds only allowed its corner to peer down on the world below. Dozens of children wandered the streets and sidewalks in groups, dressed as favorite characters or frightening creatures. Yards similarly disguised as graveyards, witches' covens, and haunted mansions filled the suburb. A mother and young son, both dressed like superheroes, walked on their own, passing by all the houses. The boy clutched a full bag of candy in his little hand.

"When we get home, you're having a bath. I don't remember the last time you had one," she said. The toddler let out a whine, but she knelt down to his level and ran her fingers through his hair. "Tell you what. I'll let you have a piece of candy afterward if you behave."

"Two!" he said, holding up two fingers.

She nodded to him. "Two pieces of candy."

Emboldened by his successful negotiation, the toddler quickly held up three fingers. "Tree!"

"Two." She stood again, but a second later her son started pulling on her arm. He pointed to a house across the street decorated like the witch's house from Hansel and Gretel.

"I wanna go that one," he said.

"No, Alex. You have enough candy." But he managed to pull his hand from hers and darted into the street. "Alex!" she called. With the two vehicles parked there, her son never saw the oncoming car. She ran after him.

"*Mom!*" I cried out in horror. The scene paused just before the car got to her. She was pushing my toddler-self out of the way.

"I'm sorry, Alex. I wasn't thinking," my Mom said, looking down. "I've watched this moment so many times it doesn't faze me any longer."

"If it makes you feel better, Alex, she did not suffer," Destiny said. "The impact killed her immediately. And she most certainly saved your life. Because of Carey's actions, I had to rewrite thousands of fates. You weren't supposed to be part of the Greater Story. Fitting you in was very difficult, but when I learned you had a soulmate, I hoped you two meeting would make up for some of the hardships."

When I was a kid, I felt like I never fit in, like I wasn't supposed to fit in. Hearing that I was meant to die that day from Destiny herself hammered home how fortunate I actually was.

"What would have happened to Amanda?" I asked.

"That is a reality too distant to know."

Mom squeezed my hand. "The world is better with you in it, Alex. I remember how badly I wanted to see you grow up, for you to have a good, happy life," she said. "I'd never wanted anything so much."

Destiny came forward and made the image in the mirror vanish. "Lady Luck and I were already nearby. Since she had so much time left in her hourglass, we offered her the chance to watch over you and brought her here."

"You've been watching over me? You've been here this entire time?" I asked.

My mother nodded. "Yes. I watched over you until Destiny won the bet, but I couldn't do anything more than watch. Now I serve her. I do not know how much time I have remaining, but I'll do what I can with what time I have left."

Destiny nudged her. "You snuck into my office and took a look at your son's fate. You're the one who begged us to change it. I'd say you've 'helped' plenty."

"So why... Why did you wait so long to bring her here!? Why *now?* Why did she have to die?" I had grown tired of being angry, but this was about more than that. This was catharsis. "I was beat up, abandoned, neglected, forgotten... Hell, I was *raped* because of you! All I wanted was to know what it felt like to have a loving parent. Damn it." I turned away from her, wiping my face dry with the back of my forearm.

Destiny stood in silence, one arm limp, the other holding its elbow. When I'd cleared the haziness from my watery eyes, I turned back around and noticed a tear falling down Destiny's cheek. My Mom put her hand on my shoulder and rubbed. It helped. I leaned into her.

"I am *truly* sorry for how things turned out," Destiny said. She took off her glasses to dry her eyes. "I really do like you, Alexander. You kept me busy rewriting things whenever you broke my expectations, which was often. Somehow, you became a good person despite the hardships you've been through. I want to give you the best possible chance at succeeding, but I am bound by the rules and by our agreement. I believe your mother will be the perfect guide for you through this uncharted territory we find ourselves in. Of course, like I said, I cannot *directly* interfere, but I think Carey has earned some vacation time, and she's welcome to spend it *however* she wishes. All I'm doing is introducing you."

I let out a slow breath. How I wanted to stay angry at her, but she appeared contrite; her sorrow looked genuine. Plus I felt an affinity toward her—a fellow writer. It took a moment before I managed to let go of it all. Neither of them spoke, they just stayed with me.

"Thank you," I said and put my hand on my mom's.

"You're wel—!" Without warning, Destiny's back went rigid and she looked behind us, at the door. "Ah! I must go," she said. "Don't lose track of your time, Alexander. You still have a chance." Her smile gave me hope. Then, she ran to the door and walked through it, leaving my mother and me alone together.

Our solitude, however, did not last long. Less than a minute after the door closed, it opened again. Lady Luck peeked her head out and scanned the room. "Psst! Is my Sister here?" she asked.

"The Dame left us a few moments ago," my mother replied.

A devious grin spread over her cheeks. "Oh, good!" She hopped over to us with a manic chuckle. "I see you've found your mom."

Before I could say something I'd probably regret, my mother answered for me. "Yes, we have found each other."

"Well, that will make this so much easier," Luck said and lowered her voice. "You see, I have in my possession a certain device which I am *not* allowed to give you, Alexander. *That* would clearly violate our non-interference clause. Instead, I had been planning on conveniently misplacing it in your vicinity, but now... now I can give it to Carey and I'm still within the terms of our agreement."

I still distinctly remembered how awful it felt when I found out Luck and Destiny had tricked me and had no intention of canceling my contract. That feeling of betrayal and helplessness stung a bit deeper when I learned that they had made a bet over my own mother's soul. They had toyed with me, yet now each was "secretly" helping me. Having their trickery work in my favor certainly felt refreshing for once. But something still didn't sit right. Luck had given me advice and hope, and now she handed my Mom a helpful tool? Destiny at least made a convincing case for her altruism. With Luck, it was getting suspicious.

"Why are you helping me?" I folded my arms over my chest.

Lady Luck lowered her glasses to look at me. I'd never looked into her eyes before. They were golden and seductive. I felt drawn to her, desiring her in every way like nothing before, but the feeling faded when she covered her gaze with her sunglasses once more. "A lady likes to have her fun. Besides, you've been through a lot. It's about time you get a little... good luck." She held a watch out to my mother. A dinosaur watch. *My* dinosaur watch. Immediately, I put my hand in my pocket and discovered a massive hole that hadn't been there earlier.

"What? How? That's—"

Luck put her finger to her lips. "Oh. Did you get a hole in your pocket? What *rotten* luck," she teased. In the past I might have asked myself when it fell and how Lady Luck got her hands on it, but at this point I simply accepted the Sisters' antics. "Don't worry. Carey will keep it safe for now. I think you'll like the improvements I made."

I'd been violated and that didn't sit well with me. The watch was important for more than one reason; it had become a comfort object to keep me calm, a fidget toy to help me focus, and a nostalgia item to make me smile. Yet, seeing it on my mother's wrist alleviated most of my anxiety. Perhaps she would fill those roles and more. "But what do you get out of helping me?" I asked.

"Don't you worry about that, love. Now listen closely. This watch is connected to your hourglass." She made sure it had a close fit as she talked. "It shows how much time you have left. I know, Chronos likes to be vague. And *so* old-fashioned. And he's *such* a drama queen. The watch can only give you an estimate, at least for now. The less time you have remaining, the more accurate it will become."

I could see the display light up for the first time in a decade. My mother looked over the watch and tapped it. "Eleven months, two weeks," she said, then gasped. "Alex, is this true?"

I lowered my gaze. Lady Luck spoke on my behalf. "I'm afraid so. A man named Hunter forced them to remove most of his sand."

"Are you serious? Won't Chronos do something about it?"

Luck shook her head. "He—"

"That bastard! Sorry." Hearing my mom curse was strange, even if we hadn't seen each other in decades. "Not Chronos. Hunter," she corrected, looking around like the Lord of Time might appear at any moment. Her expression became stern, determined. "I'll wring his little neck!" She mimicked the very action against some imaginary victim.

Lady Luck hopped backwards towards the exit. "Good luck with that. Well, I'll just leave you two to it, then. I'm sure you have a lot of catching up to do. In the meantime, I believe I must have a word with Chronos about *this*." Luck pulled out James' stopwatch from her bust. I patted my pocket out of instinct, but immediately realized that I had put it in the same pocket as the hole. "Oh don't you worry. You'll see it again. Right before you pawn it. Ta-ta!" When I realized that that was the very same watch I found on the street when I was fifteen, I'm pretty certain my jaw hit the floor. She tiptoed to the door, pressed her back against the wall, and peered into the elevator room. Then she snuck inside as best as someone can sneak while wearing that much gold.

I clicked my tongue against my teeth as I formulated the perfect question. "Mmmm... favorite ice cream?"

"Pistachio!" My mom said without hesitation. "There was this little place that made the *best* pistachio ice cream on Wenger St."

"Sweet Truth? It's still there! Pistachio is my favorite, too."

"Really? My turn then..." She did the same tongue clicking sound that I had done before she asked, "Favorite sci-fi?"

"I think... *Star Wars*."

She gave me a dazzling smile. "Which one?"

"Episode 3. *Revenge of the Sith*."

"What? Lucas made more?" Disbelief tinged her voice. "What's a 'Sith'?"

I'm sure my grin looked smug. "He did! A Sith is like an evil Jedi."

"Wow. So much I missed. And you're sure it was better than Episode 5?" I nodded. "To think, my own son prefers *Star Wars* over *Star Trek*," she said in mock indignation, the back of her hand on her forehead. My mother and I had been sitting on the floor talking for hours. As I caught her up on everything that had happened when she wasn't watching over me (she couldn't be there 24/7 after all), we began noticing similar likes and mannerisms. Like me, she worked with the written word, though as an editor. Neither of us could hold our liquor. We both clicked our tongues on our teeth. It was enough to make a guy wonder what *isn't* genetic.

"Oh, I've got one. What's my middle name?" I asked. "I only know my name because you'd written it on my underwear..." I hadn't meant to put a damper on the moment, but there was no way to ask without making us both keenly aware of how many years we'd lost.

"I like 'David'. It fits you," she said.

I smiled but shook my head. "I didn't say I was going to change it. But that was just the name of my favorite case worker. I want to know what name *you* gave me."

She looked at me appraisingly. "Marcus. Your *father* gave it to you."

I don't know why we hadn't talked about him earlier, but once she brought him up, I had to know more. "What can you tell me about Dad? Can I see him?"

A wistful smile showed on her face. "His name was Brennan. Oh, you have his eyes. I met him in Dublin. He was an engineer and inventor. A real dreamer. A defense contractor hired him right out of college. I used to go for walks through the People's Garden in Phoenix Park every day at lunch with a book in hand. One day, out of nowhere, a sharp wind picked up and ripped the book out of my hand. It was strange. I tried to catch it and literally ran into your father.

We both ended up in the pond." She sighed. "It was love at first sight. Two years later, we found out I was pregnant. So, we decided that he was going to quit his job, move to the States, and then we'd get married. After we saved enough money, that is."

"Why did you have to leave?"

"My work contract unexpectedly ended and I was transferred to Fairfax. That accelerated our plans. I moved and got a house while he continued his work in Ireland. He was supposed to join us in a year at the latest... but he was arrested shortly before you were born, accused of supplying arms to the IRA. I knew he was innocent. I died before I got a chance to go back and see him. I'm so sorry, Alex. I hadn't told anyone enough about him, so no one knew who to contact or where he was. Your grandparents and I were estranged. That Halloween, we were in a neighborhood we'd never been to, so no one recognized us or knew where you lived..."

I sat there in a deep trance, trying to imagine what it had been like. "He was *arrested?* It's like my screwed up fate started even before I was born." I leaned back and stared up at the drab, gray ceiling. "I never knew the true story of how I ended up in foster care," I said. "People had told me that my biological parents didn't want me."

Mom moved next to me and put her hand on mine. "You were *very* wanted. I wouldn't be surprised if your father still wants to meet you."

"Does he even know I'm alive? Why couldn't *he* find me?" I sat up and stared at my reflection in the mirror. The thought that I could be wanted by someone other than Amanda changed how I looked at the past, at myself.

"Well... I can't say for certain, but when you were put into the foster system, they misspelled your last name. My handwriting wasn't too clear. Destiny wouldn't let me step in and fix it."

"Are you serious? Let me guess... s-o-n?" It was such a wonderfully stupid thing to have happen that I just laughed. "What a terrible irony."

"To top it all off, you had your father's last name. Mine is still 'Andrews.'"

"Oh! What about your mirror? Can I see him that way?" I asked.

She sighed and shook her head. "No one has been able to locate it."

"What? How? Surely Chronos would be able to take you there."

Mom gave me a wistful smile. "Even *he* can't find it. No one knows why it's missing. Or if they do, they aren't telling me."

"Shit. Do you think I should try to find Dad?" I hadn't meant to say that with as much hope as I did.

"Oh, Alex. As much as I would love for you to meet and for me to get a chance to see your father again, if just for a moment, I don't think you have the time. You should be with your soulmate. I've seen how you look at her. The only other time I've seen that expression was when I saw it on your father."

She had a point, of course. "Brennan" might not be a terribly common name, at least in the States, but I had no guarantees that he still even lived in Ireland. Still, I couldn't let go of the possibility. "I could always try in my free time. Maybe he'll come to me."

"I hope so," she whispered with her hand over her heart.

"I suppose it's about time I head back." I got to my feet and turned to the looking glass. "Mirror, resume my previous timeline," I said. Amanda appeared, standing with a look of shock in the middle of my room. No sand remained there, but then again, neither did I. I'd never tried to enter a scene I wasn't in.

"Are you sure that's such a good idea?" My mom took my hand.

"No, but I've got to try. If nothing happens, I can go back to the day I stopped her from leaving with Hunter."

She shook her head. "That's not what I mean. What is going to happen two years from now? Ten? When you are gone and Hunter is released from prison, where do you think he's going to go?"

I stepped back from the mirror in shock. I could have sworn someone had just thrown a bucket of ice water over me. "I... I don't know."

"I think you do know."

"*Fuck*. Sorry. You mean, if I go back to that day, eventually Hunter will come for her?"

"With only a year left, you can't keep her safe from him."

I fell back against the wall in horror. Mom knew just what to do and put her arms around me. A sense of calm filled my soul. "Don't give up, my little one. There must be a solution," she cooed. I tried to keep myself from thinking about what would happen eleven months and two weeks later. I forced every memory I had with Amanda to run through my mind instead.

"It would have to be before he got to her," I said.

"No. It would have to be before he started to see her as his. Hunter sounds like a narcissist. The best way to deal with a narcissist is to avoid dealing with them altogether."

"Before he saw her as his? Then that means the only sure bet would be... before they were dating. They started dating *that* day." I had been avoiding returning to the day Amanda and I almost kissed for many reasons. That day I made the biggest mistake of my life, and who knew if I could undo it? Plus, I did not want to have to relive a full four years. Before Hunter threw away over a decade of my life, four years represented a decent chunk of time. If anything went wrong, it could have meant having to relive eight, maybe twelve years. But now? Now, I had nothing left to lose.

"Mirror, take me back to the day Amanda had her first kiss. That morning."

Chapter 15

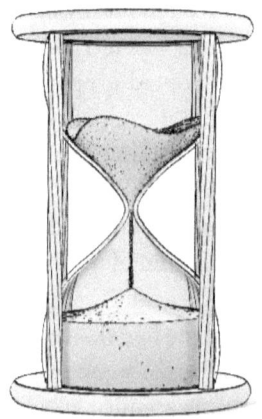

I Want Another First Kiss

Humans suck at remembering things. We either remember only the bad things or only the good things. Usually, we see the events of our past through a filter of forgetfulness and we end up glamorizing it and messing up the details. Too much of the good in that November day my sophomore year had been forgotten, perhaps on purpose.

Now that I had to live through it again, I decided I wanted to experience all of it, not just watch it go by in the mirror or torture myself at some party. I'd thought I'd remembered how cold that day had been. Snow had already collected overnight, and it continued to snow throughout the entire day. I set the mirror for when my past-self stepped out of my college dorm, then my present-self stepped into the past.

"Oh *shit* it's cold!" I remembered wrong. Even though I pulled my winter jacket tight around me, the gusts of wind cut right through it. The air stung my face, causing immediate tears to blur my vision, so I rushed to class to get out of the cold as quickly as possible. I never did look forward to going to that Gen Ed history class the university forced everyone to take, just because it was taught by the President Emeritus. On days like this, though, it meant getting away from the icy breeze. I found a seat where I could thaw, and then a moment later, someone sat in the seat next to me.

"Hey! Do you have the notes from last class?" Amanda leaned in close to me, wearing a red sweater and the matching hair band I'd given her that past Christmas. My cheeks warmed, my skin tingled. Every time I saw Amanda, I felt an exciting surge of electricity throughout my body, and often a fair amount of fear, only this was a different fear. I was terrified of letting her know how I felt. The desk screeched as Amanda scooted it up against mine, and when she was done, that exciting energy tripled. I'd completely forgotten just how powerful it had been that day. I had been wrong about Luck's gaze. Dead wrong. It couldn't compare to how I felt for Amanda.

Her foot was pressed against mine. I cleared my throat in an attempt to hide the nervousness that quickly took hold of me, then moved my foot away. "O-of course I've got them. Daydreaming again?"

Amanda blushed and showed me her sketchpad. She always had it with her, always kept it ready just in case she got some inspiration. After flipping through a few pages for me, she gave me a guilty grin. "I was drawing." Among the doodles, I saw nearly as many sketches of Hunter as there were of me. The three of us shared several classes together. My heart sank. Most of the illustrations of me looked like candid shots I had been entirely unaware of, while Hunter had that suave, flirty grin in all of his. I'd also forgotten how anxious I'd been that he would make a move on her. Too afraid to tell her, too afraid not to. Sometimes, love sucks.

"I'll get them to you after class," I said.

"Alex? What's wrong?" She said, tilting her head. "I recognize that look."

I knew she liked me, I knew what I was supposed to do, but when I stepped into this point in time, I was stepping into my nervous, young, head-over-heels-in-love, completely infatuated self with all the feelings and thoughts—and awkwardness—that came with it. "It's nothing," I said before I could stop myself.

"I think I know what it is. You're worried about the project we have in sculpture class." I remembered this conversation now. I had told her that I was and asked if she would help me with it after class, but things started deviating from my memory. "Actually, I was hoping we'd go work on it together. After class, maybe?" Amanda asked.

I could have sworn it hadn't been her suggestion the first time around. These little breaches were getting more frequent, even though I wasn't visiting the same point in time very often. In all honesty, they both concerned and intrigued me because of what they might lead to.

"I'd like that a lot," I answered.

The professor walked in and the din of conversation died down. Amanda kept her desk pressed up against mine as class began. Instead of paying attention and taking notes, like I had the first time I'd gone through this, I kept my focus on her. As the lecture went on, she began doodling but stopped when she noticed me looking at her. I quickly turned my head to the front and pretended to pay attention to the lecture. After a while, though, my eyes drifted back to her, only to find her staring at me, then blushing and looking down at her paper and the sketch she was drawing. This repeated until class ended.

*   *   *

The art studio was different from the other buildings on campus, and not just from all the art it showcased. It had a loading dock in the back that was half workspace but also featured a massive furnace set apart from everything else. The furnace provided heat for their kiln, glassworks, and smithing. Since the room we were using was nearest to the perpetually lit furnace, it was at least 80 degrees inside. Amanda and I were the only ones there, so we shed jackets and sweaters before getting to work.

I couldn't help but smile when I saw the clay, thinking back on the day we met. Normally, everyone had their own project to do, but Amanda and I got special permission. We still had to make two sculptures, only they could be a part of the same piece. By the end of the day, we would have the scene from *The Last Unicorn* where the unicorn forced the Red Bull into the sea. Of course, in my head, we'd made some amazing *coup de maître* that the great artists of the Renaissance would be jealous of. In reality, my efforts could probably have been matched by a very determined fourth-grader.

We loved it all the same.

I stared at a reference book in front of me, opened to a picture of a bull, while she fashioned her unicorn's legs. "Do you want to, um... do something? After?" I asked. God, why was this still so hard? *We were engaged, for crying out loud!*

Amanda's back straightened and she stopped working. "After? Like grab a drink or something?" she asked

"No... I mean like... something to eat, a movie... a date?"

Amanda froze. "D-date?"

"Y-yes. I'm asking... to date. If you want a date. With me. To go on. Together. With me." Oh yes, I had truly mastered the intricacies of the English tongue. "I'm asking you out!" I said loudly.

The way her eyebrows pinched together made me regret asking. "I can't tonight. There's that party I promised to go to with Hunter. I thought you said you couldn't make it." She stayed focused on the clay as she returned to her work, though it felt more like she wanted to avoid looking at me. "But... I'd love to! Maybe another time?"

Was that all it took, for her to know that I really *was* interested in her? I had to be certain. If I messed this up, she'd be dating *him* within twenty-four hours.

"Oh. Well, yeah, a-another time." We kept working, but every minute that passed I knew I would never get back. If we kept on like this, we might not even get that near-kiss. "I'm thinking... axe-throwing. A place nearby just opened..."

"Axe-throwing?" She peeked around her sculpture and smirked at me. Her green eyes looked me up and down. "You? *Axe*-throwing?"

"Well, yeah! I think it'll be fun!" I brought the book over to the desk next to her so she could see the reference I found. "How else am I going to become a proper Viking?"

Hollywood should have recorded Amanda's laugh to use in every romantic comedy they make. She put her hands on her hips, despite the clay on them, and turned to face me. "I doubt you could even hit the target! And what would your Viking name be? Alex the Beanstalk?"

"Hey! I can throw an axe!"

"Suuuure you can," she said and giggled. "But I bet not as good as me." Amanda actually rolled up her short sleeve and flexed her arm at me with a proud grin. I then did the same, which led to her poking me, which led to tickling, which led to us holding each other, clay and all, and each getting trapped in the other's eyes. Our project was all but forgotten, at least until an alarm went off in my pocket telling me the studio would be closing soon.

By the time we left, the sun had just started setting where the gray clouds failed to cover it. It had warmed up throughout the day, but our breaths still turned to dragon smoke. I thought I'd remembered this scene perfectly. It remained a permanent fixture in my mind from such constant recollection. For a while I had tried to forget it, to suppress this memory with so many others. Apparently, I really had forgotten some. The orange glow of the sunset, the soft snow catching in her bangs, the light dancing along the edges of half-frozen ripples from the nearby pond like firework fairies, the elegant arc of the snow-ladened bridge suspended over the water—they all worked together to create the most romantic scene I'd ever witnessed. We got to the fork in the path where we usually parted ways, she to a parking lot and I to my dorm. This time, we stopped and held hands.

"I hope you have fun at your party tonight," I said softly. I don't even know why I said it, when I meant to tell her not to go to it at all.

"Thanks. Sure you can't make it?"

I shook my head. "Trust me, I can't."

The day again deviated from my memory as Amanda leaned in close and whispered, "But I'll be there." My heart skipped about a dozen beats. Her arms went around me and we held each other in a tight squeeze that continued for several minutes. Long hugs made some people feel awkward, but they've never hugged Amanda.

"Please?" she asked softly.

It was a solution I'd never entertained before. What if I went *with* her? She might be able to vouch for me, or we might get kicked out together. When the embrace eased up some, our gazes locked together, sending that exciting spark through my spine. Her irises were thin, jade rings around deep, dark warmth. My resolve didn't stand a chance. "Okay. I'll come." *You* try resisting those eyes.

She let out an adorable squeal. "I'll see you there?"

I nodded. We held hands again and *the moment* came. Nerves got in my way the first time I'd lived through it, and they were still there, trying to hold me back. But I didn't need to overcome them. Amanda rose on her tip-toes and planted a light kiss against my lips. Before she had a chance to pull away, I gripped her forearms and pressed back. What had at first been little more than a peck quickly grew into more. She eased her body into mine and cupped my cheek in her hand; my arms enveloped her. This wasn't like any of our other first kisses—it wasn't awkward or passionate. It was a dance. We each responded to the other like we were perfectly in tune. Then her hungry lips came in for a second and a third.

"Screw the party," she breathed against my mouth before capturing it with hers again.

*   *   *

You've probably guessed by now that Amanda did not go out with Hunter. We stayed up late together, talking, dreaming, snuggling. The only reason she went home was because her mom called to make sure everything was okay. I may not have beat her at axe-throwing the following day, but simply being with her felt *right*, like I'd finally won. We spent as much time together as we could and only fell deeper in love each day.

For months, I rode a high like nothing I'd ever felt before. A serenity and peace of mind began growing as I realized that Hunter truly wasn't in the picture at all. Six months went by with no sign of his interference. In fact, I had stopped thinking about that entire other world altogether, like I'd never seen anything supernatural whatsoever. That had all happened to a different Alex. It's easy when you have as much experience blocking out unpleasant memories as I have. Everything was perfect—and it was going to stay that way.

At least, until the day the supernatural intruded.

"I'm so excited!" Amanda exclaimed. She held a bright yellow one-piece swimsuit up to her body with a jubilant grin.

"For the DC trip or the beach house?" I asked.

"Yes!"

"You know there will be like five other people there, right?" I had been looking through swim trunks for myself. When I turned to face her, I gave her an approving grin. "Oooh, sexy."

She squeaked. All around us, twenty-somethings prepared for summer in the store just off campus, whether that meant buying swag, browsing swimsuits, or picking up graduation gowns. Almost all of them turned to look for the source of the squeak.

"That kinda thing is only for you," she said softly. "Of course I'm excited for all of it! And also... us. It's our first big trip together." She moved a bit closer and spoke in secretive tones. "If I'd known then what I know now, I would've kissed you back in Mrs. Paladino's class." She had that impish grin that usually preceded trouble. Good trouble. But I couldn't hold back my laugh.

"Back in third grade? Ha! I'd have just run away shouting 'cooties!' or something ridiculous. Come to think of it, that might have actually happened."

She waved her hand at me dismissively and hung the swimsuit back up. "Yeah, well we gotta get to my parents' house soon or Mom'll be upset." We hadn't made it twenty feet before her hand slipped into mine and she asked, "So, have you thought about graduation at all? What you want to do after?"

"That's years away. What brought this on?" I asked.

"Oh, nothing."

"After? Like, job wise?" My mind was everywhere *but* graduation and work. Then something caught my eye. On the other side of the campus store, a student tried on his cap and gown. When he turned around, I could see the words, "Marry Me Deb?" on the top of his graduation cap in whiteout. I squeezed Amanda's hand a little tighter.

"Yeah, I mean, I know you talked about opening that home for foster kids, but that takes time. What do you plan to do first?" she asked. "I'm going to try selling my art freelance."

Six months after our first kiss and I already had marriage on my mind. After all, we knew each other better than most married couples did, and she'd already said 'yes' once before. But I wanted it to be special, and the trip seemed like the perfect time and place. I mumbled something about traveling that probably didn't make much sense, given her smile and nod.

"You're thinking about something again. I warned you about that, didn't I?" she teased. "Tell me!"

I shouldn't have been nervous. But when a woman with tanned skin and sunglasses walked by, the world I'd been trying to forget about returned to my thoughts and frazzled my mind. I would have been content if all of those memories remained nothing more than a bad dream evaporating in the morning light. "Luck?"

She disappeared among the t-shirts a few aisles away.

"Luck?"

I didn't answer Amanda at first—my mind didn't have enough power to recall repressed memories and work my tongue at the same time. When that particular memory file didn't fully load, I realized how long I'd been silently standing there.

"Oh, I'm just... lucky to have you," I said. My brief save earned me an equally brief kiss. I put my arm around her to hold her close, but I looked over her shoulder for the mysterious woman.

"Mmm, the feeling is mutual. But you know I can read you like a book. You had something else on your mind, didn't you? What's wrong?"

As easily as she could read me, I had no trouble reading her. Something worried her and she didn't want to let me know. "I suddenly remembered this nightmare I had. Just a nightmare."

"It wouldn't have anything to do with finding someone else, would it?"

"I said *nightmare*," I teased right back. "Actually, I... Amanda, do you ever think we might..." *Get married. Get married. Just SAY it!* Even though I couldn't get the words out, her sly, seductive smile told me she already knew.

She leaned against me more and whispered, "Might... what?"

I didn't have a ring yet. I hadn't asked her parents. The trip wouldn't be for a couple of weeks. But these were not the things that held me back. Out of the corner of my vision, a movement looked out of place. A mirror hung on a nearby sunglass display. Its silvery façade reflected an image—my mother. Even though she disappeared a moment later, her reflection forced the past into sharp focus. I'd been slowly convincing myself that the other world wasn't real. The key I kept in my pocket was just something I used in lieu of the watch I'd misplaced. But that false sense that everything was normal had crumbled to rubble.

"Is something wrong? You're pale."

I shook my head in reply. "I could use some food. Let's go get lunch."

That unnerved feeling didn't go away. As the day wore on, in fact, it grew into mild paranoia. Now and again, I would see Mom in the side view mirror, a window display, my cell phone. Nothing quite kills the romance like seeing your dead mother watching you wherever you go.

*   *   *

"It's only 8. Are you sure you're feeling okay? You never go to bed this early." Amanda put her hand on my forehead. "Oh. Oh doctor, the patient is burning up. Sweaty palms. Pupils dilated. Pale complexion. I've seen this before. Lonelyitis. Tsk, it's a shame. And so young, too." She folded her arms and shook her head. "I'm afraid without treatment, it's quite fatal. 0% survival rate." Never once did she break character in her delivery.

"Treatment?" I decided to humor her as we stood outside my dorm building.

"What must I do, doctor?"

She stroked an imaginary beard. "Mmmm. Plenty of fluids, three episodes of anime-ephrin, twenty ccs of snuggling, and just a touch of some 'special' medicine," Amanda slipped her arms around my neck and eased herself against me, her nose touching mine. A smile finally graced her lips. "Looks like I'm going to have to nurse the patient back to health myself."

My God, if it had been any other day, I'd have dragged her into my dorm that very moment. Men would start wars and evade their taxes for a chance to be in such a situation. But even as we held each other, I could see the reflection of my mother in the glass door to my left.

I forced a yawn. "As much as I would like that, I really don't think I have it in me tonight."

What Amanda whispered in my ear next would get this book banned in thirteen states if I printed it. My face probably looked like a ripe tomato. This wasn't fair.

"I-I- uh. Mmf." I turned up my willpower to eleven, its maximum setting. "I'm afraid we'll have to do *that* tomorrow," I said. "Assuming I survive the night."

This time, Amanda really did look worried. "If you're sure... You'll call me before you go to sleep." It wasn't a request.

"I promise." Our parting kiss was far more sweet than sorrow. As I headed inside, she waited and watched me until I got out of sight. I hadn't taken the elevator. No, I needed the time and discomfort of the stairs.

With each step, the regret at surrendering a night of bliss faded. In its place, exasperation blossomed. By the time I had made it to my dorm, I seethed. My footsteps got heavier. I slammed doors open and closed. I'm sure the downstairs neighbor appreciated it.

As soon as I got to the bathroom, I planted my hands on either side of the sink. "What the Hell do you think you are doing? Leave me alone!" As I expected, my mother stared back at me through the mirror. "Why are you here? I don't need you to be watching *everything* I do!"

Of course, I got no verbal response. Like before, I could only see into The Between. But I didn't need to hear my mother to see the attitude in her body as she put her hands on her hips.

"What? I know what I'm doing!"

Her eyes narrowed and she pointed at her ring finger.

"Is that a problem? I've been in love with her for years!"

With a frown, she jabbed several times at the dinosaur watch on her wrist.

"She told us herself she didn't know how accurate that thing is. I have *plenty* of time!"

Any anger that may have been in her expression quickly faded into pity. She shook her head, made an "x" with her forearms, then jabbed her finger towards me. When she pointed off to the side, I could clearly see her mouthing "*Amanda.*"

My anger, however, wasn't going anywhere. "Amanda? She's fine! It's fine! You'll see!" Then I turned my back to my mother and walked out of the bathroom.

I didn't sleep much that night. I stewed.

Chapter 16

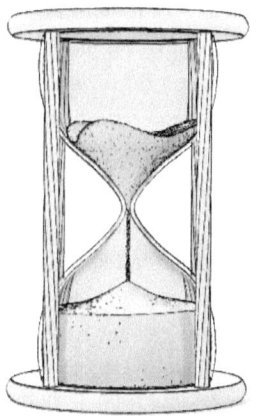

Beep Beep

"*Cariad*, did I do something wrong?"

Both the question and the pet name surprised me. Amanda hadn't used it in weeks. She looked *hurt* as she sat in the passenger seat beside me.

"Not at all! What makes you think that?"

"You've just seemed... somewhere else for the last few days," she said. "Even on the trip, you were so distracted." For some reason, the fact that we sat at a red light gave me the sensation of being under the hot-light in an intense interrogation. She put her hand on mine and I twitched. There was a distinct lack of engagement ring on it.

"Oh? I've just had a lot on my mind is all." Ever since confronting my mom, I'd felt irritated and on edge, but I didn't understand why.

Her hand pulled back into her lap and she nodded gravely. "I can tell. And I think I know what it is."

The damn light was still red. *Why did it even change? There's no one on that road!* "You do?"

"Mmm-hmm..." She drew herself into the far corner of the passenger-side seat and folded her arms over her belly. "I think it's better if we talk about it than if we just ignore it."

"Talk about what?" I asked in the age-old tradition of clueless men about to face a very angry or very upset woman. Instinctively, I tried to determine which one I would be contending with.

"About why you've been so distant!" The quiver in her voice told me I faced the upset kind. "Ever since you saw that sign…"

Red alert! Red alert! In a quarter of a second, I scanned through the memories of every sign I could remember seeing in the past month. Nothing. Granted, I'd been having difficulty keeping all the timelines separated in my mind. When Amanda didn't get an answer, she hugged herself a little tighter.

"Look, I know we've only been dating a few months and all and I know it's too early to even be thinking about it but we've known each other forever and we never talked about where this is headed and I don't want to scare you off or something I mean getting *married* is a big deal and if you don't want to then we don't have to but if you do I'm ok with that too and I know I've been dropping a lot of hints but you haven't responded to them so I want you to know that although I would prefer to get married if it's a dealbreaker we don't have to I just don't want to lose you."

How she managed to say all that in one breath still eludes me.

The CPU in my brain took quite a while to sift through the jumble of syllables and form them into words. One word stood out. *Married.* The "sign" written on the cap of one of the graduating students came to mind. "Oh. Oh! No, it's not like that. I mean, I've just been trying to find the right time to propose! I've already chickened out about a dozen times." It felt like a breath of fresh air as the panic in my head started to subside.

Her face immediately blossomed into joy. Sigmund Freud once said something about beauty being transient and that transience is beautiful. At least he got one thing right, because that smile of hers was stunning in its brilliance. And, of course, it was short-lived, interrupted by the sound of a honking truck. The light ahead of me had turned green. I put my hand up to apologize to the impatient driver behind me and pulled into the intersection.

Amanda and I spoke in unison. "Did we just get—"

*   *   *

Beep. Beep. Beep.

The sound came at regular intervals. Its high pitch didn't have the right tone for a vehicle. I had to squint when I first opened my eyes, but they eventually adjusted to the most frightening thing I could have imagined.

A ceiling.

A hospital ceiling.

*   *   *

I'm not sure how many hours I lay there listening to the beeping monitors and staring at the same 9 ceiling panels before someone came in and noticed I was awake. I'd tried to look at myself and my surroundings, but something prevented me from moving my head. I could just make out my arms in the periphery of my vision. A massive cast held my right arm in one position. Hospital sheets covered everything else. Next to me, a stand carrying medical monitors and another holding an IV bag kept their apathetic vigil over me. I could hear a TV playing old Westerns, but I could not move enough to see it. There had to be a remote somewhere, but damned if I ever found it.

"Oh, Mr. Petersen! You're awake! Let me call the doctor in. Are you warm enough?" I couldn't really get a look at the nurse talking to me, but he sounded young. When I tried to answer he quickly interjected. "Don't say anything. Just squeeze my hand once for yes." I squeezed.

It felt like another half hour passed by before the doctor leaned over me. I could feel hands moving all over my body as she talked. "Mr. Petersen? I'm Dr. Karishma. You're in the hospital. Do you know what happened to you?" I grunted eloquently in response before she took my hand so I could squeeze it. No matter how much I tried to, my jaw refused to move.

"You were in an accident. We had to perform reconstructive surgery on your jaw. Your mouth has been wired shut while the bone heals. I have you in a cervical collar as a precaution so you don't open the surgical wound. Your right arm was broken in three places. You've been in an induced coma for a little over a week. But it could have been much worse and you're recovering well. I'm sure in few months you'll be up and running." Her bedside manners weren't terrible, but they weren't exactly stellar, either. Even though I tried to form the word "Amanda," only a moan escaped. The doctor ignored it and talked to some unseen colleague using an excess of medical lingo.

When she had done everything she needed to do, she left without a word. The nurse, who looked like a high schooler, tilted my bed up so I could at least see the TV. His name-tag said "Doug." Other nurses and assistants came and went in a blur of confusion, but only Doug stuck in my mind. None of the others ever talked *to* me, only about me. I liked Doug.

"Are you in a lot pain? I can give you more—"

I managed to grunt, "Uh-uh." When I still put all my strength into squeezing his hand, he figured out that I wanted answers.

"You were in an accident, Mr. Petersen. A dump truck apparently ran a red light and sideswiped you pretty hard. I'm afraid I don't know much more than that. But don't worry; you'll make a full recovery in time. You got lucky."

Lucky? You can't say God doesn't have a sense of irony.

Doug returned to his duties without allaying my fears. I drifted between panicking about Amanda and sleep—I blame the drugs. Although my waking mind obsessed on where she was and if she was okay, I could barely move to do anything about it. On the plus side, whenever I began to feel pain, the IV's panacea—morphine—got rid of it and made me feel like I was suspended in warm water for a few hours. That night—at least I'm pretty sure it was night since they dimmed all the lights—they told me they had increased my dosage.

Doug fed me a feast of nutritionally supplemented meal replacement through a straw. At least it filled my stomach and took my mind off things. A few minutes earlier, they'd removed the breathing tube from my nose. That felt fucking *weird*. But when Doug left with the food cart, he got distracted by one of the other nurses just outside the room. They spoke softly, like that would prevent me from hearing something I shouldn't hear. With nothing else to do, a bit of gossip sounded like fun, so I listened in.

"Hey Doug, how's he doing in there?" It sounded like a young woman's voice. My drug-addled brain had started composing an imaginary hospital drama, *Recovery of the Heart* or *Paging Doctor Love*, I hadn't decided on a title yet. I tried to picture the young woman in my mind—a tall brunette with Halle Barry's body and Jennifer Connelly's face. In the last episode, her best friend, the janitor, had accidentally revealed that she had a crush on Doug.

"He's doing okay, considering. No signs of PTA, no nausea." That one was Doug. In my personal soap opera, her love remained unrequited because Doug was having an affair with an older doctor. Scandalous.

"It's a miracle he even survived. Someone's watching over him."

"Tabitha, I've been meaning to ask. Do we know if there's someone I can contact? He hasn't had any visitors since he arrived." I had a name for the mystery nurse now. Tabitha, who knew about Doug's affair and was threatening to tell his family unless he spent a night with her.

"I already tried. He doesn't have any family."

"Friends?"

"I don't even know where to start looking. The truck hit the passenger side." That soap opera ended real quick. Tabitha's voice got quieter, but in my ears she might as well have been shouting. "There wasn't enough left of his passenger to identify who they were."

"Shh! Not here!"

They kept talking, but my brain had gone numb. Somehow, I already knew. But hearing Nurse Tabitha confirm that Amanda was gone still broke my spirit.

That's what I get for eavesdropping on gossip.

∗   ∗   ∗

For the next several days, things went downhill.

Though the opioids could kill any *physical* pain I had, even their euphoric effect could not dull the soul-crushing reality and loneliness of losing my soulmate.

Doug came in and took my vitals. "Mr. Petersen, I'm going to turn you so you can get more comfortable, okay?" He started laying my bed flat.

Thank God. The TV was still on that channel that only played black-and-white sitcoms and old westerns that the world had long forgotten. They deserved to be forgotten. But since the controller was on the side with my broken arm, I couldn't reach it and since I couldn't speak, I hadn't figured out how to tell them to turn it off. I welcomed moments like these. I could still hear it, but to be honest, I preferred the canned laughter and singing cowboys over the clock.

That *fucking* clock. I *abhorred* the thing and the awful, lurching motions of its hands. Each heavy *tock* resounded throughout the room. It reminded me of the clocks in my old elementary school, only instead of counting down the time to freedom, it ticked off each remaining second of my life with a dreadful finality. I could overcome bad TV—but not time.

Once he had me laying flat, Doug started positioning my arm for the roll. "I'm going to check you for bed sores."

"I knew I'd find you eventually, you little bastard." A deep fear seized me and set all my nerves on edge. That wasn't Hunter's voice. It was Mr. Lancie's.

I tried to look in his direction, but Doug rolled me away before I could see anyone. My body tightened. I expected my former abuser to assault me at any moment. But Doug just kept working and casually talking with no concern in his tone. By the time he left, I knew Mr. Lancie hadn't actually been there, but the feeling of dread didn't go away.

Hallucinations are *fun*.

I slept a lot, despite the nightmares. They would usually involve Hunter, Mr. Lancie, Glass, or TJ. Even though I knew they would be waiting for me when I fell asleep, the imaginary fiends my mind conjured for me were better than the loneliness I felt when I was awake. I didn't get any visitors or flowers. All the families I'd ever known kept passing me around like I was the joker in a real-life game of Old Maid. The only constant in my life was now gone. Being awake just meant listening to my life tick by while waiting for the next dose of morphine.

* * *

One dream stood out. I was falling. A plain of orange sand broke my fall. The impact knocked the wind out of my lungs. By the time I could breathe again, I noticed that my hands had sunk into the sand. Pulling on one made the other sink deeper until the sand enveloped my elbows. A basin formed around me. My legs, too, were buried. I called out for help to no avail—as the basin grew deeper, the sand rose to the level of my neck, my mouth, my eyes. Under the sand, I kept slipping further down until I emerged from an opening and plummeted onto a black sand dune.

I was inside my own hourglass. More sand poured over me, heavy, forcing me down and mercilessly interring me in the grave of time. I reached out for help, even though no one was around. Just as the black sand covered my torso, Amanda fell through and landed nearby. She had rolled free of the falling sand. Without hesitation, though, she got back on her feet and pulled at me. At first, it looked like she could free me. Half of my body stuck out of the mound, but the more she pulled, the deeper she herself sank.

"Amanda! Stop! You'll get trapped!"

She smiled sadly at me. "But *you'll* be free." Then she returned to her efforts.

"Stop, I'm not worth it! You need to get out of here."

Amanda paused and looked at me. We were eye-level to each other. "It's too late for me. Let me save *you*," she softly said, her hand on my cheek. "I'll be waiting for you."

"No! I won't let you do this!" I shouted and roughly pushed her away. She flew back against the glass, no longer captured by the sand, but I sank in to my neck from the effort.

"Alex! Wake up, Alex!" Her worried expression was the last thing I saw before everything went dark. No matter how hard I tried, I couldn't move my limbs. My mouth filled with dry, choking sand.

*　　　*　　　*

I woke with a start.

For once, I wasn't alone. Naomi sat in a chair at my side, holding the remote.

"Woah, it's okay! You're okay, Alex. I've got you. I'm here." She put the remote on my lap and took my hand while stroking my hair. Her smile gave me hope. As she sat with me, telling me about her day, what the gang had gotten up to, even the memorial they were setting up for Amanda, I realized three truths.

The first was that I wasn't actually alone. A few days after we disappeared, Naomi called every hospital around until she found me. Our friends took it upon themselves to organize the memorial so Amanda's parents could grieve.

The second was that I truly did love Naomi, and I'd been doing her a disservice. Like Amanda, she'd been there for me, a constant in my life. I could tell that she loved me, too. But it wasn't romantic love. Nor was it platonic. Naomi *was* my family and I was hers, more than if we were related by blood. As a fellow foster, she knew what I'd been through in a way even Amanda couldn't really understand, because she'd been through it all, too.

Now before you get ahead of yourself, no, this isn't the story of the guy pursuing the perfect girl before realizing that the girl for him was the one at his side the whole time. Sorry, but nice thought. Naomi and I were closer than most siblings, but she was *still* my sibling.

The third truth I realized was that Amanda *wasn't* completely gone. Though I felt like part of me was simply missing, as soulmates I could still feel a part of her in me. But more than that, the dream in the hourglass didn't feel like dreams usually did. Though I couldn't prove it, I knew that girl in my dream was the real Amanda. She had a lot of time left on her hourglass, after all.

Could Amanda be in The Between right now, waiting for me? Was she in Limbo? All I needed to do to get to her was get my key.

*   *   *

By the time I'd realized that, Naomi had already gone for the night. Of course, as usual, I didn't want to wait for the next day, not when I could see Amanda now. I knew they'd put the key in a box stored away in one of the cabinets that lined the wall of my room, along with my wallet, car keys, and shoes. Doug had made sure I knew, just as he felt compelled to tell me that nothing else could be salvaged from the wreck. I waited until he left at nightfall, when the nurses changed their shift. Then I sat up.

I tried to, anyway.

One of the side effects of morphine is dizziness, a condition I hadn't noticed while lying down. I leaned against the side rail of my bed to steady myself, and that's when a small piece of plastic that kept the rail locked in place decided to snap. As it went down, so did I, all the way to the floor. Alarms of all sorts should have gone off, but I only heard my monitors keeping their rhythmic beeping.

Morphine is amazing shit. I should have been in agony, but I felt no pain at all. In the end, those hallucinations were worth it. The IV stand had wheels. I reached out and grabbed it with my good hand, then used my legs to scoot it, and me, across the floor. I didn't have enough strength in them to stand, but I could scoot just fine. The stand's wheel squeaked like a siren's call. *How do they not hear that?* I thought. If I went slow, the squeaking got quieter.

"...check on Room 8 first." It came from the hall outside.

Shit. I'm Room 8. I couldn't take my time. With all the strength I could draw, I pushed the stand toward the cabinets. That damned wheel screamed. The monitors trailed behind. Thankfully, I didn't have to go far. As soon as I reached them, I flung open the nearest cabinet door. Empty.

Footsteps approached, and fast, but my desperation was faster.

I threw open every cabinet door I could reach with the most frenetic pace possible. There was little point in keeping silent. Door after door hit its neighbor with a wooden *thunk* as I rummaged through them. Since I couldn't see their contents very well, I simply pulled it all out and onto the floor.

"Mr. Petersen?" The nurse knocked on the door.

One cabinet was almost too high for me to get to from the ground. I stretched to reach inside. Fingertips brushed plastic. With a grunt, I mustered all my strength into a lunge.

"Mr. Petersen?" The door behind me opened. At the same moment, I grabbed the handle of a bin. My weight pulled it to the floor. Everything inside spilled out—my wallet, my car keys, and the key to Chronos' manor. It skittered towards the nurse as she stepped inside.

"Mr. Petersen!" It couldn't have been hard to find me. Just follow the cords and tubes. The ninety-pound, gray-haired nurse who walked in didn't pose much of a threat to me, at least not at first. But when she went to a panel next to the door and pressed a green button on it, the entire hospital seemed to jump into action all at once. I could hear a dozen footsteps rushing down the hall. This was no hallucination.

"Code Green to Room 508. Code Green to Room 508."

I was pretty sure "Code Green" meant "stop the crazy man." I didn't want to stick around long enough to find out for sure.

With one arm, I crawled through the detritus I'd created and grabbed the key. The nurse approached me, but didn't try to stop me or anything. She said something. I was either too panicked or too drugged-up to register it. All I needed was a door with a lock. I looked up at the door to my room just as it started opening. No lock.

Orderlies rushed into the room while I frantically looked around for another lock. This is a very difficult thing to do in a neck brace, let me tell you—it's hard to do anything frantically in a neck brace. At last, I saw what I was looking for. One of the cabinet doors had a lock on it.

"Careful. He may have Post-Traumatic Amnesia. Watch his neck. And someone call Dr. Karishma." The nurse directed proceedings.

Young men in scrubs drew closer. I held the key between my lips and pushed towards the cabinet door with all the power my broken body had left. The quick tug on the wires still attached to me pulled the monitor stand onto its side. Someone tripped over it. As soon as I reached the lock, I tried to put the key into it. My body wouldn't stop shaking. Somehow, the key slid in. I opened it. The key went back between my lips. A hand grabbed the IV stand, so I let the stand go and held onto the door instead, despite the tugging of the IV line against my arm. I couldn't let any of them follow me, so when I threw my crippled body into the cabinet, I pulled the door shut behind me.

All the pain disappeared. So did the euphoric haze.

I felt the cool stone of Chronos' manor on my back.

Chapter 17

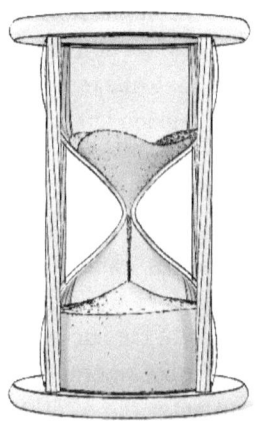

Diner Conversation

"Oh thank God!" My mother didn't even give me enough time to get my bearings before she leaned down to help me. But instead of being grateful or relieved, I was pissed off.

"Don't! I don't need your help!"

She looked like I'd just slapped her. My mother stopped, even took a step back while I got to my feet. "Alex..."

My closed fist struck the frame of the mirror. "What the fuck was that? I can't—I *won't* believe that that was a coincidence! It had to be Hunter, the little shit. I'll *kill* him."

"Alexander David Petersen!" Full name. Not good.

When I looked up, a hand struck across my face in a not-at-all-metaphorical, actual slap. It certainly knocked that vengeful spirit out of me. "You are better than that! Hunter had nothing to do with it." Tears filled my mom's eyes and streamed down her cheeks. "I was worried *sick* about you!"

Even though I only had a few memories of her, somehow she still managed to make me feel guilty. "I... I'm sorry. I'm so sorry." We held each other for a long time. I couldn't stop shaking.

Mom sniffed. "You're okay. I'm just glad you're okay."

I pulled back and shook my head. "I'm not okay. I've never felt so awful before."

She dried my sore cheek with her thumb. "You've been through something traumatic."

"I think this is... grief. I feel... incomplete without her."

"You are," she replied. "Amanda has half of your soul, just as you have half of hers. That's what having a soulmate means."

I let out a heaving sigh as the tension left my body. "That could explain why it feels like she's just in the next room." My eyes widened. "Mom, she's here! Amanda's here! She has plenty of time, and then I saw her in a dream, and she's got to be here!"

As a soft sadness filled Mom's eyes, I knew it was too good to be true. "She is in Limbo, dear. Amanda escaped it for a while, probably to get back to you. They found her in Dreamland and brought her back to Limbo. You can't see her."

"What? Why not? Where *is* Limbo, anyway? *What* is it?"

"It's where the dead wait to enter the Afterlife. It's beyond the desert, but only those who have died may enter it."

Although the prospect of seeing Amanda pleased me, I did not particularly want to hasten my departure from life. "Then... what will happen when I go to a new timeline?"

"Chronos will take care of things here. Amanda's soul will not be in Limbo once you select a new timeline. The Between sort of... resets."

"All for me?"

She smiled. "Don't ever think you aren't important."

I took some comfort in that. "What do I do now? That accident... couldn't have been an accident. Not after spending so much time thwarting Hunter, and him trying to do the same to me..." I felt and worked my jaw for a moment. Being able to open my mouth was something I'd never take for granted again.

Mom shook her head. "I don't know what caused the accident, but I know Hunter wasn't involved."

"How can we be sure? There's still at least one of him running around here somewhere. Do you know where he is?" I asked.

"No one has seen him, but there are guards posted at both of your hourglasses. And either Lady Luck or I have been here the entire time."

My shoulders slumped as I sighed. "That's not a good thing. There's no way of knowing what he's cooking up. Hmmm. The only way I know I can keep Hunter out of the scene is to go back to at least that day. But maybe this time I should keep tabs on him. And I'll have to be more careful. Mirror, take me to the day we almost kissed. Five minutes before Amanda and I parted ways."

"Alex, are you sure you should keep trying this? Isn't there something else you could do with your time?"

I stopped short, stunned. My words came slowly. "I have to keep trying. Plus, Chronos won't let me affect anything else."

She sighed. "Then you should rest, first. The accident might not have left any physical marks on you, but mental injuries are a different matter, Alex. And, if you feel the need to save her, at least don't ask her to marry you. You don't have much time left! It's not fair—"

"Don't tell *me* what's not fair!" I barked. A heartbeat later, I wished I had stayed quiet. "Sorry. But Amanda chose me, and I won't give up on her. I won't let someone else determine my fate, not Destiny, and *especially* not Hunter." I turned and faced the mirror. "Besides, Chronos said they add sand to people's hourglasses all the time. One way or another, I'm *going* to be with Amanda."

"That's not what I'm worried about." I could barely hear her voice.

The mirror showed Amanda and me getting ready to leave the pottery studio. I stepped up to it. "I know what I'm doing."

*   *   *

I had no idea what I was doing.

The moment I arrived, I felt whole again, and the sensation was heavenly. But keeping tabs on Hunter didn't leave me much time for Amanda. And if the Hunter back in The Between had a scheme, I had no way of knowing about it or stopping it.

The moments I did have with Amanda made it easy to forget him, but my mother wasn't about to let me forget *her*. Every so often I would catch a brief image of her in some reflection. It never lasted more than a split second. Not once did I acknowledge her or change any plans because of her.

A little more than a month had passed since our "first kiss." Amanda asked *me* out to dinner. This hadn't happened before. I spent the early afternoon checking in on Hunter and his goons just to make sure they stayed out of the way. Like I'd hoped, Hunter seemed to have no interest in me or my girlfriend. But an alternate version of him continued to roam The Between, so I couldn't be too careful. I even got to the restaurant early to check it out. Amanda had chosen a diner near her parents' house that we'd been to a few times before.

"Alex, I wanted to talk to you about something," she said as soon as the waitress walked away with our order.

"What's wrong?"

"You've been so... somewhere else. When we're together, you barely pay attention to me. See? Even now you're not looking at me. Is something wrong?"

"Hm? Oh, nothing. It's nothing." I'd been keeping my eye on the door as a precaution.

She sighed. "It's not nothing. You haven't been to classes. You turn your phone off and disappear for hours. I miss my *Cariad*." Her voice shook more the further she spoke. I forgot all about monitoring the door as a feeling of doom settled over me. I knew I'd messed up. If the floor collapsed beneath me at that moment, I wouldn't have been surprised.

"I didn't realize. I'm sorry." My stunned mind couldn't put more than a few words together.

"It got me thinking. I love you, Alex. I really do. And we were so good as friends. Maybe that's all we were meant to be." At this point, tears filled her eyes and formed rivulets to her chin.

I reached for her hands. She squeezed mine in return. "No, Amanda, we're meant for so much more! I know I've been preoccupied lately, but I promise that stops today."

She shook her head. "You wouldn't have your mind elsewhere without a good reason. I've been thinking about this a lot. Whatever it is that's bothering you, it must be important. And since you won't tell me what it is, it must be very private." Her lips pressed against my knuckles. "I can't give you my hundred percent until you can. You need to go take care of your problems first. Then maybe we can give 'us' a chance again."

"Y-yeah, that's a good idea," I muttered. I was prepared to do whatever it took to make 'us' work, but how long would it take to make sure Hunter stayed out of the picture? How long before we felt satisfied that I could give her the hundred percent she deserved? I let out a heavy breath. "I've been trying so hard for so long that I lost sight of the whole reason I was trying in the first place. And now I'm running out of time."

Amanda blinked in confusion and tilted her head. "I... I believe you. I have the strangest feeling that you've been fighting for me. And you can't tell me about it, even though you want to." She held my hands tighter. "If you need to rest, then rest. And when you're done with your fight, we can figure out where we stand. But I *will* be here for you."

Later that night, I quietly slipped the key over my head and stepped out of the world.

*   *   *

I'm pretty certain Alfred, Lord Tennyson first said the words, "It is better to have loved and lost than never to have loved at all." No offense to the poet laureate, but what a crock. Even though it was the strangest, most hopeful break up imaginable, it still tore me apart inside.

"I don't get it," I muttered. Mom may have been there with me, but as we sat with our backs slumped against the wall, I didn't know if I was talking to her or to myself. The chair and pile of books were no longer there. "We're soulmates.

How could this happen?"

"That's not enough," she said. Her voice soothed me, even if the message didn't. "You spent too much time worrying about Hunter and too little on her. It's not enough to simply be together, soulmates or not. Relationships take work and attention. And sacrifice. If they didn't, you two would have been together ages ago. Your father and I had to work hard for each other."

I stared at the ground. "And yet, like us, it was all for naught."

We sat beneath a heavy silence. My mother looked lost in tumultuous thought. Then she took a deep breath. "I had you. I would say that's something. But I'll be damned if I let everything you've been doing be for nothing." The air about her changed, like she filled it with an electric charge that made the hair on my arms stand on end.

"But what can we do? Nothing about this situation is fair."

"Life—"

"I know life's unfair! I know that more than anyone!" I growled.

I wish I had inherited that patience. "*Life* passes by so quickly," she continued. "We humans tend to live in blissful ignorance until most of it is in the past, then we look back and try to decide if the mistakes and regrets outnumber our joys and success. But you have a unique opportunity, Alex. If I could be in your shoes, of course I'd try to stay in Ireland and be with Brennan, try to keep him out of jail. But if I couldn't, then I'd write those stories I never had—never *made*—time for. Learn to fly a plane. Volunteer at the soup kitchen. Try my hand at painting. I'd make my time matter!"

I exhaled my breath out of pursed lips and stretched out my legs. From that position, I could just make out the watch on my mom's wrist. Most of the numbers were too hard to see clearly. Of course, the one that stood out the most was the large "zero" with a small "y." Morbid curiosity. I both wanted to know and didn't want to know. Eventually, I looked away. "What are you saying?"

"I'm telling you not to waste your time brooding. Go. Enjoy life. Do the things you always dreamed of doing."

Something about what she said bothered me in the back of my mind like an itch. I didn't know why, so I tried to ignore it, to play it off as paranoia. "My dreams... Once I graduated, I started traveling the world. I've written about amazing places. I've eaten the best food mankind can offer and seen sights most people don't even know exist. But I was alone."

She put her hand on my shoulder. "She is your soulmate. That's something *very* few people even have, let alone find. You are meant to dream *with* her. But she is not the only thing in your life. Perhaps chasing after your dream will inspire her."

"I've just been so focused on her. I'm not sure I had other dreams."

"Alex, we're selfish, busy creatures. When one dream is over, a new one almost always replaces it. Think about what motivates and drives you. If you and Amanda were together, what would you want to do *next*?"

She reminded me of the conversation Amanda and I had had in the stadium. I took a few minutes before I answered. "It's stupid. Ow! That's my ear! Okay, okay. Do you know how hard the foster system can be to survive? Most of us end up on the street after we age out. Or jail. Well, I always dreamed of starting an organization to stop all that, at least for a few kids. It would provide a safe haven for foster teens who keep getting moved from house to house like I was. They'd apprentice in a trade while living there. Not only would it teach them a lucrative skill, they'd earn money while doing it. That could help keep them off the street, maybe give them a *chance* in life."

"That's a wonderful dream. What happened? Why didn't you pursue it?"

"I always told myself I'd do it next quarter, after the next trip, the next article. I thought I had time." My voice cracked.

"Well, you could always set it up. You've already put aside the money."

I scoffed. "Chronos would never let me. He made it quite clear that I can't change anything that's not related to being with Amanda."

She leaned in closer, like she had a secret to share. "But you can. You just need to go back to your original timeline."

"What?!" The words were a punch to the gut. "I can't do that! I *won't* do that! Amanda will marry that prick and—"

"And you could end up helping hundreds, maybe thousands of kids without families. Remember what it was like?"

I didn't need the mirror to show me the terrible things I went through as a child. "I do. Of course I do. When one couple disappeared for days at a time, I had to learn how to fend for myself or starve. I was six. My twelfth foster mom started going out with a junkie who shot up in the living room and left his needles and shit all over. Bullies picked on me because I was an easy target. But worst of all was the sense of being less-than, being unloved. Even the 'good' families would dote on their real children and shirk me. More than once, I didn't even have a birthday."

Mom put her hand on my back with a little rub. "You could be the reason some child feels love, has a birthday."

The little bug that had been buzzing around my thoughts revealed itself. "Actually, I *did* always have a birthday. After I met Amanda, she *always* gave me a birthday present, even if it was something small. Once she invited me to spend Christmas break with her family. Whenever I felt unloved, she would be there making me smile again. She stood up to school bullies for me. And when we reunited in college, nothing between us had changed. She was my rock."

Mom smiled warmly at me. "Now you can be that rock for others."

"But at the cost of putting Amanda through who knows how many years of abuse at the hands of Hunter?" I asked. "Without Amanda, I don't think I'd have made it far enough to even *have* a dream. And I know she would be a good rock for *others*, too." I got to my feet and glared at the mirror. "I'm sorry, mom, but I won't let her suffer at the hands of that monster! Mirror, take me back to the day we almost kissed." As I stepped into the mirror, I kept my focus forward; the last thing I wanted was to see the disappointment in my mother's face.

Chapter 18

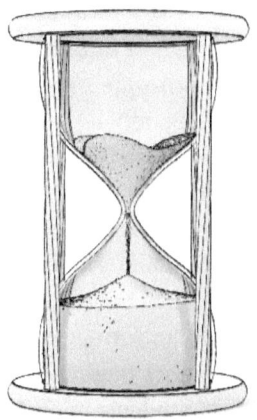

The Truth Shall Set You Free

This would be the part of the movie where the hero goes through some sort of montage. Instead of training, though, mine would be nothing but a series of failures and accidents. Each time I stepped through the looking glass, I took with me the lessons I'd learned from the previous trips. And each time, something new would happen.

The first time, weeks went by with no hangups. I had decided that I would devote my time to Amanda and leave Hunter to his own devices. It was a Sunday when it happened.

Amanda had dragged me to church with her family, though honestly it didn't take much convincing, not after what I'd seen. When it ended, we decided to spend the afternoon playing board games with Xiao and Sam. On our walk to campus, the overcast sky threatened to shed winter's tears on us, but my soulmate's smile brought spring everywhere she went.

"Tag!" Out of nowhere, she touched my shoulder and ran ahead along path towards the footbridge that overlooked the campus' frozen pond. Her giggles were contagious. "If you catch me, I'll let you pick out the first game—even that space one I suck at!"

"You mean, 'when'!" I pursued her with arm outstretched. But the laughter abruptly stopped once she got to the bridge that spanned the water. She looked back at me, so she couldn't have seen how icy the bridge itself was. Once she stepped on it, her momentum carried her off the bridge and she hit her head against the edge on the way down. Every second felt like an hour as she plunged beneath the icy façade of the pond like a rock. I jumped in right after her.

The frigid water sapped all the heat out of my bones. But I kept my mind focused on the flailing hands next to me. Amanda nearly dragged me under when I got to her, but her thrashing only lasted a few seconds before she went limp. Adrenaline kicked in fast, staving off the sapping effect of the water. Even so, the next minute spent struggling to get her to shore was a lifetime. Once on the ground, no dragon smoke came from her mouth or nose. I tried my hand at CPR, but I didn't know what I was doing. No one answered my distraught cries for help. My phone was flooded. When I tried carrying her, I discovered that I'd lost most of the feeling in my limbs and struggled to even stand. If I didn't warm up fast, the pond would be claiming two lives that day. I half-walked, half-crawled the two-hundred yards to Student Union Building 1 and barely managed to get back to Chronos' manor.

*   *   *

The next time didn't fare much better.

We had two marvelous weeks together before she ended up in a coma—a small piece of masonry from a nearby building had broken off and hit her head.

A week went by problem-free on the following attempt, until I found myself getting arrested over a case of mistaken identity. I was fortunate that they didn't think the "charm" I wore was worth confiscating when they booked me.

The time between accidents became shorter and shorter. If I tried to prevent one from happening, something else might trigger it. I admittedly spent too many days searching for her the time she disappeared without a trace. With each unfortunate outcome, I convinced myself that Hunter had something to do with it, even though there had still been no sightings of him. No reports came in as to his whereabouts in Chronos' Realm and all my personal efforts in the Between turned up nothing. My determination grew. Sometimes, I didn't even pause and talk to my mom before jumping right back in. Only a day or two would separate incidents. I got desperate, frantic. I made mistakes. I didn't eat or sleep.

And then came the day I will never forget.

I'd just witnessed Amanda get killed yet again—electrocution. Fourth death in twenty-four hours. As I took the key from around my neck, I started laughing. Nothing about this was funny, but I couldn't stop until I had returned to the manor. After so many times of this, seeing her die and trying again, the horror I should have felt just wasn't there any longer. "Mirror, take me to just before we almost kissed." Those words rolled off my tongue by rote.

"Alex!" I heard my mother's cry, felt her grab at my arm, but panic set in and I simply pulled away.

In moments, I stood before Amanda. We were just about to leave the pottery studio as we had done dozens of times before. That breath-stealing feeling I got every time I saw her was now tainted. I tried not to show it. I had to stay calm. "Do you think we could go out the back?" I asked. "There's something I've been wanting to show you."

She nodded demurely and followed. When we stepped into the lot behind the building, I immediately scanned the area. In leaving the building, we had entered into a dangerous waltz, a fatal game of Memory.

One. Two. Three.

Avoid the dumpster. Two. Three.

Van speeds past. Two. Three.

Turn left NOW. Two. Three. I couldn't afford to make a single mistake.

"What is it you wanted to show me?" she asked in her blissful ignorance.

"Well, actually it's something I've wanted to ask you," I replied. So far so good. I'd made it through this part at least five times before. "It's about the party." I reached for her hand. Her smile turned to shock for a fraction of a breath before she sank. Into a sinkhole. She disappeared so fast. I stood at the edge, hand still reaching for where she had been, and peered down, but could only see blackness and earth. Perhaps I had grown a bit desensitized, but the only thing I could think to say was, "Huh. That's a new one."

A minute later, I stepped out of the mirror again, my mind racing. "Take me back to just before we almost kissed."

"Alex, slow down!" Mom didn't even get close enough to touch me before I appeared back in the pottery studio.

"Do you think we could go out the back?" I asked. "There's something I've been wanting to ask."

"Sure. Wait. Haven't we done this before? I could've sworn..."

That stopped me. "Déjà vu?"

She nodded. "Yeah. But it felt so real."

The recent trips to my past had been so short, she hadn't displayed any knowledge she shouldn't have had in a while. But this time, it had happened so quickly that I briefly wondered if ignoring these breaches was a mistake. I got my answer a second later.

We heard a buzz and saw a brief flash, a spark, near the back door. A fire erupted faster than I thought possible. "No. *No!* This never happened before!"

"Alex, come on! We've got to get out of here!"

Amanda pushed me towards the front door but the ceiling caved in right over us. I managed to shove her back out of the way, barely. Flames engulfed the room all around her and smoke burned my eyes and lungs. Her cries for help cut through the crackling fire, but I knew it would be too late. Like always. I rushed to the front door, key at the ready.

"Mirror, take me back to just before we almost kissed!"

My mom tried to block me this time. She grabbed at my arm. My panic heightened and I roughly shoved her away without thinking, then stepped into the mirror and back into the pottery studio.

"Do you think—?"

"—No! Not out the back," Amanda quickly said and stepped away from me. "What-What the *fuck* is going on, Alex? I'm sure we've done this before! Is this some sort of trick?"

The fire broke out quicker and larger than before. This time, I couldn't shove her away from the falling debris in time. It buried her.

As soon as I stepped out of the mirror, I repeated the command. "Mirror, take me back to just before we almost kissed!"

"*Alex!*" Mom stood in front of the mirror, arms outspread.

I reached past her to touch it. But when I did, nothing happened. I was only touching its cold, smooth surface. "Mirror! Take me back to—"

"Alex, you have to stop."

"—to just before we almost kissed!" The mirror showed Amanda and me walking out of the art studio, but it barred me from entering. "-to just... before..." Mom pulled me away. I had no strength. "...we kissed..."

"Oh, my son." She held me and we sank to our knees.

Hysteria turned to shock, then sorrow, and finally, realization. "We... we were supposed to be together. It wasn't supposed to be like this. But... Oh God, what have I been doing? I've only caused her *so much pain.*" I put my face in my hands as mom rubbed my back and shoulder. I could hear and feel the soft, strangely familiar tune she hummed. It took me a moment to recognize it— *Edelweiss.* It calmed me.

I did not deserve to be calmed. "I'm a terrible person."

"Shh... You aren't. Love blinded you."

I shook my head. "Desire did. Hunter never—"

"Don't compare yourself to him," Mom interjected. "Amanda loved you. She was afraid of Hunter. You tried to support her, he wanted to control her. You helped her thrive, he held her back."

I sighed. "What a help I've been." Despite my words, I was grateful to her for her reality check. "Do you think she'll ever forgive me?"

"I'm sure if she knew the situation, she would."

I closed my eyes tightly. "I'm out of time, aren't I?"

She only hesitated for a moment. "Almost, love."

"How much?"

"Not sure. The watch says less than a day or so."

I thought when my time came that I would be scared. But I wasn't. I wasn't shocked. I wasn't angry. I was *relieved*. The fear and stress and tension left, replaced by a serene acceptance. Surrender. Peace. My body sagged. "I'm sorry."

"What for?"

"I was angry at you for no reason. I've acted like a jerk."

"You acted like an asshole." James had used the term for Hunter once, so it was only appropriate she used it on me. She slowly leaned away. "But you were mourning. You still are. You should've seen me when I first died. I tried to punch Lady Luck," she said with a chuckle. "Twice."

"Really?" I rubbed at my red-rimmed eyes. "I would've paid good money to see that."

"I'm just glad they let me see *you* since I couldn't be with you."

Under that morbid serenity, my mind had cleared and I could think more clearly than I had in weeks. "*Couldn't?*"

"Well, yes. When I read your Book of Fate, it said we would never be together again."

"But you're with me now. How? Is this in your book?"

She smiled sadly. "I've never actually seen my book. It's also been missing since I arrived. But you can't read your own book, anyway. Didn't you tell me that Destiny erased part of yours?"

"That's right... Chronos told her to. But... before, it said I wouldn't end up with Amanda. And now..."

"What? What is it?"

"She said she'd erased them from..." I rolled my eyes back in my head as the simple, obvious truth dawned on me. "Oh my God, I can't believe I'm so *stupid!*" I jumped to my feet so quickly Mom toppled over. She joined me as I left the Mirror Gallery.

"Where are the Chronowheels?" I asked.

"What's wrong?"

"Everything. I need to see Destiny."

*   *   *

"Is this your doing?" I demanded, slamming my hands down on Destiny's desk. If I had more than a few hours left to live, I might've been a bit more polite.

Her finger raised for silence. She never looked up at me, but had her eyes on an old, weathered book open on the desk before her. A quill that looked like it had been made from fire danced over the open pages of the book, writing in gold ink without her having to even touch it. After a moment, the quill lay down along the valley between the book's pages. She shut it and put it in a row of similar books on a shelf behind her desk. "Now, what is the matter, Alexander?"

"Fires where there had been none before. The random heart attack. That sinkhole. There's only *one* way all of that was possible."

"Were you not warned about anomalies? Breaches? Rifts?" she asked. "Going back to the same point over and over can cause all manner of unusual events."

"*Were* these all anomalies? Or does this have to do with my fate?" She looked at me in silence. "I mean, it was a *sinkhole!*"

From the doorway came a familiar, light laugh. "That was a good one, I'll admit." Lady Luck regarded us with amusement while lounging luxuriously against the doorframe, a martini glass in one hand. "The look on your face."

I turned toward her with renewed anger. "Are you saying they aren't breaches? *You* did it?"

She pushed off the frame and sauntered to the desk, sitting on the edge. "Might as well come clean, Sister. Of course I did. We told you, Fate writes what happens and Fortune gets to decide how. Flukes like that would've taken thousands of trips, not dozens. No, that was your fate."

Thankfully, my mother had come with me. Her presence alone kept me relatively composed. "So you're admitting to me that you interfered? You *both* interfered?!" *Relatively composed* is, of course, relative.

Destiny rose. When I look back on it now, I still can't tell if she looked more hurt at my accusation or more perturbed. "We did nothing of the sort, Alexander Petersen. This is the second time you've claimed that we wronged you and I've tried very hard to fix our... to make amends. I'm *sorry*. But you can't come barging in here every time such spurious nonsense enters your head!"

Getting rebuked by Destiny left an extremely unpleasant taste in my mouth. I felt like a kid that had interrupted their parent's work meeting to complain about not getting a cookie. It doused some of the flames in my veins, but I hadn't finished just yet. "How was this not interfering?"

"Which pages did you erase?" While Destiny and I had our heated discussion, Mom somehow found my Book of Fate up on the shelf without anyone noticing. She had it open and was idly thumbing through it. Destiny pulled the book away quickly and clutched it to her chest.

"Carey! You need to stop doing that! And we aren't lying!"

I recovered from the rebuke and ran a hand over my face in frustration. "Then please explain," I said.

Luck spoke up instead. "Silly man. I was hoping you'd have learned a few things in all our time together." She walked up to my mom and took her hand, showing off my old watch. "Tell me, does this say zero? No, it doesn't. In other words, your time isn't over. The sands of your life are still flowing."

"So?"

Destiny opened a drawer and removed a piece of paper, then carefully placed it onto the desk. She ran her finger over it as she spoke. "So, our original contract is still binding. I believe we were quite clear when we said we didn't rescind it."

"But when I accepted the offer, you agreed to erase the pages of my book. I didn't have a fate to reverse!"

"I agreed to erase the pages from that moment on, those that hadn't yet happened. But you have been delving into the *past* and I never agreed to erase *every* page in your book!"

"Only from that... that point in the *timeline* when I first came here?" I closed my eyes as the proverbial scales fell away. "Wait. You mean to tell me that no matter what I do in the past, Amanda and I can never stay together because my original fate is still reversed?"

"Ding ding ding! Jackpot, Al," Luck said.

As my knees buckled, my mom put her arm around me and guided me to a seat, then knelt down next to me. I felt my strength and my hope fade. At least I now knew how I would die in a few hours: from utter despair. "But my life... all that time... I thought you said there was a way."

"I did." None of us had noticed Chronos entering Fate's office. At some point he must have snuck inside and silently stood in the back. He was good at that. "I said that there was one way. I also cannot lie."

"What? Then... what was it? You know what, never mind. It doesn't matter now. I don't even want to know." I was sure I'd missed my chance without even seeing it. Knowing when and how would just bring more sorrow.

"Lord Chronos," my mother begged. "Please have some mercy on him. His time shortened through no fault of his own. Surely you can restore some of it."

The way he could hold his indistinctly-outlined body completely still while only moving his eyes and jaw was quite "uncanny valley" for me. He didn't even breathe. It made him impossible to read, if there was anything there *to* read. "I will not restore it. It is a repercussion of the decision Alexander made to relive his past."

"Is there nothing we can do?" She pressed him more than I dared to.

"There is." After much prompting, we finally got the full truth out of him. "If he returns to his original timeline, the agreement ends and he will not need to deal with the unexpected repercussions. The sand that was spilt will never have been spilt. In this way, he would regain the time that Hunter Pace removed, but the sand which passed naturally I will not return to him."

I perked up. "You're talking about *years* of my life. A decade, even!"

He nodded.

"You could create that charity you dreamed about!" Mom had a hopeful smile as she squeezed my hand tightly.

"With the pages of your book erased, you could even pursue Amanda," Luck added.

"But she's still going to be married to Hunter," I replied. "She'd still have gone through everything he did to her. He'll still be a threat to her and her family. And if I go back four years..."

"You will have no time left, but you might be able to keep her safe from him," Mom said.

"And my fate will remain reversed."

Destiny nodded. "Yes. You will not be with Amanda when you die. Any indication that you even *wish* to be with her will simply cause more accidents. Your intentions matter."

Luck stood behind me and put her hands on my shoulders, then leaned down and cooed into my ear. "But so far you've become rich, got to travel the world, see the sights... You do things most people only dream of. With a bit of luck it'll stay that way. If you want to *guarantee* your win, all you need to do is sacrifice your queen."

I was probably the only one, other than Chronos, without a smile. He never smiled. *Don't give up.* The words reverberated in my head. The playing card appeared in my mind's eye. Lady Luck had to have a reason for this sudden reversal. Then I recalled her earlier advice.

"It's not about *me* winning. I've been playing the wrong game," I said slowly. "I was never going to be in the bigger picture, was I? Not in hers, anyway. If I give up, he keeps her afraid of him, keeps his hold on her family, keeps cheating on her, keeps threatening to do terrible things... maybe even doing them. What if he gets even worse? However—"

"If you do not return to your original timeline, you will pass on to the Afterlife within the day. Azrael is rather anxious to meet you," Chronos said. "Not many get away from him for long."

"Yes, but once I am gone, my cursed fate will no longer pose a danger to Amanda. If I do it right, Hunter won't get the opportunity to hurt her. This might be her only chance."

Lady Luck took off her sunglasses and started putting them over my eyes. "But you'd help so many kids," she said.

I pushed the glasses off. "I'm sorry. I've made my decision."

She smiled.

Chapter 19

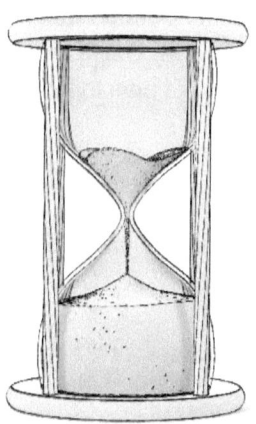

Alexander Petersen, This Is Your Life

The thing that struck me as the most odd about getting ready to see Amanda for the last time was how calm and peaceful I felt. I even made mom laugh as we rode back to the manor.

"Are you sure this is the choice you want to make?" She didn't sound too upset or worried herself. I suppose being dead and knowing the Afterlife awaits can change someone's perspective a bit.

"Yes. All those times she helped me and stood up for me... Now I get to return the favor." In moments, we were stepping out of the elevator room and into my Mirror Gallery.

"Have you thought about what you're going to say?"

I nodded and stopped in front of the looking glass. "I have."

"And you're ready for this?"

"Not in the least. Mirror, take me back to the morning of the day Amanda and I almost kissed." My old dorm bedroom came into view—I'd never see my penthouse again. I only had to step into it. But, again my legs wouldn't move. That tended to happen to me a lot.

"Alex, what's wrong?"

"This twisted fate of mine. I don't know for sure how it works. What if this fails and everything goes to Hell like all those other times?"

"If something like that happens, you can always beg Chronos to take you to your original timeline."

"I don't want her to suffer because of Hunter, but I suppose it's better than the alternative." The logic behind it did not make me feel any better. "Alright. Here we go. On the count of three. One." I stepped through. Counting any further might have given me enough time to find an excuse to back out.

*   *   *

No meteor hit the Earth. No freak tornado or plane came out of the blue. No deadly earthquake struck northern Virginia. Still, with only hours left, I knew I couldn't hang around and tempt Fate. Or Luck. Whichever one might be responsible for all that.

I found myself rather busy for most of the day, which included an important trip to the bank and an extended visit to a lawyer. Not only did I have a lot to prepare, but I had to keep away from Amanda while I did so. I didn't go to class for fear of something happening. The moment I'd finished, I sent her a text:

Meet me @ the pond

Sure enough, fifteen minutes later, her red coat came into view. I stood in front of a bench where we spent quite a bit of time together, the same one we'd fallen asleep on once. A manila envelope sat on it.

"Over here!" I waved my hand high in the air. She waved back.

"There you are! Where've you been, scruffy? Playing hooky?" As soon as she arrived, she gave me a surprisingly strong hug, which I gladly returned.

"I've been swamped. I had a lot to do." When the hug ended, she held my hands and looked at me with those large, gorgeous eyes. Scattered flakes of snow danced around us like stars moving through the galaxy. When one flake landed on her nose, she scrunched up her face and tried to blow it off. She wasn't making this easy.

"You aren't preparing to go to that party tonight, are ya?" she asked. "Or did you work on our project without me?" Her lip pushed out in a little pout.

"No. Listen, Amanda. I don't have a lot of time." I'd been replaying this conversation in my head all day, but most of my prepared speech flew away when it came down to actually saying it. I stumbled over the words. A lot.

"I... uh, Amanda, Amanda Shields, we... you and I... we can't, you know? There's an email, so—"

"Hey. *Cariad.* It's okay. It's just me," she started to reach for my hair, but I jerked my head back. After that, she looked more concerned than anything else. "We've been through this before. Right?"

"What do you mean?"

"I mean, you're going to tell me to go out the... wait. This is really weird. I could have *sworn* you were going to tell me to go out the back. Something about a fire." She put her hand to her head. "No, there *was* a fire. Or was it a truck? And I—" As she swayed, I guided her to the bench and sat with her. "I died." Her grip on my shoulder was strong, like it rooted her. "I'm dizzy. Give me a sec."

There hadn't been any random Acts of God since I arrived, but this certainly looked like more than simple déjà vu. I felt guilty for putting her through all of that. But I couldn't think of what to say.

"I'm fine now," she said after a minute. "It's passed."

"You sure?"

"I'm sure," she said unconvincingly. "You wanted to tell me something?"

With a nod, I grabbed the manila envelope from the bench and handed it to her. "Amanda Shields," I said. "God, this is a lot harder than I thought it was going to be. Amanda, I want you to have this. This is enough money to keep your family secure for a while. The smaller envelope inside is for Naomi."

She took the envelope and opened it with trembling fingers. "This wasn't in my déjà vu," she said as she glimpsed inside. "Are those all hundreds? A-Alex, I can't accept this!" She rose to her feet.

"Please do," I begged and stood as well. "And there's more. You'll be getting some documents that name you as my beneficiary. Keep them safe. I've sent you an email with legal and bank information, passwords, and some ideas of mine."

"Passwords? What is this about, Alex? You're scaring me." I could see her shaking, but I knew I couldn't comfort her without putting us both at risk.

"When I was being tossed between homes, you were my constant friend, my anchor. I wanted to be that anchor for other kids, too. But I won't be able to do it directly. The email has plans and documents I've been working on for a home to help kids who keep moving around the foster system. I know they're rudimentary, but if you and Naomi can't put this plan into action, I was hoping you could find—"

"Alexander!" She sounded on the brink of tears. "How... Is this your *lottery* money?"

"Yes. That's why I want you as my beneficiary. I'm sorry I never told you how much I had actually won."

"$7 million, but only 4.2 million after fees and taxes. ~Alex! Why do I know that?" I pressed my lips together into a fine line. She grabbed my shirt with one hand and pulled at me with each question. "Wait, beneficiary, Alex? Why do you need one? Are you sick? In trouble?"

The only answer I had for her was silence.

"I have a feeling Hunter is involved, isn't he?"

"He's part of it."

She twisted her hand into the front of my shirt, distraught and trembling. "I won't go out with him if that's what it takes to keep my best friend. To keep *you*."

Her "déjà vu" didn't seem to be going away. "And what if you *can't* keep your best friend? What will you do when I'm gone?"

Grief showed in her eyes before I'd finished talking, but they didn't focus on me; she was looking through me. She gasped. "You... You know how I feel about you. Oh! Alex, you—!"

"*When I am gone?!*" I repeated, too forcefully, too loudly.

The look of rejection she gave me felt like a knife in my heart. She let my shirt go and placed her open hand against me. "He... hurt you, didn't he? Of course I won't be with him." I had to wonder just how much she remembered from all those alternate lives. She pressed her forehead against my chest. "Is this really goodbye?"

How I wanted to tell her that I loved her, to kiss her and run away with her, but I knew that would invite disaster. Still, I figured it was acceptable to hug your best friend goodbye, so I put my arms around her and buried my face in her cinnamon hair. My shirt grew wet with her tears. Holding back my own took everything I had left. "*Cariad*," I whispered. "I'm sorry. About everything. I know I'm asking a lot of you, but do you think you could do one more thing for me?" She looked up at me and our eyes met.

"Anything."

I took a deep breath as I mustered the courage to say the three hardest words I've ever had to say.

"Forget about me."

"I can't."

The echo of a future that would never be was too much for my heart to bear. "Go." My voice was frayed. "Find happiness." Any more words would have broken me to pieces. I couldn't let her know how much I wanted to stay—as far as I knew, even a little hope that we could be together might be risky—so I let her go and walked away without another word. Her voice carried my name over the snow; I ignored it and went straight to the nearest door in SUB1.

No meteor struck, but part of me wished it had. That would have hurt less.

*　　　*　　　*

When Mom hugged me, neither of us wanted to let go. If I was about to meet Death, I might as well do it in the arms of the woman who gave me life. But I still had a few hours, and a few hours in a motherly embrace could be a bit much.

"What are you going to do now?" she asked.

I sniffed and ran my hand over my face. "When James passed, we went to his mirror to watch the most important scenes of his life. I thought that it sounded like a good way to go."

Mom nodded with a wistful smile. "Yes, it does. Let me. I've got more experience with these mirror things than you do."

She went to it and started giving it instructions. "Compile the most important and touching moments in Alex's life. Limit them to a few minutes each. Can you show them to us in no particular order, please?"

"I didn't know it could do things like that," I said softly and sat down on the floor in front of it like a kid about to watch cartoons.

"Of course it can, you just need to ask it nicely. These mirrors are a part of us, but sometimes we don't treat ourselves very nicely." She came to sit next to me as our reflection on its surface faded and my deal with Luck and Destiny under the bridge replaced it. Soon the scene changed again, to the first time Amanda and I kissed, hours before her wedding.

"Wait, this didn't happen, right? I mean, it did, but then I went even further back. She's not going to still marry him, right?"

"Not unless you go back to your original timeline. I told you, the mirror is part of you. You went through this. It doesn't matter if that reality gets erased later." We watched on in silence. It surprised me how much my memory of even so recent an event as that still got wrong. Then I heard Amanda say, "Forget about me," just as I had a few moments before. I had to brush away some tears.

"Now I understand how hard that must have been for her to say," I whispered. Memory after memory played back for me. It showed me the time I discovered that my review of the Glass Hotel had gone viral. Well, viral-ish. Some of my favorite places from around the world passed by: Versailles, the Nôgaku Theatre, La Sagrada Familia, Tower Falls. But most of the memories had Amanda in them. We'd been such a major part of each other's lives that I couldn't imagine what it would have been like without her.

A younger Alex and Amanda, about nine years old, stood in front of the bustling school hall, backpacks held on their shoulders. Alex looked panicked, like he would bolt if Amanda hadn't been beside him. As soon as a bell rang, the hall started to empty.

"Ready?" Amanda took a step forward, but Alex remained in place. "It's ok," she said. "Breathe." He inhaled. Then she took his hand and they started down the hall together to class at a brisk pace.

Without warning, an older, larger kid stepped in their way. "Orphan Boy and his substitute mommy. Can't get to class without mommy's help?"

"Beat it, Johnny," Amanda said and showed him her tight fist. Another kid appeared from behind them and shoved Alex against the lockers lining the

wall. A third grabbed Amanda by the shoulders.

"Let her go!" Alex demanded.

The trio laughed. "Hahaha! Need her to wipe your ass, too?" one taunted.

Alex balled his hands into fists. "Let her go, Jaxson!" Another bell rang in a quick chirp. "Now we're late!"

"Awww, are you afraid you'll get detention?" Johnny said, blocking Alex's view of Amanda. "My dad says you'll probably end up in jail, anyway."

Alex's fist shot at Johnny and he stumbled back. Soon the two were trading blows.

"Oh God, I remember this," I said. Even though that happened ages ago, I still felt embarrassed. And a little upset. "Guess I did throw the first punch after all..."

Amanda quickly turned and bit Jaxson on the arm. He cried out and let go, giving her the opportunity to escape... But instead, she jumped on Johnny's back and pulled on his head. The third bully grabbed her hair to pry her off. A teacher came out of the nearest classroom and broke up the fight.

"She *bit* him? I didn't know that!" I said with a chuckle. "I do remember that we ended up in detention together. More than once."

My mom nodded thoughtfully. "I recall seeing you two in there quite a few times. You had some sort of game you played when the teacher left the room."

I laughed. "Yes, we learned how to turn our pens into little launchers and tried to see whose ink chamber went the furthest. If we got caught, I'd take the blame for her. Detention just meant less time with a family that hated me."

"It's a miracle you two didn't get suspended," she giggled. "Even back then it was obvious that you both had a special connection."

A teenage Alex stared out at the line of cars coming to pick kids up at the end of the day. The line dwindled until no cars remained and Alex stood on the curb alone. Even the kids with their own cars had mostly left. A snowball struck Alex in the back of the head to the derisive laughter of some jocks, but they, too, were soon picked up by friends. Alex remained alone on the curb.

Amanda emerged from the building with a handful of others. When she saw him, she looked at him with surprise. "Alex, why are you still here?"

"Mrs. McCranie is working late tonight. What about you?" he asked, though his voice was shaky.

"I had band practice after school. We have to be ready for the Christmas concert." She stepped up to his side, but only glanced at him when he wasn't *looking. A rusty Toyota arrived. She perked up a little. "So... what are your plans for Christmas?"*

"I... uh... don't have any."

Amanda put a hand on Alex's back. "Tell me the truth. She's not really working late, is she?" When he shook his head in reply, she took both of his hands and started to pull him towards the now-waiting car. "Well then, you're going to come and have Christmas with us!"

"There was just no stopping her sometimes. When she had an idea, she went for it whole-heartedly," I said. "I admired her for that."

"Pssh! You didn't just admire her! You had a crush on her!"

"I did not! At least not yet."

Mom grinned. "When, then?"

I felt the blood rushing to my cheeks. "That Christmas. We started playing an online game, you know, the kind where you roleplay. Oh, do you know what 'online' means?"

She prodded my ribs rather sharply. "I don't live under a rock, kid."

I chuckled. "Well, we sorta started flirting through it. Our characters even got married, eventually! I didn't dare tell her it was how I really felt." Then the scene changed abruptly.

A young adult Alex sat in the back of a large lecture hall. At the front of the room, college seniors took turns giving talks about the university they went to. Behind them, on a white board, were the words, "Welcome to Orientation!"

This time Mom piped up first. "Oh, I was watching you when this happened! They're splitting the room into small groups for tours, right?" I nodded.

Alex's group headed out the door on the left. When he glanced over to the group leaving on the right, he stopped and pointed at a girl. Amanda was in the other group, pointing back at him. They simultaneously said, "It's you." Although the campus tours headed out, they stayed behind, talking.

"You two didn't even make it to the tours at all," Mom said with a grin.

"Heh, yeah, we spent the rest of the night talking and catching up. We hadn't seen each other in three years."

Mom gave me a knowing look. "You picked out that college just because she was going there, didn't you?"

"I didn't! I swear, I didn't even think she was going to college. Her parents couldn't afford it, but she got in on grants and scholarships."

The scene changed to a thirteen-year-old me sitting alone in a perfectly clean bedroom. I immediately recognized it as when I met Naomi. It was the first night her foster parents took me in as well. Thankfully, mom tugged on my arm and looked at me, because seconds later, a very confused and very naked Naomi would appear in the mirror, unaware that she now had a foster brother. I never did understand how she acted so casually that day. I'm glad she did, though, because she ended up being the only foster-sibling that I kept in touch with.

"I didn't watch all of orientation. What happened?" Mom asked.

"Oh, so you did let me have *some* privacy?" I teased. "We wandered around campus on our own for a while that night. I remember that we fell asleep on a bench together, the one by the pond."

"Didn't you go skinny dipping with her?"

"Mom! No. We didn't go skinny dipping. I... got cold feet."

"I'm betting you wish you'd gone now." Hearing my own mother say this made me embarrassed even though I hadn't done anything. No one really wants to think that their parents were once young and crazy, too.

I lost track of how much time we were spending there. It didn't matter. The mirror then showed a memory that confused me—Hunter forcing one of Chronos' workers to throw sand out of my hourglass.

"Hold on, why is it showing this?" I asked.

"It must have been a very important memory for you. Didn't this take years off your life, after all? Not all of the memories will be good ones, you know."

I got to experience James' death for a second time. And then it showed the Sisters in Destiny's office explaining to me how my fate was still reversed, and how I could get my years back.

I turned to mom and spoke softly. "I hope you aren't disappointed."

"Why would I be disappointed?"

"That I gave up ten years of my life to save Amanda."

Mom smiled. "No, Alex. I'm proud."

A soft sound, like a short breath, came from behind us. In the back of my mind I had begun to wonder just how death would come for me. Heart attack? Aneurysm? Spontaneous Combustion? With so little time remaining, I knew it had to be something sudden. I straightened and closed my eyes. It quickly became obvious.

"Hunter. I knew you'd come to finish the job. Third time's the charm, huh? But aren't you a few hours early?" I got to my feet slowly, positive that a knife would plunge into my back at any moment. When I turned around, though, the sight was far more startling than a knife-wielding lunatic.

"Amanda?!"

Chapter 20

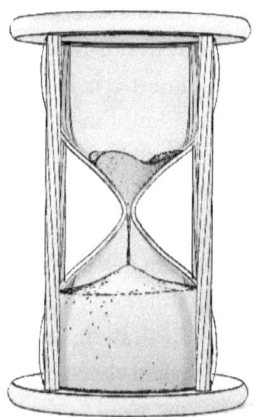

Secondhand Memories

"How did—? How long—? What did—?" With every question trying to come at once, my attempt to communicate effectively failed in a spectacular manner.

Amanda stood at the end of the short wall that separated my mirror from the mirror next to it. She held onto the end of the wall with one hand and covered her heart with the other. The poor girl shook like she'd just gotten out of a pool on a windy day. Her wild eyes darted between me, my mom, and the mirror. She shouldn't have seen any of this—it's the sort of thing that could scar a person for life. I should know.

When her eyes drifted to the mirror again, she gasped. "Hunter?" I looked back to see Hunter's truck coming down that narrow alley towards me.

"Mirror, stop please!" my mom cried out. The surface of the looking glass reflected only the three of us.

"I-I-I didn't mean to eavesdrop. Alex, what's going on? Where are we?" Amanda asked.

Mom let out a breath and stood up with a welcoming smile. "You must be Amanda. I've heard so much about you. I'm Carey, Alex's mom," she said, as if people normally made acquaintances in situations like this one.

"His dead mom?" she asked hesitantly.

Mom grinned. "But still kicking!"

Amanda stepped closer, leaving her crimson coat on the floor behind her. "Is this real?"

Mom nodded. I, on the other hand, ran through every moment the mirror had replayed to decide the appropriate level of embarrassment. It was fairly high—not quite "giving-a-presentation-on-a-subject-you-forgot-to-study-for-in-front-of-everyone-you've-ever-had-a-crush-on-while-naked" level. But close.

"We're not on campus... are we? And I'm not supposed to be here, am I?"

"Probably not..." I said. My jaw clenched as I remembered all the times she'd died.

"I imagine there are a lot of questions on both sides right now," Mom said. "Let's all sit down together and we can ask them one at a time. Does that sound good? How about you go first, Amanda?"

"Y-yeah..." Amanda said. She hesitated, though, looking me over like she couldn't be sure I was still me. But when she knelt down next to me, she wrapped me up in her arms. "I thought I'd lost you."

How could I tell her that she was still going to lose me? So I didn't; I just held her. "Are you okay?" I asked.

"I don't know," she whispered. When she finally sat next to me, rubbing her cheeks, she asked, "What is all of this? Where are we?"

My brain still hadn't recovered enough to form sentences longer than three words. Thankfully, Mom answered for me. "We're in The Between, a world set apart from Earth in time and space. Think of it as a place between the living and the dead, where immortal beings do their work."

"But what is this room? What are those for?" she pointed to the mirrors.

"This is part of Chronos' manor, and those are windows into people's pasts. This one is Alex's."

"Your past? Is that what the mirror was showing?"

I nodded. "Sort of. But it's my turn to ask a question. How did you get here? When?"

Amanda shrugged. "I followed you. I couldn't just let you go like that, otherwise I'd never see you again. Then you *disappeared* in the doorway to SUB1. I ran in before the door closed."

"Then you've been here the entire time?"

She nodded. "I came out of the mirror right there." She pointed to the one with its back to mine, in the next aisle. "When I heard your voice, I peeked over." She arched her body and pulled off her sweater, then tossed it to the red mound that was her coat. With her arms around her bent legs, she pressed her face against her knees so that only her eyes were visible. "If those were events from your past, why was Hunter trying to run you over?" she asked softly.

I shuddered at the memory. "Chronos, the Lord of Time, has been letting me

188

relive my past in order to fix a mistake I made. A lot of what you saw were times I was reliving my past." Though I had questions to ask, I knew something ate at her. "You have some more follow-ups, don't you?"

"Your past? I don't remember anything like that happening. But... why do I remember other things that haven't happened? I'm so confused." Amanda turned her eyes aside. "Is that where all these strange, new memories are coming from—your other attempts? Did they really happen?"

I had no words to explain it, so when my mother jumped in and answered for me, I silently thanked her. "Likely. *My son* refused to give up. He was determined to make sure you were safe. But when someone repeats things too often, like he did, it can have some strange effects. Which ones do you remember?"

Amanda blushed and sank her head a bit lower. "There are a lot, but there are also gaps. I remember... finding you in the church, and running away with you, and—and someone stabbing you. I remember dying a lot..."

Hearing that made me worry about what she thought of me and if all of that affected her. "I'm so sorry, Amanda. I should have stopped sooner," I whispered and lowered my gaze. "I didn't realize how much I was hurting you."

Amanda put her hand on my arm. "I also remember barely fighting off Hunter, finding out he'd been cheating on me, hearing his threats. And... I remember how happy *we* were together, our amazing trips to DC, the fun we had working on projects, dreaming with you... how it felt when you kissed me..." she mumbled.

"I, uh, well to be fair... you usually started it," I stammered.

She smiled at me and slowly lowered her legs. "I did?"

I nodded to her and then smirked. "You know it's not right to spy on someone." It was a bit of a test, to see how much she remembered, and a tease. When she scoffed and kicked me (albeit gently), I knew she remembered.

"You mentioned Chronos. Was he the tall, Middle Eastern guy with the beard and funny stare?" she asked. "You said this is his manor?" The worry in her expression grew fainter and fainter as she moved closer. I became nervous about getting too close to her, but I didn't stop her.

"This is part of it. There's a lot more. To be honest, I haven't explored much."

"I know this is a lot to absorb, but you seem to be taking it well," Mom said.

Amanda grinned. "Well I've always believed in the supernatural, but I'll admit, I didn't think it would be anything like *this*. I mean, you're either telling me the truth or I've plain gone crazy."

"I haven't ruled that last one out for myself just yet," I teased.

She leaned back and adjusted her hair band, then peered around the room. "Why haven't you explored? I'd love to see more of this place." It didn't surprised me how quickly she calmed down and accepted everything; that adventurous spirit of hers was how I discovered that I loved to travel.

"Chronos told me not to leave..."

A cute smirk graced her lips. "Since when did *you* start doing what other people told you to do? And, if you're Alex's mom, why aren't you dead?"

"I am," Mom said. "Or, I will be when Chronos returns me to Earth."

Amanda was quiet for a moment, like she'd said something wrong. "Mrs. Petersen—"

"It's 'Andrews.' But call me 'Carey.'"

"Carey... I know he used to dream about you and wonder what you would think of him. Well, I think you should be proud of your son. He's a good man. A good friend. A good... more-than-just-a-friend." I felt myself blushing at her words. "Even if he's a bit foolish at times."

Mom took her hand. "I am, and I'm grateful that you've been there for him when he needed someone the most."

Amanda blushed as well before looking to me. "Why are you reliving your past? What happened?" she asked me.

"I... did something stupid. Remember when I ran away?"

She closed her eyes. "Yeah. Mr. Lancie... he... oh God! He abused you?"

"Uh-huh. So you remember that conversation?"

"How could I not? You looked like you were dying!"

"When I ran away, Lady Luck and Dame Destiny offered me a contract to reverse my fate. I took it."

Amanda took my head in her hands and gave me a stern stare. "You're the type of guy that would eat faery food, huh? I'm not surprised you took the offer. It was stupid, but I get it. But terrible things happen to people all the time. Why did they choose you?" she asked.

I explained to her about the bet and mom's role in it. When I got to the part about giving up my soulmate, Amanda perked up like a meerkat.

"Wait. Did you say soulmates? Us? For real?" She grinned and scooched herself up against my side. Her hand moved to mine. "Does that mean... you really do love me?"

I nodded and squeezed her hand. "With all my heart," I said before I could stop myself. Thankfully, no sinkhole formed.

Amanda chewed on her lower lip for a moment. "Are you allowed to tell me all of this?"

"I suppose they never expressly said that I *couldn't* tell anyone." If the Sisters could bend the rules, why couldn't I? Not to mention, it got a whole lot easier to justify once I found out that I wouldn't be around to see any repercussions.

"Hold the phone!" she exclaimed. As Amanda's joyfulness returned, I started grinning madly. "If this is your past... then you're from the future! And I'm remembering a future me!"

I chuckled. "Yeah, an alternate future I suppose. I'm from four or so years from now. And I've been doing this another... maybe two?"

She pouted playfully. "Does this mean I'm no longer older than you?"

"Honestly, I have no idea."

Mom chimed in. "I thought you two had the same birthday."

"I was born two hours earlier!" Amanda said gleefully.

"Hey! Time zones don't count!"

"Do, too!" She stuck her tongue out and poked my side, I poked her back, but before long the frisky play turned somber. Her fingers ran through my hair as she looked at me with worry. "You're dying, aren't you? That's why you were saying goodbye." When I nodded, tears pooled in her eyes. "But I just found you! What's wrong? Is it the sand? That I saw Hunter throwing around? That was your hourglass, your life, wasn't it?"

"Yes. Yours is right next to it, you know."

"I'd never have imagined he could do something like that. And was that really his truck?" As she stared off into space, she looked horrified. "He did a lot more than just hurt you. God, what did I ever see in him?"

"He had everyone fooled," I replied. "Including me, for a long time."

Her brow furrowed as she looked at our hands. "There wasn't a lot of sand left in that hourglass. How much time do you have?"

When Mom brought the watch up to read, Amanda said, "Hey, that's the watch I gave you..."

"Yes, it is. It says he has a couple of hours," Mom responded. After seeing the alarm in Amanda's face, she meekly added, "but it might not be accurate."

"No! That can't be right! This isn't fair!" She startled me with a tug that led to her roughly shaking me and ended in an embrace. "I thought you said you fixed things!"

"I... tried. It'll be okay," I whispered, but I grew less sure of that by the moment. "Once I'm gone, my messed-up fate won't make you suffer any longer. Hunt—"

"You *fucking idiot!*" she cried. "I don't care if *I* suffer! Just as long as *you're* happy! Didn't you know that?" She moved to my lap and faced me so I could clearly see the inferno in her eyes. "You should have asked me what *I* wanted, Alex! You—you should have forgotten me like I asked."

"Wouldn't you have done the same if our situations were reversed?"

"I would have *asked* you what you wanted, Alex," she said and folded her arms. Her voice lowered to a near whisper. "And then I would have done it anyway. But I'd still have asked first!" She showed so much anger before, but it quickly turned to something almost intimate. Her hand drifted to my cheek. "Alex, I've been in love with you... almost our whole lives."

I could barely see her with how blurry my vision became. I touched my nose and forehead to hers. "Ditto."

She chuckled and sniffed. "You got to spend your lifetime with me. But, I won't get to spend mine with you. All I'll have are these... secondhand memories."

I'd never thought of it in that way. Despite my supposed fate, I still got to spend my life with her in it, at least in some capacity. "*Amanda*," I breathed.

"What if I make a contract, too?" she begged. "Maybe I can save you!"

"No, don't!" I blurted out. "They always twist it somehow."

"Then ask Chronos to put back the sand. It's not your fault Hunter spilled it!"

I shook my head. "I did. The only way he'll do that ends with you marrying Hunter."

The slap across my cheek stung like Hell, but as quickly as Amanda struck me, she had her hand there caressing the same cheek. It was the exact spot my mom had slapped. My turn for the déjà vu. "*How dare you* make that decision for me! I would rather go through *Hell* than have you die like this! You stupid—foolish—"

I surprised myself with how passionately I kissed her at that moment. She responded instantly, her kiss filled with a desperate need. It was to be our final "first kiss," and possibly our final kiss ever. It felt like we were condensing all the love and desire of our missing lifetime together into one moment. Our bodies rocked against each other and our hands roamed freely, accompanied by a steady stream of soft moans and whimpers. It ended with our foreheads together as we both gasped for air. When my mom cleared her throat, we turned deep shades of red at the unintended lewdness of our display. So much for avoiding showing affection.

Amanda tightened her hold around me. "Alex, I don't want us to end before we begin."

"*Cariad,* he threatens Jason," I said. "I honestly don't know how to keep your family safe from him any other way."

The rouge that passion had painted her flesh faded to a stark white. She searched my eyes before pressing her lips together in stubborn defiance. The first time I'd seen that expression, she had Craig Silverton in a stare down just before taking back the lunchbox he'd stolen from me. Craig never gave us trouble again after that. "If he won't do it, and you won't do it, then I'll put the sand back myself!" she announced and got to her feet.

"What? You can't! I'm sure it's all been cleaned up!"

"Then I'll get more sand!" She turned and marched towards the door of the semi-circular room. Mom and I jumped to our feet and followed her.

"You ca—"

"Yes, I can! I'm going to save my foolish soulmate even if it kills me! And don't you *dare* try to stop me, Alexander David *Marcus* Petersen!" Full-full name. This was serious. How did she even know my original middle name? She walked up to the door with determination in her every step.

"Amanda, wait!" I ran up beside her, but she didn't take her eyes off the door.

"I told you—"

"You don't know the way. But I do." Our pinkies linked and she leaned against me with a sigh.

"Thank you, Alex. All right. Lead on."

The three of us walked into the elevator room, and moments later we were leaving the manor and the garden, heading towards an out-of-place door.

Once in front of it, I said, "I don't know if this is going to work, but even if we fail, there's no one I'd rather be here with," and reached for the door's handle. It stood in the middle of a path that led away from the manor's garden, alone and without any wall to support it.

"We haven't failed yet. Say, why didn't you try this earlier?" Amanda asked.

Mom and I glanced at each other. She grinned and opened the door, stepping through and holding it for us. "Oh, I like her."

"I, uh, guess it never occurred to me. I just assumed—"

Amanda shook her head and patted my still-sore cheek. "After all this time, you still need me to look after you, huh?" When we followed Mom through the door, the open air of the garden became the still air inside the Halls of Time. The myriad rows of hourglasses I'd seen when I first arrived in The Between stretched out before us. Above, I could just make out the cathedral-like ceiling; behind us, the door sat nestled in a wall that hadn't been there from the other side. A little further down the wall, Chronowheels sat parked inside a hangar. No workers could be seen.

The three of us headed to the Chronowheels, but Amanda gazed in awe at everything around. "There truly are more things in Heaven and Earth than are dreamt of in your philosophy, Horacio," she said reverentially.

When we got to the hangar, we found that only one of the vehicles would even turn on. The others were in various states of repair and disrepair that rendered them useless. I pulled the cord to start the engine. This Chronowheel's engine wasn't covered like most others had been. It was loud and made funny sounds, popping now and then. The entire frame vibrated. We all prayed that our rattletrap stayed together long enough to do the job.

Before we got on, Mom brought us into a huddle. "Listen. We can't just go out there unprepared. You're going to need the right tools," she said. "A bag and a scoop—It won't be possible without them. But it's not going to be easy to get ahold of them."

"Why do we need them?" Amanda asked.

"Just trust me on this. Now hop on."

"Can't we take them from one of Chronos' helpers?" I asked.

She shook her head. "They've been ordered to remain somewhere safe while a 'threat' is being dealt with. But I know where to get some." After a dramatic pause, she leaned in conspiratorially. "There are more Kin you haven't met yet, such as the Twins, Dream and Fear. Just like the Sisters work closely together, so do the Twins. Dream is the master of the desert and keeps the tools we'll need, but I doubt anyone's just going to hand them over."

After all this time I'd spent in this other world, I still had so much to learn about it. "So how are we going to get to them?"

Mom winked. "I've got a few tricks up my sleeve."

Chapter 21

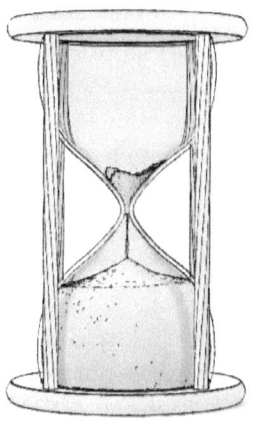

Enter Sandman

The constant, gray light gave me a low-level headache. It had been all right when I stayed in the manor, but, out here, the brightness came unrelenting from all corners of the sky and made it all the harder to see any details in the frozen waves of space-black sand that surrounded us. "Are we almost there?" I asked.

"Yes, just follow those tracks!" Mom pointed in front of the Chronowheel. The "tracks" she'd mentioned were other Chronowheel tracks, but to me they looked only like shallow indentations in the black sand. I had to lean close to the mirrors that provided a view in front of the massive wheel in order to see the tracks at all. It was a miracle I didn't lose the trail.

"It's only been a few minutes," Amanda said, but time in that place was always hard to measure. She squeezed the arm I had around her belly. I sat on the left side of the bench-seat and steered, with Mom next to me and Amanda sitting sideways in my lap. That was the only way we could all cram into one and still drive it. "How's your cheek?" Amanda asked loudly.

"Sore!"

"Good! Serves you right!" She gave me that goofy grin I loved so much.

"There!" Mom tapped my shoulder and nodded towards a large rocky outcropping on our right. The trail went from black sand to bleak, bare rocks and crags. Up ahead, a mile or so down the trail, we saw it.

Color.

There was so much it dazzled the eyes. Amanda and I may also have been in color, but not like this. Compared to the arcipluvian palette that made up the scene before us, we looked like sepia tone.

A castle stood behind a long wall that stretched out of sight. As we got closer, we could see numerous towers and balconies with crenelated parapets and every variety of heraldic flag, ribbon, and banner hanging from them. Dragons and other winged beasts flew around it and perched on parts of the roof. The gate was open, but two knights wearing shining panoplies and holding halberds stood at the entrance. Neither of them appeared to take any notice of us, despite the Chronowheel's noise.

"This is where Dream resides. Pull over. We'll go on foot from here." I did so, and in minutes we stood behind a rock just a hundred yards from the gate. Mom brought us into a huddle. "Okay, when you two get inside, go immediately to your right and follow the wall. There's a path that leads straight to a small building with a picture of an hourglass on it. The bags and scoops are in there. Once you have them, get back out here. If I'm not here, go on without me, I'll catch up."

"How dangerous is it?" I asked.

"That depends on what you run into in there. Just stay on alert and be quick. In and out."

"Then should someone stay with the vehicle and guard it?" Amanda asked. "They can have it ready to go."

"Good idea, less chance someone will get caught. Amanda, why don't you?"

"What are you going to do, Mom?"

"I'll distract the guards. I told you, I've got a trick or two. Be ready to run inside."

She didn't give us an opportunity to press her more about her plan before she turned and walked into the open, up to the guards. We held our breaths as we watched.

"What do you think she has in mind?" Amanda whispered. Mom stood in front of the guards and waved. It looked like they knew her. The three struck up a conversation. Out of nowhere, she reached for their helmets, which surprisingly came off when she pulled. Then she ran away and they gave chase, like a gazelle being pursued by a couple of rhinos.

I gaped until Amanda closed my mouth. "That? That was her 'trick'?" I asked. "A hit and run?"

She chuckled. "Well, she's definitely *your* mom, Mr. I'm-gonna-storm-the-goblin-stronghold-with-level-1-armor-on. Planning things out doesn't really run in the family, does it?"

"Hey! Tamlarian almost made it! Besides, *Praeli*, you're the one who was all gung-ho about getting the sand without even knowing where it was."

She patted my back. "As much as I'd love to stay and flirt with you more, you better get moving. Good luck." She kissed my cheek and then headed back to where the Chronowheel sat parked. I waited until I could no longer see the knights, then hustled to the gate.

* * *

Beyond the wall, Dreamland held so much beauty, fancifulness, diversity, and impossibility that it took my breath hostage until I had paid a ransom of time spent in amazement. However, that wall protected far more than just pixies and castles. I could see things I'd never imagined before, creatures like a cross between hypodermic needles and bees, a man made entirely out of crystal eyeballs, a dog with one mouth inside of another. I quickly realized that Dreamland didn't only contain good dreams.

I stayed close to the wall and tried to keep out of sight. This took little effort since the many stone buildings and thatch-roof huts that lined the streets beyond the wall made for excellent cover. At least here I wouldn't stand out due to my hue. Plenty of normal-looking people lived there as well, milling about, talking. Many headed towards the castle. As I passed by one avenue, I saw a portal like a whirlpool turned on its side, near the base of the castle. A handful of Dreamland denizens walked into it, much like I had done with the mirror. When the last entered, the portal fizzled into nothing.

A path wound just ahead of me, leading from an arrow slit in the wall towards a town square. Standing in plain view was a building with an hourglass symbol displayed on its front. The area wasn't very populated, so I headed directly for the building at a brisk walking pace.

I had nearly made it to the door when someone grabbed my attention. A street ran from the square I had just entered all the way to the distant castle. In an adjacent square, by a resplendent fountain of silver, stood a dark-robed figure with small clouds floating around it. The figure reached for one and brought it to their face before breathing it in. When they exhaled, their breath was like heavy smoke, which settled onto their outstretched palm, creating a small pile of black sand. With a vigorous motion, the figure tossed the sand away. The grains spread, then swirled around like a whirlwind in a joyous dance. It took on a shape bit by bit. In moments they had coalesced into the form of a woman with a horn in the center of her head. The small handful of sand couldn't have been enough on its own to create her.

With a second breath from her creator, color spread over the sand and it came to life. She was a ravishing young woman wearing a white gown. Her horn looked like pearl, her dark skin had no flaws, and her purple hair floated about her shoulders as if captured in a perpetual breeze.

I'd been so mesmerized by the woman that I nearly missed it when the dark-robed figure looked in my direction, straight at me. The hair on my neck stood on end. "Oh shit," I muttered and ran to the hourglass building. It had a saloon-style swinging door, so I didn't slow down at all once I got there.

I had to act fast. Thankfully, whoever managed the place did a good job keeping things organized. A ledger sat on a small pedestal. Behind it, all along one wall, hung black bags, each the size of a small trash bag and displaying an embroidered silver hourglass on it. A sign above showed a picture of one of them. The matte black thread that made up the bags absorbed all light that touched it so that I couldn't see folds in them, nor could I make out the threading. I grabbed several and stuffed them all into one bag.

On the opposite wall I saw a line of empty hooks under a picture of a glass scoop. Beneath them lay heaps of shattered glass shards and the occasional silver-threaded loop. I shuffled through the debris with my foot, then clicked my tongue on the back of my teeth. "Damn. Now what?"

There had to be another storehouse, but where? Time pressed its crescive weight on my mind. I ran out of the double doors, only to be met by the largest, thickest crowd I'd ever seen.

*   *   *

With so many moving, jostling bodies before me, panic instantly set in, quickly followed by nausea. I couldn't move, frozen in place. The mob completely obscured the far side of the square. Gradually, I realized that the people grew taller and taller until I stood at the level of their waists. I stepped back into the building; the saloon doors passed over my head. They hadn't grown—rather, I was a child.

"You aren't here to break more of my property like that other one did, are you, young man?" The voice was behind me. I spun to see the dark-robed figure from the square in the middle of the room. I still couldn't tell if it was male or female.

My hands went behind my back to hide the bags. "What? N-no! I didn't do that! I promise!"

They looked down at me with the expression of a suspicious parent. "Those do not belong to you."

Caught. "Ah! I'm just... just borrowing them," I said softly and held the bag in front of me, to my chest.

"Borrowing without asking permission is the same thing as stealing. You know that, Alex." Dream stepped closer, smiling down at me. They looked like

198

they lived in a state of perpetual daydreaming. They even had bed-head to match.

"I'm sorry," I muttered.

"Do not say what you do not mean. If you were truly sorry, you would return them. But I do not think that you will."

I didn't have time to be stalled like this, not with each passing second so precious to me. I decided to be upfront. "You're right. I intend to take them either way."

"Do you? And what if I tried to stop you?"

"I'd fight you," I said. Dream squatted to my level and held out their empty hand. I gripped the bag tighter at first but soon relaxed. "May I borrow these?" I ventured.

"You may not. Not yet. Tell me, what are your dreams?"

"Why do you want to know that?"

When Dream shook their head, that jumble of hair jiggled around. "I know them. This is for your sake. You and Amanda had a similar discussion about a year ago in your time. She told you many of her dreams, but you did not answer her in kind."

"Why should I have dreams when I'm almost out of time? What's the point?"

"Alex. That is when you need them the most! Your dreams guide you. They give your life meaning. There are no needs, not without hopes and dreams to aspire to. If you don't know what it is you truly want then you won't know what it is you truly need."

"What I need is to live!"

Dream's joyous laugh dissolved my anger and put me at ease. "Why?" I stood there in silent confusion. "You may *desire* to live, but it is not a necessity. Many have made the ultimate sacrifice to achieve their dreams."

I did not particularly like where this conversation was headed. "If I don't go soon, I won't even get to make that choice."

"This is Dreamland, not The Between. It has gates to every realm, not just the one you came through. Time here is under *my* control, Alex. Mine and my Twin's. I will not squander what is left of yours. You dreamed of happiness, and so you took a dangerous bargain because you thought you needed to in order to obtain your goal. Did you obtain it?"

I looked down at my feet. "No. Not really."

"You mean, 'not yet.' Then, you had a new dream, to be a famous writer, and you felt an education was what you needed to achieve that dream, so you went to college. But you aren't really famous, are you?"

"Not yet," I said with a bit of a smile. "Internet famous?"

Dream giggled. "Fair enough. This dream is a core part of you. But your writing may yet bring you posthumous fame, and you have desires that take priority over it."

"My foster home."

Dream nodded sagely. "A noble dream, to be sure. Yet, you've given Amanda the means to make it happen. So what is this dream that makes you feel you need to live?"

I shook my head while keeping my gaze on the floor. "I'm afraid if I say it, something bad will happen to her."

"Ah. Not even Azrael has power in Dreamland without my permission. I promise your words will not cause her harm." Dream felt both safe and comforting, in a way I imagined a loving parent would. I was utterly unprepared for it. Words just flowed freely.

"I dream that I'll live a long, happy life with Amanda."

Dream smiled at me. "You are sure?" I nodded. "I think you mean to say that you dream that Amanda will make you happy." Their words rang true. I nodded. "This dream has some good in it, but it is also selfish, don't you think? Do not fret over that. Most desires are inherently selfish. Very few are truly altruistic. Only be warned that the more selfish the desire, the less satisfying it will be once you attain it. Yet, as a dream, it is empty without a reason."

I felt like they expected me to say more. "I... dream that I'll get to spend the rest of my life making Amanda happy."

"Ah! You are getting closer. Now you have two competing dreams. It is normal to desire several things at once, but it may not be possible to achieve everything you hope for. Sometimes it takes great sacrifice. With so little time left, you may well spend the rest of *your* life making Amanda happy, but will that make her happy the rest of *her* life?"

I didn't understand why this immortal being was drilling me so, but I had a feeling it was for a good reason. I thought about my answer for a while, particularly about what Amanda had said. "I want to make Amanda happy for the rest of her life." A stern look had me quickly correcting myself. "I want her to be happy for the rest of her life. I make her happy. She wants me to be alive."

"Happiness loses its meaning when it is all that remains. What if your mutual misery is the price you must pay upfront?"

"...It would only be a few years like that. Destiny said she erased the pages of my book, from the point I came to this world onward. So after that, four years from now, our destinies would be our own to make. Right?"

Dream's gaze cut through to my core. "And what if that means you would no longer be soulmates? What if she finds happiness in the arms of another?"

I did not like that idea. It made my stomach twist. But I couldn't deny the logic—if our fates had been erased, how could we be destined to remain together? In four years of avoiding each other, waiting for the day we controlled our own fates, we could easily drift apart. I could be replaced.

"I can't know the future... but I do know I want her to be happy, whether or not it's with me. I want to be there for her, either way. It doesn't matter if we're soulmates or not. She's still my best friend. I want to be there at her wedding, when her kids are born, when she achieves her goals. I may dream of marrying her, but being her friend is no dream, it is a reality. We can still share our lives together, but not if I'm dead!"

"You are sure about this?"

"Yes. I am sure."

They got to their feet and pulled a glass scoop out from their robe, offering it to me. "Then you have my permission to take these tools, but I am unsure that you will really need them. A piece of advice, though: be honest to yourself, or you may find you have been chasing the wrong dream."

I took the scoop from their hand and put it in the bag. "Thank you! So, I can really go?" I asked, bouncing on my toes. Looking like a child made it easy to act like one.

"Yes and no. Your dreams always made me smile, Alex. Amanda's too. You are both creative and willing to go after what you want. Together you may achieve miracles—if you are willing to make sacrifices. I'm afraid my Twin, Fear, is rather fond of you as well. Fear may keep you from your dreams. So in order to leave, you two are going to need to meet face-to-face." Dream took me back to the door and showed me the throng assembled just beyond it.

I wanted to throw up.

*   *   *

No matter how many times I tried, my body wouldn't move from beyond the doorway. "Dream?" I turned around but I couldn't find them there any longer.

Come out here and face me!" It sounded like both a whisper and a scream and it came from the crowd. I searched through the bodies and found one that stood stock still, facing me. They, too, were androgynous like Dream, but instead of wearing a dark robe, Fear had no clothing on at all. While Dream seemed to encompass both genders, Fear had none. The most obvious difference between the twins, however, was that Fear did not have eyes, only scars where they might once have been.

"I can't go out there!"

"You'll never escape if you don't." People walked between us and when they'd passed, I couldn't find Fear. Almost immediately, I heard a growl coming from behind me. In one of the dark corners, coming out from under some discarded bags, prowled a deathly pale beast unlike anything on Earth. Its arms resembled thin, human arms, but they bent in too many places the wrong way, it had six of them, and it used them to crawl along the ground. Each arm ended in a hand with long, many-jointed fingers and sharp, black nails. The head looked like melting wax placed over a disfigured skull, and as more of it stepped into the light, I found that most of its flesh drooped like it would slip off its own bones any moment. Its motion as it approached was hideously serpentine.

I knew I had less than two hours left to live, yet paralysis still set in. The primal terror of being torn to pieces by this creature hadn't overcome the memories from years of abuse and neglect triggered by the crowd. I pressed my back against the inside wall and closed my eyes.

"I'm flattered that you regard me so highly. But stop being so stubborn, Al. If your dreams aren't enough to get you moving and the threat of death won't work, what *will* motivate you?" When I opened my eyes, Fear stood in front of me in place of the beast.

"Motivate me?"

Unlike the loving and doting parent Dream felt like, Fear gave off an aura of danger and even excitement. I did not sense actual animosity in their behavior, but rather a tough love that strained my pride. Yet, something in their mannerisms gave the impression that a darker, more violent side lay just beneath the surface.

"Yes. I am so often misunderstood by you mortals. I do not *mean* to hurt you. Fear is the instinct that keeps you alive! I test you, I separate the wheat from the chaff, I *want* you to overcome me. If you best me, you may yet become a better person. I am more than Fear; I am anger, desperation, and ambition. I can be an obstacle, I can be a life-saver, or I can be your drive. And still, I am hated by your kind."

"Why then? Why do you care?"

"It is my nature to care, but not coddle; I prepare you for reality. Most mortals do not like reality. That's what my Twin is for."

"Then why won't you let me leave?"

"You can leave whenever you want. It is entirely up to you."

"Wh-what do I have to do?"

"*Overcome me!*"

I looked outside. It only took a moment for the panic to get to me. "I can't!"

Fear growled. When I looked back, the beast crouched before me once more. "Why does the crowd stop you? What is it you *truly* fear?"

"I was abandoned in a crowd like this..."

The beast came close enough that I could feel its fetid breath on my neck as it chortled. "Abandonment? No. That is trauma, an emotional scar, the irrepressible *memory* of fear." The people walking past started looking familiar to me. They became the foster parents and their children from countless households who had taken me in. Beat me. Neglected me. Abused me.

When I saw Mr. Lancie, all manner of terrible feelings hit. I wanted to flee from those memories. I backed further into the storehouse only to press up against Fear.

"You were more afraid of them than of being alone. That's why you ran away. But where are you running *to*?" The question gave me pause. I knew what I was running *from* easily enough. "What reason do you have to move forward? What brought you here?"

"Amanda," I whispered without thinking.

"Alex! You've got to hurry! Hunter's here!" Amanda's voice cut through the din. Speak of the devil. I ran outside and looked for her, but couldn't see anything beyond a few feet.

"Can you come here and get the tools?" I yelled.

She screamed. I heard Hunter's laugh. "Too late, shithead," he said.

I knew that if I went, I would be walking into a trap. Either Fear wanted to play with me or Hunter waited to kill me. But it didn't matter in the end. I couldn't risk it. I bolted into the crowd. Hands grabbed at me as I wound my way between bodies. The world warped and twisted. That sense of doom ramped up, but I only went faster. I was sick, but I still kept going.

"Why are you running so fast?" I couldn't see Fear at first. The crowd stopped moving and all of them looked down at me with that same eyeless face.

"I have to save Amanda!"

"Why?"

I shoved past the people in my path until the crowd gave way. I could see Hunter and Amanda a few yards from me, just beyond the gate. Hunter stood over her as she knelt, brandishing a pistol.

"Get away from her!" Fire burned inside me.

"What scares you the most?" Fear asked in my ear.

Hunter pointed the gun at Amanda.

I stopped in my tracks. "I'm scared of losing her!"

"Too late for that," Hunter said. "I got one bullet left, so who's it going to be?"

"Then you better shoot me or I'm gonna rip you apart," I growled and moved towards him. He aimed the gun straight at me.

Before I could even blink, Amanda stood and put herself in the line of fire, hands on the pistol struggling for control. "No!" she yelled.

The blood left my face. "Amanda! Don't do it!" I cried and ran harder than I'd ever run before. I reached for her, grabbed at her arm. Then the gun went off. The sound deafened me, the muzzle flash blinded me.

A moment later, I stood just inside the gate, alone. I wasn't a child any longer.

"You found it," Fear said. When I looked behind me, I saw both Fear and Dream standing together.

"Found what?"

"The obstacle you must overcome."

"What do you mean? Losing Amanda?"

Fear shook their head and laughed. "You've already lost her."

Dream said, "You may yet find the answer if you look to your dreams."

"Can't you tell me?" I pleaded.

Fear sneered. "Perhaps I was wrong about you. You better figure it out soon, Al. I want to keep playing with you for a long time."

Chapter 22

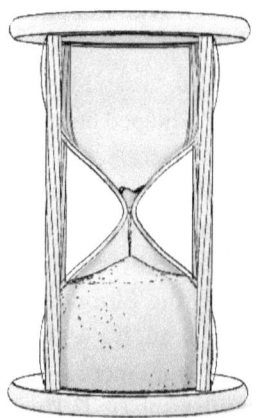

Sand Doom

"Dream A Little Dream of Me" echoed off the harsh rocks as Amanda's mellifluous voice carried it on the light breeze. Her voice cracked a little whenever she hit the high notes, but I loved hearing it anyway. When she saw me coming, she jumped out of the Chronowheel and tugged its pull cord repeatedly until the engine roared to life.

I jogged up to her and hugged her from behind before she had a chance to even turn back around. She put her hands on my arms and leaned into me.

"Miss me?" she asked.

"You have no idea. I just had the weirdest encounter and I don't know what to think of it."

"Oh? Bad dream?" she joked. "You'll have to tell me about it someday." Her optimism gave me hope. "Did you get them?"

"Plenty of bags, but just one scoop. Mom's not back yet?"

"Not yet. Do you think we should wait?"

"No. She said she'll catch up. We should probably get going." My waning time pricked at my thoughts like a needle in my mind.

"I'm driving," Amanda said. We got in and she took control of the joystick. The wheel spun around us, kicking up a dust cloud that rose high into the gray sky as we moved. The crunch of rock gradually turned to a low thrum as we reached the black sand. Amanda stopped the Chronowheel.

"This spot looks good," we both said in unison, quickly followed by Amanda saying, "Jinx! Ha! Now you have to do what I say until you buy me a coke."

I stepped onto the sand with a grin and gave a flourishing bow. "Yes, my mistress. What is your command?"

She stroked an imaginary beard. "I say I get to use the scoop to fill the bags and you have to use your hands." I helped her disembark but was thanked with an empty bag thrown in my face.

"As you wish," I said and we both got to our knees. She immediately began shoveling the sand into one of the bags while I dug my fingers in.

Only I couldn't. My fingertips did little more than make small dents in the surface. I realized that, although the Chronowheels left tracks, our footsteps were so faint I couldn't see them at all. If I wiggled my fingers back and forth, I could slowly penetrate down about an inch. It took all my strength to drag the handful of sand into the bag. "What the Hell? This stuff is heavier than lead!" As if to show off, I tried to pick up the bag. I lifted it with no problem and almost fell on my ass from overcompensating.

Amanda looked down at her glass scoop. She easily lifted the sand and poured it into the bag. When she poured some onto her palm, though, her hand immediately hit the ground. "Woah! I guess we know why they use these things, huh? They somehow make it weightless." She shook her hand free and didn't waste a second before shoveling load after load of the sand into her bag. "Better hurry!"

"If I can't scoop it in with my hands..." I said and picked the bag up. I then dragged its open end along the ground and used my hands through the bag itself to help gather the sand. With the bag between me and the sand, I had no problem. Then I had another stroke of genius. I used the third bag to scoop sand into mine even faster. Within a couple of minutes, we had all three bags bulging and ready to go. I tied the silver loop on the end of the scoop to my belt so it would hang at my side. "All right! Let's go!"

As we climbed back into the clock-like vehicle, the reality of the situation crept to the forefront of my mind. It must have taken an hour getting ahold of those tools and much of that was travel. Which meant it would take nearly an hour getting back. Add to that the fact that we had to actually *find* the hourglass. We'd be cutting it close.

As if she could read my thoughts, Amanda took the joystick and went as fast as that machine could handle, casting a spray of sand behind us.

After a few minutes passed in silence, she took my hand and guided it to the joystick over hers so we both steered. "What are you going to do when we get back?" she asked.

"What do you mean? Find the hourglass."

"No, I mean, after we've saved your life and we go back home!" She squeezed my hand a little tighter.

"Home? I... I don't know. It never occurred to me that I might see home again."

She gave me a sorrowful look, but followed it with a goofy smile. "I say we cut classes tomorrow, test your Viking mettle, and sleep in. Maybe... sleep in together?"

Nothing would have made me happier. But I had other things on my mind than fooling around. "I'm afraid we won't have that happy ending. I'll still be cursed. I've seen what happens when I try to fight it, and I'd rather not see that happen again."

A hint of despondency in her eyes threatened to damper the hope she'd been holding onto. "Oh. Right." Thankfully, the path we were on was straight and even, so she had no problem both steering and leaning her shoulder into me. "This... doesn't have to be goodbye, you know. I want to enjoy the time we do have. Maybe we could steal away a night or two." A heavy blush filled her face and ears. "Soulmates deserve that much at least, right?"

"Yeah. I would like that. A lot."

"I'm sure we can keep in touch online. If your fate says we can't be together, nothing says 'distance' like social media. And then in a few years..."

"What if this meant we won't be soulmates any longer?"

"Then it's the same as before," she said without missing a beat. "Doesn't change how I feel. How I've felt... for a while now."

"What do you mean?"

"Your little bargain kept us apart. We might as well have not been soulmates. Yet..." She brought my hand up and kissed it.

No one ever filled me with hope as easily as she did. "Yet here we are."

"Mm-hmm. Still in love. Maybe it really is possible to defy destiny."

I chuckled and kissed the back of her hand. "I don't think she'd be happy to hear you say that."

Amanda giggled and brought both of her hands to the joystick as if that might speed us up. "You know, these new memories of mine still have a lot of gaps. Tell me about our time together. The good stuff!"

"What do you want to know?"

"Hmm. Did you reeeaally shave your head to disguise yourself?"

"Ha! Yeah, I did. It felt really weird." I ran my hand through my hair, just confirming that I still had it.

"I'm pretty sure I saw right through that. I seem to recall it was at a dinner and—!"

I put my hand on her thigh and squeezed it gently. That was enough to deepen her blush and make her lose her train of thought. We didn't need to be remembering any of the bad times right then. "Ask me another one."

Her eyes darted down to my hand. "Okay. What happened in Puerto Rico?" That one had me stumped. I'm sure I stammered. "The hotel," she clarified. "I remember talking to mom on the phone. I remember kissing you on the bed. But that's it. D-did we...?"

I smirked. "A gentleman does not kiss and tell."

*   *   *

Some time passed before we dared speak again. Up ahead, I could see distant buildings spreading out like a metropolis along the edge of my vision. The sky over them seemed to gently fade from the drab, static sky of the desert to the palatial ceiling of the Halls of Time. I had to wonder if the ceiling had always been above us, only obscured by the bright light, or if the gray sky somehow turned into ceiling in some Escheresque fashion.

"I think we're close," I said.

Amanda gave my foot a playful kick. "No shit, Sherlock. But how are we going to find your hourglass? I mean, there must be billions."

She was right. When I squinted, I realized that the buildings ahead weren't buildings at all, but row after row of shelves holding hourglasses. They reminded me of crops planted in perfectly straight lines with furrows between. "Your eyes must be better than mine," I said.

"That's what you get for getting older than me," Amanda teased.

"There were signs hanging above that gave row and column."

She nodded. "Oh yeah. I remember seeing the one on the way out. 'Alpha-Beta' I think it said. All the hourglasses there were empty."

"They could be thousands of years old.'

"What was above yours?"

I sighed. "Reish and Sigma."

Amanda squinted. "Reish? That's not Greek."

"No. I looked it up once. I think it's Hebrew. Who knows how many languages those signs go through, or which order?"

"Maybe—"

I put my hand up. The roar of the engine had masked the sound, but I was sure I heard other engines *behind* us. I had to lean out to look. Sure enough, there were three Chronowheels racing towards us, each trailed by a black rooster tail of kicked-up sand. They were gaining on us.

"We've got company," I said.

"What? Didn't your mom say that everyone was told to stay indoors?"

208

"Can you go faster? I don't think we'll make it before they catch us."

"It's already at its top speed!" Amanda quickly turned, our seat staying perfectly horizontal as the tire tilted around us. We left the path and she started navigating us between the massive midnight dunes until our potential pursuers were out of sight. "We'll have to go on foot!" she said. Even though I was the one running out of time, she was the one in a rush. The moment we came to a stop, she turned to me and said, "Your belt! Take off your belt!"

I'm sure that had me blushing. When a cute girl demands that I take my belt off, I obey. Granted, no girl had ever demanded it of me before now. I took it off so quickly, I forgot about the scoop I'd tied to it. It fell and bounced off part of the wheel, gaining a large crack when it came to a rest. "Shit. I'll have to apologize to Dream. Here, what do you want my belt for?"

"Pull on the brake!" she ordered as she took the belt and started looping it around part of the metal console frame in front of the joystick. As I lifted the crank at my side, I saw her plan. I threw the bags to the ground while she brought the belt around the joystick and tightened it. The engine revved as the stick was pulled forward.

Our feet hit the sand. I released the brake. The Chronowheel took off, driverless, at high speed, wobbling between the dunes and spraying a huge black arc behind it. Even though it was getting further, the sound of engines steadily increased.

"This way!" I said and picked up the bags. It was a good thing their silver logos contrasted so well against the void-black that surrounded them, or I'd have missed them entirely. We ran away from the fresh tracks our Chronowheel had made, but we didn't have time to cross to the other side of the dune we were on to hide. I tossed her one of the bags. "Get down and hold it up in front of you!"

I fell prone, facing the tracks, and Amanda threw herself to my side. Together, we held up the bags with their logos facing us so they would block our pursuers' view of us. Their dark weave was undistinguishable from the sand, so that it was quickly impossible to tell where sand ended and bag began.

The engines grew louder. Amanda and I squeezed each other more tightly. Then we heard them zip by, the first a good deal in front of the other two. When they faded away, we peered around the bags and I could just make out a rooster tail beyond a nearby dune getting further away.

"I think we did it," Amanda whispered. We looked at each other, but our moment for elation was brief. Now we still had to make it to my hourglass and we had no conveyance. Together, we got to our feet and ran towards the Halls, bags in hand.

*   *   *

The sand gave way to stone, which soon developed a repeating pattern etched into it as we passed into the Halls. Without a word, we headed down the main aisle that the signs hung over. Every ten aisles, a new sign announced a new area. By the time we found "Sigma-Beta", I was out of breath with my hands on my knees.

"Come on, Alex! We can't stop now! We're so close!"

"Go... go on... without me..." I wheezed between breaths. Amanda was breathing hard, but not like I was. "Take the... bags..."

"Didn't you say we won't be together when you die? There's no way I'm leaving your side now. Come on!"

A Chronowheel engine rushed towards us. "Shit. Hurry, hide! Don't... touch any of them..." I said and picked up my bags, ushering Amanda down an aisle of spent hourglasses. I was wary of touching them; however, we soon discovered that without any sand in the top, they posed no threat.

The Chronowheel stopped just short of the row we hid in. A head peeked around the corner before I could get in a good hiding spot. "There you two are!"

"Mom! You got away? How did you find us?" The three of us hugged.

"I'll tell you on board!" With Amanda in my lap again, we were soon zipping down aisles. "I was following you in a Chronowheel while they chased me. That decoy was a clever idea. Did you come up with that one, Amanda?"

Amanda grinned proudly. "Yeah, but Alex kept us hidden."

"After that, I just had to look for the only people around here in technicolor. It wasn't exactly difficult," Mom said.

"We're glad you found us," I said. "I don't think we could have gone any further."

Just then I felt Amanda stiffen. Her gaze was fixed on my mom's wrist. I stupidly looked at what had caught her attention and got a glimpse of the dinosaur watch Mom wore.

But that short glimpse wasn't short enough. I'd seen the numbers on the screen perfectly:

m10:00

Chapter 23

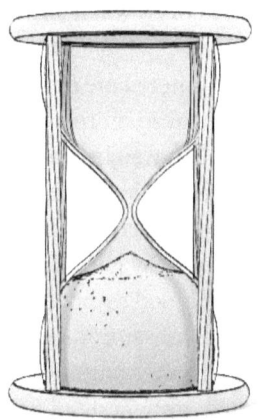

Everything Ends

When you're talking about thousands of rows and billions of hourglasses, it was bound to take time to find the exact place we had in mind, even if you knew where to go while speeding along in a Chronowheel. The entire time we sat in the vehicle, Amanda kept a tight hold of me, like she could save me if she never let go. Even her reassuring smiles were tinged with worry and fear.

"Amanda, listen," I said. "If Hunter shows up, I want you to run away. Go back to the manor."

"What? I won't abandon you!"

"Please. Get home safe. No matter what happens, I'll be waiting for you."

"Reish and Sigma. There's the sign!" Mom pointed to it. A burst of dangerous hope filled my heart. She stopped at the entrance to the row. "I can't drive this thing down there. It's too big. We'll need to make a run for it!" Our destination was almost in the very middle of the aisle.

I had been practically counting the seconds as they ticked by, but as soon as the vehicle stopped, all of that was forgotten. We jumped out, bags in hand, and sprinted past scores of hourglasses. There was nowhere to hide; Hunter wasn't here. We were home free.

"There it is!" I pointed to the one ahead that had a few grains of orange sand remaining, right next to the one mostly full of teal sand.

"With a couple minutes to spare!" Mom called out.

This was easy. As far as things like this went, I never had it easy. "Where are the guards that Chronos—"

Amanda was quite a bit ahead of us when she screamed and stumbled some hundred feet from my hourglass.

"Stop right there, asshole." Hunter came out from between two hourglasses, holding onto Amanda's hair. He looked more haggard and crazed than ever. His beard had come in fully, he had lost weight, and his clothes had holes in them. Somehow, though, he'd managed to keep himself and his clothes relatively clean. *How the Hell was he eking out a living in this place?*

As he pulled Amanda's head back by her hair, he held a jagged shard of glass up to her neck. A trail of crimson blood dripped down his hand. The spot in the lower shelf he'd come from was missing its sand timer. *No. Not missing— broken.* Its twisted remains lay mostly buried under black sand. In the empty spot on the shelf lay the twisted, gray body of young man—frozen in his final moment like James had been.

"Let her go, Hunter!" I could not mask the anguish in my voice.

"Shut the fuck up and listen! I know all about this place and what you're up to. And why. Now, put those bags of sand down. Slowly. Good. Tell that bitch to empty them. NOW!" He nodded to my mom. She looked to me, then did as he asked. After taking the bags of sand, she turned hers and mine upside-down in front of us all, making a miniature mountain of the sand. "You, too!"

Amanda hadn't dropped hers. "...No."

"*You* don't get to say 'no' to me!" He sneered and pulled the shard away from her throat, only to stab into the bag she held. She struggled as the sand spilled and the rip split itself open further. But when he dragged the tip of the glass shard along her throat, she went still. The emptier the bag became, the wider his grin did.

"When I got here, I was just going to break your hourglass," Hunter said to me. "It would have been *so easy*. But it was nearly empty, so I thought I'd wait a few minutes so I could see your face when you die."

"Why are you doing this?" I asked.

"*No one steals my things from me!*" Spittle flew from his mouth. "First, I'll watch you die, then I'll finally be able to kill my old man without you *constantly* resetting everything. And when you die, the last thing you're going to see will be me breaking your toy in front of you."

The wicked point of the glass shard left a faint scratch along Amanda's neck as it worked lower and lower, towards her chest. My stomach cramped, my heart ached; my whole world was in danger and I could do nothing about it.

Hunter jerked Amanda's head back as he started slicing her shirt from the middle of her bust. "I am *so* going to enjoy breaking you," he hissed into her ear.

With the speed of a wild wind and the fury of a tempest, Amanda grabbed his wrist and stomped on the instep of his foot. Hunter didn't have time to react. In a flash, she held the shard and faced her abuser with the point against his heart.

"You will *never* break me again!"

She pushed the shard harder against him until he released her hair. But she was too close. From her vantage point, she couldn't see him reach into his pocket and pull out a warped piece of silvery metal. It looked like he had fashioned himself a small, makeshift pickaxe.

"Amanda!" I cried and ran towards them as fast as I could. He swung the pickaxe up, which knocked the shard out of her hand and cut her palm in the process. Amanda instinctively backed up, but not fast enough to prevent the weapon from clipping her cheek, drawing a vinaceous streak of blood. He took advantage of her surprise by grabbing the front of her shirt, then raised his weapon high, ready for a fatal blow.

"I'll kill her!" he shouted at me. I stopped a few yards away. Keeping her alive was the only thing that mattered now.

She pulled at his fist and struggled. "Let! Me! Go! You're not going to kill me," she said amidst grunts. "You need me... as a hostage... to get home!"

He sneered but stayed his hand. She was right. Without a living hostage, he had no chance of escape, or he'd have done it by now.

He shook her violently and growled. "Stop struggling! *Nothing* can save him now. Or do you want to share his fate?"

Amanda looked over at me for a second, eyes growing wider. "*I* can save him! Let me *GO*, Hunter!" Her rough tugging to break his hold redoubled.

She knew something, but what? Was this the chance Chronos was referring to? Dream had told me to be honest with myself, that we'd need to be willing to make sacrifices. That made me thinking of the dream I'd in the hospital, where Amanda was pulling me out of the sand and I was trying to stop her.

And then I saw the answer, and the horrible dilemma Fear wanted me to overcome. The *only* way for me to save Amanda's life was to stay put, but that? That would rob her of her decision, *her* sacrifice. I would never again deny her of her choice.

I used nearly every last bit of strength my body had left into lunging for Hunter's raised arm. He had to let go of Amanda to stop me from taking the pickaxe. For a split second I saw his fist, then tears and pain blinded me when it slammed into my face. I let go and fell onto my ass. Amanda's footsteps hurried away into the distance.

"You just don't know when to give up," Hunter said. Opening my eyes only revealed a blur before he kicked me in the side.

"Alex!" Mom cried out. She ran and threw herself at Hunter like the superhero she was. Like the villain *he* was, he just shoved her to the ground effortlessly and stood over me, one leg on either side. My vision cleared just in time to see his harrowing stare inches away as he pulled me up by the shirt. I felt something very wrong, like my heart had lost the cadence of its dance. Without any strength left, I could scarcely lift my hand enough to grab onto his wrist. Mom crawled to me and tried to help, but even together we could not loosen his grip.

"Is that his stupid watch?" Hunter asked as he look down at Mom's wrist with a gloating grin. "Fuckin' pathetic. But it looks like you're out of time. How about I give us a countdown?"

My heart raced with a limp. I felt something squeeze painfully around my chest.

"5..." I grew dizzy and light-headed.

"4..." Breathing became difficult as the pain ramped up.

"3..." My hand slipped to the ground. The last of my strength had failed.

"2..." Hunter opened his hand and let me fall limp to the cold tile.

"1!" For the briefest of moments, a figure clad in the night sky appeared at my side. Black feathers fluttered all around, framing the figure's face. One eye remained whole but clouded over and pale; the other was just a pit in a skull. Mottled flesh, bone, sinew, and muscle were all visible in different places, displaying every level of decay. His sorrowful smile gave me a touch of comfort.

"0." A decomposing hand passed over me.

Everything ended.

I told you on the first page that I died in this story, didn't I? You didn't think that near-brush with death in the alley was actually it, did you? That would mean cheating my audience out of witnessing my promised demise, and I would never do that.

But I also never said that the story ended with my death.

Life returned to me like fire in my soul, igniting every cell in my body.

When I came to, Hunter still stood over me, but he had Mom by the forearm in a vice-like grip. "Stay outta my way, you dumb bitch." As he threw her away from him, she broke down in tears. "Now where's that two-timing whore?"

A terrible cacophony erupted nearby, like tortured wailing, fire, and screeching metal all at once. Hunter looked towards it, but the shelves stood in the way. "The fuck was that?"

I felt my strength slowly return, and just in time. I may not be the best at fighting—I believe I've proven that—and I still felt weak, but it doesn't take a lot of training or muscle to pop a guy in the nuts. Bro code be damned.

The pickaxe clattered against the floor. Hunter let out a whimper as he held his hands between his legs. With a shove, I knocked him to the ground beside me and sat up.

"Alexander?" Mom gazed at me in disbelief.

"H-how?" Hunter wheezed.

All three of us looked to my hourglass at the same time.

The hatch on top lay wide open. Amanda held up her hourglass like it weighed nothing, tipping the edge of it right over mine and sending her teal sand cascading quickly from her top bulb into mine.

"Amanda!" I cried.

When she put hers down and nudged them to help the sand settle into place, both hourglasses had about the same amount of sand—teal sand— remaining in them. She looked over at us with a huge grin. Although the right side of her face had blood all over it and more dripped from her palm, she didn't seem to notice or care. "Alex! You're alive! It—it worked!" Quick as a flash, she ran to me and helped me get up, but didn't let go after. Neither did I.

"*Cariad*. I..." With no words to describe the love, relief, turmoil, and sorrow within me, I just held her tighter.

"I couldn't see any other way to share my life with you," she said.

"Oh my babies!" I had heard that parents like to embarrass their children, but this was the first time I'd been on the receiving end. We both blushed as Mom pulled us into a hug.

Hunter must not have appreciated our little moment. "I'll kill you both," he groaned, grabbing at the pickaxe while stumbling to his feet. I didn't think he could have gotten up again any time soon, but not only could he get up, he could still run. Rather than head for us, though, he went straight for our hourglasses. He raised the weapon and aimed it at mine. It looked perfect for shattering glass.

Hunter wasn't the only one heading for it. As I hurried to catch up to him, I pulled the mourning cord off from around my neck—James' cord. How fitting.

Hunter swung his arm, but I brought the cord down over his head at the last moment and pulled it *tight* around his neck. The makeshift hammer fell from his hand in mid-arc and gently hit the glass bulb with its side, harmlessly bouncing off. Hunter let out sickening guttural croaks as he dug his fingers into his neck to grab at the garrote.

"I'm not going to kill you, Hunter. I'm not like you. But I *am* going to knock you out and tie you up until we can figure out what to do with you."

"That will be quite enough, Alexander." Chronos appeared without warning a few feet away. "Release him." I did so, but also backed up. Chances were pretty good Chronos was pissed at what Amanda and I had done. At least, as pissed as he could get. He stepped up behind Hunter and lowered the blade of his scythe menacingly, hooking it around the far side of his body so its razor edge hovered inches from his face. Hunter didn't move.

"Lord Chronos, your honor," Amanda pled as she and Mom came to my side. "Please don't take the sand out of Alex's hourglass."

"I have no such intention, Amanda Shields," Chronos said, then turned to me. "Alexander Petersen, your time in this realm is over. Now you must make your choice."

I squeezed Amanda's hand, just in case it was the last time I'd get to. "What do you mean it's over? Choose what?"

"Of course it's over, dear boy," Lady Luck spoke as she and Destiny came from the opposite direction. A Chronowheel idled at the end of the row. "What is the color of the sand in that hourglass?" the Lady asked.

Confused, I mumbled out the obvious answer. "Teal, I suppose."

"What color was your sand?" she pressed.

"Orange. Why isn't it turning orange?"

Destiny pulled out the contract I'd signed that started this whole mess. "Teal and orange are opposing colors. Your sand was originally teal, but turned orange when your fate was reversed. Now that it is teal again, it shows that our contract is finished; you have no need to remain here."

Amanda held onto my arm with poorly hidden excitement and hope. "It isn't my sand any longer?"

A knowing grin spread on Luck's cheeks. "Yes and no. You're *soulmates.* Your sand is the same, so it really doesn't matter. I'll bet you had no trouble touching his hourglass, either."

216

Chronos cleared his throat. "Now you must make your choice. Do you wish to go back to your original timeline or continue in your current one?"

"Wait. That only explains why he's still alive. How is the contract over?" Amanda asked. Chronos rolled his eyes and grunted. It had taken this long to finally get an emotion out of him.

"It's right here," Destiny said and adjusted her glasses before reading on. "'I, the undersigned, do hereby and hereon accept a full and complete reversal of my fate and fortune, so long as it does not upset the Divine Plan, to be carried out by Dame Destiny and Lady Luck until the sands of *my* life cease their flow. Signed, Alexander David Petersen.'" She looked up and pointed to the lower bulb of the hourglass. "*His* sand is all at the bottom. *Your* sand is what flows."

"How'd you figure it out?" Luck asked.

I could only shake my head. "It came to me in a dream. Sort of."

Amanda gasped with her hand over her mouth. "Hold on. He didn't actually die for real, did he?"

"Briefly," Destiny replied. "Very briefly."

As she started bouncing on her toes, Amanda asked, "And the contract is now over? You mean, we can be together?"

Destiny shrugged. "Perhaps. You'll always be soulmates, but all this meddling with your fates has left the remaining pages of your books blank. Your stories were so intertwined and convoluted, I had no choice but to erase hers as well. I'll leave it up to you two to determine your own fates." She looked over the top of her glasses at me. "You two have given me a *lot* of work. I expect great things from you both."

This time when Chronos cleared his throat, he did it loudly. "For the *last time*: now you must make your choice! Which reality do you choose?"

Amanda turned her gaze towards me, a gaze full of wonder and love. "Stay with me, Alex. I want to share our life together. Literally and figuratively."

"That's such a huge decision," I whispered.

"Not at all. I—"

I pressed the tip of my nose against hers. "Of course I will. Like you needed to ask."

She lifted on her toes to kiss me, but was interrupted by the sudden cry of terror coming from Hunter. His body was simply fading away. "What's happening to me!?" The remains of the broken hourglass and the unfortunate worker began to fade as well. When they all vanished from sight, even the echo of Hunter's voice simply stopped.

"Did you just kill him!?" I asked.

Chronos leaned on his scythe. "Now that you have decided which reality to continue in, all the other realities you created have been sealed. In your new timeline, it is very doubtful Hunter Pace will ever come to The Between."

"Does this mean James...?"

"James' reality was like yours: separate and ever-flowing. It has run its course. Azrael, Gaia, and I would need to agree to bring James back."

I heard a soft voice in my head, kind and soothing. I didn't have to wonder who it belonged to. *I will not. The hole James made in the Veil to the Afterlife closed long ago.*

"You mean you can't make a new one for him?"

That is too dangerous. But do not fret. He is happy now. You may see him again, soon enough.

"I hope not *too* soon."

However, Azrael added, *when I pulled you back through the Veil, I felt the hole you left behind grow larger. Something may have followed us through.*

"Is that what made that awful sound?" Amanda asked.

"It is possible. But if there is an intruder, we will root it out," Chronos said. "Azrael, come with me. We'll search the Halls together."

Lady Luck sauntered up to me. "You won our wager, Alexander. Do you still refuse Fortune's kiss?"

"Yes. I don't need that kind of luck now that I have Amanda." I thought back on our bet and gasped. "Our wager? Was this *whole thing* part of the game?"

I got no answer, only a sly grin.

Throughout all of this, my mother had remained silent. She put her hands on our shoulders. "It's time to go home. Come on."

As Amanda took my hand and intertwined our fingers, she asked, "Since I have all these memories... does this mean we're still engaged?"

God, I love that grin of hers.

*　　　*　　　*

Lady Luck kept her eyes on Amanda until we passed by. Then she turned to Destiny with a triumphant smirk. "Sister, I believe you now owe me two souls. Count them: uno, dos." She waved two fingers in front of her Sister.

Destiny sputtered in protest, but gave up on it and sagged her shoulders. "Yes, fine. You win."

Luck squatted and punched at the air. "Yes! I win! I *knew* that girl wouldn't let me down!"

Her Sister's pout became a smile. "I will let slide the numerous times you aided Alexander this round. I'm glad I lost this gamble. But I bet you, double or nothing, that their first will be within, say, three years?"

"Make it two and you've got yourself a bet."

Epilogue

 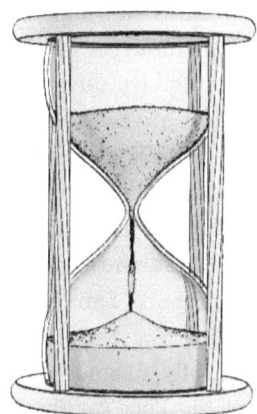

Once we started our life together, it seemed at first that my terrible luck had returned, but things were different this time around. Our trip to DC was canceled due to illness, Camden Yards didn't host the Division Series, and Amanda and I dropped out of college. Oh, and I managed to fail Professor Sapper's chemistry class again.

But we didn't care. We had each other and couldn't have been happier.

Plus, new opportunities appeared. Although I didn't do any more travel writing, Amanda and I started writing and drawing children's books. *Brian Buys A Brachiosaurus* became a bestseller. After that, we decided to make a career out of it. We didn't need college anymore.

My fortune didn't exactly go to waste. The lottery winnings all went towards making and maintaining my dream: a foster home for kids eleven and up who had been through at least seven homes. We're calling it "Carey's House." Our first kids arrive next semester, and Amanda and I are very excited. And nervous.

Amanda's memories of all those alternate timelines never went away. Quite the opposite, in fact; she seems to remember nearly everything now, sometimes better than I do. This unfortunately includes the bad with the good.

The side effects of being soulmates seem to have become much stronger. Time apart is very difficult for us both, so we usually travel together. Being together brings us incredible joy. I've also noticed that we comment on each other's thoughts now and then. My theory is that it's a result of Amanda sharing her sand with me.

We had no trouble getting information about Charles, though I only uncovered a little about James. After James passed, Charles led quite the interesting life, including a peerage. His last words were, "I am coming, my love." They are buried within sight of each other.

Hunter ended up dating Samantha for a while. It turns out he'd started hooking up with her a few weeks after Amanda and I first kissed. Funny thing I didn't tell you about Samantha, though, was that she was training to be in MMA—Mixed Martial Arts. When Hunter doted on her, she loved it. When she had been the mistress, she stayed silent. But when she caught him cheating on *her*—with Diana, again—Sam took no prisoners. I made sure to send a card to his hospital room.

He was officially diagnosed with a host of mental disorders, including narcissism, but the Pace family didn't pursue treatment—they covered it up. They didn't even press charges against Sam. My guess is that either Hunter still hasn't earned his father's approval, or they don't want to air out their dirty laundry. Maybe both.

We anticipated her father's cancer. We sadly could not prevent it, but we did catch it sooner. After some digging, we learned that he qualified for VA benefits. Between that and the Medicaid, we should have him covered for a while.

I found where my mother had been laid to rest and visit her often. I'm sure she listens whenever I'm there. As for my father, I have a lead I'm going to follow as soon as possible.

Naomi and Amanda get along like sisters, or possibly criminal conspirators. Naomi still threw that party, and got kicked out of school for it. She now spends her nights bartending, while during the day she prepares food for the kids at Carey's House. She and Xiao dated for several months but broke up amicably.

I don't want to forget everything that happened to us, so I have written it all down here in this blog for posterity. I've done my best at being accurate, but I'm sure a few details are wrong.

In a week, I marry the love of my life, two years to the day after we left The Between together and started sharing our lives. I'd love to tell you how wonderful living with her has been, but some things a gentleman does not tell.

What can I say? We're in love.

Postscript

Mom,

I'm sorry for leaving without saying goodbye. I got a lead on where to find Alex. I have no idea what's going to happen, but I'm not coming back without him. I know he's still alive, and I will keep looking until I find him, no matter what. Hopefully we will both be back in time for the wedding, but, if not, tell everyone we're sorry and that we love them.

All my heart,
            Amanda

Author's Note

Fate & Fortune is a deeply personal novel on a variety of levels. This made writing it both a pleasure and a challenge. In writing this story, I achieved some personal milestones, too. It will always hold a special place for me, just as I hope it does for you as well.

The concept for this novel came in December 2022. I've been a stay-at-home dad for 12 years now, so it is my responsibility to drive the kids to their various activities and events. I do a lot of driving. Often, I turn the radio off and let myself get absorbed in my own thoughts. You'd be surprised at how many inspirations I get while doing this. I was still figuring out my anti-depression medication then and had just finished with a difficult therapy session, so on that particular drive, I was brooding.

And when I brood, I analyze.

Now, I'm sure everyone has things in their past they regret, be it things they had done or things they wish they had done. *I should have known better. I should have kissed her. I shouldn't have kissed him. I shouldn't have gone on that trip. I should have started this years ago. I wish I'd asked how he was doing. Why did I punch that cop?*

We all look back, thinking how much better things would be if we could get another shot at them. For me, I wondered if I could have stopped my friend's death if I had just talked to her. I once lost a job over an email and asked myself if I could have prevented it. If I'd swallowed my pride, I likely wouldn't have been blocked by one of my best friends. Should I have changed universities and gone into mechanical engineering? And, yes, I do have a "what if I had kissed her?" moment. But as I thought about these things logically, I began to ask different questions: "Would things be better off? Worse? Would I have been able to change things at all?"

Looking back, I know I couldn't have saved my friend; losing that job ended up being good for me; if my friendship meant so little then he wasn't as good a friend as I thought; I couldn't really afford to change colleges; I dodged a bullet with the missed kiss.

From there, I started wondering if there are certain life events that might be fated, and if we could actually break our fate. What if someone had as many opportunities as they wanted to change something in their past, but no matter what they did, things still turned out the same, like living through the key frames in an animation?

Of course, these questions have all been asked a dozen times before. There are famous philosophers who tackled "predetermination". And there are a million time travel stories, most of which do it wrong (but not all). My mind drifted to Terry Pratchett's depiction of Death and his home, as well as Piers Anthony's depiction of Time in his *Incarnations of Immortality* series.

I wanted the hourglasses. The idea of having a contract that reverses the protagonist's fate developed early on. When I added a time limit, that someone's personal clock doesn't stop, I knew I had something. And when I thought of someone sharing the sand of their life with someone else, I pulled over and wrote it all down. Whenever I asked people what they thought of the idea, they invariably said, "I want to read that!"

I had started writing a story that I released on my blog chapter-by-chapter, and in that story I began developing my own concept of a Lady Luck and a goddess of Destiny. Is it plagiarism if you steal from yourself? I decided to give them something of a "fae" quality. It made perfect sense to me that both Fate and Fortune would bet on things, and that they would both twist whatever words are used in a contract to benefit themselves the most without actually breaking the terms. In my first draft, Lady Luck was actually the villain, not above cheating to win a bet. But as I developed the characters, it worked so much better for her and Destiny to act like sisters, and to make them more or less ambivalent to human affairs.

Chronos became the villain for a long time after that. I really did not want there to be some typical human antagonist. I wanted him to be the red herring, making everyone think he was the bad guy only to find out that it had been Chronos behind the scenes. But over time, I started to warm to the idea of a human villain. For starters, having the Lord of Time as a villain opens too many possibilities for plot holes. But then I began analyzing what sort of person would be both the opposite of the main character, but also a reflection of what he *could* be. He wouldn't be the typical jerk you usually find in stories like these. He would have to be manipulative, good at hiding his intentions, all about himself... In short, he would be the perfect specimen of a narcissist.

I started to research the condition, as well as its comorbidities. Not only does Hunter suffer from narcissism, which he developed because of his father's own narcissistic tendencies, but he also has a mild case of *obsessive compulsive personality disorder*. I'm no psychotherapist, but my understanding is that someone with OCD has things they know they must do, no matter what, and they have no choice. They know they are stupid things, might even hate that they have to do it, but that is why it is "compulsive." Someone with OCPD knows that doing a certain thing is right and good, it puts the universe in order, they are the only one that can do it, no one else can even help with it, and they'll be damned if someone defies them. I now had an antagonist with a real medical condition who is truly villainous.

Each character developed entirely on their own, though many of them were influenced by people (real and imagined). Not Alex. He was a fairly unique individual from the get-go. As I wrote Alexander, more and more of his personality and past became apparent. I started him as a sort of silent sufferer, a poster-child for foster kids, but when I researched our fostering system, I discovered how broken it is (and how much that would affect someone). The rates of abuse, homelessness, and imprisonment among fostered kids are inexcusably high. Alex had to be the guy who defied the odds and yet wasn't too hardened by the experience. He developed PTSD about halfway through the drafting process, which turned into a major characteristic of his. And yes, many fostered kids end up with PTSD.

Amanda was based on a *lot* of people all mashed together. From her protective streak and her rough-and-tumble attitude to her obsession with art and gaming, each aspect of her personality came from someone else, but all fit together perfectly. Most of her personality is based on a friend's character from an online roleplaying game I used to play. Her name was, indeed, Praeli. Unfortunately, Praeli's player disappeared, so I named Amanda's character in her honor. She was also largely influenced by a character I created in college but never got to do anything with. It goes to show that sometimes a good character just needs the right story.

One thing I wanted to do with this novel was mess around with the classical ideas of *protagonist* and *hero*. In the Hero's Journey, the protagonist starts passive, with something happening *to* them, which sets them off. At the turning point they take the story in a new direction by taking an active role. At the climax, they must make a sacrifice to overcome the villain. By those rubrics, both Alex and Amanda are the protagonist and hero of this story, but each in their unique way. Throughout most of the novel, Alex takes the initiative while Amanda is passive. However, she takes the initiative when she enters The Between and he becomes more passive. Alex sacrificed getting his time back in order to keep Amanda out of Hunter's clutches, while Amanda surrendered half of her life to keep Alex alive. Like proper soulmates, they were designed to complement each other, essentially taking different parts of the same role at different times. However, there is even a point at which Alex becomes both his own and Amanda's villain, causing them each more harm than good.

Once I figured out the characters, the story practically wrote itself, like it *wanted* to get out. I started writing it using an iPad and a portable keyboard during an 11-hour car ride to visit family after Christmas. (No, I was not driving; I was in the passenger seat). Within 5 months, I had the rough draft finished and was already going through editing. You must understand that this is an incredible accomplishment for me, considering the number of years it took to finish my first book, *A Sinister Love*. It was after I finished this one that I realized I really *could* be a novelist. I've worked all sorts of jobs, from waiting tables to data entry to grant writing to door-to-door sales, but this is the first time I felt like I might be in a true career, like I've found my calling.

However, writing this story was not all fun (just mostly fun). I believe I put poor Alex through the wringer a number of times in this book, and Amanda along with him. Just like there are method actors, I am a method writer. I truly get into the head of each character, sharing their emotions and reactions. On top of that, several of the scenes are either based on things that I went through, or that people I know went through. So at times, writing this novel became emotionally taxing. Yes, I've cried over James' death more than once.

I did quite a bit of research for this novel as well, mostly delving into a variety of mental and medical conditions. As previously stated, Hunter has *narcissism* and *OCPD*, while Alex has *PTSD* and has developed *enochlophobia* (a general fear of crowds – unlike *ochlophobia* which is a fear that a crowd will turn mob-like) as a result. Amanda's father develops a specific, persistent form of cancer. Both Eliza and James perish from tuberculosis. I tried to accurately portray an actual hospital visit as well. Because of this desire for accuracy, I had to be very careful with my words. But no matter how much I researched or how careful I was, I'm sure there are still mistakes. I invoke artistic license in those cases.

The hardest part was probably revealing Hunter's narcissism and how it works. Some of the tools narcissists use are gaslighting (insisting that something you know or witnessed is not true), guilt trips, threats, faux promises, blaming the other person, isolation, violent outbursts, smear campaigns, and lying, but there are many different forms of narcissism. There are some things they all have in common: an inflated sense of self, a lack of empathy, and a willingness to exploit or demean others. It is something of an oxymoron, however, in that this inflated sense of self may very well stem from a deeper hatred of oneself. They often use *trauma bonding* to keep their victims from leaving.

Hunter's narcissism comes in three (unofficial) flavors. As a covert narcissist, he gets passive-aggressive, cannot abide criticism, and tries to cover up his condition so others don't know. He is also a malignant narcissist, characterized by paranoia, sadism, and risk-taking. Finally, vindictive narcissists never let go of grudges and will sometimes go to an extreme to get revenge. Most narcissists start to show their true colors after four to six months (when Hunter tries to get Amanda on his yacht), and have no problem quickly replacing someone they have lost interest in (thus Hunter's claim that he is just having fun with her).

His father, though this is never described in the novel, is a communal narcissist, using the Pace family's connection to local charities to give himself a feeling of superiority and appear altruistic, though he is negligent of others in his family and foments conflict.

If you believe you know or might be someone with narcissism, the best thing to do is seek professional help immediately.

*   *   *

While designing The Between, I cannot claim that anything in particular influenced me. The Halls of Time came easily, with the need to house the hourglasses and an easy way to access someone's past. Dreamland and the Desert of Life (the black sand desert's proper name) are completely my own invention. The sand appears to Dream as clouds—powerful desires by humans. Dream gives them form. When a dream dies, it is either turned into a new dream, or, in the case of dreams that fulfilled their purpose, they go to the desert and turn into sand—the more fulfilling the dream, the more sand. This sand is then used to give life to mortals. Those mortals dream and the process starts again. Much revolves around the sand. There is more, such as how the hourglasses are made and different properties of the sand, but that is for later novels.

Fortune's Folly, which is where Lady Luck presides, is clearly based on Las Vegas, while The Library of Fate is based on Trinity College Library in Dublin (we will get to see much more of it in the next book). Attached to the desert is also Limbo. This is where Azrael, the Angel of Death, rules. Limbo is a reflection of Earth, a way to access the spirits. As it was a place of waiting when the Immortals had not yet fallen (depicted in my first book, *A Sinister Love*), it is again a place of waiting. Those who die before their time are taken to Limbo until their time is up, unless they are first recruited by one of the Kin. We will get to see Limbo in the next book as well.

I designed the Kin to be immortal aspects of the universe which interact with humans, and have thus come together. With 2 exceptions, they are distinct from other Immortals (and, in fact, are **not** completely immortal). Azrael and Gaia, though, are angels. I have plans for them in the future. As the angel of Death, I wanted Azrael to display all the stages of decay, not simply be a skeleton. I wanted Chronos to be old, yet young, not always in this reality (mentally), and devoid of most emotions. He not only embodies time, but space, order, and reason. He carries a scythe because he uses it to cut through time, and he is the one who ultimately determines when one's time ends. In contrast, Azrael carries a lantern, for he is a guide to the Afterlife, a *psychopomp* (but more on that in the next novel). Lady Luck was modeled after the typical sort of person you'd imagine would visit a place like Vegas. She likes making everything into a game.

She also embodies playfulness, sexuality, chaos, and risk-taking. Destiny is meant to be like a "sexy librarian" type, self-controlled and yet concerned for others. There is a dichotomy to her. She embodies knowledge, law, math, and science, but she is surprisingly the most in-tune with humans, for she writes and keeps their stories. She is the focus of the next novel and will play a rather central role in the future. I wanted the Twins to be non-binary but in opposing ways. Dream embodies both genders while Fear embodies neither. Dream is a hodgepodge of similar characters in fiction and represents desires, goals, imagination, and hope. Fear comes from some of the creatures from horror films I watched when I was younger. They represent instinct, drive, motivation, but also anger, weakness, pain, and hunger. Unlike Dream, whose interactions with mortals are personal and unique to each, Fear is universal and impartial (and thus needs no eyes to see who they are affecting). Don't let anyone tell you writers don't put subtle things into their works. There is one more Kin that has not been mentioned yet, but we will meet him and Gaia in the next novel.

The relationships between the Kin were important to get right. All of them, in some way, interact with the others, yet each has their own purview. Sort of like a system of checks and balances. I wanted them to be both opposing and complementary. They all work together in some way, but some more than others. Luck and Destiny have the closest relationship, to the point where even they sometimes aren't sure who is in charge of what. Dream and Fear are a close second, one being the goal and the other being the drive. As a twin myself, I can tell you that there is a balance between wanting to be alike and wanting to be different.

I am a big fan of Neil Gaiman's work. It is an unintended coincidence that the Kin bear any resemblance to some of Neil's most well-known characters. I did not even realize it until I had finished the rough draft and was in the process of editing. I hope it is apparent that this is a case of *convergent evolution* as it were, and nothing more. If it wasn't for his example and inspiration, I might not be writing novels.

*   *   *

During the writing and editing of this novel, I had many personal and family issues to attend to, which undoubtedly made it harder to write. My cat, Terra, died after 15 years of being the sweetest animal and best pet I'd ever known. We don't give the loss of animal companions enough importance. I suffered a random attack of something like vertigo, where my eyes constantly drifted to the left (nystagmus). This made writing stop for a while—it took months to go away (and still isn't completely gone). For most of the year, I made regular 5-hour trips to my sister's house to help set up all the furniture in my parents' new house so they could move in (it's a whole thing, don't get me started). Then, my father passed away from Lewy Body Dementia. He was an amazing, brilliant man, a rocket scientist (literally), Air Force veteran, musician, Eagle Scout, and devoted father and husband. I miss him every day. But watching his mental decline put the fear of God into me—nothing sobers you up like looking down a 40-year long gun barrel aimed at you. Like Alex, I need to make the time I have left count, to leave this world a better, happier place than it was when I came into it.

Hopefully, I have achieved that in some small way by making you, dear reader, smile, laugh, cry, and possibly throw this book across the room. If you've fallen in love with these characters the same way I have, I trust you will pick up the sequel, *A Date With Destiny*.

I have every intention of writing novels and stories until I die. Perhaps one of them is your future favorite book. Perhaps something *you* write will become my future favorite book.

The only way to find out is to write it.

Thank You

...to my Kickstarter backers, for supporting my writing and helping to make this book, and all my books, possible!

Robert Windsor	*Tony Lawhorne*
Bri May	*David Holzborn*
Bob Hooper	*Andrew B*
Billye Herndon	*Irinel Finco*
Cat Gerbo	*Jessica Worgo*
The Duke of BAzlandia	*Karl Musser*
Bryce	*Julia Olmstead*
Joel White	*Paul Irons*
Daniel Davis	*A. Sturniolo*
Marlene Renteria	*Bouke de Boer*
Rosa Thill	*Jennifer Fulton*
Sarah Hixon	*Julie Hixon*
KF	*Shery Rouss*
Mark van Wassenhove	*Keion Robinson*
Jennifer Podrasky	*Chanel Holm*
Darby Harn	*Samantha Newberry*
Rachael Hixon	*Tempo*
Tony M	*Lucius Cohen*
Parakeet Griffin Games	*Caleb Smith*

*Please take a moment to **rate** and **review** this novel on Amazon, Goodreads, Librarything, your blog, social media, or wherever you go to buy books or talk about them. It is the #1 best way to show you appreciate an author's hard work.*

Chapter 1: Rotworm

"Don't you dare do it, Jeremy!" Scribble muttered at the mass market romance she huddled over while hiding under her desk. She turned the page so fast it almost tore, then covered her mouth to soften her gasp. "No! I can't believe you actually did it! Kim is too good for you."

"Subordinate #8281."

Scribble completely missed the robotic-sounding voice coming from just above her head. She bit her lip and turned to the next page. "Oh no! Kim! Don't kiss him!" When a book had its fangs in her, not much else registered.

"Subordinate #8281!!" The electronic voice sounded urgent, irate.

"What? Who? Ow!" In her rush to respond, Scribble stood up too quickly and rammed the stubby horns on her head into the underside of her desk. They got stuck... that is until she heard the voice again.

"If you do not answer me, #8281, I will have you flayed!"

The threat worked. It took a few tugs, but Scribble managed to break free and step out from under her desk. Her gray, swirling eyes opened wide at the sight of a computer sitting on top of it. She examined it with wonder—the sleek design, the corners twisted into little points, the logo of a serpent twisting around a partially eaten apple. The faint sound emanating from it reminded her of the agonized screams she often heard from the mortal souls she dealt with on a regular basis, only worse. On the monitor, a window displayed the dark silhouette of a distant figure.

"B-B-B-Belphegor! Sir!" Scribble said, straightening herself. Her barbed tail curled around her body, but when she tried to grab it and saw the book still in her hand, she let out a squeak and tossed the book under the desk.

"#8281. You're fired."

The words felt like piano wire around her neck. Her face, normally a pleasant shade of red, grew pale.

"Have your office cleared out by—"

"F-fired!?" Her voice cracked as she spoke. "B-but why? I've always been a good worker!"

"*You're too far behind!* Fifty million souls find their way to Purgatory every year, and you're in charge of monitoring them. Yet I find you slacking off with a book. A *human* book."

Scribble's pointed ears swiveled back at being caught. She wrung her tail in both hands. "It's my first break in a year. Sir."

"And your last. You don't have any more human contraband, do you?"

235

In the corner of the small office stood a cabinet full of all manner of knick-knacks. It held comics, dice, a collection of lights, playing cards, and even a rusty sword, but the books brought her the most joy. Just thinking about one of her coworkers opening it and discovering her stash made Scribble tremble. "N-n-no, sir."

"Hmm. Besides, the old methods are just too slow. A whole year of backlog has built up. Typing everything out by hand just won't do it. That's why I've decided to upgrade. This computer will be doing your job now. I doubt you were even aware it was installed." On cue, the computer opened a new window. A list of names appeared, each with a date of death and an empty bar labeled "processing." The bar for the first name was filled in a matter of seconds, then the name beneath moved up to replace it and its bar started filling. Scribble had to admit it; the computer did her job much faster than she ever could.

"I-I can learn! This job is all I know! I've worked here for thousands—"

"—*You are incapable of learning, imp!*" The distant silhouette moved closer until Scribble could see Belphegor in exquisite and stomach-churning detail. Numerous scars, lesions, pustules, and pockmarks marred his pale flesh. His emaciated limbs had wires in them, strung to some vast, dark machine filling most of the scene's background. The wires even penetrated the skin of his face. Whenever he moved, instead of using his muscles, the appropriate wire pulled on him. The voice box in his chest did all the talking for him so he didn't have to. Scribble couldn't imagine a better paragon of slothfulness. "You are a coward, and you have no ambition. It disgusts me."

She cowered and lowered her ears subserviently. "Wh-what's going to happen to me?"

"I don't care."

The window closed, leaving the imp alone in her office with the machine that had replaced her. She felt tears welling in her eyes, but tried to contain herself and straightened her posture. *Deep breaths, Scribble. That's it. I'll just gather my things.* She adjusted her blouse and pencil skirt before heading to the cabinet. Several large demons wearing security outfits appeared at the door just as she reached out to open it. She certainly did not need the guards to see her collection and add to her troubles, so she stepped back.

"On second thought, I do have a job for you." Belphegor's silhouette appeared in a little window on the computer's screen once more.

Scribble felt a twinge of hope and turned to the monitor. "Y-yes, sir?"

"Since you love humans so much, report to Rotworm on Level 1. From now on, you will be tempting a human."

"I'm going to be a Sinister? But I've never even *seen* a living human!"

Belphegor drew closer to the screen again, lips pulled into a disturbing smile.

"Then you better prove me wrong and learn fast. But I'm not doing this to be nice. I want you to provide me a soul for my experiments. You're already on thin ice, 8281. I've had to cover for several of your mistakes. I have it on good authority that one of the souls in Purgatory has been *gaining* weight, not losing it! Imagine if the Order catches wind of this!"

"B-b-but sir, I haven't seen any evidence—"

"This debacle puts me in a precarious situation, so I suggest you avoid messing up again, or I'll be using *your* soul to tinker on."

The image on the screen changed to a new scene. A lanky demon lay strapped to a metal table, all manner of mechanical devices sticking out of him. His torn wings hung from hooks, his limbs appeared broken, and he cried out in agony.

"I'm nearly done with this one. You have until the computer finishes processing your backlog."

Any hope Scribble harbored disappeared. A number showed up on the computer screen, "15 minutes." She gasped in horror, but a moment later, it changed. "22.4 hours." "3.7 hours." "90,027 hours." It eventually settled near 1000. Belphegor's window closed and the security demons escorted her outside. As they guided her along, she stole glances at the windows passing by. Far below, millions of human souls suffered rehabilitation to prepare them for Heaven, each occupying their own small cubicle. From her vantage point, the myriad cubicles melted into a hauntingly beautiful Fibonacci Sequence of pain and redemption.

*   *   *

The gates of Hell stood before Scribble like the open maw of some dark and twisted leviathan. It dwarfed every soul that passed through it, but Scribble, in particular, keenly felt the insignificance of her three and a half feet. A hot breath from within flowed over her soft red skin as each step brought her closer to its sharp, ruthless fangs. But only when the two luminous guards moved to block her way did the imp cower in fear.

"State your business," one of them said in a melodic voice—a voice that did not seem to match the rest of the angel. Each wore golden armor and held a weapon of divine nature—a blade made of a dancing tongue of steel flame, a hoarfrost-covered spear that chilled the air and created its own descending fog. Their helmets completely covered their faces, but four eyes that looked like some ancient artist had painted them into existence floated in orbit around them in eternal vigilance.

"I-I-I'm Scribble. I was sent here... by B-Belphegor, my boss." The ensuing quiet egged her on. "He told me to report to... Rotworm?"

"The Order has not received word of a reassignment. No one has been reassigned from Purgatory in thousands of years." One of the floating eyes paused and examined Scribble, from her professional office clothing to her diminutive wings. She felt exposed as it darted around her, but soon, it returned to its place and the two angels stepped aside. "I sense no threat. Proceed."

Scribble quickly slipped past them. Immediately, the ambiance changed from that of a vast cavern filled with the sounds of pain to a busy hub filled with chatter. Long hallways stretched out from the center. Demons filled the place, some in business suits and some wearing nothing at all. They huddled in groups, stood in queues, or rushed about haphazardly. Signs and overhead screens directed the traffic and displayed tidbits of news or other information. Vendors lined the walls, selling various Infernal Devices and diabolical contraptions like spiked clubs and travel pillows. A painting of a rather severe-looking angel pointing at the observer overlooked it all from a mural high above with the words, "Report contraband. St. Michael is watching," printed beneath.

"It's like an airport!" Scribble said to herself.

"A wot?" The voice came from an overweight demon behind an "information" desk.

"An airport! I read about them in books! Oh, I hope I get to see my collection again." Despite the despondency in her voice, she gazed in awe at all the comings and goings around her.

"Books, eh? Ain't those, y'know... illicit-like?" the overweight demon asked with immediate interest and a menacing grin.

Scribble turned pale and looked between him and the mural of St. Michael behind him. She backed away but tripped and fell on her rear. Before she could get back on her feet, she felt a sudden tug as if an invisible rope pulled her back towards Purgatory.

The larger demon laughed. "Yer soul ain't weigh nothin'!"

In the back of her mind, Scribble vaguely remembered what she'd learned about soul weight long ago. She flapped her wings and, immediately, the tug stopped. "Ah... I never had to do this back home."

"Hmph. Must be one of 'em Purgat'ry types. Hardly demons, if ya ask me."

"We are too!" she protested. When she got to her feet, she found that all it took was a single flap every now and again to keep that pulling force at bay.

"No self-respectin' demon would let 'imself be seen there, I tell ya. Yer gonna need a soul stone if ya wanna go past Level 1, wot with yer tiny wings."

"Level 1?"

"Green, eh? This is Level 1. Gets ya where ya wanna be. Them's the tunnels to the other levels that way—Ministry o' 'ternal Torment over there—and Outgoing on the other side." He pointed a sausagelike finger at signs for each.

"Outgoing?"

"Yeah, Mor'al Realm mostly."

"Is that where I'll find Sinisters?" Scribble asked.

"Could be, could be." As he spoke, Scribble brightened and started moving towards the sign that had a picture of a globe on it. "Now, why the rush? Tell me more about them, ah, books o' yers." He glanced over at a few other large demons that began to approach her slowly. She noticed them just in time to keep them from completely surrounding her.

"Ah!" she squeaked. "Th-th-that's okay! I d-d-don't know what you're talking about. I better be... going... now..." As Scribble walked away, one of the other demons stepped in her path to block her. She stopped short and tried moving in another direction but to the same effect. Suddenly, her ears flattened and she began trembling in fear as she looked towards a new, imaginary assailant. "Wh-what do you want?!" she cried out.

The bluff worked. The nearest demon looked behind him to see who, or what, had chilled her so. That gave her the opening she needed. Scribble dashed between her would-be assailant's legs and ran as fast as her own legs could carry her down one of the hallways. By the time she came to a stop, she couldn't see any of the others.

When she caught her breath, Scribble realized she was lost. All along the walls, she saw doorways with labels on them in languages she'd never seen and could not even begin to read. She wandered from sector to sector, the signs changing languages until she found some that she recognized. "London" displayed over one doorway, "Paris" above another.

Nearby, a tall, moderately handsome demon with a long, bent nose and red skin took notice of her meandering. His greasy black hair was slicked back, exposing two small horns. The perfectly tailored and pressed suit he wore gave him a chic, cut look. Behind him sprouted a pair of strong, black wings covered in lizard-like scales. With one hand, he held a black briefcase; with the other, he held up a sign with the word "Doodle" scrawled across it. As Scribble moved closer, he smiled the kind of smile that could sell curtains to the homeless.

"Doodle?" he asked before she could get too far away.

"What? N-no, I'm sorry, you have the wrong person," Scribble said as she tried to move on. He followed her, easily keeping pace and looking her over.

"Short, dumpy, shy, lost... you fit the description. You're Doodle, all right." With the level of conviction in his voice, she almost believed him.

"Dumpy?" Her voice got quieter as she suddenly became self-conscious. "I'm not..."

"Oh, it's nothing a makeover or two can't fix." He smiled at her again, his deep red eyes looking into hers uncomfortably. She half-wanted to buy whatever he was selling just to get rid of him.

"My name isn't Doodle, it's Scribble, and I'm looking for—"

"Rotworm? At your service." He took her hand in a firm, confident grip and shook. "Doodle, Scribble... whatever. It's a terrible name. You should change it." He talked fast, making it hard for her to get a word in edgewise.

"You're Rotworm? Oh... I was told—"

"Yes, yes," he interrupted again. "Bel told me all about you. Come with me and we'll get you set up." Without pause, he began walking towards one of the portals. Scribble followed close behind him. "So, you don't have any experience with humans?" he asked as they walked.

"N-not really, sir." She thought better than to mention her books this time.

Rotworm "tsked" and shook his head at no one in particular. To Scribble, it felt like she had already failed at her new job. He turned a corner sharply and spoke without so much as a glance back at her. "The primary job of a Sinister, your job, is to *persuade* the human, your client, to add a little more weight to its soul."

"But don't their souls always get lighter?" Scribble asked as if making a meaningful contribution to the conversation. "They always end up in Heaven sooner or later."

"That's only in Purgatory, and that won't be the case for much longer if... hmm. Here we are." Before Rotworm could explain himself, he stopped at a doorway that led to a long, curved tunnel. It had buzzing, fluorescent lights along either side and a beige and blue carpet with a simple block pattern that repeated frequently. Rotworm stepped behind the small, vacant desk next to the portal and put his briefcase on top of it. With a pair of mechanical clicks, the case swung open, obscuring him entirely from her view. "Before we visit Earth, there are some rules that you must know. Don't get me wrong, I couldn't care less if you break them. I am *required* to give them to you."

A hand shot out from behind the briefcase, holding a piece of paper for Scribble to take. On it, she saw a list of official regulations printed in gold ink that seemed to shift upon the page just beyond the word her eyes focused on. Even as she read it, Rotworm started speaking them aloud to her. "Rule number 1: Don't attack another Immortal. Angel or demon, it doesn't matter. The Order will find you. Rule number 2: You cannot kill a human or save a human's life. The Order will find you. Rule number 3: Do not reveal yourself to the humans. The Order will find you."

"But what if it happens by accident?" Scribble asked in a soft voice.

Rotworm lowered the lid of the briefcase far enough to peer down his nose at her. "Rule number 4: No accidents. Look, most of them won't believe it even if you *do* reveal yourself. Just... don't say or do anything stupid, like showing the way back here or possessing one of them. And take breaks... we shouldn't spend too much time there. It's not healthy." He waved his hand dismissively. "You can read the others. These are all just formal rules—you won't even be dealing with most of them."

Scribble already felt overwhelmed as she scanned through the rules once more. Her grey eyes suddenly turned to Rotworm when he shoved an accordion-like folder into her hands. It contained nearly half a foot of papers inside of it. *How did that fit in his briefcase?* she wondered.

"One more thing before I throw you to the wolves," Rotworm said as his smile twisted. The slight bend in his long nose made it appear more diabolical, lending him the look of someone about to enjoy watching two men fight to the death. "This is your client's dossier."

"What about a... a training period?" Scribble asked.

"That *was* your training period."

"Y-you mean..."

"Sink or swim, baby. I'm *required* to go with you on your first run, but don't expect me to do any of the hard work. Your client's name is Peter or Patrick or something like that." He nodded towards the dossier. "This is where you'll be keeping track of every decision it makes. I recommend you memorize everything; that'll help you tempt it better."

On the front, in stamped lettering, was the name 'Paul Taylor'. Scribble glanced inside. She found photographs, handwritten notes, typed pages, and endless post-its scattered throughout. The hodgepodge was a monument to inefficiency and disorganization. "Th-there's so much! What happened to his old Sinister?" she asked.

"Grimtooth? Oh, he didn't do a very good job. He was fired... into a pit. Of actual fire. Don't worry about him, worry about yourself. Because if you disappoint me, I'll have to hand you over to Bel in pieces, and he doesn't like it when bitsss go misssssssing," Rotworm said. Along with the new sibilance, a forked tongue slithered from his lips and his horns grew a little longer. He turned his briefcase so she could see inside it as he slowly lowered the lid. On top of some papers sat a collection of demon horns, each one unique. His eyes followed Scribble with a bestial quality, like a predator playing with its food. "Shall we get ssstarted?"

About the Author

Spencer Hixon (with an x-o-n) is a writer of many things, but primarily urban fantasy novels and short stories. When he isn't writing, he's either driving his two children all over God's Green Earth or playing board games (the kind with rulebooks that need indexes).

He lives in Mishawaka, Indiana with his nuclear scientist soulmate and all the book characters still living in his head. His debut novel, *A Sinister Love*, was published in 2024. Visit spencerhixon.com for more.

Oh, and he has an identical twin.

Yes, really.

www.ingramcontent.com/pod-product-compliance
Lightning Source LLC
Chambersburg PA
CBHW050409260626
47156CB00003B/937